鐵路特考 英文高分特快車
Railway Special Examination

作者序…

　　在競爭激烈的考試中，能用最短時間獲得最大得分效果往往就是勝出的關鍵，而綜觀歷次鐵路特考英文試題，其深度並不超過高中英文，但如果考生因離開學校過久或英文學習中斷，造成對英文的疏離，使該拿的分數沒拿到，影響考試結果，那真是令人扼腕。有鑑於此，本書出版的目的在於使考生能在短時間內掌握鐵路特考英文考試準備方向及應考技巧，並加強解題能力。

　　所謂知己知彼，百戰百勝，尤其是參加國家考試，對考古題的掌握更是快速累積應考實力的重要關鍵。本書蒐集自民國98年至102年歷屆鐵路特考英文試題，並加上部分公務考試試題等共22份，將試題逐題詳細解析，使讀者能充分掌握考古題。本書依考試命題方向及重點加以分析，整理出考試常考之單字及文法觀念。其中單字部分，精選考試常用相關的16類型單字，配合例句說明用法；在文法部分，將考試最常用的文法觀念濃縮為11個單元，內容除文法觀念說明外，並有常見錯誤及常考重點提示。在閱讀測驗方面，本書除提供閱讀測驗應考技巧，教導考生如何在有限考試時間中精確掌握題目及文章重點。本書另準備2回模擬試題，並配合完整之分析解答，供考生自我挑戰及磨練。

　　筆者編寫本書是希望以一己之力貢獻社會。然筆者畢竟知識有限，雖殫竭心力，然書中仍難免有不夠周全之處，期盼各位讀者先進不吝與以指正，並預祝讀者在激烈的考場中能順利金榜題名！

方定國

編者序...

　　《鐵路特考英文高分特快車》一書問世，希冀可以提供鐵路特考的考生們一本內容精華的考前備考書。在有系統的規劃、清楚易學習的架構讓考生能在有限的準備時間裡爭取高分。此書的特點如下：

　　（一）、清楚建立文法觀念，學會最重要的考試文法重點。羅列一定要知道的重點，捨去枝節末節的文法規則。常見的文法學習盲點破解，見到考題方能有信心下筆作答。

　　（二）、精選必備單字片語讓閱讀速度與技巧同步提升，單字片語細分16大方向方便學習者記憶，並附上中英對照例句不必死背活吞。各單元後有練習題可測驗吸收。

　　（三）、共22回近年來鐵路相關考古題練習與中譯解析，每題均附上流暢的中文翻譯與詳細解析，知道正確答案是什麼之外也知道為何錯誤的選項不能選。並指出從文章哪裡可以導出答案。解題的同時也是複習常考文法與單字，仔細的解題讓您複習常考的文法與單字，一次又一次地複習再複習，讓解題的能力更加爐火純青。

　　（四）、特別收錄2回模擬考題，可考前自我測驗，找出學習弱點並多加練習；亦包含閱讀測驗解題要領，強化閱讀策略與技巧使答題更準確快速。配合閱讀測驗實戰練習，培養英語閱讀測驗答題的語感與速度。

　　期盼此書能成為一本效度高的應考書籍。然編輯工作若有缺失也祈望各界不吝批評指教。

倍斯特出版編輯部

目 錄 •••

Chapter 01 重要文法觀念

Chapter 02 重要單字片語

CONTENTS

Chapter 03　閱讀測驗解題要領

Chapter 04 近年考題與中譯解析

CONTENTS

Chapter
05

模擬考題與中譯解析

Chapter
06

附錄

01
CHAPTER

重要文法觀念

UNIT 01 五大句型與八大詞類

一、英文八大詞類

單字是構成英文語句的單元，單字本身及根據其在句子中的語意或功能，可以分為八大詞類。需注意的是，一個單字並不限定僅有一種詞類，許多單字具有兩種以上的詞類，以下為八大詞類及其意涵。

（一）、名詞

名詞是人、生物、事物等的名稱，在句子中可以作為主詞、受詞、補語等用途，同時具有數量、型式的變化。例如：child（小孩）、dog（狗）、newspaper（報紙）等字。名詞需注意其單複數型式，有些集合名詞是為整體，無複數型。

（二）、代名詞

代名詞是用以替代某一特定名詞的字。可以當作主詞、受詞、補語，並具有性別數量、人稱、等變化。例如：I（我）、you（你）、she（她）、this（這）、what（什麼）、who（誰）等字。

（三）、形容詞

用來表示名詞、代名詞的性質、狀態、數量，也可以用來修飾名詞、代名詞，或是當作補語使用，並具有比較級、最高級的變化。例如：beautiful（美麗）、small（小）、white（白色）等字。

（四）、動詞

動詞為表示主詞的動作及狀態。具有時式、人稱、數量、語態等變化，例如：eat（吃）、look（看）、read（閱讀）等字。動詞分及物與不及物動詞，但多數動詞同時可為及物與不及物，但意義可能不同。

（五）、副詞

用來表示時間、場所、樣態、程度、頻率等，具有修飾動詞、形容詞及全句的功用。具有比較級、最高級的變化。例如：very（非常）、often（偶爾）、fluently（順暢地）等字。

（六）、介系詞

　　可放於名詞之前，以表示該名詞的方向、場所等，或與名詞、動詞組成片語等。
例如：at（在）、on（在...之上）、with（一起）等字。

（七）、連接詞

　　具有連接字與字、片語與片語、子句與子句作用的詞。從屬連接詞並具有引導從屬
子句的作用。例如：and（及）、but（但是）、because（因為）等。

（八）、感嘆詞

　　表達驚訝、喜悅、憤怒或悲傷等用詞。與其他詞類較無關連且無變化。例如：hi
（嗨）、oh（啊）等字。

◤二◢、英文句子的五大基本句型

　　句子最重要的兩個部分就是主詞和動詞，正確完整的英文句子二者缺一不可，其它
部分就是字詞之間相互的修飾及說明的功用。所以在英文句子中，依據主詞及動詞的變
化可以歸納出五種基本句型，再複雜的句子幾乎都可歸類為這五種基本句型，故稱之為
五大基本句型。

（一）、主詞（S.）＋動詞（V.）

　　本類型句子基本上就只有主詞和動詞，但動詞為不及物動詞（Vi.，Intransitive
Verb），也就是該動詞可以單獨發生、不需要牽涉到其它人事物，即可表達一個動作的
意義。

> **例句**
>
> She sings.（她在唱歌。）
> He ran away.（他跑走了。）
> Nothing happens.（什麼事都沒發生。）

（二）、主詞（S.）＋動詞（V.）＋受詞（O.）

與第一類句型相比，本句型多了動詞的受詞，句型中的動詞為及物動詞（Vt.，Transitive Verb），也就是該類動詞需要牽涉到其它人事物，如果沒有受詞，則意義便會不完整。

例句

She likes roses.（她喜歡玫瑰花。）

The cat drank some water.（那隻貓喝了點水。）

John bought a cell phone.（約翰買了一隻手機。）

注意：底線標示的部分為動詞的受詞，試著看看如果沒有這些受詞，文句意義是否完整？

（三）、主詞（S.）＋動詞（V.）＋補語（C.）

本類句型中的動詞，因為本身不具意義，只是把主詞和補語畫上等號，所以叫它「連綴動詞」，意思就是連繫前後者，讓它們產生關係。「連綴動詞」主要是be動詞及感官動詞（均屬於Vi），其補語為主詞補語，通常為名詞或形容詞（或其片語，子句），其作用為補充說明主詞狀態、形貌等。

例句

She is a teacher.（她是老師。）

They are students.（他們是學生。）

You look great.（你看來很好。）

注意：底線標示的部分為主詞補語，試著看看如果沒有補語，文句意義是否完整？

（四）、主詞（S.）＋動詞（V.）＋受詞一（O1）＋受詞二（O2）

本類句型和第二種很像，都是「主詞＋動詞＋受詞」，差別是在第四種比第二種多了一個受詞，原因是這類型的動詞必須牽涉到兩個人事物，因此這類型的動詞又可以叫做「雙賓動詞」。

例句

I gave you a book.（我給你一本書。）

He bought Mary flowers.（他買花給瑪莉。）

She cooks her husband dinner everyday.（她每天幫她先生煮晚餐。）

注意：以第一個例句而言，「給」的動作通常牽涉兩件事：給誰？給何物？故該動詞就需要兩個受詞，否則句子的意思就不完整了。

（五）、主詞（S.）＋動詞（V.）＋受詞（O.）＋補語（C.）小標

相較於同樣具有補語的第三種句型，本類句型的動詞後面接了受詞，所以該補語稱為受詞補語，通常是名詞或形容詞，用以補充說明受詞。

例句

I believe her a teacher.（我相信她是老師。）

She calls them students.（他叫他們是學生。）

You make me happy .（你讓我感到快樂。）

注意：

比較第四及第五種句型會發現，句子前面都是主詞（S.）＋ 動詞（V.）＋ 受詞（O.），在來接下的部份到底是應該是另一個受詞（屬於句型四）還是受詞補語（屬於句型五）呢？當然，如果該部分是形容詞，那很明顯的就是受詞補語，但如果同為名詞呢？這時一個判斷的技巧就是在動詞後面的兩個詞中間加個 Be 動詞（或畫上等號），再來看結果合不合理，如果合理→受詞補語，如果不合理→第二個受詞，以實際上述例子分析如下：

I gave you a book.→ you （are） a book.→不合理（人不會是一本書）→a book是第二個受詞。

I believe her a teacher.→ she （is） a teacher.→合理（她可能會是老師）→a teacher 是受詞her的補語。

再複雜的句子拆解到最後，一定是其中一種。例如可以加很多形容詞，也可以加很多副詞，或是合併很多個句子，但是增加的形容詞和副詞只是豐富句子的內容，最本質的主詞和動詞還是不變，所以每一個句子也還是要符合這五種基本句型。

三、應試重點

（一）、運用句型原則判斷詞性

如該空格在句中的作用為何？應用何種詞性。運用五大句型原則，抽絲剝繭將句子中的主詞及動詞找出來，並確認各修飾語間的關係，即可確認題目中所需的詞性，並配合單字能力加以解題，例如以下實際考題：

The Colosseum in Rome and sites in the historic walled town of Urbino have
　　　　　　　　　　　　　　　　　　　S.
suffered damagedue to （　　） snow-fall.
　　　V.　　O.　　　　　O.C.

故該句為句型中所提之第五型，due to（由於）後面需接受詞，故空格中可用名詞或形容詞（修飾後面snow-fall）。

（二）、集合名詞應注意單數複數用法

集合名詞（people, family, furniture, staff, crowd, team, class…）視為整體時應用單數動詞，但如指群體中的構成分子則用複數。

> **例句**

X The furniture in this house were all piled up.

　　說明：furniture在此指整個屋子的家俱，只能視為一整體，故不能用複數be動詞（were；are的過去式）。

O The furniture in this house was all piled up. （房子裏所有的家俱都堆起來了。）

> **例句**

　　The family is living in this area for a long time. （這家人住這區域很久了。）

　　We are a large family. （我們是一個大家庭。）

（三）、及物動詞與不及物動詞用法

注意有些動詞只能用不及物，後面需接介系詞，有些只能用及物，後面不需接介系詞。

> **例句**

X She arrived the train station last night.

　　說明：arrive（抵達）只能用做不及物動詞，後面需接介系詞片語當主詞補語。

O She arrived at the train station last night. （她昨晚抵達火車站。）

> **例句**

　　After dinner, we usually listen to the news. （晚飯之後我們通常都收聽新聞。）

　　Will you come with me to the department store? （你要跟我去百貨公司嗎？）

（四）、不定代名詞（one, another, the other, others）的區別

　　one是指不特定的物，有三者時分別以one, another, the other來表示

> **例句**

X Tom wants to sell his notebook computer, and I want to buy one.

　說明：句中的意思應該是要買湯姆的那一台筆電，而不是買隨便一台，所以不能用one，應該用it（指前面提過的特定物）。

O Tom wants to sell his notebook computer, and I want to buy it.（湯姆想賣他的筆電，而我想買下來。）

> **例句**

She has three pens. one is red, another is black, and the others is blue.（他有三隻鉛筆，一隻是紅的，一隻是黑的，還有一隻是藍的）

I have three cats.one is black, and the others are white.（我有三隻貓，一隻是黑的，其餘是白的。）

（五）、不可數名詞

　　可數名詞有複數型，如主詞為複數時，其動詞要配合用複數型，而不可數名詞沒有複數型，動詞一律用單數，所以不可數名詞前面不能使用冠詞 a / an 等或數字，但可用 this / that，表示許多的時候可用 much。

> **例如**

X We would appreciate any advices you can offer.

　說明：advice（勸告）是屬於不可數名詞，所以沒有複數型，應改為單數。

O We would appreciate any advice you can offer（我們感謝您所提出之任何忠告。）

X His knowledges of English and Mandarin are quite extensive .

　說明：knowledge（知識）是屬於不可數名詞，所以沒有複數型，應改為單數，動詞也必須配合用單數。

O His knowledge of English and Mandarin is quite extensive.（他在英語及國語上的知識十分淵博。）

隨堂練習！

(　) 1. The sick baby was _____ all the night.

　　　(A) wake 　　　(B) awaking 　　　(C) awake 　　　(D) to wake

(　) 2. The _____ for four guides have been going on since 8:00.

　　　(A) interviewers (B) interviews 　　(C) interviewing 　(D) interviewer

(　) 3. _____ are investigating the shooting accident.

　　　(A) The police 　(B) A police 　　(C) The polices 　(D) A police officer

(　) 4. It is said that the enemy is _____ the village.

　　　(A) marching to (B) marched to 　　(C) marching 　(D) march

(　) 5. The price of the real estate in this area has _____ since last quarter.

　　　(A) raised 　　　(B) raises 　　　(C) risen 　　　(D) rose

(　) 6. The segment of the chart indicates the _____ of soybean.

　　　(A) produce 　　(B) productive 　(C) producing 　(D) production

(　) 7. To finish the job, the company required two _____.

　　　(A) machineries (B) machinery 　(C) machine 　　(D) machines

(　) 8. There are four apples on the table. Paul is going to take one of them.
　　　Kelly is going to take _____ .

　　　(A) the other 　(B) the others 　(C) anothers 　(D) others

中譯解析

1. C；中譯：生病的嬰兒整晚沒睡。

解析：空格前面是be動詞，故需填入一個形容詞當主詞補語，故需用awake（醒著的），答案為 (C)。

2. B；中譯：對這四位導遊的面談從早上八點鐘到現在。

解析：interview當名詞「面試」之意，本句後面已經有完成式動詞，故空格需填入名詞，作為主詞的一部分，且需用複數，故答案為 (B)。

3. A；中譯：警方正在調查槍擊案件。

解析：the police 是集合名詞，應視為複數，所以句中be動詞用are，故答案為 (A)。另如果是表示一個警察時，要用a police officer，動詞就用單數is。

4. A；中譯：據說敵軍即將前進到這村莊。

解析：由於空格前有表示現在進行式的be動詞，且現在進行式可表未來時間的事物，故空格需用分詞，且march（前行，行軍）為不及物動詞，後面需有介系詞，故答案為 (A)。

5. C；中譯：這區域的不動產價格自上個季度來就已經上揚了。

解析：看到since…，就需考慮到用現在完成式，表示從過去到現在的一段時間，且rise（上升）的過去分詞是risen，故答案為 (C)。

6. D；中譯：這份比例圖顯示出大豆的產量。

解析：segment（部分），chart（圖表）。空格部分前面有 the，後面又有of soybean，因此需填入名詞，故答案為 (D)。

7. D；中譯：為了完成這項工作，這家公司需要二台機器。

解析：空格前面是量詞，故需填入一個複數可數名詞，machinery 泛指一般機具，為不可數名詞，machine 才是可數名詞，故答案為 (D)。

8. B；中譯：有四顆蘋果在桌上，保羅將要拿走其中一個，凱利將拿走其他的。

解析：The other(s)可用來表示一定數量的同類物品中剩下的最後幾個，在這邊 the others = the other apples，故答案為 (B)。

UNIT 02 時態

時態是指句子動詞用來表示動作（情況）發生時間的各種形式。不同時間發生的動作，要用不同形式的動詞來表示。因此，每個句子都要考慮時態問題，選用適當的動詞時態。

時態一時間分為現在式、過去式及未來式三類，另表示動詞動作的狀況有一般式、進行式、完成式即完成進行式四類，故上述二類之組合即有十二種時態產生，分別如下表所示。

	一般式	進行式	完成式	完成進行式
現在式	一般現在式	現在進行式	現在完成式	現在完成進行式
過去式	一般過去式	過去進行式	過去完成式	過去完成進行式
未來式	一般未來式	未來進行式	未來完成式	未來完成進行式

▶ 一、時態句型

（一）、一般式

1. 現在式：He works for the company.（他為公司工作。）
2. 過去式：He worked for the company last year.（他去年為公司工作。）
3. 未來式：He will work for the company next year.（他明年將為公司工作。）

（二）、進行式（be+Ving）

1. 現在進行式：He is writing the report now.（他正在寫報告。）
2. 過去進行式：He was writing the report when I called him yesterday.（我昨天打電話給他時他正在寫報告。）
3. 未來進行式：He will be writing the report tomorrow afternoon.（他明天下午將會寫報告。）

（三）、完成式（have / has+Vp.p）

　　1. 現在完成式：He has just finished the report.（他剛才完成報告。）

　　2. 過去完成式：He had finished the report when I came.（我來時他已經完成報告。）

　　3. 未來完成式：He will have finished the report by tomorrow afternoon.（他明天下午前將會寫完報告。）

（四）、完成進行式（have / has+been+Ving）

　　1. 現在完成進行式：He has been studying English for a long time.（他長時間以來一直都在讀英文。）

　　2. 過去完成進行式：He had been studying English when he was in college.（他在大學時代一直都在讀英文。）

　　3. 未來完成進行式：He will have been studying English for 10 years by next month.（到下個月的時候，他學習英文時間將滿十年。）

二、應試重點

（一）、表時間或條件的副詞子句中，需以現在式表示未來時間，不可用未來式

　　由when，if，after，before，as soon as，even if，in case，though，till，until，unless，so long as等引導的副詞子句，需以一般現在式來表示未來時間。

　　例如

　　　○ When she will leave for Tokyo tomorrow, I will take her to the airport.

　　　　說明：when副詞子句指未來將發生的事，不用未來式，需用現在式替代未來式。

　　　○ When she leaves for Tokyo tomorrow, I will take her to the airport.（當她明天離開前往東京時，我會載她到機場。）

　　例句

　　　If it rains tomorrow morning, you should put your rain coat on.（假如明天早上下雨，你就要穿上雨衣。）

　　　As Mary comes in later, we should cheer her.（當瑪莉等一下進來後，我們要為她喝采。）

（二）、時態的一致性

主要子句與從屬子句的時態需一致，不可相互矛盾（如現在式與過去式混用），若主要子句的動詞是過去式，則從屬子句的動詞亦需配合主要子句用過去式。

例句

O She said she had too much work to do.（她說她有太多工作要做。）

X She said she has too much work to do.

O He says he has visited the company.（他說他拜訪過那家公司。）

X He says he had visited the company.

注意：以下狀況不適用上述時態一致性：

1. 子句中表示自然規律、客觀真理、科學事實等內容

例句

The teacher told us that the earth revolves round the sun.（老師告訴我們地球繞著太陽轉動。）

He once said to me that actions speak louder than words.（他曾經對我說過行動勝於雄辯。）

2. 主要子句出現表示要求、勸告、主張、必須等意思的動詞時，後續子句內的動詞需用原形。

例句

The doctor ordered that we stay at the hospital.（醫師要求我們待在醫院。）

The director insisted that they work overtime.（導演堅持要他們加班工作。）

（三）、注意過去式與現在完成式的區別

1. 一般過去式表示事件或狀態必定發生在過去，從其完成到現在之間有一段間隔。

2. 現在完成式只要用來表示開始於過去而延續至今的動作（有可能繼續延續下去）或重複性的事件。

3. 兩種時態的動作都發生在過去，現在完成式強調動作現在的結果，過去式著眼過去的動作或狀態本身。試比較：

I have read this book.（說明已經讀過。）

I read this book yesterday.（敘述昨天做的一件事，與現在無關。）

4. 過去式用於描述過去一個特定時間點發生的事，現在完成式則為描述過去一段時間起至目前已完成的事物，兩者使用時機可以用表示時間的副詞來加以區別分辨。

需用完成式：since last month（從上個月以來）, for seven days（7天期間）…表示過去一段持續的時間。

需用過去式：yesterday, three days ago, in 1997, when…（當…時候）…表示過去某特定的時間。

例句

O I have worked for this company for over 10 years.（我已經在這家公司工作超過10年了。）

X The famous store was here since 1960 .

說明：句中並沒有提到這家店現在已經關了或不存在，故視為繼續存在經營，故為從過去到現在持續的意義，動詞時態應用完成式。

O The famous store has been here since 1960.（這家有名的店從1960年起就在這裏了）

例句

O They came here one year ago.（他們一年前來到這裏。）

X They came here since last year.

O Wehave been here for five days.（我們已經在這邊五天了。）

X We have been here five days ago.

（四）、注意過去時間的表示法

表示過去時間的二個先後動作，較先發生者用過去完成式，較晚發生者用過去式。另如表示過去一個動作發生的時候另一個動作又發生，則通常副詞子句的時間用過去式，主要子句用過去進行式。

例如

O The train already left when she arrived at the station.

說明：句中意思應該是火車先離開（較早發生），她才趕到（較晚發生），故較早發聲者需用過去完成式，而非過去式。

O The train already left when she arrived at the station.（火車早已離開她才趕到火車站。）

例句

He had already called the police when I get there.（我到那裏實他早已報警了。）

I was eating dinner when John called me.（我吃早餐的時候約翰找我。）

隨堂練習！

(　) 1. I _____ money for a few years since we started working in New York.
　　　 (A) saved 　　(B) has saved 　　(C) had saved 　　(D) have saved

(　) 2. She _____ a bath when I call her last night.
　　　 (A) took 　　(B) have taken 　　(C) was taking 　　(D) had been taken

(　) 3. It was believed from 200 years ago that the earth _____ round.
　　　 (A) was 　　(B) is 　　(C) to be 　　(D) should be

(　) 4. I _____ smoke a lot when I was young , but now I don't.
　　　 (A) was used to 　(B) am used to 　　(C) use to 　　(D) used to

(　) 5. This construction project _____ out for over 10 years.
　　　 (A) carries 　　　　　　　(B) carried
　　　 (C) had carried 　　　　　(D) have been carried

(　) 6. John _____ the bus home after finishing all his works.
　　　 (A) took 　　(B) takes 　　(C) will take 　　(D) taking

(　) 7. Will you go shopping at SOGO when it _____ a big sale?
　　　 (A) have 　　(B) has 　　(C) will have 　　(D) should have

(　) 8. How long _____ TV before you went to bed last night?
　　　 (A) had you watched 　　　　(B) have you watched
　　　 (C) you had watched 　　　　(D) you have watched

中譯解析

1. D；中譯：自從在紐約工作以後，我這幾年才有存錢。

   解析：since只從過去到現在的一段時間，所以要用現在完成式，且主詞為I，故要用have saved，答案為 (D)。

2. C；中譯：我昨晚打電話給她時她正在洗澡。

   解析：洗澡表示過去時間已持續的動作，所以用過去進行式最恰當，故答案為 (C)。

3. B；中譯：早在 200 年前就認為地球是圓的。

   解析：表示真理的敘述一律用簡單現在式即可，不論其提到的時間為何，故答案為 (B)。

4. D；中譯：我年輕時習慣抽菸，但現在我不抽菸了。

   解析：used to 表示過去經常的習慣，均需用過去式，故本答案為 (D)。be used to（習慣於）用在此句中語意不符。

5. D；中譯：這項建設工程已經執行超過 10 年了。

   解析：carry out（執行），表示從過去到現在的一段時間，且可能會持續下去，需用現在完成式，且句中主詞project（工程）是需要被執行，所以也必須用被動式，故空格內用被動完成式，答案為 (D)。

6. A；中譯：約翰在做完他所有工作後坐公車回家。

   解析：由句意來看，該句應該是指發生在過去的事，不牽涉到習慣或是時的描述，故動詞用簡單過去式，答案為 (A)。

7. B；中譯：當 SOGO 百貨有特價時，你會去採購嗎？

   解析：本句為疑問句型式，但 when 引導的副詞子句人需謹守以現在式代替未來的原則，所以動詞搭配第三人稱單數需用 has，答案為 (B)。

8. A；中譯：在上床睡覺前，你看電視多久了？

   解析：明確表示過去時間先後發生的二件事，較早發生的用過去完成式，較晚發生的用過去式。以本題而言，先看電視後睡覺，所以看電視需用過去完成式，睡覺則用過去式，在依疑問句型使用導裝，故為 had you watched…，答案為 (A)。

UNIT 03 動詞

　　動詞是一個英文句子的核心，也是最複雜的部分。考試中有關動詞方面的考題重點主要以動詞時態、動詞與句型、動詞性質（使役動詞、感官動詞…）、動詞三態的變化等為主，其中動詞時態、動詞與句型已於前面提過，以下再分別介紹動詞應注意的要點：

一、及物動詞（Vt.）與不及物動詞（Vi.）

　　不及物動詞後面不接受詞，及物動詞後面一定要接受詞，需注意及物動詞需直接接受詞，故將介係詞放在及物動詞後面是錯的，即使意思是相同，使用及物與不及物動詞，與有無介係詞有關，例如talk about與discuss均是討論之意，但discuss只能當及物動詞，故不能用discuss about，另外discuss可當及物動詞或不及物動詞使用，但意思不同，如當談話時，必須用talk about，這時就將talk about稱為一組片語動詞。片語動詞是一種慣用語，整個片語應該當做動詞來看。

（一）、相同意思的及物動詞與不及物動詞

　　以下列句數組常見的動詞及片語動詞，例如talk about=discuss, arrive at =reach…

　不及物動詞

　O Let's talk about the next issue.（談談下一個議題吧。）

　X Let's talk the next issue.

　及物動詞

　O Let's discuss the issue in the meeting.（會議中討論這議題吧。）

　X Let's discuss about the issue in the meeting.

其他類似情形尚有

　O She came into the room.（她走進房間。）

　O She entered the room.

　X She entered into the room.

　O A group of tourists arrived at the hotel.（一團觀光客到達飯店。）

　X A group of tourists arrived the hotel.

（二）、看來相似卻易混淆的及物動詞與不及物動詞

以下列舉數組意混淆的動詞，需特別注意。

1. rise/raise

rise動詞變化：rise-rose-risen（Vi.昇起）

The sun rises in the east.（太陽從東方升起。）

raise動詞變化：raise-raised-raised（Vt.將…提升）

Raise your hand if you have any question.（有問題請舉手。）

2. lie/lay

lie動詞變化：lie-lay-lain（Vi.躺著；位於）

The book lies on the desk.（書本擺在書桌上。）

lay動詞變化：lay-laid-laid （Vt.放置於）

She laid a package on the floor.（她將包裹放置地上。）

3. wake/awake

wake動詞變化：wake -woke -woken （Vi.醒來；Vt.叫醒）

I woke to the wailing of a police siren.（我聽到警車的響聲就醒來了。）

awake動詞變化：awake -awoke -awaken （Vi.醒來；Vt.喚起）

The shooting awoke our old fears.（槍擊喚起我們往日的恐懼。）

4. fall/fell

fall動詞變化：fall -fell -fallen （Vi.跌落）

She fell on the ground.（她跌倒在地上。）

fell動詞變化：fell -felled -felled （Vt.砍倒。）

The old oak tree was felled.（老橡木被砍倒了。）

5. marry

marry可作為及物及不及物動詞二種用法

及物動詞：

John married Mary last month.（約翰和瑪莉上個月結婚。）

不及物動詞：

They got married in June.（他們六月結婚。）

Sam is married to my sister.（山姆與我妹妹結婚。）

二、使役動詞

使役動詞是指具有「讓人…」或「使人…」之意的動詞，用法說明如下。

（一）、使役動詞make、have、let後面的動詞需用原形

例句

I made him drive on the way home.（我讓他在回程路上開車。）

We need to have someone take care of those things.（我們需有人來處理那些事情。）

Let me introduce the speaker of today's speech.（我來介紹今天的演講人。）

（二）、get、allow、cause、force等在受詞後面的動詞需為不定詞（to+V）

例句

She got me to fill the application sheet.（她要我填申請表單。）

They did not allow me to go home then.（當時他們不讓我回家。）

The police forced the suspect to confess.（警察強迫嫌犯要招供。）

（三）、使役動詞後面的受詞用於接受動作時，動詞用過去分詞，表示被…。

例句

I had my clothes washed yesterday.（我昨天送洗衣服。）

It is very difficult to make ourselves understood to others.（要讓別人了解自己是很難的。）

三、感官動詞

所謂「感官動詞」是指使用我們的感覺器官的動詞，而最常見的感官動詞，莫過於是「看」和「聽」了。這類的動詞，計有 hear、see、watch、hear、feel、notice等。

和其它的動詞不太一樣的地方是，感官動詞的後面第二個動詞，可以是「原形動詞」，也可以是「現在分詞」（V-ing）的形式。

（一）、感官動詞+受詞+原形動詞：用於強調感受到的事實

例句

I saw a bird fly.（我看到鳥飛。）

I heard him shout in the street.（我聽到他在街上大聲叫。）

We watch him work in the garden yesterday.（我們昨天看著他在園子裏工作。）

（二）、感官動詞+受詞+動名詞V-ing：用於強調該項動作的發生。

例句

I saw a bird flying.（我看到鳥正在飛。）

She heard someone knocking loudly.（她聽到有人正在大聲叫。）

I felt the wind blowing.（我感覺到風正在吹。）

（三）、如同使役動詞，感官動詞用於被動式時，原形動詞會變成不定詞（to+V）

例句

主動：Someone saw her leave that building.（有人看見她離開那棟大樓。）

被動：She was seen to leave that building (by someone).（她被看見離開那棟大樓。）

四 、應試重點

（一）、片語動詞

片語動詞是一種慣用語，它是在動詞後面加上介系詞或副詞而形成與原來動詞不同意義的片語，整個片語應該當做動詞來看。常用片語例如：take advantage of, hang up, turn off, give up, come up with, fall in, lead to, come up with, passed away, look after, look into, come across, prevent from, suffer from, connect with, take acre, make sure, put off…等，需注意有些可分開，有些不可分開。

Ⅹ The police are looking this accident into seriously.

說明：片語動詞 look into（＝investigate）調查，不能被受詞 the car accident 分隔。

Ｏ The police are looking into this accident seriously.（警方正嚴肅地在調查這場意外。）

例句

The old lady passed away peacefully.（老婦人安詳地去世了。）

She came up with some good ideas for the product promotion .（她想出一些推廣產品的好方法。）

He asked me to look after his child while he was away. （他要我當他不在的時候照顧他的孩子。）

（二）、使役動詞

A（主詞）+使役動詞（have, make let）+B受詞（通常是人）+原形動詞，其意思為A讓B去做某事，但如B受詞為物且後面接動詞過去分詞，二者意思不同，須分辨清楚不要混淆。

例句

XLet them training the new guide dogs.

　　說明：句中let為使役動詞，後面應用原形動詞，稱省略to的不定詞。。

O Let them train the new guide dogs. （讓她們訓練這隻導盲犬。）

XMary had her car repair yesterday.

　　說明：句中had為使役動詞，受詞her car 為受詞，補語應用過去分詞表示被修理，不可用原形動詞。

O Mary had her car repaired yesterday. （瑪莉昨天將車子送去修理。）

（三）、表示建議、要求的動詞

及物動詞（suggest, request, order）+名詞子句（動詞原形），不論前面動詞為現在式或過去式。

例如

XThe manager suggested that we gave up that project yesterday.

　　說明：suggest後面接名詞子句當受詞，子句內的動詞應用原形（或稱省略should），與前面suggest時態無關。

O The manager suggested that we give up that project yesterday. （經理建議我們應該放棄那個計畫。）

例句

He had requested that the door to his room be closed. （他要求關閉通向他房間的門。）

The mayor ordered that relief supplies be distributed immediately. （市長命令馬上發放救濟品。）

(四)、易混淆動詞

以下列舉常見的意思易混淆動詞,考試時需留意。

項次	單字	例句
1	schedule (V) 將…列入計畫表;安排 (N) 時間表	The tourist group is scheduled to arrive tomorrow.(旅行團定於明日到達。)
	scheme(V) 策劃;密謀 (N) 計畫;方案	My scheme for raising money should be practicable.(我籌款的計畫應是可行的。)
2	affect (V) 影響(造成改變)	Smoking will affect your health.（抽煙會影響你的健康。）
	effect (N) 引響(造成的結果)	Their quarrels had a bad effect on their son.（他們的爭吵對兒子有不良的影響。）
3	lie (V) 說謊(三態:lies;lied;lied)	He lied to his wife.（他對妻子說謊。）
	lie (V)臥、躺(三態:lies;lay;lain)	He lies on the sofa and fell asleep.（他躺在沙發上睡著了。）
	lay (V) 置放;鋪設;下蛋(三態:lays;laid;laid)	I laid plastic carpets on the floor.（我在地板上鋪了塑膠地毯。）
4	rise (V) 上升;(沒有外力)	The sun is rising above the sea.（太陽正升到海平面上。）
	raise (V) 舉起;提高;(有外力)	Raise your hands if you agree.（如果同意就舉起手來。）
5	attend (V) 指參加會議、婚禮、典禮;聽報告、講座等	He'll attend an important meeting tomorrow.（他明天要參加一個重要會議。）
	join (V) 指加入某個組織成為其中一員。	She joined the guitar club two years ago.（她二年前加入吉他社。）

✏ 隨堂練習！

(　) 1. Jefferson unexpectedly _____ his secretary last week.
　　(A) married　　(B) married to　　(C) married with　　(D) was married

(　) 2. You _____ sleepy today. Didn't you have a good sleep last night?
　　(A) see　　(B) seem　　(C) say　　(D) hear

(　) 3. Each of the four divisions _____ its own office in our company.
　　(A) has　　(B) have　　(C) had　　(D) having

(　) 4. The auditorium can _____ more than 500 people.
　　(A) accommodate
　　(B) accommodate for
　　(C) accommodate to
　　(D) accommodate as

(　) 5. The guests have already _____ in the from desk.
　　(A) checking　　(B) check　　(C) checks　　(D) checked

(　) 6. The hurricane is _____ this area soon.
　　(A) approached to
　　(B) approaching to
　　(C) approaching
　　(D) approach

(　) 7. The boss lets his employee _____ a vacation every summer.
　　(A) take　　(B) to take　　(C) taking　　(D) taken

(　) 8. The mayor was determined to set up public safety and promised such a tragedy never to happen again.
　　(A) The mayor decided to set up public safety and compromised such a tragedy never to happen again.
　　(B) The mayor decided to set up public safety but was compromised by such a tragedy happening.
　　(C) The mayor resolved to establish public safety to prevent from such a tragedy again.
　　(D) The mayor resolved to establish public safety by preventing such a tragedy not happening.

中譯解析

1. A；中譯：傑弗遜上星期突然和他的秘書結婚。

   解析：unexpectedly（突然地），結婚marry為及物動詞，後面可以直接接受詞，故答案為 (A)。另可以用get married to（與某人結婚）。

2. B；中譯：你今天好像很睏，你昨晚沒有睡好嗎？

   解析：have a good sleep（睡好覺），sleepy 為形容詞，故前面要用連綴動詞seem，不能用一般動詞see，答案為 (B)。

3. A；中譯：我們公司裏四個部門各自有自己的辦公室。

   解析：主詞具有each of +sth, every+sth, ever yone, each one等字眼，其動詞均需用單數，故答案為 (A)。

4. A；中譯：這間禮堂能容納超過500人。

   解析：accommodate為及物動詞，表示可容納，後面加數量作為受詞，不需有介系詞，故答案為 (A)。其他常見類似情形者尚有enter, discuss, approach…等。

5. D；中譯：客人們已經在櫃台辦好報到了。

   解析：題目中出現助動詞have，故空格中動詞應用現在完成式，答案為 (D)。

6. B；中譯：颱風不久就會接近這個區域了。

   解析：空格前有表示現現進行式的be動詞is，所以可以現在用進行表示未來的意思，所以答案為 (B)。另注意approach為及物動詞，後面不需有介系詞。

7. A；中譯：這老闆每年夏天都會讓員工休假。

   解析：let為使役動詞，所以受詞後面的動詞需用原形動詞，答案為 (A)。

8. C；中譯：市長決心要建立公共安全並承諾這樣的悲劇不會再發生。

   解析：be determined to的意思是決心要做…，句中需注意動詞promise（承諾），compromise（使…屈服），題目意思主要是說市長決心要建立公安系統讓悲劇不會再度發生，故答案應為 (C)。

   (A) 市長決心要建立公共安全並妥協了這樣的悲劇不會再發生。

   (B) 市長決心要建立公共安全但被這樣悲劇的發生所屈服了。

   (C) 市長決心要建立公共安全來預防這樣的悲劇不會再發生。

   (D) 市長決心要以防止這樣的悲劇不會發生的方式來建立公共安全。

UNIT 04 形容詞與副詞比較級

　　形容詞與副詞比較形變化有原形、比較級級最高級等三種，要瞭解這些句子需從as或than等關鍵字中找出哪一種變化，並牢記各種比較級句子的正確型態。

一、基本型

（一）、原形：as+形容詞或副詞+as…（與…一樣）

例句

　　She sings aswell today as she did yesterday.（她今天唱得和昨天一樣好。）

　　Listening is as important as speaking in learning English.（學英文時，聽與說一樣重要。）

　　He speaks English as well as she.（他英語說得和她一樣好。）

（二）、比較級：形容詞或副詞比較級+than…（比…還要）

　　She sings much better today than she did yesterday.（她今天唱得比昨天好多了。）

　　My brother is shorter than my sister.（我哥哥比我姊姊還要矮。）

　　The population of Taipei is less than that of Tokyo.（台北的人口比東京要少。）

（三）、最高級：the+形容詞或副詞最高級+of / in…（在之中…最）

　　Mary is the kindest of all.（瑪莉是所有人中最親切的。）

　　Jason is the most ambitious in our department.（傑森是我們部門中最積極的人。）

　　She reads the most distinctly of all the girls.（在所有女孩子中她讀得最清楚。）

（四）、比較級的單字變化：

　　1. 規則型

　　　　(1)單音節形容詞或副詞在字尾加er構成比較級，加est構成最高級，以e結尾的加r和st。如:fast→faster→fastest；big→bigger→biggest；close→closer→closest等。

　　　　(2)大多數雙音節和多音節形容詞或副詞在前面加more構成比較級，加most構成最高級。例如：seldom→more seldom→most seldom；

beautiful→more beautiful→most beautiful等。

2. 不規則型

以下列舉數個不規則的比較級變化，應隨時牢記在心。

good → better → best

bad → worse → worst

ill→worse→worst

little→less→least

far→farther→farthest（指距離更遠）

far→further→furthest（指更進一步）

三 、其他常用的比較級句型

（一）、原形

1. .not as +形容詞或副詞原形+as…（不像…那麼）

例句

August is not as hot as July.（八月不像七月那麼熱。）

He drives not as fast as she does.（他開車不像她一樣快。）

He does not study as hard as she does.（他學習不像她那麼努力。）

2. 表示倍數：倍數+as+形容詞或副詞原形+as…（…的幾倍）

例句

The laptop is twice as expensive as the desktop.（筆記型電腦的價格式桌上型電腦的二倍。）

Mary works three times as hard as Jenny.（瑪莉比珍妮多三倍努力工作。）

3. as +形容詞原形+a/an+名詞+as…（與…一樣是…）

例句

Tom is as experienced a carpenter as his father used to be.（湯姆也和父親一樣是個老經驗的木匠。）

He is as excellent an engineer as his brother had been.（他也和她哥哥過去一樣是個優秀的工程師。）

（二）、比較級

1. 比較級+than any other+名詞…（比其它所有的…還…）

本句型雖用比較級用法，但意義卻是最高級（超過其他所有，那就是無人能敵了。）

例句

She is smarter than any other worker in her office.（她比辦公室其他人更聰明。）

She sings better than anyone else in her class.（她在班裡唱得最好。）

He works harder than anyother employees.（他是所有僱員中工作最努力的。）

2. no other+單數名詞+比較級…（沒有其他像…那麼的）

例句

No other hotel is more economic than Hotel 6.（沒有其他旅舍像Hotel 6那麼經濟划算了。）

He said no otherman is kinder than him.（他說沒有人比他更仁慈了。）

3. 部分比較及後面介系詞不用than，而是用to，包括：superior, inferior, senior, junior等。

例句

Mr. Walker is senior to me in the company.（華克小姐在公司裏比我資深。）

Her sister is superior to her in maths.（她妹妹數學比她還要好。）

4. the+比較級，the+比較級…（越…就越…）

例句

The more haste, the less speed.（欲速則不達。）

The harder she worked, the more progress she made.（她越努力工作就越有進步。）

（三）、最高級

1. 用現在完成式來表示「到目前為止…中最…」之意

例句

The mansion is the most impressive place I have ever visited.（那座大樓是我參觀過最印象深刻的。）

That girl is the most beautiful one he has ever seen.（那女孩是他看過最漂亮的一個。）

2. make the most of…（將…做最大程度利用）

例句

We should make the most of this good chance.（我們應充分利用這個好機會。）

I will make the most of the precious time to study.（我將充分利用寶貴時間來看書。）

3. at least（至少應該）

例句

You need to submit your outline at least.（你至少應該交你的大綱出來。）

He should return one half of his debt at least.（他至少應該還一半的債務。）

三、比較級常見的錯誤

（一）、注意形容詞的用法

需注意常見形容詞用法的區別，以免用錯形容詞，是列舉如下：

　1. high與tall：

　　說人、動物或樹木的要用tall，指建築物的高時用tall或high均可，但指離地高度等需用high。

例句

Tom is taller than everyone else in his class.（湯姆比班上其他的人都高。）

The Taipei 101 is higher than any other building in Taiwan.（台北101比台灣任何其他建築都來得高。）

　2. further 與farther：

　　further 通常是指進一步的（進度），farther 通常是指更遠的（距離）。

例句

There was nothing further to be done for this man.（對於這個男人再沒什麼能做的了。）

He can throw the ball farther than I can.（他能擲這個球比我擲得遠。）

　3. big 與large：

　　large是指大的，寬大的，大規模的（三維空間尺寸有關）

　　big是指在面積，體積，數量，程度等方面的大的、巨大的（與程度有關）。

例句

I'd like to change this dress for one in a larger size. （我想把這件洋裝換成更大的。）

This city got a lot bigger when the railroad came in the 1960s. （在1960年代通了火車之後，這座城市變大了許多。）

（二）、比較對象需為一致

要作比較需為同樣的事物才能進行，否則就不合邏輯，所以在比較級句子中一定要注意比較的對象是否對等，也就是橘子比橘子，蘋果比蘋果，不可以拿橘子比蘋果。

例句

X The rooms at the Regency Hotel are larger than the Rex Hotel.

本句的中文翻譯為：Regency飯店的房間都比整個Rex飯店來的大。常識判斷這應該不合邏輯，本句錯誤的原因是比較的對象不對，不可拿飯店的房間跟整個飯店來比，應該要房間比房間，所以該句需修正為：

O The rooms at the Regency Hotel are larger than those at the Rex Hotel. （Regency飯店的房間都比Rex飯店房間來的大。）

例句

X John's academic performance is better than Mary.

O John's academic performance is better than Mary's. （約翰課業比瑪莉來的好。）

X He sees me more often than his father.

O He sees me more often than he sees his father. （他見我比見他父親的時間多。）

四 ▶ 、應試重點

（一）、形容詞比較句型

說明：除上述提到之比較句型外，亦需注意以下常考句型

1. so+adj+enough：有夠…的

2. such a +n：就是如此的（一個東西）

3. too+adj（adv）+to：太…因而

4. the +比較級, the +比較級：愈…愈是（怎麼樣）

✗ The lady was so enough beautiful that everyone was attracted by her.

說明：enough需放在被修飾的形容詞後面，不可擺前面，另如果沒有enough，則so…that 亦可成立（如此…以致於）。

○ The lady was so beautiful enough that everyone was attracted by her.（這位女士真是漂亮而吸引每個人的目光。）

例句

He is such a nice teacher, and every student likes him.（他是如此一位好老師班上每位同學都喜歡他。）

The weather is too cold to go to school.（天氣太寒冷而無法上學。）

The more excellent she was, the more modest she became.（她愈優秀就變得愈謙虛。）

（二）、比較級的比較基礎

說明：比較需有相同的比較基礎，也就是人比人，物比物，不可人比物。

✗ Mary's shoes are smaller than Cindy.

說明：句中本意應該是比較鞋子的，但依句子的解釋卻是拿瑪莉的鞋子和莘蒂本人來比，明顯不相稱，故應改為鞋子比鞋子，要用所有格。

○ Mary's shoes are smaller than Cindy's.（瑪莉的鞋子比莘蒂的鞋來得小。）

例句

I ski more frequently than Peter (does).（我比彼得更常滑雪。）

My brother is three years older than I (am).（我哥哥年紀比我大三歲。）

☑ 隨堂練習！

( ) 1. Mike runs _____ of all the man.

    (A) fast   (B) faster than   (C) fastest   (D) the fastest

( ) 2. They do not believe in the manager's story _____ .

    (A) any long   (B) no longer   (C) any longer   (D) longer

( ) 3. The number of visitors of the art gallery is _____ than 150 a day.

    (A) less   (B) fewer   (C) lesser   (D) little

( ) 4. Charles is teller than _____ boys in the class.

    (A) all the   (B) all the other   (C) the all   (D) all

( ) 5. The tree is _____ that one over there.

    (A) two times as high as   (B) two times as tall as

    (C) higher two times as   (D) taller two times as

( ) 6. The distance from my house to the rail station is _____ .

    (A) further than her   (B) further than that of her

    (C) farther than her   (D) farther than that of her

( ) 7. The membership fee for that golf club is _____ than that of any other one in the town.

    (A) cheap   (B) cheaper   (C) cheapest   (D) more cheaper

( ) 8. The presentation was as useful _____ we had expected.

    (A) as   (B) than   (C) to   (D) more

中譯解析

1. D；中譯：麥克在所有人中跑的最快。

   解析：本題考副詞最高級，所有人中表示最快要用最高級級副詞，並要加the，所以答案為 (D)

2. C；中譯：他們再也不相信經理說的話。

   解析：需記住not…any longer=no longer（已經不再），故答案應為 (C)。

3. A；中譯：這藝廊的參觀人數每天不滿150人。

   解析：空格後面有than，表式空格內需用比較級，再由句意判斷用less than作適當，所以答案為 (A)。注意：lesser為較小的，在此處不宜使用。

4. B；中譯：查理斯比班上其他男孩子都來的高。

   解析：該句為比較級句型，表示比班上其他男孩子高，其實就是指班上最高，空格部分可填入all the other或any other，故答案為 (B)。

5. B；中譯：這棵樹是那邊那棵的二倍高。

   解析：本題為形容詞比較級，表示樹木高度應用tall，不能用high，故兩倍高度應用two times as tall as，答案為 (B)

6. D；中譯：我房子到火車站的距離比她房子到火車站的距離來的遠。

   解析：比較句型中應注意比較的對象需一致，句中比較的對象式房子到車站的距離，所以需用farther than that of her，以that 來替代The distance from my house to the rail station，答案為 (D)，且注意far（遠的）表距離時，比較級為farther。

7. B；中譯：這家高爾夫俱樂部的會費比鎮上任何一家都來得便宜。

   解析：空格後面有than，應該用比較級cheaper，than any other（比甚麼都來的…）雖是比較級型式，但意義上為最高級，答案為 (B)。需注意比較的對象需一致，就本題而言，需以這家的會費比其它家的會費才合理。

8. A；中譯：這份簡報跟我們預期的一樣有用。

   解析：A as+形容詞或副詞+as B （A和B一樣的…），所以空格內需用as，答案為 (A)。

UNIT (05) 現在分詞與過去分詞

分詞是由動詞演變而來，分詞有現在分詞與過去分詞兩種。現在分詞可以與be動詞形成進行式，過去分詞可以與be動詞形成被動式外，分詞本身並扮演著形容詞的角色，可用來修飾名詞或代名詞，或是當補語使用。

 、分詞種類與用法

（一）、現在分詞（V+ing）

1. 用於進行式（be+Ving）

   She is teaching English at school.（她正在學校教英文。）

   We were watching TV when she called me last night.（她昨晚打給我時我們正在看電視。）

2. 當形容詞使用，修飾名詞，表示主動之意

   There lay a sleeping baby.（這裡躺著個沉睡的嬰兒。）

   This is an interesting article.（這是一篇有趣的文章。）

   The fiercely barking dog frightened the robbers.（狗猛烈的叫聲嚇到了強盜。）

3. 當形容詞使用做為補語，表示主動之意

   He sat reading a book.（他坐著讀一本書。）

   I found him standing at the door.（我發現他站在門上。）

   Eric's story about this trip was amusing.（關於艾瑞克這趟旅行的事是有趣的。）

4. N＋分詞，由形容詞子句簡化而來的，稱為分詞修飾語或分詞片語

   People living in Taipei are usually rich.（生活在台北的人通常很有錢。）

   =People who live in Taipei are usually rich.

   The man carrying a briefcase is Jan's brother.（那個手拿公事包的男人是珍的哥哥。）

（二）、過去分詞

1. 用於完成式（have/has/had+Vpp）

I have finished the work.（我已完成工作了。）

She has done her homework.（她已完成家庭作業了。）

We had already completed the project by last Sunday.（我們早在上禮拜天就完成那項計畫了。）

2. 用於被動式（be+Vpp）

English is spoken all over the world.（全世界都可說英語。）

She was attacked by a robber yesterday.（她昨天被一個強盜攻擊。）

My room was cleaned yesterday.（我的房間昨天被清理過。）

3. 當形容詞使用，修飾名詞

Never touch a broken window.（不要碰破掉的窗戶。）

The broken bike is mine.（這壞掉的腳踏車是我的。）

This newly equipped laboratory is ready now.（這新裝設完成的實驗室已經被使用了。）

4. 當形容詞使用做為補語，表示被動之意

I was surprised at the news.（我很驚訝聽到這消息。）

I had my car washed yesterday.（我昨天洗車子。）

Some of the soldiers seem dissatisfied.（有些士兵似乎不滿意。）

5. N＋分詞，由形容詞子句簡化而來，稱為分詞修飾語或分詞片語

It is hard for him to understand a letter written in English.（看懂一封英文信對他來說是一件困難的事。）

= It is hard for him to understand a letter which was written in English.

The driver hurt in the accident were taken to the hospital.（意外中受傷的駕駛已被送往醫院了。）

Did you hear the concert presented by the university band?（你聽過這所大學樂團的演奏嗎？）

注意

當分詞作為形容詞使用修飾名詞，或當補語時，如果被修飾者或賓語為人時，要用過去分詞，反之，如果被修飾者或賓語為物時，要用現在分詞。

例如

His response to the question was quite disappointing. I felt disappointed at his response.（他對這問題的反應相當令人失望，我對他的反應感到失望。）

二、分詞構句

分詞構句由副詞子句及and所引導表附帶狀況的子句轉換而來，用以表示時間、原因、條件、讓步、附帶狀況。

（一）、一般分詞構句

兩邊主詞相同時，將副詞子句的從屬連接詞及子句的主詞去掉，再將子句內的動詞依主動改為Ving，被動改為Vp.p。用法：副詞子句/and子句+主要子句

例句

While I walkedalong the street, I met my ex-girlfriend.（當我延著街上走時，我遇見我前任女友。）

→Walking along the street, I met my ex-girlfriend.

Animals can do lots of amazing things when they are properly trained.（當施以適當的訓練，動物可以做很多令人驚異的事。）

→ Animals can do lots of amazing things when properly trained.

Not knowing what to do, she began to cry.（由於不知道怎麼辦，她開始哭了起來。）

注意

（1）完成式的主動中，直接將has/have/had +Vpp改為 having +Vpp

（2）如果需要連接詞的意思時，可以將連接詞保留。

例句

Having finished my work, I went to play basketball.

After having finished my work, I went to play basketball.（在完成我的工作之後，我就去打籃球。）

（二）、獨立分詞構句

兩邊主詞不同，保留兩邊主詞，將副詞子句的從屬連接詞去掉，再將子句內的動詞依主動改為Ving，被動改為Vp.p。

例句

If the weather permits, we will have a picnic tomorrow.（如果天氣允許，我們明天將舉辦野餐。）

→Weather permitting, we will have a picnic tomorrow.

As school was over, they went home.（學校放學後，他們就回家。）

→School being over, they went home.

As the moon has risen, we put out the light.（當月亮升起，我們就熄燈。）

→The moon having risen, we put out the light.

（三）、慣用語

以下為一些常用分詞構句型成的分詞片語，可直接視為慣用語置於句首使用。generally speaking（一般說來）; roughly speaking（大致地說）; strictly speaking（嚴格地說）; frankly speaking（坦白地說）;speaking of（說到）; judging from（由…看來）

例句

Generally speaking, man is stronger than woman.（一般說來，男人比女人強壯。）

Roughly speaking, there are three possible solutions to our problems.（大致來說，我們的問題有三個可能的解決方式。）

Strictly speaking, your composition is not good enough.（嚴格地說，你的作品還不夠好。）

Frankly speaking, I don't like him.（坦白說，我不喜歡他。）

Speaking of cooking, my mom is the best.（說到廚藝，我媽是最好的。）

Judging from his abilities, he is qualified for the position.（由他的能力看來，他可以勝任這個職位。）

、應試重點

（一）、分詞使用

1. 現在分詞Ving當形容詞使用，修飾某事物的，置於被修飾物之前

例如

The speaker was given a standing ovation.（觀眾向演講者起立鼓掌。該詞是指鼓掌的象徵或方式。）

2. 過去分詞Ved當形容詞使用，修飾某事物的時候，置於修飾物之前，有被動的意味。

例如

The couple has rented a furnished apartment.（這對新婚夫婦租了一間有家具的公寓。）

3. 當分詞作為形容詞使用修飾名詞，或當補語時，如果被修飾者或賓語為人時，要用過去分詞，反之，如果被修飾者或賓語為物時，要用現在分詞。

例句

She was disappointed by her sister's birthday gift.（她對於她姐給的生日禮物感到失望。）

My brother's birthday gift was disappointing.（我弟弟的生日禮物令人失望。）

✗This beautifully decorating house belongs to Mr. Brown.

說明：動詞decorate（裝潢）應為被動概念，在此應用過去分詞Ved當形容詞來修飾。

○ This beautifully decorated house belongs to Mr. Brown.（這棟裝潢漂亮的房子是伯朗先生的。）

✗The movie we saw yesterday was very excited.

說明：主詞The movie是無生物，故要用現在分詞當主詞補語，說明主詞movie的狀態。

○ The movie we saw yesterday was very exciting.（我們昨天看的電影很刺激。）

例句

Company A has some expertly trained employee.（A 公司有一些受過專業訓練的員工。）

He could not quite the laughing woman.（他無法制止那位大笑的婦人。）

I'm very interested about the novel which my brother gave me as a gift.（我對我弟弟送我的那本小說感覺很有趣。）

（二）、分詞構句表示法

說明：分詞可以形成片語，當作副詞用來修飾主要子句，稱為分詞構句，可置於句首、句中、或句尾，表原因、結果條件或讓步等。

例如

✗ Coming home earlier, we should leave tomorrow morning with her.

說明：如果分詞子句與主要子句主詞相同，改為分詞構句時主詞可省略，如不同時，主詞需保留，以免混淆。本句應原為：If she comes home earlier, we should leave tomorrow morning with her.，兩邊主詞不同，故主詞需保留

O She coming home earlier, we should leave tomorrow morning with her （她早一點回來的話，我們明天早上就可以和她一起離開。）

例句

Accepted by the company, I need to demonstrate my capability.（即使被公司採用了，我還是必須證明我的能力。）

I sat in the sofa, reading the newspaper.（我坐在沙發上看著報紙。）

📝 隨堂練習！

( ) 1. I was _____ to hear about the earthquake in Japan. I have a lot of friends who live there.
 (A) devastating (B) devastated
 (C) being devastated (D) devastate

( ) 2. It was _____ to know that I didn't get a good grade.
 (A) disappoint (B) disappointing
 (C) disappointed (D) being disappointing

( ) 3. _____ the way to take, he went on his journey with courage.
 (A) Telling (B) Having been told
 (C) Having told (D) Have told

( ) 4. I ought to get my laptop _____ , or I can't do my report.
 (A) repeat (B) repeated (C) repair (D) repaired

( ) 5. The boss blocked the fresh ideal _____ by a younger employee.
 (A) submitting (B) submitted (C) to submit (D) submit

( ) 6. Thegovernment was blamed for being ill-equipped to deal with the economic crisis.
 (A) Because of being no capability to deal with the economic crisis, the government was blamed.
 (B) Because of being no capability to deal with the government economic crisis, the critic was blamed.
 (C) Thegovernment was blamed for being lacking good equipment to deal with the economic crisis.
 (D) For being ill-equipped to deal with the economiccritic, thegovernment was blamed.

( ) 7. No matter how frequently _____ , the works of Beethoven always attract large audiences.
 (A) performing (B) performed
 (C) to be performed (D) being performed

中譯解析

1. B；中譯：聽到日本地震我極為震驚，我有許多朋友住那邊。

   解析：空格內需填入主詞補語，主詞為人，所以表事情緒的形容詞應該用過去分詞來當形容詞，故答案為 (B)。

2. B；中譯：知道我沒有得到好成績真令我失望。

   解析：句中主詞 it 指的事指後面的名詞子句 that…，屬於事物，故應當用現在分詞來形容，故答案為 (B)。

3. B；中譯：在被告知即將去的道路後，他鼓起勇氣踏上旅程。

   解析：主要子句為過去式，從屬子句比過去時間更早，且為被告知，需用被動的過去完成式，選項中顯示該具需用分詞構句，故用 Having been told，答案為 (B)。

4. D；中譯：我得去把我的筆記型電腦修好，否則無法寫報告。

   解析：電腦是要被人修好，可以用 get / have +受詞+過去分詞（當形容詞用），所以答案為 (D)。

5. B；中譯：老闆阻止了年輕員工所提出的新案。

   解析：由形容詞子句 which is submitted 省略成 submitted，所以答案為 (B)。

6. A；中譯：政府因為缺乏有效工具來因應經濟危機而備受責難。

   (A)政府因為沒有能力去處理經濟危機而受責難。

   (B) 評論家因為沒有能力處理政府的經濟問題被責難。

   (C)政府因為缺乏良好的設備來處理經濟危機而受責難。

   (D) 政府因為沒有效工具來應付經濟評論者而受責難。

   解析：ill-equipped 在題目中是指準備不足，或政府沒能力之意，故最接近答案為 (A)，注意：需區別 critic（評論者）與 crisis（危機）之不同。

7. B；中譯：不論如何反覆演奏，貝多芬的作品總是能吸引多數的聽眾。

   解析：本句中貝多芬的作品被反覆表演，分詞與句子的主詞之間是被動關係，應該用過去分詞，故答案為 (B)。

UNIT 06 動名詞與不定詞

　　動名詞（V+ing）與不定詞（to+V）結構中都含有動詞，可視為是動詞的一種變型，在句子中的地位可當作主詞、受詞或補語，也就是與一般名詞的地位無異，但因其含有動詞，該動詞後面可接受詞或補語，是兼具動詞與名詞的一種結構。需注意是動名詞與現在分詞結構相同（均為V+ing），但其用法不同，動名詞因具有名詞的性質，但現在分詞是作為形容詞用修飾名詞。

一、不定詞

　　不定詞可以分為有to的不定詞及原形不定詞（也就是動詞原形），不定詞可以作為名詞、副詞及形容詞等用法。

（一）、名詞用法

　　可作為句中的主詞、受詞或補語之用。

> **例句**
>
> 主詞使用：To find a good used car is very difficult.（找一部好的二手車是很困難的。）
>
> 受詞使用：After work everyone wanted to go swimming.（工作完成後每個人都想要去游泳。）
>
> 補語使用：Our plane is to leave Saturday by noon.（我們的計畫是星期六中午前離開。）

（二）、副詞用法

　　不定詞的副詞用法為表示「為了」、「變成」、「由於」等意思。

> **例句**
>
> She came to Taipei to learn Chinese.（她為了學中文而來到台北。）
>
> I'm very glad to hear that I he can get a promotion.（我因得知他可以晉升而很高興。）

（三）、形容詞用法

不定詞的詞用法詞用於表示「為了…的」或「應該…的」，主要作為補語使用。

例句

Would you like something to eat now?（你現在要不要吃點甚麼嗎？）

We expect our visitors to stay for a week.（我們希望的訪客們應該待一個禮拜。）

（四）、不定詞的否定

不定詞否定用法是在to前面加上not。

例句

They decided not to postpone the meet.（他們決定不延長會議。）

He warned the travelers not to drive at night.（他警告遊客不要晚上開車。）

（五）、原形不定詞（也就是動詞原形）

使役動詞（make、have、let）及感官動詞（hear、see、watch、hear、feel…）後面動詞需接原形不定詞（也就是動詞原形）。

例句

He felt someone touch his ear.（他感到有人摸他耳朵。）

Please help me (to) find the front door key.（請幫我找前門的鑰匙。）

注意

help 後面可接不定詞或原形動詞。

二、動名詞

動名詞（V+ing）具有動詞及名詞雙重特性，因此可接受詞，也可以用副詞修飾，且在句子中可以當主詞、受詞、補語級介系詞受詞等功用。

例句

主詞：Driving at night makes him nervous.（晚上開車讓他感到緊張。）

受詞：We enjoy getting together on weekends.（我們喜歡周末聚在一起）

補語：His favorite sport is driving car at top speed.（他最喜歡的運動就是高速駕車。）

介系詞受詞：I am interested in learningJapanese.（我對學習日文有興趣。）

（一）、動名詞或不定詞當動詞受詞之使用

一般而言，以不定詞當動詞的受詞，意思為實現未來意向的動作，為較積極性的含意，而如果接動名詞的話，則為實現過去意向動作之消極性含意。

（二）、後面需接不定詞作為受詞之動詞

afford, agree, aim, arrange, ask ,claim, dare, decide, decline, desire, determine, except, expect ,fail, guarantee, hesitate, hope, learn, manage, mean, offer, plan, prepare, pretend, promise, refuse, seek, take, want, wish…等動詞後面需接不定詞。

　例句

He managed to complete the sales report.（他設法完成銷售報告。）

She asked us never to come to class unprepared.（他要求我們上課要有準備。）

（三）、後面需接動名詞作為受詞之動詞

admire, appreciate, avoid, consider, delay, deny, discontinue, dislike, enjoy, escape, finish, forgive, give up, mind, miss, permit, postpone, practice, prohibit, put off, quit, recommend, regret, spend ,suggest ,resist,……等動詞後面需接動名詞。

　例句

The guard denied letting the prisoner escape.（警衛否認放走囚犯。）

Have you considered taking a different kind of job?（你有考慮到做個新工作嗎？）

（四）、後面可接動名詞或不定詞作為受詞之動詞

attempt, begin, cease, commence, continue, decline, dare, intend, like, love, mean, need, neglect, plan, prefer, propose, stop, remember, try…等動詞後面需可接動名詞或不定詞，但意思可能會有不同，一般而言，接不定詞表示「接下來要做的事」，而接動名詞表示「已經做過的事」。

　例如

1. Remember：

remember to do（不要忘記做…）

Remember to buy a bottle of soy-bean sauce on your way home.（回來時不要忘了買瓶醬油。）

remember+Ving（忘記做過…）

He can't remember buying soy-bean sauce in the grocery store.（他不記得有在這雜貨

店買過瓶醬油。）

2. Forget：

　forget to do（忘記要去做…）

　Mary forgot to return this book to the library.（瑪莉忘了要把這本書還給圖書館。）

　forget + Ving（忘記做過）

　Mary forgot returning this book to the library last month.（瑪莉忘了上個月還過這本書還給圖書館了。）

3. Stop

　stop to do（為了…而停止）

　I stopped to have a lunch.（我停下來吃午餐。）

　stop+ Ving（停止…）

　He decided to stop smoking.（他決定要戒菸。）

☰ 、應試重點

不定詞片語當副詞使用

　　說明：不定詞to+V.經常用來作為表示目地的副詞使用，指出某一行為的目地是另一行為，有in order to+V.之意。

例如

　I have come here to apologize.（我已經來道歉了。表示我來是為了要道歉。）

　I sent her a bunch of flowers to thank her for a party.（我送她一束花以感謝她辦這場宴會。送花的目的是為了要感謝。）

　✗ Some speakers would hesitate choosing the right word.

　說明：hesitate後面能接不定詞或動名詞當受詞，但句中的意思應該是停頓下來選擇用字，含有動作的目的之意，故應用不定詞。

　○ Some speakers would hesitate to choose the right word.（有些演講者會停頓一下以選擇正確用字。）

例句

　He stopped to talk to me after the lecture.（他演講完後停下來跟我說話。）

　We were all tired, so we stopped to take a rest.（我們都累了，所以停下來休息。）

📝 隨堂練習！

( ) 1. Marry enjoyed _____ with her boyfriend last Sunday.

(A) to dance　　(B) to be danced　(C) dancing　　(D) had danced

( ) 2. In order _____ a peace agreement, the two countries need to make a compromise.

(A) make　　(B) making　　(C) to make　　(D) made

( ) 3. My wife always spends a lot of money _____ makeup.

(A) buy　　(B) buying　　(C) to buy　　(D) bought

( ) 4. Remember _____ the poor old man when you pass by there.

(A) seeing　　(B) to see　　(C) see　　(D) seeing

( ) 5. We are planning _____ up a oversea branch in Taiwan.

(A) set　　(B) to set　　(C) setting　　(D) sets

( ) 6. John is a lazy boy. We do not expect him _____ all of the homework by tomorrow.

(A) complete　(B) to complete　(C) completing　(D) be completed

( ) 7. The patient stopped _____ sweet dessert for diabetes.

(A) to eat　　(B) eat　　(C) eating　　(D) to be eating

( ) 8. She was scared of Billy being in crowds after 9/11 terrorist attacks.

(A) She scared Billy out of being in crowds after 9/11 terrorist attacks.

(B) She was scared by Billy for being in crowds after 9/11 terrorist attacks.

(C) After 9/11 terrorist attacks, she was scared of Billy when he was in crowds.

(D) After 9/11 terrorist attacks, she was scared when Billy was in crowds.

中譯解析

1. C；中譯：瑪莉上星期天和她男朋友跳舞跳得很愉快。

   解析：及物動詞 enjoy 後面的動詞需用動名詞，故答案為 (C) ，其它此類的動詞尚有avoid, consider, dislike, finish, mind…等。

2. C；中譯：為了要簽訂和平協議，這兩個國家必須妥協。

   解析：compromise（妥協），表示目的的不定詞 in order to 是很常用的，在此作為副詞片語使用，故答案為 (C) 。

3. B；中譯：我太太總是花大錢買化妝品。

   解析：makeup（化妝品），及物動詞 spend 後面的動詞需用動名詞，故答案為 (B)

4. B；中譯：當你經過那邊時，記得去看一下那可憐的老人。

   解析：remember 後面可接動名詞，表示記得做過某事，也可接不定詞，表示記得要去做某事。本題句意應為記得要去看之意，所以用不定詞 to see，答案為(B)。

5. B；中譯：我們正計畫要在台灣設立海外分公司。

   解析：set up（設立），動詞 plan 後面需接不定詞，所以答案為 (B)。其他類似者計有 decide, hope, promise, want 等。

6. B；中譯：約翰是個的懶惰的孩子，我們不期待他明天之前可以完成家庭作業。

   解析：except 後面需接不定詞，故答案為 (B)。

7. C；中譯：這個病人因為糖尿病而停止吃甜點。

   解析：diabetes（糖尿病），由句意可判斷應該是要停止吃甜點（已經得糖尿病了），而不是停下來去吃甜點，所以要用動名詞，答案為 (C)。

8. C；中譯：在 911 恐怖攻擊後，她會擔心比利待在群眾之中。

   (A) 在911恐怖攻擊後，她會嚇得比利不敢待在群眾之中。

   (B) 在911恐怖攻擊後，她會因待在群眾之中而被比利嚇到。

   (C) 在911恐怖攻擊後，當比利在群眾之中時她會擔心。

   (D) 在911恐怖攻擊後，當比利在群眾之中時她會被嚇到。

   解析：be scared of 在句中解釋為擔心害怕，題目主要表達的是如果比利待在群眾之中她就會擔心（怕被攻擊），所以答案為 (C)。

UNIT 07 連接詞與介系詞

 、連接詞

連接詞主要功用為連接句子中的各種結構，包括主詞、動詞、形容詞、受詞及子句等，並可引導從屬子句。連接詞區分為對等連接詞、從屬連接詞、相關連接詞及連接副詞等四類，以下分別敘述期用法及使用時機。

（一）、對等連接詞

對等連接詞使用於連接具有相同類的字、詞、片語及子句等，主要有and, or, but, so, for, yet, nor等。

1. 詞的連接

We decided to eat steak and eggs. （我們決定吃牛排與蛋。）

You or your sister should visit Aunt. （你或你姐姐要去看伯母。）

2. 片語的連接

How do you go to downtown, by taxi or by bus? （你如何到城裡去，座計程車或搭巴士？）

The meat at the restaurant is too rare or too well done. （那家餐廳的肉不是太生就是太熟。）

3. 句子的連接

Melissa screamed and then fainted. （瑪莉莎先尖叫然後安靜下來。）

You tell him, or he'll get into the trouble. （你告訴他，否則他會惹上麻煩。）

注意

使用對等連接詞時，連接的詞性及時態等需一致。

例如

X His latest novel is long, tiresome, and bore.

O His latest novel is long, tiresome, and boring. （他最新的小說冗長、無趣且無聊。）

X The director likes to ski and skating.

O The director likes to skiing and skating. （這位導演喜歡滑雪及溜冰。）

（二）、從屬連接詞

　　從屬連接詞用於主要子句與從屬子句間之連接，依子句的性質分類，有用於名詞子句的that, if , whether…等，用於副詞子句的although, as soon as, because, though, when, while, if…等。

　　依連接詞的意思可大略分為7大類型：

1. 表示「讓步」: although, though, even if, even though, while ,whereas, whether, no matter what。

　　例句

　　Although the quality of this product is excellent,the price is too high. （雖然產品品質良好，但價格太高了。）

　　While this plant is downsizing, others are expanding their operation. （當這家工廠在精簡員工同時，其它的工廠仍擴張營業。）

　　I'll go swimming whether it rains or not. （不管下雨與否，我都會去游泳。）

2. 表示「目的」: so that, in order that, lest…should

　　He is so weak that he can't walk to the bathroom by himself. （他如此虛弱以致於無法自行走到浴室。）

　　They evacuated the building lest the wall should collapse. （他們撤離這棟建築以房牆壁倒塌下來。）

3. 表示「條件」: if, in case （that）, provided （providing） that, suppose （supposing） that, unless

　　If you have good education, you will be in high demand by employer. （如果你受良好的教育，雇主就會很需要你。）

　　I won't call you unless something important happens. （我不會打給你除非有重要事情發生。）

4. 表示「時間」: when, while, as, since, till, until, before, after, once.

　　Since John became the CEO, our company has made a lot of money. （自從約翰成為公司的 CEO 後，我們賺了不少錢。）

　　Look before you leap. （三思而後行。）

5. 表示「原因」: because, as, since, now that （since）, in that （because）

　　Because we have to arrive there on time, we take a taxi. （因為要準時到達那邊，我們就坐計程車。）

　　Now that you mention it, I do remember. （既然你已提到了，那我會記住。）

6. 表示「結果」: so

The car broken down, so they had to take the bus.（車輛壞了，所以他們必須搭乘巴士。）

7. 表示「比較」: than, as…as

A bad excuse is better than none at all.（一個爛藉口比沒有藉口來的好。）

She is as tall as you.（她與你一樣高。）

（三）、相關連接詞

有些連接詞與其他字結合來形成所謂的相關連接詞。它們總是成雙成對，以對稱來處理的不同句子元素連接起來；換言之，相關連接詞兩邊的文法關係必須對稱。

1. Both A and B（A 與 B 都…）

Both our salary and our benefits are not satisfactory.（我們的薪水與福利都無法令人滿意。）

The man finished the jobs both quickly and well.（這個人把工作做的既快又好。）

2. Not only A（but）also B（不只 A，還有 B）

Their new home is not only beautiful but also large.（她們的新家不只大還很漂亮。）

Not only James, but Peter also got a prize.（不只是詹姆士還有彼得也得獎。）

3. A as well as B（A 像 B 一樣好）

The ceremony as well as the reception was gorgeous.（這場典禮與接待都很好。）

Those students seem intelligent as well as eager.（那些學生看來聰明且求知慾望高。）

4. Either A or B（A 或 B 都）

She is usually either upset or sad.（她通常不是煩悶就是悲傷。）

Either coffee or tea will be served soon.（茶或咖啡馬上會端出來。）

5. Neither A nor B（A 和 B 都不）

Stan neither drinks nor smokes.（斯坦不喝酒及抽菸。）

Neither Mike nor his wife goes to church on Sunday.（麥克及他太太星期天皆不上教堂。）

注意

上述連接詞用於連接主詞時，需注意動詞的單複數變化：

（1）A as well as B 必須與 A 一致

例句

The teacher as well as the students wants to take the tour.（老師與學生們都要參加旅遊。）

The words as well as the music are beautiful.（文字與音樂都很優美。）

（2）Not only A（but）also B, Either A or B, Neither A nor B 需與 B 一致

例句

Either fruit or vegetables are good for a snack.（水果或蔬菜都是很好的點心。）

Not only the plants but also the grass is very dry.（不只數目連草地都很乾燥。）

（3）Both A and B必須為複數

例句

Both Mary and Tom were hurt in that accident.（瑪莉與湯姆都在意外中受傷。）

Both sing and dancing are her favorite hobby.（唱歌與跳舞是他最喜歡的嗜好。）

（四）、連接詞副詞

連接詞副詞如 however, moreover, nevertheless, consequently, as a result 被用來產生兩個觀念之間的複雜關係，但需特別注意的是連接副詞與連接詞不同，無法連接兩個句子，且使用於兩個子句間時，前面須加「;（分號）」以表示連接。

例句

O Although I was tired, I worked overtime.（雖然我很累，我還是加班了。）

O I was tired; nevertheless, I worked overtime.（我很累，然而我還是加班。）

XNevertheless I was tired, I worked overtime.（Nevertheless 為連接副詞，不可連接子句。）

O While Larry is a good husband, he's also a good father.（勞瑞是個好丈夫，也是個好父親。）

O Larry is a good husband; moreover, he's a good father.（勞瑞是個好丈夫，除此之外，他也是個好父親。）

XLarry is a good husband, moreover he's a good father（moreover 為連接副詞，不可連接子句）

二、介系詞

介系詞在英文中分類主要分為三類，也就是表示時間概念的in, on, at , before等，表地點概念的，如 inside, on, at 等級表示動作或方向概念的，如 toward, up, down 等，另介系詞常與名詞或動詞結合形成介系詞片語或片語動詞，在英文句中均佔有非常重要地位，需加以注意。

（一）、表時間的介系詞

1. 表示時間線上的某一特定點：

介系詞	用法	例句
in	年份，如：in 2012	I was born in 1968.
	季節，如：in summer	It is hot in summer.
	時間，如：in the night	She usually comes here in the night.
	月份，如：in August	He was born in July
on	日期（特定日期點） on Sunday on 6th July	We are off on Sunday. Mary's birthday is on 6th July.
at	時間（特定時間點） at 09:00 at that moment at present	The train will be leaving at 09:30 We didn't know what happen at that moment. She is still calm at present.

注意

若同時有多個時間點需在同一句子中表達，則一般由小到大排列，即時間幅度幾點鐘 → 上下午 → 日期。

例如

He was born at 6 a.m. in the morning on Monday.（他是星期五上午六點出生的。）

2. 表示一段延續的時間：

介系詞	用法	例句
since	since＋時間＋ago	She has studied English since 5 years ago.
	since＋過去某時間點	She has studied English since 2005.
	since＋過去式子句	She has studied English since she went to junior high school.
for	for＋一段持續時間	She has studied English for 5 years
from	from…to（肯定句）	She works hard from morning to afternoon.
until till	until（till）否定句	I won't be back until 9 p.m.
during	during＋一段時間	What did you do during your Christmas vacation?
by, in, with	by , in ,with＋一段時間	I will see her by 4 o'clock.（四點鐘之前）I will see her in 10 minutes.（十分鐘之後）I will see her within 10 minutes.（十分鐘之內）

注意

since與for 皆用於完成式。

（二）、表地方的介系詞

　　表地方的介系詞需考慮一基準點來比較，該基準點可以是實體的東西，如公園，也可能是虛有的東西，如能力等，但以下先以實體來舉例說明。

介系詞	用法	例句
基準點上	in（表示較大地方）	She lives in Taipei.
	on	She is walking on the street.
	at（表示較小地方）	She bought his shoes at the store.
基準點上方或下方	over , above, under, underneath	He had a bruise just above his left eye. There is a cat under the table. He jumpedover the ditch.
基準點附近	near, next to, between,	There is a small park next to her house. The house is located between two tall buildings. His house is near a river.

（三）、表方向的介系詞

　　表示標示某個方向時使用，這方向可為具體（東西南北，或物體，如建築物等），或是虛有的（如人生目標），較常用有to / from（去/從），for（朝向…目的），toward（朝向），away from（從…離開），in （to） / out of（進去／從…出來），up / down（上／下），around（環繞）等。

例句

He always walks to school from his home. （他總是從他家走到學校。）

Some of the employee have prepared for the ceremony for several weeks. （有些員工已經為了這典禮準備了好幾個星期。）

They moved away from their old community. （她們從舊社區搬走了。）

（四）、介系詞片語與片語動詞

　　介系詞片語是由介系詞起頭，名詞或代名詞結尾的兩個或兩個以上的字群所組成。可當名詞、當形容詞或當副詞使用，修飾動詞、形容詞、其他副詞或修飾整句，例如at first（一開始），except for（除…以外），at a cost of（以…價格）…等。片語動詞則是動詞與介系詞的習慣性用法組合，例如account for（導致於），make up for（賠償），take part in（參加）…不勝枚舉，平時就應留意記憶。

> 例句

　　I'm in charge of this store.（我管理這家店。）

　　In case of an earthquake, turn off the gas and stove.（當地震時，關閉瓦斯及爐子。）

　　Turn in your assignment by the end of this weekend.（在周末前交出你的作業。）

　　Our president contribute money to charities.（我們董事長捐款給慈善機關。）

（五）、連接詞與介系詞

　　連接詞可以引導子句，介系詞只能接片語。常考的連接詞有 while , when, except , though, although, if , even though, whether 等, 另外易與連接詞混淆的介系詞有 in spite of , despite, in case of, because of 等需注意。

　　✗ Despite I like the color of that hat, I don't like its shape.

　　說明：本句中主要子句是I don't like its shape.前面應該是要由連接詞引導的副詞子句來修飾全句，但 despite (=in spite of) 是介系詞，它也有「雖然」之意，但無法引導子句，只能接片語，故需用適當的從屬連接詞。

　　○ While I like the color of that hat, I don't like its shape.（雖然我喜歡這帽子顏色，但我不喜歡它的款式。）

> 例句

　　Although many difficulties are still ahead, we are certain to make a great achievement.（雖然前面還有許多困難，但我們確認能獲得偉大成就。）

　　Whether sick or well, he is always cheerful.（不管有沒有生病，他總是快樂的。）

📝 隨堂練習！

( ) 1. The office will be closed tomorrow _____ it is a holiday.

      (A) although   (B) because   (C) with   (D) but

( ) 2. Notify us immediately _____ you do not received all pages.

      (A) unless   (B) if   (C)and   (D) but

( ) 3. They won the contest, _____ the other team was very strong.

      (A) when   (B) if   (C) though   (D) than

( ) 4. The city government announced the budget would be cut 30% this year.

      (A) by   (B) in   (C) at   (D) on

( ) 5. _____ the disagreement between management and labor, the new regulations have been carried on.

      (A) Despite   (B) Although   (C) Even if   (D) In spite

( ) 6. _____ his tight schedule, the manager take the responsibility with pleasure.

      (A) In spite of   (B) Despite of   (C) Although   (D) Even though

( ) 7. I have been looking forward to _____ you again soon.

      (A) see   (B) seeing   (C) have seen   (D) having seen

( ) 8. _____ Keiven, no one objects to the construction plan.

      (A) Except   (B) Except for   (C) Besides   (D) In addition to

中譯解析

1. B；中譯：因為是假日，辦公室明天將關閉。

   解析：空格前後為二個獨立子句，所以需用連接詞，辦公室關閉應該是因為假日，為因果關係，所以答案為 (B)。

2. B；中譯：如果沒有收到全部頁數，立刻通知我們。

   解析：空格應用表示條件的連接詞 if，其它連接詞均語文亦不符，所以答案為 (B)。

3. C；中譯：雖然其他隊伍很強，他們還是贏得那場競賽。

   解析：空格內應用從屬連接詞，表式讓步的雖然之意，故應用選項中的 though，答案為 (C)。

4. A；中譯：市政府宣佈今年預算將會削減 30%。

   解析：空格後面表示消減的幅度為 30%，故應填入表示程度的介系詞 by，答案為 (A)。

5. A；中譯：儘管勞資雙方對新的規則有不同的意見，新規則還是會繼續執行下去。

   解析：空格後面為名詞片語，故空格內只能填具有讓步意思的介系詞而不能用連接詞，選項中以介系詞 despite（儘管）最恰當，答案為 (A)。注意：in spite of = despite。

6. A；中譯：雖然行程緊湊，經理基於職責仍欣然允諾。

   解析：空格後面為片語，空格不可用連接詞（需接子句），需用介系詞。選項中 Although 及 Even though 均為連接詞不符合，另 In spite of = Despite（雖然、儘管）均為介系詞，且符合題意，故答案為 (A)。

7. B；中譯：我一直期盼著不久後能再見到你。

   解析：片語 look forward to 中，to 為介係詞，所以後面需接名詞或動名詞，故答案為 (B)。

8. B；中譯：除了凱文之外，沒有人反對這個建築計畫。

   解析：介系詞 Except（除…之外）用法等同於 except for，但如置於句首需用 except for。其它選項 Besides（除…之外還有），In addition to（除了…尚有）均與題意不符，故答案為 (B)。

UNIT 08 關係子句

關係詞分為關係代名詞及關係副詞,其引導的子句則依其用途為形容詞子句。關係詞具有連接二個子句的連接詞,及代替名詞或副詞之雙重功用。

一、關係子句

(一)、關係代名詞及其先行詞之關係

使用關係代名詞時,其前面一定會出現一個名詞(或代名詞),稱之為先行詞,而關係代名詞的作用則為修飾、說明該先行詞,同時做為該關係子句之主詞或受詞,下表為關係代名詞及其先行詞之關係。

先行詞	主格	所有格	受格
人	who	whose	whom
物	which	whose(of which)	which
人或物均可	that		that

例句

主格用法:This is the soldier who fought to defend our country before.(這個士兵他以前挺身保為我們國家。)

所有格用法:The workers whose salaries were cut were very angry.(薪水被削減的員工非常生氣。)

受格用法:She was the woman whom everyone admired.(她就那個人人稱讚的婦人。)

(二)、what 的用法

what 為包含先行詞的關係代名詞,前面不需加先行詞,

也就是:what = the thing(s) which (or that)

例句

What you do now is useless.（你現在做的事是沒用的。）

I don't know what you're talking about.（我不知道你在說甚麼）

其它與 what 有關之慣用語有 what we call（我們所說的）, what is call（所謂的）,
what is more（再者）等

（三）、關係代名詞與介系詞

　　關係子句中，時常因為使用片語動詞而出現動詞後面有介系詞出現，此時常將此介
系詞提於關係詞前，此時關係詞變成介系詞的受詞。另外，關係代名詞 that 前面不可加
介系詞（需用 which）。

例

The office which I used to work in is next to the train station.（我以前工作的辦公室
在火車站旁邊。）

= The office in which I used to work is next to the train station.

= The office where I used to work is next to the train station.

Here comes the man who I am waiting for.（來的這個人就是我要等的人。）

= Here comes the man for whom I am waiting.

I don't know the reason which he told a lie for.（我不知道他說謊的原因。）

= I don't know the reason for which he told a lie.

= I don't know the reason why he told a lie.

（四）、複合關係代名詞

　　包含先行詞的關係代名詞稱為複合關係代名詞，最常見者為 what, whoever,
whomever, whichever, whatever 等。可以引導名詞子句與副詞子句。

例句

Whatever happens to you, we will be glad to help you.（不管你發生甚麼事，我們都
樂意幫助你。）

Give this message to whoever is in charge.（把這訊息給所有負責的人。）

He gave whoever would ask some help.（他給任何要求他幫忙的人。）

（五）、關係副詞

關係副詞為表示原因、地點、理由等的關係詞，有一般常用的when, where, why, how 等。

You should tell me the day when he will come back.（你應該告訴我他將回來的日子。）

This is the house where I have lived for many years.（這就是我已經住過好幾年的房子。）

This is the way how she solve all problems.（這就是她解決所有問題的方法。）

Can you tell me the reason why you did so?（你能告訴我你會如此做的原因嗎？）

We talked about our project in the parking lot where I park my car every morning.（我們在我每天早上停車的停車場討論我們的計畫。）

（六）、複合關係副詞

複合關係詞類似複合關係代名詞，前面不需有先行詞，有whenever, wherever, however三種。

Whenever you are not sure, you should ask me.（當你不確定的時候，你可以問我。）

Take a seat wherever you want.（找任何一個你喜歡的位置坐下。）

However tired we are, we need to complete all our work.（不管有多累，我們都必須完成所有工作。）

三、關係詞應注意事項

（一）、why, where, which

當先行詞為表示場所或指原因的名詞時，這時可能用關係副詞（why 或 where），也可能用關係代名詞 （which）。當使用關係副詞時，後面需接完整子句。用關係代名詞時，因為關係代名詞代是代替先行詞（有可能是主詞或是受詞）所以接不完整的子句（少主詞或是少受詞）。

例句

My boss didn't understand the reason why I quit the job.（我老闆完全不瞭解為什麼

我要離職。）

My boss didn't understand the reason which I told him.（我老闆完全不瞭解我告訴他的理由。）（I told him 句子不完整，不知道 told 什麼，所以用關代 which）

The company where you saw yesterday is owned by my father.（你昨天看到的那家公司是我爸爸的。）

The shop which has many interesting goods is owned by my father.（那家有許多有趣商品的店是我爸爸的。）（has many interesting goods is owned by my father 句子不完整，沒有主詞，所以用關代 which）

（二）、that 與 which

在先行詞為物的狀況下，that 與 which 在形容詞子句中均能用於主格及受格，但二者並非完全通用。例如當先行詞是不定代名詞時（one, all, everything, anything…），不能用 which，應改用 that，另先行詞如有最高級形容詞修飾，亦只能用 that。

例句

You can buy anything that you want.（你可以買任何你想要的東西。）

Everything that he said means a big question.（他講的每件事情都是一大問題。）

That is the tallest tree that exists today in this area.（那棵樹是這區域目前活著最高大的樹。）

（三）、關係代名詞的省略

在某些句子中，並沒有看到關係代名詞，表示關係代名詞是可以省略的。關係代名詞能否省略的原則是：省略以後句子意義是否清楚完整、會不會造成誤解。一般而言，受格可以省略，主格不能省略。

例句

I like the book which you bought yesterday.（我喜歡你昨天買的書。）

= I like the book you bought yesterday.

O The man who is watching TV is my brother.（這個正在看電視的人是我哥哥。）

X The man is watching TV is my brother.

O The manager who had proposed his suggestion was transferred to the head office.（提案的經理被調到總公司去了。）

X The manager had proposed his suggestion was transferred to the main office.

三、應試重點

（一）、what , whatever 用法

說明：what = the thing(s) which（所…的事物或人），whatever（任何…事物；凡是…的東西），均不需先行詞。

❌ What happens to us, we will be able to handle it.

說明：句中應是指所有發生的任何事情，而不是發生的事，故語氣上應用 whatever 為對。

⭕ Whatever happens to us, we will be able to handle it.（不管發生甚麼事，我們都能應付。）

例句

What you said was right.（你所說的事是對的。）

Whatever I have is yours.（我所有的東西都是你的。）

You can eat whatever you like.（你可以吃任何想要的東西。）

（二）、形容詞子句簡化成分詞片語

說明：分詞片語是由一個分詞加上一些字所組成，可以用來修飾名詞跟代名詞。分詞片語是由形容詞子句縮減而來。先把形容詞子句中的關係代名詞去掉（只有關係代名詞為主詞時），再把 be 動詞去掉，主動動詞改為現在分詞，被動動詞改成過去分詞。

❌ She sat down in a corner was formed by two houses.

說明：句中應該有依形容詞子句 which was formed by two houses，which 為主格，不可單獨省略，但本句中可與 be 動詞同時省略。

⭕ She sat down in a corner（which was）formed by two houses.（她在二間房子形成的角落裏坐了下來。）

例句

People who buy lottery tickets are often found at bingo.

→簡化成：People buying lottery tickets are often found at bingo.

（通常會買樂透的人喜歡玩賓果。）

The man who was elected was very popular.

→簡化成：The elected man was very popular.

（當選的那個男人很受歡迎。）

（三）、介系詞＋關係詞用法

　　說明：當形容詞子句中有用到動詞片語，其介系詞常常提到關係詞前面。

　　✗Here is a magazine in that you are interested.

　　　說明：句中形容詞子句原為 that you are interested in，介係詞提至關係詞前面時，不能用that，應改用which。

　　○ Here is a magazine in which you are interested.（這裏有一本你喜歡的雜誌。）

　　例句

　　That is the boy of whom we have just speaking.（這就是那個我們剛剛談到的男孩。）

　　This is the room in which I was born.（這房間就是我出生的地方。）

（四）、which 與 that

　　說明：對關係代名詞的先行詞為物時，that 與 which 均可用於主格及受格，但二者並非完全通用。

　　✗Anything which you see here can be divided between you.（你們都可以平分在這裏看到的任何東西。）

　　　說明：關係詞先行詞是不定代名詞時（one, all, everything, anything…），不能用which，應改用that，另先行詞如有最高級形容詞修飾，亦需用 that。

　　○ Anything that you see here can be divided between you.（你們都可以平分在這裏看到的任何東西。）

　　例句

　　We should avoid mentioning anything that may embarrass him.（我們應該避免提到任何會使他尷尬的事。）

　　Which was the first steamship that crossed the Atlantic?（何者是第一艘橫越大西洋的蒸汽船?。）

📝 隨堂練習！

(   ) 1. The police questioned a driver _____ had been caught speeding.
  (A) why   (B) whose   (C) who   (D) whom

(   ) 2. _____ you come to Taipei, let us know in advance.
  (A) Wherever   (B) Whenever   (C) However   (D) Whomever

(   ) 3. The teacher _____ we met yesterday will retire next month.
  (A) to who   (B) whom   (C) whose   (D) which

(   ) 4. He was respected by the people _____ he studied because he
  worked so hard.
  (A) with who   (B) whom   (C) with whom   (D) that

(   ) 5. Previous failures, _____ the manager had caused, discouraged us
  from working hard.
  (A) who   (B) whom   (C) that   (D) which

(   ) 6. People _____ have dogs usually get more exercise than those who
  do not.
  (A) who   (B) whom   (C) whose   (D) which

(   ) 7. He was the man whom all his friends admired and who won the respect
  even of his enemies.
  (A) All his friends admired him, and even he is respected by his enemies.
  (B) He was admired by all his friends and those who won the respect of
    his enemies
  (C) He was the man of whom his enemies respect, and then was admired
    by all his friends.
  (D) All his friends who won the respect of his enemies admired him, even
    though he is respected by his enemies.

(   ) 8. Do not move anything _____ you see in the room. All of them are
  Alex's favorites.
  (A) what   (B) who   (C) which   (D) that

中譯解析

1. C；中譯：警察盤問一個超速被逮的司機。

解析：speeding 超速。空格後面是動詞，需填入主格的關係代名詞，先行詞是 a driver（人），所以答案為 (C)。

2. B；中譯：不管何時你到台北來，事先讓我們知道。

解析：選項中除 However 外，其餘均為複合關係代名詞，依句意應用表示無論什麼時候的 Whenever，所以答案為 (B)。

3. B；中譯：我們昨天見到的那個老師下個月就要退休。

解析：先行詞是 teacher，是關係子句的受格，所以關係代名詞要用 whom，答案為 (B)。

4. C；中譯：他被跟他一起學習的人所尊重，因為他十分努力。

解析：本句中關係詞需用受格 whom，且將原來形容詞子句中的介系詞（whom he studies with…）提於關係詞前面，形成 with whom，答案為 (C)。

5. D；中譯：之前經理造成的失敗造成我們無心工作。

解析：空格中需填入為關係代名詞，先行詞為 Previous failures（屬物），故關係詞可用 that 或 which，但因此處為非限定用法，只能用 which，不可 that，所以答案為 (D)。

6. A；中譯：有養狗的人通常比沒有養狗的人有較多的運動。

解析：空格後面是動詞，所以研判空格應該填入主格的關係代名詞當作主詞，因先行詞是 people，所以關係詞用 who，答案為 (A)。

7. A；中譯：他是一個所有朋友都欽羨的人，也是個贏得敵人尊敬的人。

（他是一個受他所有的朋友都讚賞且甚至被他的敵人所尊敬的人。）

解析：

(A) 他所有的朋友都讚賞他甚至也被他的敵人所尊敬。

(B) 他受他所有的朋友及那些受他的敵人所尊敬的人的讚賞。

(C) 他是一個受敵人所尊敬的人，且因此被所有朋友所讚賞。

(D) 雖然他被敵人所尊敬，所有受他的敵人所尊重的朋友都讚賞他。

本句題目需注意各關係子句間的關係，才不會被混淆，題目主要意思是他受到他的所有朋友及他的敵人的尊重或讚賞，所以答案為 (A)。

8. D；中譯：不要碰任何你在房間看到的東西。那些全部都是艾利克斯最喜歡的東西。

解析：此句缺少一個關係代名詞，前面有 anything 所以不能選 (C) 要選 (D) that。

UNIT 09 被動語態

　　英文句子分為主動語態與被動語態。主動語態的主詞是動作的執行者，其句子結構為主詞＋動詞（及物）＋受詞…，而被動語態的主詞是動作的承受者（受詞），其句子結構受詞+be 動詞+動詞過去分詞＋by （或to）主詞…，而該動作的執行者（原來的主詞）常常是被省略。

一、被動語態

（一）、現在式的被動語態：is / am / are + 及物動詞的過去分詞

例句

Our classroom is cleaned every day.（我們的教室每天被清掃。）

I am asked to study hard by my mother.（我被我母親要求要用功念書。）

（二）、過去式的被動語態：was / were + 及物動詞的過去分詞

例句

A new shop was built last year.（去年一間新的店被創立了。）

During the storm, several trees were uprooted.（許多樹木在那場風暴中被連根拔起。）

（三）、現在完成時的被動語態：has / have + been + 及物動詞的過去分詞

例句

A lot of soldiers have been wounded.（有許多士兵已經被傷了。）

This book has been translated into many languages.（這本書已經被翻譯成許多種語言了。）

Many artificial satellites have been sent up into space by many countries.（許多人造衛星已經被許多國家發射上太空了。）

（四）、未來式的被動語態：will+ be + 及物動詞的過去分詞

例句

The house will be sold in July.（這房子七月要被出售。）

A new hospital will be built in our city.（一間新的醫院要蓋在我們城市。）

Theywill be married next month.（他們下個月要結婚。）

（五）、現在進行式的被動語態：am / is / are + being + 及物動詞的過去分詞

例句

The machine is being fixed right now.（這機器現在正在被修理中。）

Trees are being planted over there by them.（樹木正被種植在那邊。）

Some toys are being played by a boy there.（一些玩具正被一個男孩玩著。）

（六）、不定詞的被動語態：to + be + 及物動詞的過去分詞

例句

There are two books to be read.（有二本書要念。）

There are twenty more trees to be planted.（有二十多棵樹木要種。）

She still has three assignments to be handed in.（她有三個作業要交。）

（七）、不能用於被動語態的動詞

1. 不及物動詞，意即不加受詞的動詞，則多無被動語態。

例句

Birds can fly.（鳥會飛。）

He became a good teacher.（他成為一個好老師。）

She arrived at New York last night.（她昨晚抵達紐約。）

2. 部分表示狀態而非動作的及物動詞（例：have, cost, want, lack, fit, have, hold, marry, own, wish, cost, notice…）不能用被動式。

例句

O The new captain's smile lacks warmth.（這位新艦長的微笑缺乏溫暖。）

X Warmth is lacked by the new captain's smile.

O Eric has an old scooter.（艾瑞克有部舊的摩托車。）

X A scooter is had by Eric.

O The wallet cost 500 dollars. (這皮夾價值 500 元。)

X The wallet is cost 500 dollars.

3. 表示瞬間或消失意義的動詞，如appear, die,disappear, end, fail, happen, last, lie, remain, sit, spread, stand，就算是可當及物動詞用，仍不可用被動式。

例句

O Gradually a smile appeared on the father's face. (這父親的臉上漸漸地露出笑容。)

X Gradually the father's face was appeared a smile on.

O Tom failed history last semester. (湯姆上學期歷史考試不及格。)

X History was failed by Tom last semester.

O She sat the child in the chair. (她把孩子放在椅子上。)

X The child was sat in the chair by her

注意

rise, fall, happen是不及物動詞；raise, seat是及物動詞。

例句

O The price has risen. (價格已經上揚。)

X The price has been risen.

O The accident happened last week. (意外上週發生。)

X The accident was happened last week.

O The price has been raised. (價格已經被抬高。)

X The price has raised.

O Please be seated. (請就坐。)

X Please seat.

（八）、被動語態特殊用法

Get + 過去分詞構成的被動語態

Get + 過去分詞也可以構成被動語態，用這種結構的句子側重于動作的結果而不是動作本身，在此 get 可以看成 be 動詞使用。

例句

The man got hurt on his way home. (那個男人在回家的路上受傷了。)

How did the glass get broken? (杯子怎麼破了？)

His dog got run by a car. (他的狗被車輾過去了。)

二、授與、感官、使役動詞的被動語態

（一）、授與動詞為可接受兩個受詞動詞（如give,bring,send,teach…），其主動語態有兩
種型態：

A.主詞＋授與動詞＋人（間接受詞）＋物（直接受詞）

例句

The father sent his son a new bicycle.（這父親送他兒子一輛腳踏車。）

B.主詞＋授與動詞＋物（直接受詞）＋介系詞＋人（間接受詞）

例句

Julie sent a letter to George.（朱麗寄一封信給喬治。）

（二）、授與動詞之被動語態亦有兩種型態：

1. 以間接受詞為主詞：

人（間接受詞）＋be動詞＋授與動詞p.p.＋物＋by 動作的施予者.

例句

The boy was sent a new bicycle (by his father).

George was sent a letter (by Julie).

2. 以直接受詞為主詞：

物（直接受詞）＋be 動詞＋授與動詞 p.p.＋to＋人＋by 動作的施予者.

例句

A letter was sent to George (by Julie).（一封信被寄給喬治。）

A new bicycle was sent to the boy (by his father).（一輛新腳踏車被送給那男孩。）

（三）、感官動詞的被動語態（hear、see、watch、hear、feel、notice等）

主動：主詞＋感官動詞＋受詞＋原形動詞

被動：受詞＋be＋過去分詞＋to 原形動詞（不定詞）＋by 主詞

例句

主動：I saw him do it.（我看到他做的。）

被動：He was seen to do it by me.（他被我看到有做。）

主動：I could hear her come into the room.（我能聽到她走進房間。）

被動：She was heard to come into the room.（她被聽見走進房間。）

（四）、使役動詞的被動語態（make、let、have）

使役動詞用被動型式時，make 後面動詞用不定詞，let 用 be allowed 代替被動型式，但have不能做被動使用。

主動：主詞+使役動詞+受詞+原形動詞

被動：受詞+ be p.p+to 原形動詞 + by 主詞

例句

主動：He made me wait outside.（他要我在外面等。）

被動：I was made to wait outside.（我要求在外面等。）

主動：Mother made me clean my room.（我母親要我清理房間。）

被動：I was made to clean my roomby my mother.（我被我母親要求要清理房間。）

主動：She let me enter her office.（她讓我進她辦公室。）

被動：I was allowed to enter her office.（我被允許進她辦公室）

、應試重點

（一）、各時態被動式表示法

說明：注意每一種動詞時態被動式用法，尤其是被動進行式及被動完成式需特別注意，因為其牽涉到二個be動詞的用法搭配。

✗My car will have being fixed for 5 day until tomorrow morning.

說明：句中應該用未來完成式的被動時態，未來被動完成式句型是will have been +p.p。

○ My car will have been fixed for 5 day until tomorrow morning.（到明天上午為止，我的車子將已送修達五天了。）

例句

Meat is being eaten by me now.（現在肉正被我吃掉。）

Meat has been eaten by me already.（肉已經被我吃掉了。）

（二）、使役動詞或感官動詞被動式

說明：注意使役動詞或感官動詞被動式時，原形動詞的補語會變成不定詞。

✗His secretary was made typing those files by his boss this morning.

說明：本句主動式應該為The boss made his secretary type those files this morning.改為被動式後，type原形動詞應該改成不定詞to type表被動。

O His secretary was made to type those files by his boss this morning.（秘書今天早上被老闆要求把這些文件打字。）

> **例句**
>
> The poor fellow was seen to stay outside last night.（昨天晚上這可憐的傢伙被看到待在外面。）
>
> The vice-president was made to meet us in person.（副總裁被要求單獨來見我們。）

（三）、常用的被動型態片語

說明：注意常用的被動型態片語，例如：be depressed to, be referred to, be determined to, be addicted to, be covered with, be satisfied with, be surprised at, be worried about, be accustomed to…等

> **例句**
>
> The lion is referred to as king of the jungle.（獅子被稱為叢林之王。）
>
> David is addicted to reading detective novels.（大衛沉迷於看偵探小說。）
>
> I was surprised at his passing that math exam.（我對他能通過數學考試感到驚奇。）

✓ 隨堂練習！

( ) 1. The historical building _____ after the earthquake.

    (A) repaired   (B) was repaired   (C) repair   (D) to repair

( ) 2. Today, more computer games for children _____ than ever.

    (A) is sold   (B) sold   (C) are being sold (D) sell

( ) 3. Goods that _____ in China are exported all over the world.

    (A) are manufactured   (B) manufactured

    (C) being manufactured   (D) have manufactured

( ) 4. About 80% of the shoes in this store _____ from China.

    (A) importing   (B) are imported   (C) import   (D) has imported

( ) 5. The car accident which _____ right here two days ago killed 3 people in the end.

    (A) wasoccurred   (B) had been occurred

    (C) had occurred   (D) occurred

( ) 6. Does this umbrella _____ you?

    (A) belong to   (B) be belonged to (C) belong for   (D) belong by

( ) 7. His new job is very busy and he _____ working late until 10 or 11 p.m.

    (A) is used to   (B) used to   (C) uses to   (D) was used to

( ) 8. Livestock in this farm was raised only by the grain and _____ grass in the past.

    (A) wasrisen   (B) rose   (C) was raised   (D) raised

中譯解析

1. B；中譯：這座歷史建築在地震後被修復了。

    解析：房子不會自行修復，故需要用被動式才合理，故動詞要用 was repaired，答案為 (B)。

2. C；中譯：今日，孩子的電腦遊戲銷售的比過去多。

    解析：句中有 today，故需用現在式，且東西是被銷售，需用被動，再考慮該情形不屬於習慣或規律性，故用進行式表示現在趨勢，故答案為 (C)。

3. A；中譯：在中國製造的貨品被銷往世界各地。

    解析：句中空格處為形容詞子句的動詞，因其先行詞 goods（貨品）需備製造出來，所以用被動式，答案為 (A)。

4. B；中譯：這家店大約百分之八十的鞋子是從中國進口的。

    解析：主詞是代表物的鞋子，所以與動詞進口是被動關係，故應用被動語態，答案為(B)

5. D；中譯：三天前發生在這邊的車禍意外最終造成三人死亡。

    解析：空格內需用表示車禍發生的動詞occur，但注意不可用被動式（不及物動詞），在此表示過去時間用過去式即可，答案為 (D)。

6. A；中譯：這隻傘屬於你的嗎?

    解析：belong to somebody（屬於某人），此片語不可用被動語態（如 is belonged to），故答案為 (A)。

7. A；中譯：他的新工作非常忙，他已經習慣於工作到十點或十一點。

    解析：used to +V 表示過去曾經…，be used to + Ving 表示習慣於，依題意是指現在已經習慣於工作到十點或十一點，且應該用現在試表示一種習慣，所以答案為 (A)。

8. C；中譯：在過去這家農場的牲畜只有用穀物及草餵養。

    解析：牲畜是被用飼料餵養的，所以需用被動過去式，並注意動詞三態：rise（升高）-rose-risen，raise（養育，抬起）-raised-raised.所以答案為 (C)。

UNIT 10 假設語氣

　條件句有三種語氣表達，分別是 1.祈使語氣 2.直說語氣 3.假設語氣。

　假設語氣是指在一種特定的情況下，推斷（或必定）會發生的事情的一種句子結構，其句子結構包含條件子句（或稱 if 子句）及主要子句（或稱結果子句）。在不同的假設下，要用不同的時態來表達。if 子句是副詞子句的一種。假設法有三種 1.與現在事實相反 2.與過去事實相反 3.與未來事實相反，需要注意動詞的變化。

一、直說語氣條件句

　if 子句引導的子句為現在式，它的結果子句可能為現在式（通常表習慣）、未來式（多用 will 加原形）、表達語態（使用語態助動詞 might, should等）。所以假如在結果子句看到現在式，未來式等句型，也可推得前面條件句一定是現在式，表示說話者心中並未與事實相反的狀況。

（一）、句型：If + S + V（現在式），S + V（現在式）
　　表示現在的事實或常理。

　　例句
　　　If it rains, my dog barks.（如果現在下雨，我的狗就會吠。）
　　　If I get up at 6am, I usually get to work on time.（如果我六點鐘起床，通常我就可以準時上班。）

（二）、句型：If + S +V（現在式或Be + V-ing），S + will + V
　　表示未來的事實。
　　注意
　　　因 if 子句屬於副詞子句，會用現在式來代替未來式，所以 if 子句不可能用未來式。
　　例句
　　　If it rains tonight, the concert will be canceled.（如果今天晚上下雨，音樂會就會被取消。）

If she comes tomorrow, I will tell her about our plan.（如果她明天有來，我會告訴她我們的計劃。）

（三）、句型：If + S + V（現在式）, S + 助動詞 + V（原形）

表示未來有可能的事實。

If Cindy hands in her proposal early tomorrow, she might take a break.

（如果辛蒂明天早一點交案，她可能可以休息。）

If he comes home in August this year, he could bake a birthday cook for you.

（如果他今年八月回家，他可以烤一個生日蛋糕給你。）

三、假設語氣條件句

（一）、與現在事實相反

句型：If + S + V（過去式）, S + would / could / might / should + V

if子句的動詞一定是過去式，結果子句也一定是would+ V。該類句型表示如果現在沒有發生甚麼事情（或未來肯定不會發生），現在則結果就不會這樣…，所以與現在的真實情況是相反的。

例句

If I had a billion dollars, I would buy you a house.（如果我有一百萬元，我就會買間房子給你。）【但事實上我沒有一百萬，所以現在我沒有買】

If I were you, I would tell the truth.（假如我是你的話，我就會說實話。）【但事實上我不是你，所以現在我沒有說實話】

If he had studied hard, he could pass in the examination.（假如他有用功的話，他就會通過考試。）【但事實上他沒有用功，所以現在他沒有通過考試】

注意

在此情況中，如果 if 子句出現 be 動詞，不論何種名稱身分，正式用法一律需使用were。但一般口語可以用was。

例句

If I were you, I would buy that house.（如果我是你，我就會買那房子。）

If he were not here, Mary could speak loudly.（假如他不在這裏，瑪莉就會大聲講

話。）

（二）、與過去事實相反

句型： If + S + had + V.pp（過去分詞）, S + would / could / might / should + have + V.pp（過去分詞）

句子中看到假設子句動詞是過去完成式，就知道後面會有would have的句型，表示該假設子句中談到的事情事發生在過去，主要子句要表達要是當時不是怎樣…，現在就不會是如此…所以是與過去的真實情況相反的（當然，主要子句中敘述的情況也沒發生）。

例句

If we had gone to the movie last night, we would have seen your favorite actress.（如果我們昨晚有去看電影，我們就可以看到你最喜愛的女演員了。）【但事實上他們昨晚沒有去看電影，且沒看到喜愛的女演員】

If he had driven slower at that time, the accident would not have happened.（如果當時他開慢一點，這意外就不會發生了。）【但事實上他開很快，且發生車禍】

We would have won the game if he had not broken his arm.（如果他沒有摔斷手臂，我們就會贏得比賽。）【但事實上他摔斷手臂，且沒有贏比賽】

（三）、與未來事實相反

1. 句型：If + S + were to + V（原形）, S + would / could / might / should + V（原形）
表示完全不可能在未來發生的事。

例句

If I were to go abroad, I would go to the U.S.（倘若有一天我能出國，我要去美國。）

【事實上，說話者未來幾乎不可能出國】

If the sun were to rise in the west, I would love you.（如果太陽從西邊升起，我才會愛你。）

【事實上，太陽根本不可能從西邊升起】

2. 句型：If + S + should + V（原形）, S + would/will + V（原形）
可能性極小，機會渺小的是，萬一。

例句

If it should rain tomorrow, I would not go.（萬一明天下雨，我就不去。）

【下雨的機率很低，但還是有可能】

If he should come, he would write a letter to tell us.

（萬一他會來，他會寫一封信給我們。）

【他會來的機率很低，但是還是有可能】

（四）、省略 if 的假設句

假設子句的if可以加以省略，原子句中的結構變成倒裝句，但主要子句完全不變，句型如下：

1. Were + S. + Adj./ N. …, S+ would +V（原形）

2. Had + S + P.P. …, S + would + have+ V（過去分詞）

3. Should + S + 原V. …, S + would +V（原形）

例句

If I were you, I would learn to cook.（如果我是你，我就會學煮飯。）

= Were I you, I would learn to cook.

If I had been there, I would have helped you.（如果我有在那裡，我就會幫忙你。）

= Had I been there, I would have helped you.

If it should rain, she would not come.（萬一下雨天，她就不會來了。）

= Should it rain, she would not come.

（五）、其他類型假設語氣

1. 表但願（wish）的假設法

（1）S. wish (that) S. + were/ V-ed →與現在事實相反

（2）S. wish (that) S. + had + P.P. →與過去事實相反

例句

I wish I were a doctor.（但願我是個醫生。）

I wish I had studied hard in my youth.（我但願我年輕時有用功念書。）

2. 表好像（as if）的假設法

（1）S. + V. + as if + S. + were / V-ed →與現在事實相反

（2）S. + V. + as if + S. + had + P.P. →與過去事實相反

例句

The child talks as if he were a man.（這小孩講話就好像是個大人。）

He talks as if he had known the news yesterday.（他講的就如同他昨天就知道這消息。）

≡、應試重點

（一）、假設句時態判斷運用

說明：判別是一般假設或與事實相反，用主要子句的時態，並注意假設語句的變型。

✗If you have parked your there, they would have towed it away.

說明：本句依判斷應為與過去事實相反的假設（因主要子句用 would +現在完成式），故if子句需用過去完成式來表示與過去相反的事實。

○ If you had parked your car there, they would have towed it away.（假如你有在那邊停車，你就會被拖吊。）【但事實上沒有停在那】

例句

I wish that I had never met her before.（我要是以前沒遇見過她就好了。）

【但事實上是有見過她】

If john were here now, we could play tennis.（如果約翰有在這裡，我們就能打網球了。）【但事實上他不在】

（二）、假設句的省略

說明：假設句中的if子句中的連接詞if可以省略，其條件句則需變成倒裝結構（例如 Had I +…, I would…）

✗Have he known your address, he would have written you.

說明：本句依判斷應為與過去事實相反的假設（因主要子句用 would + 現在完成式），且省略掉 if，但子句需用過去完成式，助動詞需用 had，且需倒裝。

○ Had he known your address, he would have written you.（假如他知道你的地址，他就會寫信給你。【但事實上他不知道】

例句

Were I in your position, I would make the same decision.（假如我在你位子上，我也會做相同的決定。）【但我不在你位子上】

Had you informed us earlier, we would have taken the necessary steps.（假如你早一點通知我們，我們就可以採取必要措施。）【但你沒有通知】

句型	錯誤樣態	正確樣態	說明
if only 要是…該有多好	If only you are here.	If only you were here. (要是你現在在這裏該有多好。)	if only +過去式，表示與現在事實相反 if only +過去完成，表示與過去事實相反。
	If only you were here yesterday.	If only you had been here yesterday. (要是你昨天在這裏該有多好。)	
it is time 該是…時候了	It is time we tell her the truth.	It is time we told her the truth. (該是我們告訴他實話的時候了。)	it is time+過去式，表示現在該做而沒做，有時用high time來更加強調。
would rather 寧願	I would rather you do it now.	I would rather you did it now. (我寧願你現在做它。)	would rather +過去式，表示與現在或未來事實相反 would rather +過去完成，表示與過去事實相反。
	I would rather you did it yesterday.	I would rather you had done it yesterday. (我寧願你昨天做它。)	

隨堂練習！

(　　) 1. If Mr. Brown _____ you, he would make use of the Internet.

　　　(A) is 　　　(B) are 　　　(C) will be 　　　(D) were

(　　) 2. If they _____ employee will be reimbursed for their expenses.

　　　(A) request 　　(B) requested 　　(C) had request 　　(D) can request

(　　) 3. I wish that he _____ there when my boss came in yesterday.

　　　(A)were 　　　(B) was 　　　(C) have been 　　　(D) had been

(　　) 4. If it _____ tomorrow, we won't go to picnic.

　　　(A) rain 　　　(B) rains 　　　(C) will rain 　　　(D) shall rain

(　　) 5. But for air, we _____ live today.

　　　(A) can 　　　(B) can not 　　　(C) could 　　　(D) could not

(　　) 6. _____ I not so busy now, I would do it for you.

　　　(A)If 　　　(B) Was 　　　(C) Are 　　　(D) Were

(　　) 7. He seemed as if he _____ to ski then, but actually he didn't.

　　　(A) learn 　　　(B) learned 　　　(C) have learned 　　(D) had learned

(　　) 8. _____ I known you earlier, I would have given you some
suggestions.

　　　(A) Have 　　　(B) Had 　　　(C)If 　　　(D) Was

中譯解析

1. D；中譯：如果伯朗先生是你的話，他就會使用網路。

   解析：該句由後面主要子句用 would+V，知其為與現在事實相反之假設句，故空格內 be 動詞一律用 were，答案為 (D)。

2. A；中譯：假如她們要求，員工必須賠償她們的費用。

   解析：這是表示直說語氣的條件句未來的狀況，條件子句（if 子句）用一般現在式，主要子句用 will+V（原形），故答案為 (A)。

3. D；中譯：我但願昨天我老闆進來時他能在那裏。

   解析：wish（但願），通常是用在一個不可能實現的願望，或與事實相反的假設，由此句亦可看出是與過去事實相反，故要用 had+Vp.p，答案為 (D)。

4. B；中譯：假如明天下雨，我們就不會去野餐。

   解析：條件子句（if 子句）用現在式表未來時間，主要子句用 will+V（原形），won't = will not，故答案為 (B)。

5. D；中譯：要不是有空氣，我們今天就不能活了。

   解析：but for（要不是），是一個與現在事實相反的假設用語，故後面主要子句用 could+V（原形），故答案為 (D)。

6. D；中譯：我當時要不是那麼忙，我就會幫你做。

   解析：由後面主要子句知這是一個與現在事實相反的假設用語，且用倒裝句，故空格需用 be 動詞 were，故答案為 (D)。

7. D；中譯：他看起來似乎學過滑雪，但事實上沒有。

   解析：由句中知他事實上沒有學過滑雪，as if（似乎）其用法與 if 假設句一樣，對與過去事實相反時，as if 後面用 had+Vp.p，故答案為 (D)。

8. B；中譯：假如我早一點認識你，我就可以給你一些建議了。

   解析：由主要子具可看出是與過去時事相反 （would have+Vp.p），故條件句應用要用 had+Vp.p，但需倒裝，故答案為 (B)。

UNIT (11) 特殊句型

　　英文中除了五大句型及被動、假設等用法外，尚有其他特殊句型，本章介紹強調句型、附加問句、祈使句、There be句型、倒裝句、感歎句及省略句等句型，這些句型部分常見於口語會話中，考試中亦不時可見。

一、句型解說

（一）、強調句型

1. 句型結構：It is（was）+adj+…+to+V（或Ving或that子句）
   句子強調的是後面to+V（或Ving或that子句）的事，it 是虛主詞，be的時態的一般是現在式，當它後面的句子為過去式時，才用過去式。

   例句

   It was nice to see him again.（能再次看到他真好。）

   It is my great pleasure meeting such a nice speaker.（能會見這麼好的演講者是我的榮幸。）

   It is evident that he's telling a lie.（他很明顯的正在說謊。）

2. 除此之外，不要忘記 it 通常用在句子中表示時間、距離及天氣等。

   例句

   It's lunchtime.（現在式午餐時間。）

   It is a six-hour drive to Dallas.（到達拉斯需要六小時車程。）

   It was rain last night.（昨晚有下雨。）

（二）、附加問句

　　附加問句指附帶於直述句句尾的簡單問句，通常只有兩個字。前面直述句若為肯定，則句尾簡單問句需為否定，反之亦然。

　　例句

   Thereis a taxi outside, isn't there?（外面有一輛計程車，不是嗎？）

   Tom doesn'twork very well today, does he?（湯姆今天沒有做的很好，是吧？）

She has beautiful eyes, doesn't she?（她有雙漂亮的眼睛，不是嗎？）

注意

當附加問句的語調向下時，則發問者目的並不是真的在問一個問題，而只是要對方同意你的談話，這時回答者會被期望回答的立場（否定獲肯定）是與發問者相同的，而語調上揚時，則說話者附加問句就是一個真正的問句，回答者可依自己立場選擇回答。

A：Tom doesn't look very well today, does he?↓【語調下降】

B：No, he looks awful.【被期待與 A 相同立場】

C：You couldn't do me a favor, could you?↑【語調上升】

D：It depends what it is.【視狀況回答，不需考慮 C 的立場】

（三）、祈使句

1. 祈使句的主詞是you，但一般被省略，句子直接以動詞原形開頭。

例句

Take this note to the commander.（拿這份通知給指揮官。）

Tell the patient that the doctor has been delayed.（告訴病人醫生被耽誤了。）

Please give me a call tomorrow about noon.（大約明天中午請給我個電話。）

2. Let's 句型

有些稱之第一人稱祈使句（有別於上述第二人稱you），let's=let us，表示建議、請求或者命令之意。

Let's have a celebration.（我們來慶祝一下。）

Let's finish the project as soon as possible.（我們盡快把這計畫完成。）

Let's not stay at home tonight.（今晚不要待在家裏。）

（四）、There +be 動詞句型

There be結構中，there 為虛主詞，be動詞在此意義為「存在」之意，真正的主詞為be動詞後面的名詞，故其動詞單複數的形式應配合該名詞。

例句

There is some sugar in the bowl.（碗裏面有一些糖。）

There were three students absent today.（今天有三位學生缺席。）

There are some people upstairs.（樓上有許多人。）

（五）、倒裝句

1. 倒裝句型結構：否定副詞+ 助動詞+主詞 +動詞+受詞…

倒裝結構是指一般敘述句的詞語位置變動而形成的句子。就是將強調的部分結構放在句首，並且將主詞與助動詞倒置，以達到「強調」作用之句型。

例句

一般句：We had hardly started when it started to rain.（當開始下雨時我們都還沒開始。）

倒裝句：Hardly had we started when it started to rain.← 強調副詞 hardly（幾乎不）

2. 以下所列的副詞（或片語）因強調而提到句子最前面時，須使用倒裝句，也就是將主詞與助動詞倒置。

（1）否定性副詞片語/子句

例：Seldom will you see such an enthusiastic student.（你很少會看到如此熱心的學生。）

常見的否定副詞（片語）有hardly, scarcely, barely, rarely, never, seldom, little, nowhere, no longer, not until …, no sooner…(than) , not only…(but) also, in rare cases, on no account, under no circumstances…等。

（2）Only 帶頭的副詞/副片/副詞子句

Only in recent years have people begun to realize the importance of wildlife conservation.（直到最近人們才瞭解到野生動物保護的重要性。）

（3）表「位置」或「處所」之副詞/介詞片語

At the east side of the hill stood an old house.（一間老房子座落於山的東邊。）

（六）、感歎句

感歎句結構：What + a(n) + adj.（或 N.）+ N. ! 或 How + adj.（或adv.）+S.+V. !

感歎句主要為對原句中的主詞補語表示讚嘆，故將其提於句首，常見於日常口語會話中。

例句

What a terrible accident it is!（多恐怖的意外事件啊！）

What a beautiful girl she is!（她是多麼漂亮的一個女孩啊！）

How terrible it is!（這是多麼恐怖啊！）

（七）、省略句

在上下文中，為避免重複，任何句子成分都有可能省略，根據具體語境進行理解。

1. 在時間、條件、讓步等從屬子句中，當從屬子句的主詞跟主要子句的主詞一致時，從屬子句的主詞可以省略，同時將從屬子句的動詞變為分詞形式。

例如

When I walked on the street yesterday, I met a friend of you.（當我昨天在街上走時，我遇到你一個朋友。）

Walking on the street, I met a friend of you.

2. 在時間、地點、條件、讓步等從屬子句中，當從屬子句的主詞跟主要子句的主詞一致或從屬子句的主語是 it 後接 be 動詞時，從句的主語、謂語可以省略。

例如

If (he is) given the same treatment, he is sure to get well.（假如他被施以同樣的治療，確信他可以好轉。）

If (it is) possible, I will visit you tomorrow.（假如可以的話，我明天將拜訪你。）

3. 當省略不定詞的內容時，須保留 to。

例如

A：Alice, why didn't you come yesterday?（愛麗絲，你昨天為什麼不來？）

B：I was going to, but I had an unexpected visitor.（我要去，但是突然有人來拜訪我。）

二、應試重點

（一）、It is that+…句型

說明：It is that +…句型中，it 為需主詞，真正主詞為後面的名詞子句或片語，為非常常見的結構，需能明白辨識出 it 所代表的含意，尤其是句子很長時，應把握句型分析原則才不會被搞混。

ＸIt is obvious for modern society in Taiwan to hold part-time jobs has become a growing tendency among university students.

說明：看到開頭本句是 It is 的句子就要注意後面要找 that 引導的名詞子句、不定詞 to+V 或動名詞 Ving，找出主詞，才能解題或看懂句子意思。本題的題目很長,尤其 it is 到後面看到 to 已經隔很遠,其實這一串都只是主詞補語,真主詞在後面,且 to 無法引導一名詞子句,應改為 that 子句,正確方式如以下正解所示。

O It is obvious for modern society in Taiwan that holding part-time jobs has become a growing tendency among university students. (在現代台灣社會中,擁有兼差已經成為大學生之間成為一個成長趨勢是很明顯的。)

例句

It is compulsory for all motorcyclists to wear helmets. (所有騎摩托車的人都必須戴安全帽是強制性的。)

It is possible to discern many different techniques in her work. (從她的作品中可以識別出許多不同的創作手法。)

(二)、倒裝句(否定副詞開頭、問句型)

說明:倒裝句考題最常出現在以否定副詞開頭的句中,把握住倒裝就是將主詞動詞順序對調的大原則即可。

X No sooner he had arrived at his home than it began to rain.

說明:錶是否定的副詞級片語用(hardly, neither, nor, never, no, not, scarcely, seldom…)於句首時,需用倒裝句型,故句中應將註動詞提至主詞前。

O No sooner he had arrived at his home than it began to rain. (她一抵達他家就馬上下起雨來。)

例句

Not until last week did the chance come to visit the school (一直到上個禮拜才有機會拜訪這所學校。)

On no condition must you go alone. (不論如何你都要單獨前往。)

隨堂練習！

(　) 1. I failed in the final examination last term and only then _____ the importance of studies.

(A) I realized　(B) I had realized　(C) had I realized　(D) did I realize

(　) 2. Of the making of good books there is no end; neither _____ any end to their influence man's lives.

(A) there is　(B) there are　(C) is there　(D) are there

(　) 3. Scientists say it may be five or six years _____ it is possible to test this medicine on human patients.

(A) since　(B) after　(C) before　(D) when

(　) 4. It was with great joy _____ he received the news that his lost daughter had been found.

(A) because　(B) which　(C) since　(D) that

(　) 5. It was _____ back home after the experiment.

(A) not until midnight did he go　(B) until midnight that he didn't go
(C) not until midnight that he went　(D) until midnight when he didn't go

中譯解析

1. D；中譯：我上學期期末考不及格，且到那時我才了解讀書的重要性。

解析：當 only 修飾狀語置於句首時，句子要用倒裝，且該句是過去某時的動作，需用過去簡單式。故正確答案為 (D)。

2. C；中譯：好書的創作是無止盡的，而好書對人類的影響也是無止盡的。

解析：根據句子結構，neither 等否定詞提前時，句子倒裝，再根據 there be 句型中 be 的形式要求，可知答案選 (C)。

3. C；中譯：科學家說可能還要再過五到六年這種新藥才能在人體上試驗。

解析：根據句子的意思，科學家對藥品先要進行反復試驗後才能用於病人身上，因此答案選 (C)。

4. D；中譯：他收到他失蹤的女兒已經被找到的消息後非常高興。

解析：強調句型，答案選 (D)。

5. C；中譯：他一直到半夜實驗完以後才回到家。

解析：對句型 It is not until + sth. + that 子句+進行強調時，故答案選 (C)。

02
CHAPTER

重要單字片語

與人格特性、健康相關

Active [`æktɪv] *adj.* 主動的；活躍的

例 She is an **active** member of the school's dancing club.
她是學校舞蹈俱樂部的一名活躍會員。

Addiction [ə`dɪkʃən] *n.* 成癮

例 John is now fighting his **addiction** to alcohol.
約翰現在正努力戒除酒癮。

Aggressive [ə`grɛsɪv] *adj.* 積極的；侵略性的

例 An **aggressive** young man can go far in our company.
有進取心的青年人在本公司能大展鴻圖。

Allergy [`ælədʒɪ] *n.* 過敏

例 Every spring, the blossoming flowers aggravate her **allergy**.
每年春天盛開的花朵會加重她的過敏。

Ambulance [`æmbjələns] *n.* 救護車

例 We helped her into the **ambulance**.
我們扶她上了救護車。

Antipathy [æn`tɪpəθɪ] *n.* 憎惡；反感

例 Jim has an **antipathy** against Mary.
吉姆對瑪莉有反感。

Appearance [ə`pɪrəns] *n.* 外貌；外觀

例 He was very insecure about his **appearance**.
他對自己的外貌沒有信心。

Arrogant [`ærəgənt] *adj.* 傲慢的；自大的

例 You'r so **arrogant** to assume you'll win every time.
你以為每次都能贏未免太自大了。

Captious [`kæpʃəs] *adj.* 吹毛求疵的；挑剔的

例 His criticisms are always **captious**, never offering constructive suggestions.
他的評論通常都吹毛求疵，且從不提出有建設性的建議。

Cancer [`kænsə] *n.* 癌症

例 Smoking is usually responsible for many cases of lung **cancer**.
吸煙通常是許多人患肺癌的致病因素。

Cautious [`kɔʃəs] *adj.* 小心的

例 She was very **cautious** about committing herself to anything.
她謹小慎微，從不輕易表態。

Characteristic [‚kærəktə`rɪstɪk] *adj.* 特有的；獨特的

例 He accepted the prize with his **characteristic** modesty.
他以他特有的謙遜態度接受了獎勵。

Cholera [`kɑlərə] *n.* 霍亂

例 The village is now suffering from the **cholera** epidemic.
這個村莊現在正流行霍亂。

Clinic [`klɪnɪk] *n.* 診所

例 The baby **clinic** is always held on Tuesday afternoons.
嬰兒門診通常都在週二下午。

Compassion [kəm`pæʃən] *n.* 同情；憐憫

例 He shows no **compassion** for his patients.
他對病人沒有任何同情心。

Considerate [kən`sɪdərɪt] *adj.* 體貼的

例 It was very **considerate** of you to send me such a nice gift.

你真體貼送我如此精美的禮物。

Contagious [kən`tedʒəs] *adj.* 傳染性的

例 It is mandatory to isolate people with **contagious** diseases.
傳染病患者應予以強制隔離。

Dedicated [`dɛdə͵ketɪd] *adj.* 專注的；獻身的

例 I don't think Sandy's sufficiently **dedicated** to stay the course.
我認為珊蒂不夠堅定，不會堅持到底的。

Depression [dɪ`prɛʃən] *n.* 沮喪；消沉

例 Her mood varied from optimism to **depression**.
她的情緒由樂觀變為消沉。

Diabetes [͵daɪə`bitiz] *n.* 糖尿病

例 The poor old man was afflicted with serious **diabetes**.
那可憐的老人受到嚴重的糖尿病所折磨。

Diagnose [`daɪəgnoz] *v.* 診斷

例 The doctor **diagnosed** me with a kidney infection.
醫生診斷我為腎臟感染。

Diligent [`dɪlədʒənt] *adj.* 勤勉的

例 Philip is a **diligent** student and should do well in the examinations.
菲力浦是一個勤奮的學生，他會考出好成績的。

Disappointment [͵dɪsə`pɔɪntmənt] *n.* 失望；挫折

例 In spite of her **disappointment**, she managed a weak smile.
儘管很失望，她還是勉強露出一絲淡淡的微笑。

Embarrassing [ɪm`bærəsɪŋ] *adj.* 尷尬的

例 I was **embarrassing** to completely forget her name.
當時我完全忘記了她的名字真是尷尬。

Enthusiastic [ɪn͵θjuzɪ`æstɪk] *adj.* 熱心的；熱情的

例 I am **enthusiastic about** a project for building a new house.
我熱衷於修建一座新房子的計畫。

Epidemic [͵ɛpɪ`dɛmɪk] *adj.* 流行的；傳染的 *n.* 流行病

例 The magnitude of the **epidemic** was extraordinarily frightening.
這種流行病傳播範圍之廣異常地令人驚惶不安。

Exhausting [ɪg`zɔstɪŋ] *adj.* 筋疲力竭的

例 Business trip can be very **exhausting**.
公務旅行是非常累人的。

Flu [flu] *n.* 流感

例 Mary was absent from school today because she got a serious **flu**.
瑪莉今天因為得到嚴重流感而沒到校上課。

Frustration [͵frʌs`treʃən] *n.* 挫敗；挫折

例 He thinks it to be a great **frustration** to fail in that examination.
他認為在那場考試不及格是個很大的挫折。

Furious [`fjʊərɪəs] *adj.* 狂怒的；狂暴的

例 I was so **furious** I couldn't control myself.
我氣極了以致無法克制自己。

Generous [`dʒɛnərəs] *adj.* 慷慨的；大方的

例 It was **generous of you** to share your delicious food with me.
你真慷慨把美味食物與我分享。

Hesitant [`hɛzətənt] *adj.* 猶豫的

例 She's **hesitant about** signing the employ contract.

她對是否簽這個雇用契約還猶豫不決。

Hostile [`hɑstɪl] *adj.* 敵對的；敵方的n.敵對

例 Cindy found his manner towards her distinctly **hostile**.
辛蒂覺得他對她的態度極不友好。

Humble [`hʌmbl] *adj.* 謙卑的

舉 The man is not **humble**, but puts on an affectation of humility.
這個人並不謙遜，但裝出一副很謙卑的樣子。

Humorous [`hjumərəs] *adj.* 幽默的；滑稽的

例 Mary's husband is a **humorous** man.
瑪莉的丈夫是一個幽默的人。

Immune [ɪ`mjun] *adj.* 免疫的

例 I'm **immune** to smallpox as a result of vaccination.
我種過疫苗了所以對天花有免疫力。

Infectious [ɪn`fɛkʃəs] *adj.* 傳染的

例 **Influenza** is a kind of infectious disease.
流感是一種傳染病。

Irritable [`ɪrətəbl] *adj.* 易怒的

例 My elder sister was rather **irritable** today, and was angry about what I said or did.
我姊今天很易怒，我不管說甚麼或做甚麼她都不高興。

Nutrient [`njutrɪənt] *n.* 養分；營養品

例 These **nutrients** are helpful to your health.
這些營養品對你的健康有幫助。

Optimistic [ˌɑptə`mɪstɪk] *adj.* 樂觀的

例 Jenny was always **optimistic**, even when things were at their worst.
珍妮即使在最糟糕的時候也總是非常樂觀。

Pessimistic [ˌpɛsə`mɪstɪk] *adj.* 悲觀的

例 He is very **pessimistic about** the future.
他對未來感到非常悲觀。

Poisonous [`pɔɪznəs] *adj.* 有害的；惡毒的

例 This medicine will be **poisonous** if it is taken in large quantities.
這種藥如果服用過量是會中毒的。

Prescription [prɪ`skrɪpʃən] *n.* 處方

例 These pills can only beobtained by **prescription**.
這些藥丸只有憑醫生處方才能買到。

Regret [rɪ`grɛt] *n.* 遺憾；悔恨

例 We told her with **regret** of our decision.
我們遺憾地把我們的決定通知她。

Remedy [`rɛmədɪ] *n.* 藥物；治療法

例 The **remedy** is worse than the disease itself.
這種療法比疾病本身更讓人難受。

Sensitive [`sɛnsətɪv] *adj.* 敏感的；易受傷的

例 He is very **sensitive about** his failure.
他對他的失敗感到很受傷。

Stubborn [`stʌbən] *adj.* 頑固的；固執的

例 He incurred blame for his stubborn attitude.
他態度頑固而招致責難。

Sympathy [`sɪmpəθɪ] *n.* 同情；同情心

例 The miserable story stirred her **sympathy**.
這悲慘的故事激起了她的同情心。

Symptom [`sɪmptəm] *n.* 症狀；徵兆

例 The **symptoms** of flu include headache and vomiting.
流感的症狀包括頭痛和嘔吐。

隨堂練習！

(　　) 1. The Prime Minister expressed her _____ at the failure of the talks.
　　　　(A) awe　　　　　(B) regret　　　　　(C) fatigue　　　　　(D) greed

(　　) 2. Smiles and laughter are very _____ . Share them with a friend.
　　　　(A) contagious　　(B) dangerous　　(C) generous　　(D) cautious

(　　) 3. Being sorry for his mistake, he took a _____ step towards her.
　　　　(A) hearty　　　　(B) hesitant　　　(C) active　　　　(D) diligent

(　　) 4. The physician made a _____ against sea-sickness for him.
　　　　(A) description　　(B) proscription　　(C) prescription　　(D) destination

(　　) 5. My fever has gone, but I have a _____ .
　　　　(A) cause　　　　(B) cough　　　　(C) cost　　　　(D) caution

中譯解析

1. B；中譯：首相對談判失敗表示遺憾。
   解析：(A) awe 敬畏 (B) regret 遺憾 (C) fatigue 疲勞 (D) greed 貪婪
   本題考名詞。Express at（對⋯表達），talk 有商談、會談之意，本題表示對會談失敗的反應，故答案以 (B) 最恰當。

2. A；中譯：微笑與笑聲是很有感染力的，將它們與你的朋友一起分享吧。
   解析：(A) contagious 感染性的 (B) dangerous 危險的 (C) generous 大方的 (D) cautious 小心的
   本題考形容詞，表示歡笑可與朋友分享，所以用contagious（感染性）來形容最適合，故答案為 (A)。

3. B；中譯：對所犯的錯誤感到抱歉，他猶豫著向她走近了一步。
   解析：(A) hearty 衷心的 (B) hesitant 猶豫的 (C) active 主動的 (D) diligent 勤勉的
   本題考形容詞。有分詞結構Being⋯知，該句主詞是指 he，也就是他對自己的錯誤感到抱歉，所以主要子句中用 hesitant（猶豫的）來表達他的行為最洽當，故答案為 (B)。

4. C；中譯：醫生給他開了個暈船的藥方。
   解析：(A) description 描述 (B) proscription 放逐 (C) prescription 藥方 (D) destination 目標
   本題考名詞。sea-sickness（暈船），對抗（against），暈船的藥是一種處方，所以用 prescription（藥方）最為適當，故答案為 (C)。

5. B；中譯：我退燒了，但是還有點咳嗽。
   解析：(A) cause 原因 (B) cough 咳嗽 (C) cost 價值 (D) caution 警告
   本題考名詞。感冒症狀有發燒及咳嗽等，需注意其單字，本題為 cough（咳嗽）最為適當，故答案為(B)。

與運動、嗜好、興趣相關

Amateur [ˋæməˌtʃʊr] *n.* 業餘者

例 Although Tom's only an **amateur** he's a first-class player.
雖然湯姆只是個業餘愛好者，但卻是一流的高手。

Amusement [əˋmjuzmənt] *n.* 娛樂

例 If you need an **amusement** from work, you could go swimming during your lunch break.
想在工作之餘找點樂子，就在午休時間去游個泳吧。

Antique [ænˋtik] *n.* 骨董

例 He saw the vase in the window of an **antique** shop downtown.
他在市區一家古董店的櫥窗裡看見了這個花瓶。

Badminton [ˋbædmɪntən] *n.* 羽毛球

例 John just played **badminton** for sport.
約翰打羽毛球只是打著玩的。

Band [bænd] *n.* 樂團

例 The **band**'s success has encouraged hundreds of would-be imitators.
樂團的成功激勵了數以百計未來的追隨者。

Barbecue [ˋbɑrbɪkju] *n.* 戶外烤肉

例 We had a **barbecue** on their yard on Sunday.
星期天我們在院子裡烤肉。

Bowling [ˋbolɪŋ] *n.* 保齡球

例 He often takes to **bowling** with a few of his friends.
他還常常跟幾個同事去打保齡球。

Camp [kæmp] *n.* 露營；*v.* 紮營

例 Our **camping** trip was spoilt by a typhoon.
颱風破壞了我們的露營旅行。

Canvas [ˋkænvəs] *n.* 油畫；帆布

例 The painter painted an oil painting on the **canvas**.
這位畫家在畫布上畫了一幅油畫。

Cartoon [kɑrˋtun] *n.* 卡通

例 The **cartoon** completely diverted the children's attention.
那部卡通片完全地轉移了孩子們的注意力。

Comic [ˋkɑmɪk] *n.* 漫畫；*adj.* 滑稽的

例 I saw my daughter reading a science fiction **comic**.
我看見女兒在看一本科幻連環漫畫雜誌。

Concert [ˋkɑnsət] *n.* 音樂會

例 The singer's decision to cancel the **concert** is bound to disappoint many fans.
這位歌手取消這場音樂會的決定肯定會使很多歌迷失望。

Cultivate [ˋkʌltəˌvet] *v.* 耕種

例 He also **cultivated** a small land of her own.
她還耕種了一片屬於自己的小園子。

Dart [dɑrt] *n.* 飛鏢；標槍

例 The boy hit the target with his first **dart**.
那男孩第一鏢就擊中了目標。

Drama [ˋdrɑmə] *n.* 戲劇

例 He acted his part very well in the French **drama**.
他在這齣法國戲劇中演得很成功。

Exercise [ˋɛksəˌsaɪz] *n.* 運動；練習；*v.* 練習

Regular exercise can improve blood circulation.
經常運動會促進血液循環。

Fan [fæn] *n.* 熱情影、歌迷

例 Both the father and theso nare baseball **fans**.
父子兩人都是棒球迷

Foul [faʊl] *n.* 犯規；*adj.* 卑鄙的

例 The player was taken out for committing a **foul**.
那個選手因犯規被判下場。

Golf [gɑlf] *n.* 高爾夫球

例 Jones enjoyed a round of **golf** on Sunday morning.
瓊斯喜歡星期天的上午打一場高爾夫球。

Guitar [gɪˋtɑr] *n.* 吉他

例 She sat on the sofa idly plucking the strings of her **guitar**.
她坐在沙發隨意地撥著吉她的弦。

Handicraft [ˋhændɪˌkræft] *n.* 手工藝品

例 His hobbies include music, reading and **handicraft**.
他的愛好包含音樂、讀書和手工藝品。

Heritage [ˋhɛrətɪdʒ] *n.* 傳承；遺產

例 The ancient statues are part of the national **heritage**.
這些古代雕像是民族遺產的一部分。

Hike [haɪk] *n.* 健行

例 We went on a ten-mile **hike** through the forest last week.
我們上週做了一次穿越森林的十英里健行。

Hobby [ˋhɑbɪ] *n.* 嗜好

例 Mary takes up gardening as a **hobby** after she retired.
瑪莉退休後從事園藝為嗜好。

Hurdle [ˋhɝd!] *n.* 障礙；圍籬

例 Her horse fell at the final **hurdle**.
她騎的馬在最後一個跨欄倒下了。

Instrument [ˋɪnstrəmənt] *n.* 樂器；儀器

例 He can play nearly every musical **instrument**.
他幾乎會彈奏每一種樂器。

Jog [dʒɑg] *n.* 慢跑；*v.* 慢跑

例 She goes for a **jog** in the park every morning.
她每天早晨我在公園裡慢跑。

Lyric [ˋlɪrɪk] *adj.* 抒情的

例 This is a good example of **lyric** poetry.
這首詩是抒情詩的範例。

Opera [ˋɑpərə] *n.* 歌劇

例 She's one of the leading lights in the **opera** world.
她是歌劇界的一位要角。

Outing [ˋaʊtɪŋ] *n.* 戶外郊遊

例 Sunday afternoon is a perfect time for a family **outgoing**.
星期天下午適合全家外出郊遊。

Pastime [ˋpæsˌtaɪm] *n.* 娛樂

例 Playing chess is his favorite **pastime**.
下棋是他最喜愛的娛樂。

Photographer [fəˋtɑgrəfɚ] *n.* 攝影師

例 The **photographer** snapped a nice picture of her.
攝影師給她拍了一張很棒的照片。

Puzzle [ˋpʌz!] *n.* 猜謎遊戲；*v.* 使迷惑

例 I don't know the key to the **puzzle**.
我不知道這個謎語的答案。

Race [res] *n.* 競賽；賽跑

例 He came fifth in the **race**.

他在賽跑中獲第五名。

Recreation [ˌrɛkrɪˈeʃən] *n.* 休閒

例 There are excellent facilities for sport and **recreation** in this sport center.
在運動中心有完善的體育娛樂設施。

Rehearsal [rɪˈhɝs!] *n.* 排練；彩排

例 They are in **rehearsal** now. You may come later.
它們正在彩排，你可以晚一點再來。

Relay [rɪˈle] *n.* 接力比賽

例 As a kid, I love running in **relays** with my friends.
我小時候喜歡和朋友玩接力賽。

Resort [rɪˈzɔrt] *n.* 度假勝地

例 Congratulation, you've won a five-day vacation at a **resort**.
恭喜您獲得度假村五日遊。

Rhythmic [ˈrɪðmɪk] *adj.* 旋律的

例 I gradually fell asleep to the **rhythmic** ticking of the clock.
我聽著時鐘的滴答聲漸漸入睡了。

Rival [ˈraɪv!] *n.* 對手；*adj.* 競爭的

例 She contested with her **rival** for a big prize.
她為了獲得鉅額獎品與對手一較高低。

Skate [sket] *v.* 溜冰

例 It took Mary just three days to learn to **skate**.
瑪莉只花三天時間就學會了滑冰。

Soccer [ˈsɑkɚ] *n.* 英式足球

例 **Soccer** is the American word for football.
在美國，足球叫做"soccer"。

Softball [ˈsɔftˌbɔl] *n.* 壘球

例 Did you have a **softball** game after school today?
今天你們是不是放學後有個壘球比賽呀？

Spectator [spɛkˈtetɚ] *n.* 觀眾

例 Some **spectators** would throw the ball back to the players.
有些觀眾會把球擲回給球員。

Sprint [sprɪnt] *v.* 衝刺

例 At the end of the race, all the runners **sprinted** for the finish line.
在比賽終點，所有跑者向終點衝刺。

Spur [spɝ] *n.* 踢馬刺；*v.* 踢；刺激

例 It is the bridle and **spur** that makes a good horse.
要把馬練好，韁繩靴刺不可少。

Surf [sɝf] *v.* 衝浪；上網

例 You'r welcomed to come and **surf** in the ocean in front of our hotel.
歡迎你在我們旅館前的大海裡盡情的衝浪吧。

Symphony [ˈsɪmfənɪ] *n.* 交響樂

例 The Ninth **Symphony** of Beethoven is very famous.
貝多芬的第九交響樂非常有名。

Tournament [ˈtɝnəmənt] *n.* 錦標賽

例 This **tournament** is open to both amateur and professional runners.
這次錦標賽業餘選手和職業選手均可參加。

Violin [ˌvaɪəˈlɪn] *n.* 小提琴

例 Mary persevered with her favorite **violin** lessons.
她孜孜不倦地學習她喜愛的小提琴。

Volleyball [ˈvɑlɪˌbɔl] *n.* 排球

例 All the children are playing **volleyball** on the lawn now.
現在所有孩子們都在草地上打排球。

隨堂練習！

( ) 1. _____ can be played by two or four people.
 (A) Golf (B) Volleyball (C) Badminton (D) Softball

( ) 2. Learning a musical _____ introduces a child to an understanding of music.
 (A) equipment (B)instrument (C)sentiment (D)instruction

( ) 3. His symphony was laughed off the stage at its first _____ .
 (A) refresh (B) rehearse (C) rehearing (D) rehearsal

( ) 4. The industrial secrets were retailed to a _____ concern.
 (A) rival (B) lyric (C) thrill (D) river

( ) 5. For _____, we go to the movies once a week.
 (A) amateur (B) assistance
 (C) abasement (D) amusement

中譯解析

1. C；中譯：羽毛球可由兩人或四人來打。
 解析：(A) Golf 高爾夫 (B) Volleyball 排球 (C) Badminton 羽毛球 (D) Softball壘球
 本題考球類名稱。這四種球類中，只有羽毛球可以兩人或四人來打，答案為 (C)。

2. C；中譯：學一種樂器能引導孩子瞭解音樂。
 解析：(A) equipment 設備 (B) instrument 樂器 (C) sentiment 感情 (D) instruction 教育
 本題考名詞。introduce（引導），選項中以instrument（樂器）填入空格最合理，即經由學習音樂的樂器，答案為 (C)。

3. D；中譯：他的交響曲在第一次預演時就受到嘲笑而不能上演。
 解析：(A) refresh v.翻新 (B) rehearse v.排練 (C) rehearing n.【法】覆審 (D) rehearsal n. 排練
 本題考名詞。laugh off（恥笑），stage（舞台），表示在第一次排練時就被恥笑，選項中應填入rehearsal（排練），答案為 (D)。

4. A；中譯：工業秘密被洩露給一家對立的公司。
 解析：(A) rival 敵對的 (B) lyric抒情的 (C) thrill 使興奮 (D) river 河流
 本題考名詞。retail（轉述），concern（利害關係），在此表示相關的公司，故選項中以rival（敵對的）最恰當，表示是對立的公司，答案為 (A)。

5. D；中譯：我們的娛樂是每週去電影院看一次電影。
 解析：(A) amateur 業餘者 (B) assistance 幫助 (C) abasement 卑微 (D) amusement 娛樂
 本題考名詞。for 開頭表示為了甚麼理由，後面提到電影，所以研判選項中應為 amusement（娛樂），表示為了娛樂的緣故，答案為 (D)。

與旅遊相關

Accommodation [əˌkɑməˈdeʃən] *n.* 居住；適應

例 **Accommodation in** this city is relatively expensive.
這個城市住房相對地昂貴。

Airline [ˈɛrˌlaɪn] *n.* 航線

例 The **airline** services operate daily.
這條航線每天都有班機飛行。

Airsick [ˈɛrˌsɪk] *adj.* 暈機的

例 Last time when I took a plane, I got **airsick**.
上次我乘飛機時暈機了。

Baggage [ˈbæɡɪdʒ] *n.* 行李

例 They piled all the **baggage** in and drove off.
他們把全部行李塞進去就開車走了。

Bellman [ˈbɛlmən] *n.* 服務員

例 The **bellman** will take your baggage up for you.
服務員會替你把行李送上去的。

Boarding [ˈbordɪŋ] *n.* 登機

例 Where is the **boarding** gate for this flight to Taipei?
這班往台北班機的登機門在哪裡？

Connecting flight [kəˈnɛktɪŋ] [flaɪt] *n.* 轉接航班

例 You must confirm **connecting flight** reservations in advance.
你必須事先確認轉接航班的訂位。

Currency [ˈkɜ·ənsɪ] *n.* 流通；貨幣

例 What kind of **currency** do you want to change?
你想要換哪種貨幣？

Customs [ˈkʌstəmz] *n.* 海關〔複數〕

例 The **customs** are looking for such things as drugs or alcohol.
海關人員查察毒品、酒類這樣的東西。

Delay [dɪˈle] *v.* 延誤；*n.* 延遲

例 We apologize for the **delay** and regret any inconvenience it may have caused.
我們對此次延誤以及因此可能造成的所有不便表示道歉。

Departure [dɪˈpɑrtʃə·] *n.* 離開

例 Guests are requested to vacate their rooms by noon on the day of **departure**.
房客務請在離開之日的中午以前騰出房間。

Destination [ˌdɛstəˈneʃən] *n.* 目的地；目標

例 I eventually arrived at my **destination**.
我終於到達了目的地。

Dining room [ˈdaɪnɪŋ] [rum] *n.* 餐廳

例 The hotel features an impressive **dining room** overlooking the lake.
這家旅店特別設很棒的餐廳可以俯瞰湖面。

Doormen [ˈdorˌmæn] *n.* 門廳應接員

例 The hotel **doormen** are usually considered front desk employees.
飯店門廳應接員通常被認為是櫃台員工。

Economy class [ɪˈkɑnəmɪ] [klæs] *n.* 經濟艙

例 How much does it cost for **economy class**?
經濟艙要多少錢？

Escalator [ˈɛskəˌletə·] *n.* 電扶梯

例 Take the **escalator** over there and turn right, and you'll see the sign.

到那邊乘坐電扶梯然後往右轉，您就會看到指示。

Immigration [ˌɪməˈgreʃən] *n.* 移民

例 Because of all red tape at **immigration**, I missed my connecting flight.
由於移民局令人討厭的繁瑣公事程序，我誤了轉機航班。

Information [ˌɪnfəˈmeʃən] *n.* 資料；情報

例 You can get all the tourism **information** in the desk.
你可以在服務台獲得所有旅遊資訊。

Insurance [ɪnˈʃʊrəns] *n.* 保險

例 We recommend that you buy travel **insurance** on all holidays.
我們建議您為所有假期都購買旅行保險。

Itinerary [aɪˈtɪnəˌrɛrɪ] *n.* 行程表

例 A visit to Paris must be included in the **itinerary**.
巴黎之行必須列入預定行程。

Lobby [ˈlɑbɪ] *n.* 大廳

例 Mary is in the **lobby** of that hotel now.
瑪麗現正在那旅館大廳。

Luggage [ˈlʌgɪdʒ] *n.* 行李

例 Will you keep an eye on my **luggage**? Please!
勞駕您幫我看一下行李，好嗎？

Menu [ˈmɛnju] *n.* 目錄；菜單

例 Do you have a **menu** in Japanese?
你們有日文菜單嗎？

Museum [mjuˈzɪəm] *n.* 博物館

例 Photography is forbidden inside the **museum**.
博物館內嚴禁攝影。

Order [ˈɔrdə] *n.* 次序；訂購 *v.* 命令；點菜

例 May I **order** now? Please.
我現在可以點菜了嗎？

Pass [pæs] *n.* 通行證；經過

例 This **pass** enables me to travel half price on buses.
我用這張通行證可以半價乘巴士。

Passenger [ˈpæsndʒə] *n.* 乘客

例 Each **passenger** was allowed two 30-kg pieces of baggage.
每位乘客可帶兩件30公斤的行李。

Passport [ˈpæsˌport] *n.* 護照

例 Check the expiration date on your **passport** before you leave.
檢查一下你護照上的截止日期。

Photograph [ˈfotəˌgræf] *n.* 照片 *v.* 為…照相

例 This **photograph** is too small to see. Please enlarge it for me.
這張照片太小看不清楚，請把它給我放大。

Registration [ˌrɛdʒɪˈstreʃən] *n.* 登記；報到

例 Would you fill in this **registration** form?
你可以填寫這張登記表嗎？

Remittance [rɪˈmɪtns] *n.* 匯款

例 How much of the **remittance** do you want to convert into U.S. dollars?
你要把多少匯款換成美金？

Rental [ˈrɛntl̩] *n.* 租金；出租

例 We had a **rental** car when we were on summer vacation.
我們暑假時租了一輛車。

Reservation [ˌrɛzəˈveʃən] *n.* 預訂

例 I'll call the restaurant and make a **reservation**.
我要給餐廳打個電話預訂座位。

Restaurant [ˋrɛstərənt] *n.* 餐廳

例 Could you recommend a nice **restaurant** near here?
你是否可介紹一家附近口碑不錯的餐廳？

Round-trip *n.* 來回旅行

例 I'd like a **round-trip** ticket to Taipei, please!
我要一張台北來回車票。

Route [rut] *n.* 路線；航線

例 The coastal path is a popular **route** for walkers.
這條海濱小路是散步者很喜歡走的路線。

Scenery [ˋsinərɪ] *n.* 景色；場景

例 The village is celebrated for its beautiful **scenery**.
這村莊以其美麗的風景著名。

Shuttle [ˋʃʌt!] *n.* 來回運輸，接駁

例 There's a **shuttle** service from the train station to the airport.
火車站和飛機場之間有接駁服務。

Sightseeing [ˋsaɪtˏsiɪŋ] *n.* 觀光；遊覽

例 Can we get a ticket for the **sightseeing** bus here?
我們是否可在此購買觀光巴士券？

Souvenir [ˋsuvəˏnɪr] *n.* 紀念品

例 I bought the ring as a **souvenir** of Greece tour.
我買了一枚戒指留作對希臘的紀念。

Stopover [ˋstɑpˏovɚ] *n.* 中途停留

例 We had a two-day **stopover** in Singapore on the way to Australia.
我們去澳大利亞時中途在新加坡停留了兩天。

Terminal [ˋtɝmən!] *n.* 航廈

例 Passengers are transported by bus to the air **terminal**.
用公共汽車載送旅客前往航站樓。

Timetable [ˋtaɪmˏteb!] *n.* 時刻表

例 You can find out the times of your trains in this **timetable**.
你可在這一時刻表上查到你的火車時刻。

Tip [tɪp] *n.* 小費；提示

例 I gave the taxi driver a **tip**.
我付小費給計程車司機。

Tour [tʊr] *n.* 旅遊；導覽

例 The **tour** included a visit to the Aerospace Museum.
這次遊覽包括參觀航太博物館。

Tourism [ˋtʊrɪzəm] *n.* 旅遊

例 This city is heavily dependent on **tourism**.
這個城市非常依賴旅遊業。

Tourist [ˋtʊrɪst] *n.* 觀光客

例 The town depends almost on the **tourist** trade.
這座城市幾乎完全靠旅遊業維持。

Traveler's check [ˋtrævlɚs] [tʃɛk] *n.* 旅行支票

例 I am sorry. We do not accept any **traveler's check**.
對不起，我們不收旅遊支票。

Visa [ˋvizə] *n.* 簽證簽證；*v.* 簽證

例 I obtained a **visa** to visit Korea.
我獲得訪問韓國的簽證。

📝 隨堂練習！

( ) 1. Computerized _____ systems help airlines profits in several ways.
(A) reservation   (B) instruction   (C) attention   (D) immigration

( ) 2. The youth gave me his hand when I was lifting my _____ .
(A) bagger   (B) bagman   (C) baggie   (D) baggage

( ) 3. When Uncle Bill went abroad to sightsee, he bought me a watch as a

_____ .
(A) souvenir   (B) solution   (C) senior   (D) scenery

( ) 4. The _____ policy covers sudden death or disablement.
(A) ascription   (B) assumption   (C) instance   (D) insurance

( ) 5. Are you looking for furnished _____ ?
(A) accommodation   (B) destitution
(C) constitution   (D) organization

💬 中譯解析

1. A；中譯：電子訂票系統經由多種方式讓航空公司獲利。
解析：(A) reservation 訂位 (B) instruction 教導 (C) attention 注意 (D) immigration 移民
本題考名詞。Computerized（電腦化），in several ways 以多種方式，依題意指電腦化的訂位最合理，故答案為 (A)。

2. D；中譯：當我提行李時，那個年輕人過來幫我提。
解析：(A) bagger 裝袋工 (B) bagman 收取贓款的人 (C) baggies 游泳短褲 (D) baggage 行李
本題考名詞。Give someone a hand（幫助某人），依題意是指提行李最合理，故答案為 (D)。

3. A；中譯：比爾叔叔出國去玩時買了錶給我作為紀念品。
解析：(A) souvenir 紀念品 (B) solution 溶液 (C) senior 年長者 (D) scenery 風景
本題考名詞。buy somebody something（買某物給某人），買下手錶當作紀念品最合理，故答案為 (A)。

4. D；中譯：保險單內容涵蓋了突然死亡或傷殘保險。
解析：(A) ascription 歸因於 (B) assumption 假設 (C) instance 事例 (D) insurance 保險
本題考名詞。policy 一般解釋為政策，方針，在此意思為內容，cover（包含）。因句中提到死亡或傷殘，與保險有相關聯，應故本題選項應為 (D)。

5. A；中譯：你在找備有傢俱的出租房間嗎？
解析：(A) accommodation 居住 (B) destitution 窮困 (C) constitution 構成 (D) organization 組織
本題考名詞。looking for（找尋），由空格前的形容詞 furnished（具傢俱的），研判應是與居住有關係，故答案為 (A)。

與尺寸、度量、金錢相關

Abundance [ə`bʌndəns] *n.* 大量；豐富

例 There was an **abundance** of soybean last year.
去年大豆豐收。

Account [ə`kaʊnt] *n.* 帳戶；計算

例 The interest is added to your **account** every year.
每年的利息都加到你的存款中。

Altitude [`æltə‚tjud] *n.* 高度

例 The airliner flew at an **altitude** of 30000ft.
客機在三萬英尺的高度飛行。

Amplify [`æmplə‚faɪ] *v.* 放大；擴大

例 The new manager wants to **amplify** the company.
新經理想要擴大公司。

Approximate [ə`prɑksəmɪt] *adj.* 大約的 *v.* 接近；近似

例 The builder gave me an **approximate** cost for fixing the roof.
房屋修建商給我修理房頂粗略地估計了一個價錢。

Billion [`bɪljən] *n.* 十億

例 The bank has assets of more than 1 **billion** U.S. dollars.
該銀行有超過10億美元的資產。

Bottle [`bɑt!] *n.* 一瓶量

例 She upset a **bottle** of ink.
她打翻了一瓶墨水。

Bundle [`bʌnd!] *n.* 一捆；一束

例 He sold a **bundle** of old magazines to the second hand store.
他把一捆就雜誌賣給了二手店。

Cash [kæʃ] *n.* 現金 *v.* 付現金

例 Credit cards eliminate the need to carry a lot of **cash**.
信用卡省了攜帶很多現金的必要。

Centimeter [`sɛntə‚mitə] *n.* 釐米；公分

例 The scale of this map is 5 **centimeter** to the kilometer.
這個地圖的比例是用五釐米代表一公里。

Change [tʃendʒ] *n.* 零錢；*vt.* 改變

例 Please give me small **change** for this five dollars note.
請把這五塊錢換成零錢。

Chunk [tʃʌŋk] *n.* 一大塊

例 I've almost completed a fair **chunk** of my article.
我已經幾乎把文章的一大部分寫完了。

Cluster [`klʌstə] *n.* 一群；叢

例 We can see stars in **clusters** in the night sky.
我們可以看到夜空中的星群。

Compute [kəm`pjut] *n.* 估算；*v.* 計算

例 I **computed** my losses at about 500 dollars.
我估計我的損失約有五百元。

Deposit [dɪ`pɑzɪt] *n.* 保證金；儲蓄 *v.* 放置；淤積

例 We've put down a 5% **deposit** on the car.
我們已支付了車款的5%作為訂金。

Dimension [dɪ`mɛnʃən] *n.* 尺寸；範圍

例 Length is one **dimension**, and width is another.
長是一種度量，寬又是另一種度量。

Diminish [də`mɪnɪʃ] *v.* 降低；縮減

例 We must **diminish** the administrative expenditure.
我們必須縮減行政開支。

Equation [ɪ`kweʃən] *n.* 平衡；方程式

例 I can't make this dual **equation** come out.
我不會解這個二元方程式。

Fraction [`frækʃən] *n.* 片段；小部分

例 Only a small **fraction** of a bank's total deposits will be withdrawn.
一家銀行的總存款只有少量會被提取。

Gap [gæp] *n.* 缺口；差距

例 How can we bridge the **gap** between the rich and poor?
怎樣才能縮小貧富之間的差距？

Huge [hjudʒ] *adj.* 巨大的

例 The company's results show a **huge** jump in annual profits.
公司的結算顯示年度利潤大增。

Immense [ɪ`mɛns] *n.* 無盡的

例 The universe isso **immense** that no one knows where it ends.
宇宙是無窮盡的，沒有人知道盡頭在哪裡。

Inferior [ɪn`fɪrɪə] *adj.* 低劣的；次級的

例 I admit that I am **inferior** to him in many respects.
我自認在許多方面比他差一截。

Interest [`ɪntərɪst] *n.* 利息

例 What's the **interest** rate for the savings account?
儲蓄存款的利率是多少？

Layer [`leə] *n.* 層；階級

例 A thin **layer** of dust covered everything in this room.
這房間所有的物品上都積了薄薄的一層灰塵。

Lessen [`lɛsn] *v.* 減少

例 The noise from the outside began to **lessen**.
外面的噪音開始減弱。

Liter [`litə] *n.* 公升

例 The bottle holds a **liter** ofwine.
這個瓶子裝一升葡萄酒。

Lot [lɑt] *n.* 一堆

例 Mary spends a **lot** of money to follow the fashion.
瑪莉趕時髦花費了不少錢。

Lump [lʌmp] *n.* 一塊；團

例 How many **lumps** do you take in your drink?
你喝飲料加幾塊方糖？

Massive [`mæsɪv] *adj.* 大的；重的

例 Cindy ate a **massive** amount of chocolate ice cream.
辛蒂吃大量的巧克力霜淇淋。

Maximum [`mæksəməm] *adj.* 最高的；最多的

例 The car has a **maximum** speed of 130 kilometers per hour.
這車最高速為每小時130公里。

Mileage [`maɪlɪdʒ] *n.* 里程數

例 Car rental usually charge daily fee by the **mileage** driven.
租車通常用每日開車的里程數來計費。

Million [`mɪljən] *n.* 百萬

例 The population of this city has increased from 1.2 **million** 10 years ago to 1.6 million now.
城市的人口從10年前的120萬已增加到現在的160萬。

Minimum [`mɪnəməm] *adj.* 最小的；最低的

例 Repairing charge for your car will cost a **minimum** of 100 dollars.
修理你的汽車最少要100美元。

Negative [`nɛgətɪv] *adj.* 否認的；負面的

例 He gave me a **negative** answer.
他給了我一個否定的回答。

Negligible [`nɛglɪdʒəb!] *adj.* 可以忽略的

例 There was a **negligible** amount of rain in that region last year.
去年在那個地區只有極輕微的雨量。

Outnumber [aʊt`nʌmbɚ] *v.* 比…多過

例 The latter **outnumber** the former by about a fifty to one.
後者在數量上超過前者，比率約為50：1。

Package [`pækɪdʒ] *n.* 包裝；包裹

例 A large **package** has arrived for you.
你有一個大包裹來了。

Positive [`pɑzətɪv] *adj.* 確定的；正的

例 An electron has a negative charge, and a proton has a **positive** charge.
電子帶負電荷，質子帶正電荷。

Quantity [`kwɑntətɪ] *n.* 數量

例 The exact **quantity** cannot be determined yet right now.
確切數量目前尚不能確定。

Quarter [`kwɔrtɚ] *n.* 四分之一；一刻鐘

例 We walked a **quarter** of a mile down the mountainside.
他們沿山坡下行了四分之一英里的路程。

Radius [`redɪəs] *n.* 半徑；輻射

例 They are measuring the **radius** of the circle.
他們正在測量圓的半徑。

Redundant [rɪ`dʌndənt] *adj.* 過多的；多餘的

例 These words here are **redundant**. They can be left out.
這些字是多餘的，可以去掉。

Revenue [`rɛvəˌnju] *n.* 收入；歲收

例 There was an increase of 5% in tax **revenues** last year.
去年的稅收有百分之五的成長。

Shortage [`ʃɔrtɪdʒ] *n.* 缺少；不足

例 There is a serious **shortage** of water.
水嚴重短缺。

Rate [ret] *n.* 比率

例 The unemployment **rate** is rising in Spain.
西班牙的失業率正在上升。

Stack [stæk] *n.* 一堆；堆疊

例 There is a **stack** of clothes to be washed in the basket.
籃子裡還有一大堆衣服要洗。

Statistics [stə`tɪstɪks] *n.* 統計學；統計表

例 We have **statistics** data for the last year.
我們有去年的統計資料。

Surplus [`sɝpləs] *n.* 過剩；*adj.* 過剩的

例 Wheat was in **surplus** last year.
去年小麥過剩。

Tiny [`taɪnɪ] *adj.* 極小的

例 Unfortunately, I found that your work had a **tiny** flaw.
很不幸，我發現你的作品有一處微小的瑕疵。

Volume [`vɑljəm] *n.* 卷；冊；數量

例 The number of accidents is proportionate to the increasing **volume** of traffic.
交通事故的數字與交通量的增長成正比。

隨堂練習！

( ) 1. There is an _____ of commodity supplies on the markets.
(A) abandon　　(B) announce　　(C) abundance　　(D) allowance

( ) 2. A _____ of files awaited me on my desk.
(A) stack　　(B) chunk　　(C) layer　　(D) fraction

( ) 3. If you cancel your flight, you will forfeit your _____ .
(A) deposit　　(B) change　　(C) account　　(D) package

( ) 4. A：Excuse me! What is the exchange _____ between NT and US dollars?
B：The rate is 30.01:1 right now.
(A) money　　(B) treasury　　(C) finical　　(D) rate

( ) 5. How do you measure the _____ of a gas?
(A) liter　　(B) lump　　(C) package　　(D) volume

中譯解析

1. C；中譯：市場上商品供應充足。
　解析：(A) abandon 放棄 (B) announce 宣佈 (C) abundance 充足 (D) allowance 補助
　本題考名詞。Commodity（商品，日用品）。依句意應為市場上面商品供應充足，故答案應為 (C)。

2. A；中譯：我桌上有一堆文件正待我去處理。
　解析：(A) stack 堆、疊 (B) chunk 大塊 (C) layer 層、級 (D) fraction 小部分
　本題考計量單位用語。在此表示一大堆文件（files），應用a stack of，故答案應為 (A)。

3. A；中譯：如果你取消航班訂位，訂金概不退還。
　解析：(A) deposit 訂金，押金 (B) change 零錢 (C) account 帳號 (D) package 包裹
　本題考名詞。Forfeit（v.喪失）。表示取消航班則你會喪失你的訂金，故答案應為 (A)。

4. D；中譯：A：請問一下，現在台幣與美元為多少？
　B：現在匯率是 30.01：1。
　(A) money 金錢 (B) treasury 國庫 (C) finical 財政 (D) rate 比率
　解析：本題考貨幣匯率說法，匯率為 exchange rate，故答案為 (D)。

5. D；中譯：你如何計量氣體的體積？
　解析：(A) liter公升 (B) lump團，塊 (C) package包裝 (D) volume體積
　本題考計量單位用語。Measure（v.測量），氣體是以體積為單位來測量的，故答案為 (D)。

與住宅、公寓相關

Aisle [aɪl] *n.* 通道；走道

例 She walked up and down the **aisle** to stretch her cramped muscles.
她在樓道裡走來走去以舒展痙攣的肌肉。

Apartment [ə`partmənt] *n.* 公寓住宅

例 Someone has been snooping around my new **apartment**.
有個人一直在我新住所周圍窺探。

Architecture [`arkə͵tɛktʃɚ] *n.* 建築物；建築學

例 My elder brother majored in **architecture** at college.
我哥哥在大學是主修建築。

Attic [`ætɪk] *n.* 閣樓

例 I found this old picture when I was clearing the **attic**.
我在清掃閣樓時發現了這張舊照片。

Basement [`besmənt] *n.* 地下室

例 It is relatively damp in the **basement**.
地下室相對的潮濕。

Bathroom [`bæθ͵rum] *n.* 浴室

例 There are two two large and beautiful **bathrooms** in this house.
這房子有兩間漂亮的大浴室。

Block [blɑk] *n.* 區塊；街區

例 The entire **block** will be knocked down for new buildings.
整個街區將被拆除以造新的房子。

Cabin [`kæbɪn] *n.* 小木屋；船艙

例 They built a new **cabin** in a couple of hours.
他們在幾小時之內就建起了一座新的小木屋。

Ceiling [`silɪŋ] *n.* 天花板

例 A lamp is suspended from the **ceiling** above us.
我們頭頂上的天花板上吊著一盞燈。

Commodity [kə`madətɪ] *n.* 日用品；商品

例 There is an abundance of **commodity** supplies on this super market.
這家超市商品供應充足。

Condo [`kando] *n.* 公寓房間

例 She moved into a new **condo** on the East side of town.
她搬到東城一間出租公寓去了。

Corridor [`kɔrɪdɚ] *n.* 通道；走廊

例 You can stay in our guest room at the left end of the **corridor**.
你可以住在我們的客房，它就在這走廊的盡頭。

Cosmetic [kaz`mɛtɪk] *n.* 化妝品

例 The kit consisted of twenty **cosmetic** items.
整套工具包括20種化妝用品。

Cottage [`katɪdʒ] *n.* 農舍；小屋

例 Although the **cottage** is tiny, it's charming.
雖然這間小屋很小，卻十分迷人。

Couch [kaʊtʃ] *n.* 躺椅；長沙發椅

例 We were sitting on the **couch** watching TV.
我們正躺在沙發上看電視。

Curtain [`kɝtn] *n.* 窗簾；簾幕

例 The new **curtains** and carpet match pretty well.
新窗簾與地毯搭配非常諧調。

Cushion [`kʊʃən] *n.* 軟墊；靠墊

例 Mary embroidered flowers on the **cushion** covers.
瑪莉在這些靠墊套上繡了花。

Decoration [ˌdɛkə`reʃən] *n.* 裝飾；裝潢

例 The color of curtains does not match with the **decoration**.
窗簾顏色與室內裝潢不相配。

Drainpipe [`dren͵paɪp] *n.* 排水管

例 The **drainpipe** conducts the excess water from the well.
排水管把多餘的水從井中排出。

Drawer [`drɔə] *n.* 抽屜

例 The little boy took his books from the desk **drawer**.
小男孩從書桌抽屜取出他的書。

Elevator [`ɛlə͵vetə] *n.* 電梯；升降機

例 She lives on the fifth floor, so we'd better take the **elevator**.
她住在五樓上，我們最好乘電梯。

Faucet [`fɔsɪt] *n.* 水龍頭

例 Water was falling out from the **faucet**.
水正從水龍頭流出。

Floor [flor] *n.* 樓層；樓板

例 Don't jump up and down on the **floor**. It will disturb others who live underneath.
不要在樓板上下跳動，會影響到住在樓下的人。

Foundation [faʊn`deʃən] *n.* 基礎；地基

例 This mansion has a very solid **foundation**.
這棟大樓有非常結實的地基。

Furniture [`fɜnɪtʃə] *n.* 傢俱

例 They have rearranged the **furniture** in the bedroom.
他們重新擺放了臥室裡的傢俱。

Garage [gə`rɑʒ] *n.* 車庫

例 The ball ended up on the **garage** roof.
這球最後落到了車庫頂上。

Garden [`gɑrdn] *n.* 庭園；花園

例 The **garden** is completely overgrown with weeds and flowers.
花園裡長滿了雜草及花朵。

Gate [get] *n.* 大門

例 Tell him to wait for us at the **gate**.
告訴他在大門口等我們。

Landlord [`lænd͵lord] *n.* 房東

例 The **landlord** promised to do my apartment over.
房東答應翻修我的公寓房子。

Lawn [lɔn] *n.* 草地；草坪

例 The **lawn** needs mowing immediately.
草坪需要立即修剪。

Lease [lis] *n.* 租約；契約

例 When does the **lease** of the apartment run out?
這公寓的租約何時到期？

Lodge [lɑdʒ] *n.* 小屋 *v.* 寄宿

例 My family rented a mountain **lodge** at a ski resort for holiday.
我家人在一家滑雪飯店租一間山間小屋來度假。

Lumber [`lʌmbə] *n.* 木頭；木料

例 They built a cabin out of old **lumber**.
他們利用舊木料草草地蓋起了一間小屋。

Mansion [`mænʃən] *n.* 大廈；宅第

例 It is well-known that the **mansion** on the hill is haunted.
眾人皆知那座山坡上的豪宅鬧鬼。

Mattress [`mætrɪs] *n.* 床墊

例 She doesn't like white **mattress**.
她不喜歡白色床墊。

Mortgage [`mɔrgɪdʒ] *n.* 抵押

例 We're paying out 300 a month on our house **mortgage**.
我們每月要付300英鎊房屋貸款。

Parlor [`pɑrlə] *n.* 客廳；起居室

例 They were conversing in the **parlor** at that time.
他們正在客廳談話。

Penthouse [`pɛnt͵haʊs] *n.* 閣樓

例 The family has booked the **penthouse** suite for summer vacation.
這個家庭已預定了閣樓套房來過暑假。

Pillar [`pɪlə] *n.* 柱子；廊柱

例 This **pillar** is a little tilted.
這柱子有點斜，需要加以修理。

Residence [`rɛzədəns] *n.* 住處；住宅

例 We finally have a comfortable new **residence**.
我們終於有了一個舒適的新居

Stairs [stɛr] *n.* 樓梯；階梯

例 He had run up and down the **stairs** many times.
他已上上下下樓梯好幾回了。

Suburban [sə`bɝbən] *n.* 郊區

例 They are now living in **suburban** Washington.
他們現正住在華盛頓的郊外。

Suite [swit] *n.* 套房

例 We have a very nice air conditioned **suite** for rent.
我們有裝修漂亮並配有空調的套房可供出租。

Threshold [`θrɛʃhold] *n.* 門檻

例 The groom carried his beautiful bride over the **threshold** of their new house.
新郎牽著他美麗的新娘跨過新房的門檻。

Tile [taɪl] *n.* 磁磚

例 The bathroom is faced with colorful **tile**.
浴室鋪著鮮豔的瓷磚。

Toilet [`tɔɪlɪt] *n.* 廁所；沖水馬桶

例 He usually wants to go to the **toilet** after breakfast.
他通常早餐後想上廁所。

Villa [`vɪlə] *n.* 別墅

例 David invited all of us to stay at his new **villa** in the south of island.
大衛邀請我們去住在他位於這個島南方的別墅。

Wardrobe [`wɔrd͵rob] *n.* 衣櫥

例 He bought a new **wardrobe** after he graduated from college.
在他專科學校畢業後他買一個新衣櫃。

Warehouse [`wɛr͵haʊs] *n.* 倉庫；大賣場

例 Some trucks waited at the **warehouse** to pick up their loads.
一些貨車在倉庫等著裝載貨物。

Yard [jɑrd] *n.* 院子

例 Children always play in the back **yard** after dinner.
晚餐後孩子們總是會在後院遊玩。

隨堂練習！

(　) 1. The historic _____ was presented by the owner to the city, and is kept up by the local authority.
(A) menace (B) mention (C) mission (D) mansion

(　) 2. This _____ is fine for two people, but not more.
(A) investment (B) department
(C) apartment (D) management

(　) 3. The sheep got into the field through a gap in the _____ .
(A) hedge (B) wall (C) lumber (D) lawn

(　) 4. The authorities took measures to roll _____ price back.
(A) commodity (B) community
(C) commissary (D) commodore

(　) 5. Do you own the house or are you a _____ ?
(A) lease (B) temp (C) landlord (D) tenant

中譯解析

1. D；中譯：這幢有歷史意義的宅邸是房主送給城市的, 現在由地方當局保養維修。
解析：(A) menace 脅迫 (B) mention 提及 (C) mission 任務 (D) mansion 宅邸
本題考名詞。Keep up（保存），local authority（地方當局）。依句意應為歷史宅邸，現在由政府來維護，答案應為 (D)。

2. C；中譯：這公寓房子適合兩個人住，但人再多就不行了。
解析：(A) investment 投資 (B) department 部門 (C) apartment 公寓 (D) management 管理
本題考名詞。fine for（適合），二個人適合住的地方應為公寓房子，答案應為 (C)。

3. A；中譯：羊群從樹籬的缺口跑向田野。
解析：(A) hedge 籬笆 (B) wall 牆壁 (C) lumber 木頭 (D) lawn 草地
本題考名詞。got into（進入），羊可以穿過的地方應該為籬笆，答案應為 (A)。

4. A；中譯：當局採取措施使物價全面回降。
解析：(A) commodity 商品 (B) community 社會 (C) commissary 物資供應站 (D) commodore 海軍准將
本題考名詞。Measures 指各種方法，roll 為起伏、轉動，為當局控制使價格回穩的東西應為商品，故答案應為(A)。

5. D；中譯：你是擁有這幢房子還是租住的?
解析：(A) lease 契約 (B) temp 臨時員 (C) landlord 房東 (D) tenant 房客
本題考名詞。房子不是自有就是租賃，租賃的身分就是房客 tenant，故答案應為 (D)。

與辦公室商務相關

Access [`æksɛs] *n.* 進入

例 Only a few people have **access** to the whole facts of this case.
只有少數幾個人能看到有關該案全部事實。

Administration [ədˌmɪnəˋstreʃən] *n.* 管理；行政

例 The Chief Executive should have experience in business **administration**.
總經理應有企業管理經驗。

Agreement [əˋgrimənt] *n.* 同意；協定

例 They must come to an**agreement** on salary before the papers could be signed.
在簽訂文件前他們必須就薪資完成協定。

Assurance [əˋʃʊrəns] *n.* 擔保；保險

例 He already has a life **assurance**.
他早已經投保了人壽保險。

Benefit [`bɛnəfɪt] *n.* 利益；利潤 *v.* 使…得利

例 You must study hard for the **benefit** of yourself.
為了你自己好你必須努力用功。

Boycott [`bɔɪˌkɑt] *n.* 抵制；*v.* 抵制

例 We should put the company under a **boycott**.
我們應該聯合抵制該公司。

Cabinet [`kæbənɪt] *n.* 櫃子；內閣

例 There is no roomforan other filing **cabinet** in our office.
我們辦公室裡沒有地方可再擺一個檔案櫃。

Capacity [kəˋpæsətɪ] *n.* 能力；容量

例 She was employed in the **capacity** of management.
她因其管理才能而被聘用。

Capital [`kæpət!] *adj.* 主要的 *n.* 資金；首都

例 He got business **capital** for his new venture through his father.
他從他父親那邊獲得資金來從事他的新投資。

Characteristic [ˌkærəktəˋrɪstɪk] *n.* 特徵；特性

例 One **characteristic** of a good purchase is a solid warranty.
一個好的買賣的特性就是要有堅強的保固服務。

Circulation [ˌsɝkjəˋleʃən] *n.* 流通；循環

例 There is a large **circulation** in the pop music.
流行音樂銷路很廣。

Code [kod] *n.* 法規；準則

例 Our company's address **code** is to wear formal suit in the office.
我們公司的法規是在辦公室時必須穿著正式套裝。

Commerce [`kɑmɝs] *n.* 商業；貿易

例 Close **commerce** binds the two countries together.
密切的貿易把這兩國結合在一起。

Commission [kəˋmɪʃən] *n.* 傭金；委員會

例 The sales clerks work on **commission** only.
銷售人員只根據銷售量收取傭金。

Competition [ˌkɑmpəˋtɪʃən] *n.* 競爭；比賽

例 They need to keep all their ideas confidential as **competition** was fierce.
由於競爭激烈，他們必須要對所有他們的計畫保密。

Conference [`kɑnfərəns] *n.* 協商；會議

例 After the interview, they held a **conference** together.
會談後他們共同舉行會議。

Convince [kən`vɪns] *v.* 說服；使確信

例 It requires a lot of talking to **convince** the judge he is innocent.
要說服法官他是無辜很費口舌的事。

Corporation [ˌkɔrpə`reʃən] *n.* 公司；團體

例 The **corporation** was founded in 2006.
這個公司成立於2006年。

Crisis [`kraɪsɪs] *n.* 危機

例 The **crisis** had a negative effect on this trade.
這次危機對此次交易產生了負面的影響。

Develop [dɪ`vɛləp] *v.* 發展

例 With proper training, the intern could **develop** into a leader.
經由適當訓練實習生也能發展成為一個領導者。

Dismiss [dɪs`mɪs] *v.* 解雇；解散

例 The committee of the company has decided to **dismiss** her.
公司董事會已決定辭退她。

Document [`dɑkjəmənt] *n.* 文件；證書

例 Jenny asked her secretary to make a copy of the **document**.
珍妮叫秘書把檔複製一份。

Economic [ˌikə`nɑmɪk] *adj.* 經濟的

例 An **economic** crisis was hanging over some countries in that area.
一場經濟危機正在威脅著那個區域的一些國家。

Employment [ɪm`plɔɪmənt] n.雇用；職業

例 The expansion of the factory means the **employment** of sixty or more workers.
工廠的擴建意味著將增雇超過六十名工人。

Endorsement [ɪn`dɔrsmənt] *n.* 背書；保證

例 The cashier would not accept the check without an **endorsement**.
收銀員不會接受未獲背書的支票。

Engagement [ɪn`gedʒmənt] *n.* 約會；約定

例 I can't see you on Monday because I have a previous **engagement**.
星期一我不能見你因為我有約在先。

Experience [ɪk`spɪrɪəns] *n.* 經驗；*vt.* 經歷

例 No previous **experience** is mandatory for this job.
這一工作無需相關的經驗。

Expiration [ˌɛkspə`reʃən] *n.* 屆滿；期限

例 John wants to renew his account before the **expiration** date.
在有效期限來到前，約翰必須更新他的帳號。

Fee [fi] *n.* 費用

例 The **full** fee must be payable on enrollment.
所有費用必須在入學時繳清。

Files [faɪl] *n.* 檔案；文件

例 This folder can easily holds twenty **files**.
這檔案夾可以輕易的容約20個檔。

Financial [faɪ`nænʃəl] *adj.* 財務的；財政的

例 The enterprise was in deep **financial** difficulties.
該公司陷入了嚴重的財務困難。

Forecast [`for͵kæst] *n.* 預測 *v.* 預測

例 The sales **forecast** for the next year is very optimistic.
下一年度的銷售是非常樂觀的。

Gain [gen] *v.* 取得；增進 *n.* 增加；獲利

例 The company is eager to **gain** a stronghold in Asia.
這家公司急於在亞洲取得一席之地。

Hire [haɪr] *n.* 租金；酬金 *v.* 雇用；租借

例 An employer cannot afford to **hire** incapable workers.
一個雇主不會出錢雇用沒有能力的工人。

Interest [ˋɪntərɪst] *n.* 利息

例 Mary lent me the money as 5 percent **interest**.
瑪莉以五分的利息借我一筆錢。

Investment [ɪnˋvɛstmənt] *n.* 投資；授權

例 Any **investment** must involve an element of risk.
任何投資都有一定的風險。

Loan [lon] *n.* 貸款；借出

例 The firm is in default on the **loan**.
這家公司拖欠借款。

Location [loˋkeʃən] *n.* 地點

例 This is a good **location** for a trade show.
這是一個交易展的好地點。

Management [ˋmænɪdʒmənt] *n.* 經營；管理

例 John has stepped up into the **management** of the company.
約翰已升入公司的管理部門。

Merchandise [ˋmɝtʃən͵daɪz] *n.* 商品；貨品

例 Toothpaste is common **merchandise** in a drugstore.
牙膏是藥局裡的常備商品。

Negotiation [nɪ͵goʃɪˋeʃən] *n.* 協商；談判

例 We closed the deal in sugar after two weeks of **negotiation**.

經過兩個星期的談判，我方關於糖的生意成交了。

Professional [prəˋfɛʃən!] *n.* 專業人士；*adj.* 專業的

例 He needs a **professional** to sort out his finances.
他需要專業人士為他管理財務。

Profit [ˋprɑfɪt] *n.* 盈餘；獲利

例 They actually had a **profit** of $ 582.68.
他們的收益事實上是$582.68。

Profitability [͵prɑfɪtəˋbɪlətɪ] *n.* 利益

例 The product manager should be responsible for product **profitability**.
產品經理應對產品的盈利狀況負責。

Register [ˋrɛdʒɪstɚ] *n.* 登記；註冊 *v.* 記錄

例 He is looking over a hotel **register** now.
他正在檢查旅館住宿登記。

Salary [ˋsælərɪ] *n.* 薪水

例 My **salary** is paid directly into my bank account.
我的工資直接撥到我的銀行帳號。

Scheme [skim] *n.* 計畫；方案

例 Can you project a new working **scheme** for me?
你能為我設計一個新的工作計畫嗎？

Staff [stæf] *n.* 職員；工作人員

例 We were impressed by the professionalism of the **staff** of the company.
這家公司職員的專業素質給我們的印象很深。

Strategy [ˋstrætədʒɪ] *n.* 策略

例 What achievements should our marketing **strategy** have achieved?
我們的銷售策略應該取得了哪些成果呢？

隨堂練習！

( ) 1. Due to low _____ , industrial output has remained stagnant.
    (A) commission   (B) investment   (C) invention   (D) agreement

( ) 2. The money is to be used for the _____ of the poor.
    (A) benefit   (B) profit
    (C) capacity   (D) engagement

( ) 3. In running a company, strict _____ management means everything.
    (A) physical   (B) economical   (C) financial   (D) fiscal

( ) 4. The company was pouring around $30 million into the _____ .
    (A) schedule   (B) circulation   (C) negotiation   (D) scheme

( ) 5. A：Hello, John, I've been waiting for you for more than two hours.
    Do you forget our _____ ?
    B：I'm sorry, but my boss had me arrange an emergency schedule to America, so I can't go away now.
    (A) investment   (B) assignment   (C) engagement   (D) enrollment

中譯解析

1. B；中譯：由於投資少，工業生產一直停滯不前。
解析：(A) commission 委託 (B) investment 投資 (C) invention 發明 (D) agreement 協議
本題考名詞。output（產出），stagnant（停滯的），工業生產停滯的可能原因應該是低落的投資，故答案應為 (B)。

2. A；中譯：這筆錢用來為窮人謀福利。
解析：(A) benefit 利益，福利 (B) profit 盈餘 (C) capacity 能力，容量 (D) engagement 約定
本題考名詞。be used for（被用來做），錢可用來幫助窮人，也就是給窮人作為福利，故答案應為 (A)。

3. C；中譯：經營一家公司，嚴格的財務管理是至關重要的。
解析：(A) physical 有形的 (B) economical 經濟的 (C) financial 財務的 (D) fiscal 財政上的
本題考形容詞。Running 在句中解釋為經營，營運之意，要經營一家公司牽涉到的事財務管理，故答案應為 (C)。

4. D；中譯：該公司要向該計畫注資約 3,000 萬美元。
解析：(A) schedule 進度表 (B) circulation 循環 (C) negotiation 協商 (D) scheme 計畫
本題考名詞。pouring 在句中解釋為注入資金之意，錢要投注在計畫中，故答案應為 (D)。

5. C；中譯：A：哈囉，約翰，我已經等你超過二個鐘頭了，你忘了我們之間的約了嗎？
B：很抱歉，我老闆要我安排一個緊急到美國的行程，所以我現在還無法脫身。
解析：(A) investment 投資 (B) assignment 分配 (C) engagement 約會 (D) enrollment 登記。go away（離開），對話顯示 A 和 B 之間有約定碰面，但 B 一直沒出現，所以推斷空格應為 engagement（約會），故答案為 (C)。

與職業工作相關

Accountant [ə`kaʊntənt] *n.* 會計師；會計人員

例 She was satisfied with her earnings as an **accountant**.
她對自己會計師的收入很滿意。

Administrator [əd`mɪnə͵stretɚ] *n.* 管理人員

例 He has **administrators** under him, but takes the crucial decisions by himself.
他手下有管理人員，但重要的決策仍由他自己來做。

Analyst [`ænlɪst] *n.* 分析師

例 The collected evidence has been sent to the **analyst** for further analyses.
收集到的證據已經送給分析師做進一步分析。

Announcer [ə`naʊnsɚ] *n.* 解說員；廣播員

例 A radio **announcer** may have millions of audience.
一個廣播員可能擁有數百萬名聽眾。

Architect [`ɑrkə͵tɛkt] *n.* 建築師

例 The new building was built from the design of a famous **architect**.
這座新建物是由一位著名建築師設計建成的。

Astronauts [`æstrə͵nɔt] *n.* 太空人

例 **Astronauts** had brought back specimens of rock from the moon.
太空人已經從月球帶回了岩石標本。

Attendant [ə`tɛndənt] *n.* 服務員；侍者

例 The flight **attendant** helped me find my seat.
空服員協助我找到我的座位。

Attendee [ə`tɛndi] *n.* 參加者

例 This **attendee** has tentatively accepted the meeting requirement.
與會者已暫時接受了會議要求。

Bachelor [`bætʃələ] *n.* 學士

例 I graduated from university and got a **bachelor** for engineering.
我大學畢業並取得工程學士學位。

Blacksmith [`blæk͵smɪθ] *n.* 鐵工；工匠

例 The **blacksmith** forged a bar of iron into a knife.
鐵匠把一根鐵條鍛造成一把刀。

Cashier [kæ`ʃɪr] *n.* 出納員；收銀員

例 The check must be signed in front of the **cashier** of the bank.
必須當著銀行出納員的面前簽這些支票。

Celebrity [sɪ`lɛbrətɪ] *n.* 名聲；名氣

例 She found herself something of a **celebrity**.
她意識到自己已小有名氣了。

Chef [ʃɛf] *n.* 大廚

例 The **chef** asked his assistant to take care of the roasting.
大廚叫他的助手負責燒烤。

Clerk [klɝk] *n.* 辦事員；職員

例 The **clerk** attached the price tag to each article.
店員給每一件商品系上標價簽。

Colleague [kɑ`lig] *n.* 同事

例 Mary is held in high esteem by her **colleagues**.
瑪莉深受同事的敬重。

Committee [kə`mɪtɪ] *n.* 委員會

例 The **committee** is composed mainly of lawyers and doctors.
委員會主要由律師及醫師所組成。

Consultant [kən`sʌltənt] *n.* 顧問；商議者

例 He is a **consultant** on law affairs to the mayor.
他是市長的一個法律顧問。

Contractor [`kɑntræktɚ] *n.* 承包商

例 My company was the **contractor** of this construction.
我的公司是這項工程承包商。

Corporation [ˌkɔrpə`reʃən] *n.* 公司；團體

例 It takes brains to manage a large **corporation**.
管理一家大公司需要智慧。

Correspondence [ˌkɔrə`spandəns] *n.* 通信

例 A secretary comes in twice a day to deal with his **correspondence**.
一個祕書每天來兩次處理他的信件。

Customs [`kʌstəmz] *n.* 海關〔複數〕

例 The **customs** have seized large quantities of smuggled amphetamine.
海關查獲了大量走私的安非他命。

Deputy [`dɛpjətɪ] *n.* 代理人；*adj.* 副手的

例 John will act as a **deputy** for him during his absence.
他離開期間約翰將代理他的職務。

Distributor [dɪ`strɪbjətɚ] *n.* 分發者；經銷商

例 I'll take some back with me to show to our **distributor**.
我要帶一些回去給我們的經銷商看看。

Donor [`donɚ] *n.* 捐贈者

例 The **donor** engraved the inscription upon a marble plate.
捐獻者在一塊大理石板上面刻下了銘文。

Employee [ˌɛmplɔɪ`i] *n.* 雇員；受雇者

例 The **employee** was dismissed by his boss.
老闆解雇了那個雇員。

Freelance [`fri`læns] *n.* 自由作家

例 Many people prefer to be a **freelance** from home.
許多人願意在家當自由職業者。

Intern [ɪn`tɝn] *n.* 實習生

例 I worked as an **intern** in that company last year.
去年我在那家商行實習。

Investigator [ɪn`vɛstəˌgetɚ] *n.* 調查員

例 John was a special **investigator** for the FBI.
約翰是聯邦調查局的特別調查員。

Juvenile [`dʒuvən!] *n.* 青少年

例 To everyone's surprise, two of the robbers were **juvenile**.
讓人驚訝的是搶匪的其中二個是青少年。

Labor [`lebɚ] *n.* 勞力；疲勞

例 You need to rest from your **labor**. You look very tired.
你的樣子很疲勞，需要放下工作休息一下。

Legislator [`lɛdʒɪsˌletɚ] *n.* 立法委員

例 The new **legislators** are a bunch of worthless politician.
新的立法委員們是一群毫無用處的政客。

Mechanic [mə`kænɪk] *n.* 機工；技工

例 He's neither an electrician nor a **mechanic**.
他既不是電工也不是技工。

Musician [mju`zɪʃən] *n.* 音樂家

例 An aspiring **musician** must practice many hours a day.
有抱負的音樂家每天要練習很多小時。

Opponent [ə`ponənt] *n.* 對手；敵手

例 He beat his **opponent** in the campaign.
他在選舉中擊敗了對手。

Participant [par`tɪsəpənt] *n.* 參加者

例 He has been an active **participant** in the seminar.
他在研討會中一直積極參與。

Physician [fɪ`zɪʃən] *n.* 醫生；內科醫生

例 Jeffrey is under the care of a **physician**.
傑弗瑞正接受一位內科醫生的治療。

Principal [`prɪnsəp!] *n.* 首長；校長；*adj.* 主要的

例 Is your uncle a high school **principal**?
你的伯父是中學校長嗎？

Professor [prə`fɛsə] *n.* 教授

例 The committee was composed of **professors** and engineers.
委員會由教授和工程師組成。

Referee [ˌrɛfə`ri] *n.* 裁判員；仲裁者

例 The team was very angry at the **referee's** decision.
隊員們對裁判員的裁決感到非常氣憤。

Representative [rɛprɪ`zɛntətɪv] *n.* 代表；代理人

例 John is a **representative** for a large steel firm.
約翰是一家大型鋼鐵公司的代理人。

Specialist [`spɛʃəlɪst] *n.* 專家

例 The farmers looked up to him as a **specialist**.
農民們尊他為專家。

Sponsor [`spansə] *n.* 贊助者

例 A **sponsor** came to our rescue with a generous donation.
有個贊助人慷慨捐贈來解救我們。

Subordinate [sə`bɔrdnɪt] *n.* 部屬；*adj.* 下級的

例 She was always friendly to her **subordinate** officers.
她對部屬一向和藹可親。

Supervisor [ˌsupə`vaɪzə] *n.* 監督者；主管

例 The clerk said he needed to get his **supervisor** to authorize my refund.
櫃員說必須讓他的主管批准我的退款。

Technician [tɛk`nɪʃən] *n.* 技術員

例 Our country needs more engineers, scientists, and **technicians**.
我們國家需要有更多的工程師、科學家和技術人才。

Teller [`tɛlə] *n.* 出納員

例 Rachel worked as a **teller** in a newly opened bank.
瑞秋在當地一家新開的銀行當出納。

Veteran [`vɛtərən] *n.* 老兵；老手

例 My grandfather is a **veteran** of the World War II.
我祖父是二戰時的老兵。

Volunteer [ˌvalən`tɪr] *n.* 志願者

例 We have enlisted a few **volunteers** to help clean the lobby.
我們已經找到幾個人自願協助打掃大廳。

隨堂練習！

(   ) 1. I have a meeting with my _____ about my research topic.
         (A) investigator   (B) supervisor   (C) administrator   (D) mechanic

(   ) 2. He wants to work for a newspaper; he is a _____ writer.
         (A) freelance   (B) technical   (C) intern   (D) veteran

(   ) 3. The sacred duty of a _____ is to heal the sick.
         (A) physical   (B) physician   (C) physicist   (D) physics

(   ) 4. A good _____ can analyze an unprofitable operation quickly.
         (A) accountant   (B) accounting   (C) account   (D) accouter

(   ) 5. A: I have a job interview today.
         B: You do? _____
         A: Thanks. I'll do my best.
         (A) Really?   (B) Good luck!   (C) Don't worry!   (D) You'll see!

中譯解析

1. B；中譯：我要就我的研究課題與我的指導者見一次面。
　解析：(A) investigator 研究者 (B) supervisor 指導人 (C) administrator 管理員 (D) mechanic 技工
　本題考名詞。要討論研究計畫，最有可能是與指導者或導師討論，選項中以supervisor具有監督、指導者之意，故答案應為 (B)。

2. A；中譯：他想去報社工作，他是一名自由作家。
　解析：(A) freelance 自由作家 (B) technical 專門技術人員 (C) intern 實習生 (D) veteran 退伍軍人
　本題考名詞。句中提到他想從事有關報紙的寫作工作，選項中以 freelance（自由作家）最符合，故答案應為 (A)。

3. B；中譯：醫生的神聖職責就是治癒病人。
　解析：(A) physical 身體的 (B) physician 內科醫生 (C) physicist 物理學家 (D) physics 物理學
　本題考名詞。sacred（神聖的），heal（治療），會治療病人的人是醫生，故答案應為 (B)。

4. A；中譯：一名優秀的會計師能迅速分析出沒有效益的作業。
　解析：(A)accountant 會計師 (B) accounting 會計 (C) account v.計算 (D) accouter v.裝備
　本題考名詞。unprofitable（沒效益的），會分析作業效益者應為會計師，故答案為 (A)。

7. B；中譯：A：我今天要面談一個工作。
　B：是嗎？(A) 真的？(B) 祝你好運！(C) 不要緊張！(D) 你會明白！
　A：謝謝你。我會全力以赴。
　解析：B 知道 A 有新的面試機會後，A 最後說謝謝你，表示 B 有說祝福他的話，故以 Good luck!（祝你好運！）最恰當故答案為 (B)。

與交通運輸相關

Acceleration [æk͵sɛlə`reʃən] *n.* 加速

例 The train drivers use the speedometer to monitor the rate of **acceleration**.
火車駕駛員由速度計來監控加速度。

Accident [`æksədənt] *n.* 意外事故

例 He said the **accident** could have been avoided.
他說這個事故本來是可以避免的。

Anchor [`æŋkɚ] *n.* 海錨；*vt.* 錨泊

例 The sailor coiled the rope around the **anchor**.
水手把繩子盤纏在海錨上。

Aviation [͵evɪ`eʃən] *n.* 飛行；航空

例 If you want to learn **aviation**, you must have perfect eyesight.
如果你要學習飛行，你必須有好視力。

Boulevard [`bulə͵vɑrd] *n.* 大道

例 Sunset **Boulevard** is a wide main road.
日落大道是一條寬廣的主要道路。

Canal [kə`næl] *n.* 運河

例 The cargo ship is sailing towards Europe through the Suez **Canal**.
這艘貨輪正通過蘇伊士運河駛往歐洲。

Captain [`kæptɪn] *n.* 船長；首領

例 The **captain** made a decision to abandon the ship.
船長決定下令棄船。

Collide [kə`laɪd] *v.* 碰撞

例 Two ships **collided** in the rough seas and finally sank.
兩艘船在波濤洶湧的海面上相撞且最後沉默了。

Commute [kə`mjut] *n.* 通勤

例 She spends much less time on her **commute** to work now.
她現在工作通勤時間節省好多。

Congestion [kən`dʒɛstʃən] *n.* 交通擁擠

例 The **congestion** in the downtown area gets even worse during the summer.
夏天市中心交通阻塞尤為嚴重。

Crossing [`krɔsɪŋ] *n.* 十字路口

例 The policeman usually stands in the middle of the **crossing**.
員警通常佔在十字路口的中間。

Crosswalk [`krɔs͵wɔk] *n.* 行人穿越道

例 We should go across a road at the **crosswalk**.
我們應該在行人穿越道過馬路。

Cruise [kruz] *n.* 郵輪；*v.* 巡航

例 I'd love to go on a round-the-world **cruise**.
我很想乘郵輪環遊世界。

Destination [͵dɛstə`neʃən] *n.* 目標；目的地

例 I eventually arrived at my **destination**.
我終於到達了目的地。

Domestic flight [də`mɛstɪk] [flaɪt] *n.* 國內航線

例 Can I see a **domestic flight** schedule?
我能看一看國內航班時刻表嗎？

Driveway [`draɪv͵we] *n.* 車道

例 The car idled and parked in the **driveway**.
這輛車引擎發動著停在行車道上。

Engine [ˋɛndʒən] *n.* 引擎

例 The car's got sort of **engine** trouble again.
這車子的引擎又再度故障。

Fare [fɛr] *n.* 運費；車費

例 A single **fare** to New York is 170 dollars.
到紐約的單程票價為170美元。

Ferry [ˋfɛrɪ] *n.* 渡輪；渡口

例 The **ferry** carriers freight on this river.
渡輪在河中裝載貨物。

Freeway [ˋfrɪˏwe] *n.* 高速公路

例 We were driving on a California **freeway**.
我們正沿著加州的一條高速公路行駛。

Gasoline [ˋgæsəˏlin] *n.* 汽油

例 There is still some **gasoline** left in the car's tank.
汽車油箱裡還剩下一些汽油。

Helicopter [ˋhɛlɪkɑptɚ] *n.* 直升機

例 She was rushed to the nearest hospital by **helicopter**.
她由直升機火速送到最近的醫院。

Helmet [ˋhɛlmɪt] *n.* 頭盔；安全帽

例 The woman on the motorcycle wore a nice **helmet**.
騎摩托車的婦人戴了一頂漂亮的安全帽。

Interchange [ˋɪntɚˏtʃendʒ] *n.* 交流道

例 We should leave the freeway at the next **interchange**.
我們應該在下一個交流道駛離高速公路。

Intersection [ˏɪntɚˋsɛkʃən] *n.* 交叉路口

例 There is a stop sign at an **intersection**.
在交叉路口處有停車標誌。

Limousine [ˋlɪməˏzin] *n.* 豪華轎車

例 The movie star stepped out of the **limousine** and waved at her fans.
這位電影明星從豪華轎車下來並向影迷揮手。

Navigate [ˋnævəˏget] *v.* 航行

例 Such boats can **navigate** on the Nile.
這種船可以在尼羅河上航行。

Non-stop *n.* 直達

例 This is a **non-stop** flight to Tokyo.
到東京的直達航班。

Passenger [ˋpæsndʒɚ] *n.* 乘客；旅客

例 The ticket was handed back to the **passenger**.
票還給旅客了。

Path [pæθ] *n.* 小徑

例 Go through the arch and follow the **path**, you'll find a toilet.
穿過拱門沿小徑往前走，你就會發現一間廁所。

Pedestrian [pəˋdɛstrɪən] *n.* 行人

例 Not only the driver but also the **pedestrian** should obey the traffic law.
行人及駕駛人都必須遵守交通規則。

Penalty [ˋpɛn!tɪ] *n.* 罰款；懲罰

例 The traffic **penalty** for speeding is 500 dollars.
超速的交通罰款是500元。

Pier [pɪr] *n.* 碼頭；防坡堤

例 The public **piers** are crowded with fishermen.
公共碼頭上擠滿了漁夫。

Pilot [ˋpaɪlət] *n.* 飛行員；領航人

例 The **pilot** was not given clearance to land by air traffic controller yet.
飛行員尚未得到空中管制員發出的著陸許可。

Platform [`plæt͵fɔrm] *n.* 講台；月臺

例 What **platform** does the train to Kaohsiung leave from?
到高雄的火車從哪個月臺發車？

Rail [rel] *n.* 鐵路

例 The new **rail** link has shortened an hour off the traveling time.
新鐵路連線把旅程縮短了一個小時。

Scooter [`skutɚ] *n.* 摩托車

例 In Taiwan, there are many people riding **scooters** to work every day.
在台灣許多人每天騎摩托車上班。

Sedan [sɪ`dæn] *n.* 轎車

例 My parents own a Honda **sedan**.
我父母有一輛本田牌轎車。

Ship [ʃɪp] *n.* 船；*v.* 運送

例 Did he **ship** the goods by train or by plane?
他是用火車還是用飛機運送那批貨物的？

Shortcut [`ʃɔrt͵kʌt] *n.* 捷徑

例 I tried to take a **shortcut**, but got lost.
我本來想抄近路，結果卻迷路了。

Sidewalk [`saɪd͵wɔk] *n.* 人行道

例 Don't park your car on the **sidewalk**.
不要把你的車停人行道上。

Steer [stɪr] *v.* 掌舵；駕駛

例 What is it like to **steer** a ship this size?
駕駛這麼大的船感覺怎麼樣？

Subway [`sʌb͵we] *n.* 地下鐵

例 Where is the nearest **subway** station?
最近的地鐵站在那裏？

Ticket [`tɪkɪt] *n.* 車票；入場卷；罰單

例 Do you want a single or a round-trip **ticket**?

你要單程票還是往返票？

Toll [tol] *n.* 通行費

例 You have to pay a **toll** to drive on a turnpike.
在收費公路上開車要繳通行費。

Traffic [`træfɪk] *n.* 交通；來往 *v.* 在…通行；交易

例 The **traffic** in downtown area is heavy tonight.
今夜市區交通繁忙。

Transit [`trænsɪt] *n.* 通行；*v.* 通過

例 The canal can **transit** a total of 50 ships daily.
這條運河每天能通過50條船。

Transportation [͵trænspɚ`teʃən] *n.* 運輸；運送

例 The airline gives free **transportation** for a certain amount of luggage.
航空公司免費運送一定數量的行李。

Truck [trʌk] *n.* 卡車

例 The **truck** driver was stopped by the police.
卡車司機被員警攔了下來。

Tunnel [`tʌn!] *n.* 隧道

例 They are digging through the mountain to make a **tunnel**.
他們正在鑿山建一條隧道。

Underpass [`ʌndɚ͵pæs] *n.* 地下道

例 You can use the **underpass** over there. It's safe.
你可以使用那邊的地下通道，那是安全的。

Wheel [hwil] *n.* 方向盤；輪狀物

例 The driver of the taxi was slumped exhausted over the **wheel**.
計程車司機疲憊得趴在方向盤上睡著了。

隨堂練習！

( ) 1. Attempts to restrict parking in the city centre have further aggravated the problem of traffic _____ .
　　(A) accident 　　(B) congestion 　　(C) commute 　　(D) destination

( ) 2. The bus had to deviate from its usual _____ because of a road closure.
　　(A) road 　　(B) driveway 　　(C) rail 　　(D) route

( ) 3. It's a long _____ from New York to Boston.
　　(A) rental 　　(B) commute 　　(C) commence 　　(D) ship

( ) 4. The large ship could not _____ on the river.
　　(A) transport 　　(B) steer 　　(C) navigate 　　(D) drive

( ) 5. The city built a _____ overpass over the highway.
　　(A) pedestrian 　　(B) acceleration 　　(C) aviation 　　(D) crosswalk

---

中譯解析

1. B；中譯：在城市中心限制停車的嘗試使塞車的問題更加嚴重。
　　解析：(A) accident 意外 (B) congestion 阻塞 (C) commute 通勤 (D) destination 目的
　　本題考名詞。aggravate（使惡化），在市中心限制停車造成的交通問題，選項中以congestion（阻塞）較合理，故答案應為(B)。

2. D；中譯：因為道路封閉，公共汽車只得繞道而行。
　　解析：(A) road 道路 (B) driveway 車道 (C) rail 鐵路 (D) route 路線
　　本題考名詞。deviate from（從…脫離），road closure（道路封閉），巴士行駛的路線用 route，故答案為 (D)。

3. B；中譯：從紐約通勤到波士頓路程很長。
　　解析：(A) rental 租賃 (B) commute 通勤 (C) commence v.開始 (D) ship 船運
　　本題考名詞。兩地間例行的往返為 commute（通勤），故答案為 (B)。

4. C；中譯：那艘大輪船不能在河裡航行。
　　解析：(A) transport 運輸 (B) steer 駕駛 (C) navigate 航行 (D) drive 開車
　　本題考動詞。船在河面上航行用navigate，故答案為 (C)。

5. A；中譯：城裡在公路上建了一座人行天橋。
　　解析：(A) pedestrian 行人的 (B) acceleration 加速度 (C) aviation 航空 (D) crosswalk 行人穿越道
　　本題考名詞。overpass（天橋），高速公路上方的天橋用 pedestrian overpass（行人天橋），故答案應為 (B)。

與國家、地區相關

Ambassador [æm`bæsədɚ] *n.* 大使

例 The **ambassador** did his best to prevent the outbreak of hostilities.
這位大使竭盡全力防止戰事的爆發。

Antarctic [æn`tɑrktɪk] *n.* 南極

例 The **Antarctic** is one of the world's last great wildernesses.
南極洲是世界上最大的荒原之一。

Arctic [`ɑrktɪk] *n.* 北極圈

例 The so-called **arctic** is the large region surrounding the North Pole.
所謂的北極是指環繞地球北部及點的廣大區域。

Atlantic Ocean [ət`læntɪk][`oʃən] *n.* 大西洋

例 The **Atlantic Ocean** separates America from Europe.
大西洋把美洲和歐洲分隔開來。

Autonomy [ɔ`tɑnəmɪ] *n.* 自治權；人生自由

例 I prefer being single because it give me so much **autonomy**.
我寧願單身因為那讓我有更多自主權。

Ballot [`bælət] *n.* 投票；選票

例 The presidential candidate received over 50% of the **ballot** and won the election.
這位總統候選人獲得超過50%選票而贏得選舉。

Buddhism [`budɪzəm] *n.* 佛教

例 **Buddhism** was introduced into China about 67 AD, and spreaded all around the country from then on.
佛教是在西元67年左右傳入中國的，並從那時起傳遍全國。

Capitalism [kæpət!ɪzəm] *n.* 資本主義

例 **Capitalism** lays stress on innovation, competition and individualism.
資本主義重視創新、競爭和個人主義。

Catholicism [kə`θɑlə͵sɪzəm] *n.* 天主教

例 He is a convert to **Catholicism**.
他改信天主教。

Christianity [͵krɪstʃɪ`ænətɪ] *n.* 基督教

例 My wife and I were initiated into **Christianity**.
我太太與我被介紹加入了基督教。

Colony [`kɑlənɪ] *n.* 殖民地

例 Before independence, many **colonies** were governed by the British.
許多殖民地在獨立前受英國政府統治。

Communism [`kɑmju͵nɪzəm] *n.* 共產主義

例 People who believe in **communism** think government should control the production of everything.
信仰共產主義的人認為政府應控制一切生產。

Congressman [`kɑŋgrəsmən] *n.* 國會議員

例 You can express your concerns by writing a letter to your **congressman**.
你可以寫信給國會議員表達你的意見。

Constitution [͵kɑnstə`tjuʃən] *n.* 憲法

例 These people's rights are enshrined in the country's **constitution**.
這些人民的權利已載入國家憲法。

Continental [͵kɑntə`nɛnt!] *adj.* 大陸性的

例 A **continental** climate type is quite different from an insular one.

大陸性氣候型態大不同於島嶼氣候。

Corruption [kəˋrʌpʃən] *n.* 貪汙

例 **Corruption** is like a ball of snow, once it's set a rolling it must increase.
腐敗如同一個雪球，一旦滾動就會愈滾愈大。

Dictator [ˋdɪkˌtetɚ] *n.* 獨裁者

例 The **dictator** ruled the country. He gained his power by force.
這位獨裁者統治這國家，他是用武力取得政權。

Dynasty [ˋdaɪnəstɪ] *n.* 朝代；王朝

例 Opium was imported from England in the Qing **Dynasty**.
清朝時鴉片從英國進口過來。

Equator [ɪˋkwetɚ] *n.* 赤道

例 The beautiful island of Tahiti is situated in south of the **Equator**.
美麗的大溪地位於赤道以南。

Ethnic [ˋɛθnɪk] *n.* 少數民族；*adj.* 種族的

例 The Thao tribe is considered the tenth **ethnic** group among Taiwan's indigenous peoples.
鄒族在台灣原住民族群列為第十個少數民族。

Globalization [globəˌlaɪˋzeʃən] *n.* 全球化

例 Because of **globalization**, different cultures around the world share many same features.
全球化使世界上不同文化有了更多的相同點。

Hemisphere [ˋhɛməsˌfɪr] *n.* 半球狀

例 In southern **hemisphere**, winter begins on June 21.
在南半球，冬天始於6月21日。

Imperial [ɪmˋpɪrɪəl] *n.* 帝國的

例 We firmly made an objection to the **imperial** system.
我們堅決反對帝制。

Insular [ˋɪnsələ] *adj.* 海島的；孤立的

例 Having lived in one place all his life, his views are **insular**.
他一輩子住在一個地方，所以思想狹隘。

Islam [ˋɪsləm] *n.* 回教；伊斯蘭教

例 **Islam** is one of the great world religions.
回教是世界上幾大宗教之一。

Latitude [ˋlætəˌtjud] *n.* 緯度

例 Winters are long and snowy in the high **latitude**.
高緯度區的冬天是時間長且多雪。

Longitude [ˋlɑndʒəˋtjud] *n.* 經度

例 The city is at **longitude** 21° east.
這個城市位於東經21度。

Majesty [ˋmædʒɪstɪ] *n.* 威嚴；陛下

例 We beg Your **Majesty** to show mercy to him.
我們懇請陛下對他發發慈悲。

Mediterranean [ˌmɛdətəˋrenɪən] *n.* 地中海；*adj.* 地中海的

例 Those houses near the seashore are **Mediterranean** in character.
這些房子都屬地中海風格。

Middle East [ˋmɪd!] [ist] *n.* 中東

例 The topics today will focuse on the crisis in the **Middle East**.
今天課題集中於中東危機。

Migrant [ˋmaɪgrənt] *n.* 移民

例 Thousand of **migrants** moved from Vietnam to this country to find jobs.
數以千計的移民從越南到這個國家來找工作。

Missionary [`mɪʃənˌɛrɪ] *n.* 傳教士

例 Later Dr.Mackay went to Taiwan as a **missionary**.
後來馬偕醫生以傳教士的身份去了台灣。

Oriental [ˌorɪˋɛnt!] *adj.* 東方的

例 Her research is focused on how **oriental** culture is spreading to the west.
她的研究著重於東方的文化如何逐漸傳到西方。

Pacific Ocean [pəˋsɪfɪk] [ˋoʃən] *n.* 太平洋

例 The **Pacific Ocean** is the biggest oceanon the earth.
太平洋是地球上最大的海洋。

Patriot [ˋpetrɪət] *n.* 愛國者

例 The solider is a **patriot**. He is really to defend it against the enemy.
這位士兵是一位愛國者，他將為國家抵禦敵人。

Peninsula [pəˋnɪnsələ] *n.* 半島

例 Korean **peninsula** lies to the west of Japan.
朝鮮半島在日本以西。

Province [ˋprɑvɪns] *n.* 省；州

例 A railways system has spread over the **province**.
鐵路網已遍佈全省。

Reef [rif] *n.* 礁岩

例 Australia's Great Barrier **Reef** is the world's largest living creature.
澳洲大堡礁是世界最大的活實體。

Refugee [ˌrɛfjʊˋdʒi] *n.* 難民

例 The **refugee** was condemned to a life of wandering and homeless.
這個難民註定要過流浪居無定所的生活。

Regime [rɪˋʒim] *n.* 政權；統治

例 The **regime** was finally overthrowed after 20 years of misrule.
在施行了20年的暴政後，這個政權最終被推翻了。

Senator [ˋsɛnətɚ] *n.* 參議員

例 A **senator** has the right to draft regulations.
參議員有權力起草法案。

Sovereignty [ˋsɑvrɪntɪ] *n.* 主權

例 Many countries claimed **sovereignty** over the new island.
許多國家聲稱對新的島嶼擁有主權。

Taoism [ˋtaʊˌɪzəm] *n.* 道教

例 He explained the beliefs of **Taoism** to us.
他向我們講解了道教教義。

Terrorist [ˋtɛrərɪst] *n.* 恐怖份子

例 Two soldiers were killed in a **terrorist** attack.
兩名士兵遭到恐怖分子攻擊而死亡。

Tyranny [ˋtɪrənɪ] *n.* 暴政；專制

例 Many people came to America in order to escape **tyranny**.
許多人為逃避暴政而來到美洲。

Universal [ˌjunəˋvɝs!] *n.* 一般的；宇宙的

例 The infinite of the **universal** is very attractive to human beings.
宇宙的無限對於人類很有吸引力。

隨堂練習！

(　　) 1. Economic _____ brings not only opportunities for development but also challenges.
　　(A) regulation　　　　　　　(B) inflation
　　(C) Contamination　　　　　(D) globalization

(　　) 2. The _____ personally conveyed the president's message to the king.
　　(A) amateur　　(B) patriot　　(C) ambassador　　(D) legislator

(　　) 3. China is an _____ country with a long history.
　　(A) oriental　　(B) ethnic　　(C) criminal　　(D) radical

(　　) 4. In the east, they have a dry _____ climate with severe winters.
　　(A) conventional　　　　　　(B) contentious
　　(C) continental　　　　　　　(D) conditional

(　　) 5. The _____ first step was to strangle the free press.
　　(A) doctor's　　(B) dictator's　　(C) missionary's　　(D) terrorist's

中譯解析

1. D；中譯：經濟全球化所帶來的不僅僅有發展機會，也有嚴峻的挑戰。
   解析：(A) regulation 規則 (B) inflation 通貨膨脹 (C) contamination 汙染 (D) globalization 全球化
   本題考名詞。not only…but also（不僅…而且），指會帶來發展機會跟挑戰的事物，選項中以globalization（全球化）最恰當，故答案應為 (D)。

2. C；中譯：大使將總統的口信親自轉達給國王。
   解析：(A) amateur 業餘者 (B) patriot 愛國者 (C) ambassador 大使 (D) legislator 立法委員
   本題考名詞。convey（轉達），轉達二國元首之間訊息的人應為大使，故答案為 (C)。

3. A；中譯：中國是一個有著悠久歷史的東方國家。
   解析：(A) oriental 東方的 (B) ethnic 少數民族 (C) criminal 犯罪的 (D) radical 激進的
   本題考形容詞。中國是在東方的一個具有悠久歷史的國家，故答案為 (A)。

4. C；中譯：他們東邊是乾燥的大陸性氣候，冬季嚴寒。
   解析：(A) conventional 平常的 (B) contentious 好爭吵的 (C) continental 大陸性的 (D) conditional 有條件的
   本題考形容詞。用來說明氣候的特徵中，選項中唯有continental（大陸性的），可以用來表示大陸性氣候，故答案為 (C)。

5. B；中譯：獨裁者的第一步是扼殺新聞自由。
   解析：(A) doctor 醫生 (B) dictator 獨裁者 (C) missionary 傳教士 (D) terrorist 恐怖份子
   本題考名詞。strangle（扼殺），會扼殺新聞自由的人，選項中以dictator（獨裁者）最適宜，故答案為(B)。

與社會議題相關

Abolish [ə`bɑlɪʃ] *v.* 廢除

例 The tax will be **abolished** by the end of this year.
這稅將在今年底將被廢除。

Academy [ə`kædəmɪ] *n.* 學院

例 This is an **academy** of music.
這是一所音樂專科學院。

Adversity [əd`vɝsətɪ] *n.* 逆境；苦難

例 Those who do not desert you in time of **adversity** are the real friends.
在患難中不棄你而去的人才是真正的朋友。

Aggression [ə`grɛʃən] *n.* 攻擊；侵略

例 It will be considered as **aggression** to shut missile on the border.
在邊界設飛彈將被視為一種攻擊。

Announcement [ə`naʊnsmənt] *n.* 宣告；聲明

例 The **announcement** had provoked a storm of anti-goverment protest.
這個聲明激起了反政府抗議的風潮。

Annual [`ænjʊəl] *adj.* 每年的；*n.* 年度

例 Usually, the **annual** rainfall in this area is less than 100 mm.
本地區通常年度的降雨量不足100毫米。

Assassinate [ə`sæsɪnˌet] *v.* 暗殺

例 The police uncovered a plot to **assassinate** the president.
警方偵破了一個行刺總統的陰謀。

Assault [ə`sɔlt] *n.* 攻擊

例 They were charged with **assault**.
他們被控侵犯他人身體罪。

Assistance [ə`sɪstəns] *n.* 援助；幫助

例 Is there public **assistance** in your country?
在你們國家是否有公共援助機構？

Ban [bæn] *v.* 禁止

例 The sale of private alcohol was once **banned** in Taiwan.
在台灣，私人酒類的販賣曾經被禁止過。

Bankruptcy [`bæŋkrəptsɪ] *n.* 破產

例 The company is on the brink of **bankruptcy**.
該公司已瀕臨於破產的邊緣。

Candidate [`kændədet] *n.* 候選人

例 The **candidate**'s speech was non-specific.
這位候選人的講話只是泛泛之談。

Certificate [sə`tɪfəkɪt] *n.* 證書

例 Will we be awarded a **certificate** after the course?
學習結束後會頒發文憑或者證書嗎？

Charity [`tʃærətɪ] *n.* 慈善、仁愛

例 Cindy isa very generous giver to **charity**.
莘蒂是慈善事業的慷慨捐助者。

Citizenship [`sɪtəznˌʃɪp] *n.* 公民權

例 You can apply for **citizenship** after five years' residency.
居住五年後可申請公民資格。

Competitive [kəm`pɛtətɪv] *adj.* 競爭的

例 My boss is both **competitive** and honourable.
我的老闆既有競爭性又很誠實。

Contamination [kənˌtæməˈneʃən] *n.* 汙染

例 There is a high level of water **contamination** here.
水污染的程度已經很高。

Controversy [`kɑntrə‚vɝsɪ] *n.* 爭議

例 There was much **controversy** over the mayor candidate.
這市長候選人的爭議很大。

Convict [kən`vɪkt] *v.* 宣告有罪

例 The man was **convicted** of drug dealing and sentenced to 10 years in prison.
這個人被宣告販毒並判刑10年。

Copyright [`kɑpɪ‚raɪt] *n.* 著作權

例 Who owns the **copyright** on this song?
誰擁有這首歌曲的版權？

Criminal [`krɪmən!] *n.* 罪犯

例 The **criminal** robbed a pedestrian and ran away.
罪犯搶奪了一個行人並逃跑了。

Deficit [`dɛfɪsɪt] *n.* 赤字；虧損

例 The authorityis ready to cut the budget **deficit** for the next fiscal year.
官方已準備好削減下一財年的預算赤字。

Discriminate [dɪ`skrɪmə‚net] *v.* 歧視；區別

例 The law **discriminates** against woman.
這條法律歧視婦女。

Duration [djʊ`reʃən] *n.* 持久；期間

例 The school was used as a hospital for the **duration** of the war.
戰爭期間這所學校被用作醫院。

Environmental [ɪn‚vaɪrən`mɛnt!] *adj.* 環境的

例 All the parties disputed against the **environmental** issues.
各方都對對環境問題爭論不休。

Franchise [`fræn‚tʃaɪz] *n.* 選舉權

例 The country did'nt granted the **franchise** to women until 1950.
這個國家直到1950年才給予婦女選舉權。

Fraud [frɔd] *n.* 欺騙；詐欺

例 The man was revealed to be a **fraud**.
這男人被揭露是個騙子。

Hijack [`haɪ‚dʒæk] *v.* 劫持

例 The airplane was **hijacked** this morning when it was en route to Berlin.
這班航機今天上午飛往柏林途中被劫持了。

Inflation [ɪn`fleʃən] *n.* 通貨膨脹

例 The Government's main aim is to beat **inflation**.
政府的主要目標是減低通貨膨脹。

Institution [‚ɪnstə`tjuʃən] *n.* 機構；協會

例 They built a charitable **institution** for the young children.
他們建立了一個兒童慈善機構。

Kidnap [`kɪdnæp] *v.* 綁架

例 Those who **kidnapped** the child should be sentenced to death penalty.
綁架小孩的人應該被處以死刑。

League [lig] *n.* 聯盟；社團

例 How many baseball **leagues** are there in this city?
在這城市裏有多少棒球聯盟？

Legislation [‚lɛdʒɪs`leʃən] *n.* 立法

例 The newspaper reported the **legislation** had been passed by the Congress.
報紙報導有關這個立法已由國會通過。

Majority [mə`dʒɔrətɪ] *n.* 大多數

例 The candidate believes his supporters are in the **majority**.
這位候選人相信支持他的人占多數。

Nominee [ˌnaməˋni] *n.* 被提名人

例 The presidential **nominee**is prone to choose a woman as a running mate.
總統提名人傾向於找一位女性競選夥伴。

Objection [əbˋdʒɛkʃən] *n.* 反對

例 If you have no **objection**, the agenda is adopted.
如果你沒有意見，議程就通過了。

Obligation [ˌabləˋgeʃən] *n.* 義務

例 Everyone is under an **obligation** to keep the game rules.
每個人都有遵守這些運動規則的義務。

Overturn [ˌovəˋtɝn] *v.* 推翻

例 They are secretly plannning to **overturn** the government.
他們正秘密計畫推翻政府。

Parliament [ˋparləmənt] *n.* 國會

例 The new bill was rushed through **Parliament**.
新的議案很快在國會中通過了。

Pension [ˋpɛnʃən] *n.* 養老金

例 The country provided a **pension** to the elder.
國家給長者們提供養老金。

Precedent [ˋprɛsədənt] *n.* 先前；慣例

例 The judge's decision will set a **precedent** for the similar murder cases.
這法官的判決將立下類似謀殺案的慣例。

Prohibition [ˌproəˋbɪʃən] *n.* 禁止

例 The **prohibition** against drunken driving can save many innocent lives.
禁止酒後開車將會拯救許多無辜的生命。

Prosecute [ˋprasɪˌkjut] *v.* 對…提起訴訟；執行調查

例 The man was **prosecuted** for drug

dealing after the court prosecutor proved he was guilty.
在經過法院檢察官確認有罪後，這個人被以販毒起訴。

Recruit [rɪˋkrut] *n.* 新兵；*v.* 募兵

例 The country is **recruiting** for the Army.
國家正在為陸軍徵募新兵。

Reimburse [ˌriɪmˋbɝs] *v.* 補償

例 The restaurant will **reimburse** the customer for any loss or damage.
這家餐廳願賠償顧客受到的一切損失和損害。

Resource [rɪˋsors] *n.* 資源；方法

例 All trash is simply an unused **resource**.
所有的垃圾只不過是一種未被利用的資源。

Responsibility [rɪˌspansəˋbɪlətɪ] *n.* 責任

例 To uphold certain basic principles is the **responsibility** of government.
政府均有責任維護護某些基本原則。

Survey [sɚˋve] *n.* 調查；*v.* 審視

例 A recent **survey** shows that most people are worried about the increasing crime.
一份最近的調查顯示大多數人對不斷增長的犯罪率表示憂慮。

Suspect [səˋspɛkt] *n.* 嫌犯

例 The witness said that **suspect** has brown hair and green eyes.
嫌犯有著一頭棕髮和一雙綠眼睛。

Utility [juˋtɪlətɪ] *n.* 水電費

例 The rent does not include **utilities**. You must pay it by yourself.
房租不包括水電費用，你必須自付。

隨堂練習！

( ) 1. The policeman advised the _____ to interact with the police.
(A) referee　　　(B) juvenile　　　(C) candidate　　　(D) criminal

( ) 2. The decision to build a dam here was criticized by _____ groups.
(A) cooperative　　　　　(B) contaminative
(C) competitive　　　　　(D) environmental

( ) 3. It is unjust and unlawful to _____ against people of other races.
(A) reimburse　　(B) discriminate　　(C) assassinate　　(D) prosecute

( ) 4. There is a danger of serious _____ from radioactive waste.
(A) contamination　　　　(B) conversation
(C) contention　　　　　(D) condensation

( ) 5. The mayor will try to accord the _____ over the housing scheme.
(A) adversity　　(B) controversy　　(C) utility　　(D) precedent

中譯解析

1. D；中譯：員警勸罪犯與警方合作。
   解析：(A) referee 裁判 (B) juvenile 青少年 (C) candidate 候選人 (D) criminal 罪犯
   本題考名詞。interact with（與…相互配合），警察請某人配合調查，選項中以criminal（罪犯）最適宜，故答案為 (D)。

2. D；中譯：這個建水壩的決定受到了環保團體的批評。
   解析：(A) cooperative 合作的 (B) contaminative 汙染的 (C) competitive 競爭的 (D) environmental 環境的
   本題考形容詞。建水壩會影響環境，所以應該是會受環保團體的批評，故答案為 (D)。

3. B；中譯：歧視外族人是不公正的，也是違法的。
   解析：(A) reimburse 賠償 (B) discriminate 歧視 (C) assassinate 暗殺 (D) prosecute 控告
   本題考動詞。people of other races指其他種族的人，對他人歧視用discriminate against，故答案為 (B)。

4. A；中譯：放射性廢棄物有嚴重污染的危險。
   解析：(A) contamination 汙染 (B) conversation 會話 (C) contention 競爭 (D) condensation 濃縮
   本題考名詞。radioactive waste（放射性的廢棄物），放射性的廢棄物是一種環境的污染，故空格應填入 contamination（汙染），答案為 (A)。

5. B；中譯：市長試圖調解在住房建築規劃方面的爭議。
   解析：(A) adversity 苦難 (B) controversy 爭議 (C) utility公共事業 (D) precedent 前例
   本題考名詞。accord…over（協調），市長應該是要解決紛爭，故空格應填入 controversy（爭議），答案為 (B)。

與自然、科學相關

Aerospace [`ɛrəˌspes] *n.* 航空；太空

例 The entire **aerospace** industry is feeling the chill winds of economic recession.
航空航太工業都感受到了經濟衰退的寒意。

Agricultural [ˌægrɪ`kʌltʃərəl] *adj.* 農業的

例 He attended an **agricultural** college to study animal husbandry.
他進入農業學院去研讀畜牧系。

Atmosphere [`ætməsˌfɪr] *n.* 大氣；氣氛

例 The **atmosphere** on earth consists of more than 70 % of nitrogen.
地球的大氣中含有70%以上的氮氣。

Celestial [sɪ`lɛstʃəl] *adj.* 天文的

例 The sun, moon, stars, etc. are all called **celestial** bodies.
太陽、月亮、星星等都稱之為天體。

Clone [klon] *v.* 複製

例 Scientists **cloned** a sheep and named her Dolly.
科學家們複製了一頭綿羊並把它命名為桃莉。

Compatible [kəm`pætəb!] *adj.* 相容的

例 This computer software is **compatible** with that one, and they can be used together.
這電腦軟體與那個式相容的；他們可以同時使用。

Coral [`kɔrəl] *n.* 珊瑚

例 She wore a white dress with a pair of **coral** shoes.
她穿著一雙點綴著白色珊瑚的鞋子。

Cosmos [`kɑzməs] *n.* 宇宙

例 Our world is only a tiny part of the **cosmos**.
我們的世界僅僅是宇宙的一極小部分而已。

Drought [draʊt] *n.* 乾旱

例 Despite the **drought**, some plants are growing in again.
儘管乾旱，一些植物又長出來了。

Ebb [ɛb] *n.* 退潮 *v.* 退潮

例 As the tide **ebbs**, it flows away from the shore.
當潮水退去，它就從海岸邊浮現。

Eruption [ɪ`rʌpʃən] *n.* 爆發

例 The **eruption** of the volcano caused many damages.
這場火山爆發造成許多損害。

Evolution [ˌɛvə`luʃən] *n.* 演化；演進

例 It must have passed through an interesting procedure of **evolution.**
它必定經過了一個有趣的進化過程。

Extinct [ɪk`stɪŋkt] *adj.* 絕種的

例 It has been more than 250 years since the wolf became **extinct** in Britain.
狼在英國已經滅絕250年了。

Flourish [`flɝɪʃ] *v.* 茂盛；猖獗

例 In Africa, the illegal trade of animal products continues to **flourish**.
在非洲，野生動物製品的非法交易仍舊猖獗。

Genetic [dʒə`nɛtɪk] *adj.* 基因的；遺傳性的

例 It's very difficult to treat **genetic** diseases.
遺傳性疾病治療起來很困難。

Glacier [`gleʃɚ] *n.* 冰山

例 Global warming threatens to melt the Earth's **glaciers.**
地球暖化使得地球上的冰山融化。

Habitat [`hæbə‚tæt] *n.* 棲息地

例 Animals driven out of their natural **habitat** are more vulnerable to disease.
被迫離開牠們原來棲息地的動物很容易被疾病感染。

Hover [`hʌvɚ] *v.* 翱翔；盤旋

例 The sea birds **hover** over the surging waves.
海鳥在驚濤駭浪上翱翔。

Kindle [`kɪnd!] *v.* 點燃

例 To keep himself warm, the man **kindled** a fire with matches and some newspaper.
為了取暖，這男人用火柴及一些報紙點一把火。

Livestock [`laɪv‚stak] *n.* 牲口；家畜

例 He raises cows, pigs and other **livestock**.
他養殖牛、豬和其他家畜。

Literacy [`lɪtərəsɪ] *n.* 識字，讀寫能力

例 Some adults have some problems with **literacy** and numeracy.
例：一些成年人在讀寫和計算方面都有困難。

Lizard [`lɪzɚd] *n.* 蜥蜴

例 The **lizard's** tongue flicked out and caught an insect.
蜥蜴突然伸出舌頭，捉到一隻昆蟲。

Lotus [`lotəs] *n.* 蓮花

例 **Lotus** grows in Africa and Asia.
蓮花產于非洲和亞洲。

Mammal [`mæm!] *n.* 哺乳動物

例 The whale is the largest **mammal** on earth.
鯨魚是地球上最大的哺乳動物。

Maple [`mep!] *n.* 楓木

例 Maple sugar is refined from the sap of **maple** trees.
楓糖是由楓樹的樹液製成的。

Marine [mə`rin] *adj.* 海上的；海生的

例 **Marine** creatures are those which live in the sea.
海洋生物是生存在海裡的生物。

Missile [`mɪs!] *n.* 飛彈

例 The **missile** hit the target at 2000 miles away.
飛彈命中2000浬外的目標。

Molecule [`malə‚kjul] *n.* 分子

例 A **molecule** of water is made up of two atoms of hygrogen and one atom of oxygen.
一個水分子是由兩個氫原子和一個氧原子構成的。

Octopus [`aktəpəs] *n.* 章魚

例 It is said that **octopus** is the most intelligent marine creature.
據說章魚是最聰明的海中生物。

Odor [`odɚ] *n.* 氣味

例 The herb has a special taste and **odor**.
藥草有種獨特的味道和氣味。

Orbit [`ɔrbɪt] *n.* 軌道

例 The satellite was launched into **orbit** around the moon.
這顆衛星被發射進入環繞太陽的軌道。

Ozone [`ozon] *n.* 臭氧

例 They will press for international action to protect the **ozone** layer.

他們將督促國際社會採取行動保護臭氧層。

Pesticide [`pɛstɪ‚saɪd] n. 農藥

例 The **pesticide** was spread over the land.
田裡撒上了農藥。

Radiation [‚redɪ`eʃən] n. 輻射線；放射

例 In that accident, many workers received heavy dose of **radiation**.
在那次事故中，許多工人受到大劑量的輻射。

Reptile [`rɛpt!] n. 爬蟲類

例 Snake, lizard, and other **reptiles** warm their bodies by the sun light.
蛇、蜥蜴及其它爬蟲類生物靠陽光來溫暖身體。

Sacred [`sekrɪd] adj. 神聖的

例 In India, the cow is treated as **sacred** animal.
在印度，牛是被視為神聖的動物。

Salmon [`sæmən] n. 鮭魚

例 We saw a **salmon** jumping in the waterfall.
我們看見一條鮭魚在那邊瀑布中跳躍。

Satellite [`sæt!‚aɪt] n. 衛星

例 People were astonished by the pictures the **satellite** sent back to earth.
人們對人造衛星送回地球的圖片歎為觀止。

Shark [`ʃɑrk] n. 鯊魚

例 Henry was just about to dive when he saw two **sharks**.
亨利正要潛進水裡時他看見二條鯊魚。

Simulation [‚sɪmjə`leʃən] n. 模擬

例 The **simulation** allows him to test various functions of this control system.
這模擬使他能夠試驗這控制系統的各種功能。

Spectrum [`spɛktrəm] n. 光譜；頻譜

例 After the rain, a rainbow emerged with the full **spectrum** of bright colors.
下過雨後，色彩繽紛的彩虹浮現。

Superstition [‚supɚ`stɪʃən] n. 迷信

例 It's a general **superstition** that black cats are unlucky.
認為黑貓不吉祥是一種很普遍的迷信。

Swarm [swɔrm] n. 一大群

例 A **swarm** of buzzing hornets flew out of the hive.
一群的嗡嗡叫的黃蜂飛離巢穴。

Torch [tɔrtʃ] n. 火炬

例 We could see the **torch** flared in the darkness.
我們看到火炬在黑暗中閃光。

Tornado [tɔr`nedo] n. 龍捲風

例 The **tornado** barreled across the field and downtown.
這場龍捲風橫掃郊區及城鎮。

Update [ʌp`det] v. 更新

例 If you want to keep your computer from being attacked, renew and **update** your anti-virus software constantly.
如果你要使你的電腦能免於駭客攻擊，你必須持續不斷地更新你的防毒軟體。

Vibration [vaɪ`breʃən] n. 振動

例 This instrument can detect the slightest **vibration** on the ground.
這部儀器能探測出地表上極微弱的震動。

Virus [`vaɪrəs] n. 病毒

例 It is mandatory for blood banks to test all donated blood for the **virus**.
血庫必須檢查所有捐獻的血是否含有這種病毒。

隨堂練習！

( ) 1. The new system will be _____ with existing equipment.
    (A) comparable   (B) companionable (C) computable   (D) compatible

( ) 2. The farmers used manure to keep up the _____ of their land.
    (A) capability   (B) fertility   (C) faculty   (D) faucet

( ) 3. The pilot's skills are tested through _____ .
    (A) stimulation   (B) simulation   (C) stimulant   (D) stink

( ) 4. Darwin eventually put forward a model of biological _____ .
    (A) evocation   (B) revolution   (C) convention   (D) evolution

( ) 5. A：My computer seems to be out of order. Can you look it over?
    B：Sure, let me see. Oh! _____ You must reinstall it.
    (A) It looks good!
    (B) It's a nice work!
    (C) The software is out of date.
    (D) I've done it over.

中譯解析

1. D；中譯：新的系統將與現有的設備相容。
   解析：(A) comparable 可相比的 (B) companionable 友善的 (C) computable 可計算的 (D) compatible 相容的
   本題考形容詞。新的系統與舊的系統可能有相容性的問題，故空格應填入 compatible（相容的）為宜，答案為 (D)。注意：不要與 comparable（可相比的）混淆。

2. B；中譯：農夫們用肥料保持其土質的肥沃。
   解析：(A) capability 能力 (B) fertility肥沃 (C) faculty 教職員 (D) faucet 水龍頭
   本題考名詞。manure（肥料），keep up（保持），要耕作土地需要有肥料，故空格應填入 fertility（肥沃），答案為 (B)。

3. B；中譯：飛行員的技術是通過模擬飛行來檢測的。
   解析：(A) stimulation 刺激 (B) simulation 模擬 (C) stimulant 刺激物 (D) stink 惡臭
   本題考名詞。tested through 表示經由（方法）來試驗，飛行員的技巧需先經過模擬訓練，故空格應填入 simulation（模擬），答案為 (B)。

4. D；中譯：達爾文最終提出了生物進化的模型。
   解析：(A) evocation喚起 (B) revolution革命 (C) convention 集合 (D) evolution 進化
   本題考名詞。put forward（提出），biological（生物學的），我們都知到達爾文提出生物進化論，故空格應用evolution（進化），答案為 (D)。

5. C；中譯：A：我的電腦似乎故障了，你能幫我檢查一下嗎？
   B：沒問題，我來看一下，喔！ _____ ，你必須重灌。
   (A) 它看起來是好的 (B) 做的很好 (C) 軟體已經過期了 (D) 我已經重做了。
   解析：look it over（檢查一下），reinstall（重灌）。A 認為他的電腦故障了，請 B 幫他檢查看看，B 說到要重灌軟體，所以表示軟體有問題，故答案以 (C) 最適宜。

與地點、位置相關

Alongside [ə`lɔŋ`saɪd] *prep.* 在…旁邊

例 There is a barber shop **alongside** the theatre.
劇院旁邊有一家理髮店。

Auditorium [ˌɔdə`torɪəm] *n.* 禮堂

例 The **auditorium** is mainly used for concert and public meeting.
這座禮堂主要是用來舉辦音樂會和會議。

Bakery [`bekərɪ] *n.* 麵包店

例 We usually walk to the **bakery** to buy donuts.
我們通常步行去麵包店買甜甜圈。

Booth [buθ] *n.* 亭子；小攤子

例 The girls wearing their sunglasses went into the **booth**.
帶著墨鏡的女孩們走進去攤子裏。

Bottom [`batəm] *n.* 底部

例 The ship was buried at the **bottom** of the sea.
船已葬身海底。

Boundary [`baʊndrɪ] *n.* 邊界

例 This river forms the **boundary** of the two countries.
這條河流形成了兩國的分界線。

Brink [brɪŋk] *n.* 邊緣

例 The old elm tree grew on the **brink** of the cliff.
那棵老榆樹生長在峭壁的邊緣。

Cemetery [`sɛməˌtɛrɪ] *n.* 墓地

例 Some of the soldiers were buried in the **cemetery**.
一些士兵葬於那個公墓。

Central [`sɛntrəl] *adj.* 中央的

例 This is the central area of the whole city.
這是整個城市的中心區域。

Contemporary [kən`tɛmpəˌrɛrɪ] *adj.* 現代的

例 There is an exhibition of work by **contemporary** British artists.
這裏有一場當代英國畫家作品展。

Counterclockwise [ˌkaʊntə`klɑkˌwaɪz] *adj.* 逆時針方向

例 All the cars moved in a **counterclockwise** direction.
所有車子按逆時針方向移動。

Culture center [`kʌltʃə][`sɛntə] 文化中心

例 The concert will be held at the **Culture Center**.
音樂會將在文化中心舉行。

Department [dɪ`partmənt] *store* 百貨公司

例 We went to nowhere else but the **department store** yesterday.
昨天我們除去了百貨公司其他什麼地方也沒去。

Dome [dom] *n.* 圓頂建築物

例 The **dome** of that cathedral is gorgeous.
那座大教堂的圓頂美極了。

Downward [`daʊnwəd] *adj.* 向下

例 His house is situated at the **downward** slope of a hil.
他的房子座落於向下的山坡。

Drugstore [`drʌgˌstor] *n.* 藥房

例 I will bring stuff from the **drugstore** for your hands.

我到藥局去給你的手弄點藥來。

Exterior [ɪk`stɪrɪə] *adj.* 外部的

例 The **exterior** of the house needs to be painted.
房子外牆需要油漆了。

Factory [`fæktərɪ] *n.* 工廠

例 This **factory** is scheduled to be demolished next year.
這個工廠定預計明年拆除。

Frontier [frʌn`tɪr] *n.* 偏遠地帶

例 The wagon train traveled slowly across the **frontier**.
貨運馬車緩慢駛過偏遠地帶。

Gas station [gæs][`steʃən] 加油站

例 He forgot to stop by at the **gas station**.
他忘了到加油站順便加油。

Gorge [gɔrdʒ] *n.* 峽谷

例 Wind was funneling through the **gorge**.
風吹過峽谷。

Gymnasium [dʒɪm`nezɪəm] *n.* 健身房

例 He goes to the **gymnasium** to exercise every day.
他每天都去健身房訓練。

Horizontal [ˌharə`zant!] *n.* 地平線；*adj.* 水準的

例 She changed her position from the **horizontal**.
她從水平姿勢變換成其他姿勢。

Inland [`ɪnlənd] *n.* 內陸；內地

例 Canals and rivers form the waterways system of the **inland** country.
運河和江河構成了這內陸國家的水路系統。

Interior [ɪn`tɪrɪə] *adj.* 內部的

例 There is water in the **interior** of the cave.
在山洞的內部有水。

Interval [`ɪntəv!] *n.* 間格

例 The **interval** between the two trees is 10 meters.
這兩棵樹的間隔是10公尺。

Isle [aɪl] *n.* 小島

例 The boat sails for a paradise **isle**.
小船駛向天堂一般的小島。

Laundry [`lɔndrɪ] *n.* 洗衣店

例 Please send clothes to the **laundry**.
請把這些衣物送往洗衣店。

Local [`lok!] *adj.* 在地的

例 He put an advertisement in the **local** news paper.
他在當地報紙上登了一則廣告。

Lounge [laʊndʒ] *n.* 大廳

例 Some guests are watching TV in the hotel **lounge**.
有些客人在飯店會客廳看電視。

Mainland [`menlənd] *n.* 大陸

例 Birds from the **mainland** visit the southern islands every winter.
每年冬天，大陸上的飛鳥飛往南邊島嶼過冬。

Metropolitan [ˌmɛtrə`palətn] *n.* 大都會；*adj.* 大都會的

例 There are many tall buildings in the center of a **metropolitan**.
大都會市中心有許多高樓建築。

Middle [`mɪd!] *adj.* 中間的

例 The equator is an imaginary line around the **middle** of the earth.
赤道是一條假想的環繞地球中間的線。

Nation [ˈneʃən] *n.* 國家；國民

例 The President gave an address to the **nation** over the radio.
總統向全國發表廣播演說。

Northeastern [ˌnɔrθˈistən] *adj.* 東北部

例 Heavy floods rage **Northeastern** Indonesia.
大洪水肆虐了印尼東北部。

Parallel [ˈpærəˌlɛl] *adj.* 平行的；*n.* 平行

例 The railway and the canal are **parallel** to each other.
鐵路是與運河平行。

Plateau [plæˈto] *n.* 高地

例 The family has been herding sheep on the **plateau** for generations.
他們世世代代在這高原上放牧羊。

Square [skwɛr] *n.* 廣場

例 Across the busy **square**, vendors sell hot dogs and sandwiches.
在熱鬧廣場的另一邊，攤販叫賣著熱狗和三明治。

Polar [ˈpolə] *n.* 極地；*adj.* 極地的

例 If we can't find a way to stop global warming, the **polar** bears will soon extinct.
如果我們再不設法阻止地球暖化，北極熊很快就會消失。

Ranch [ræntʃ] *n.* 農場

例 The **ranch** is in the bottom of a hill.
該牧場位於一個小山坡底下。

Reverse [rɪˈvɝs] *adj.* 相反的；*v.* 使反相

例 He wrote down his name on the **reverse** side of the used paper.
他在用過的紙的背面寫下他的名字。

Ridge [rɪdʒ] *n.* 山脊

例 They walked along the mountain **ridge** for two hours.
他們順著山脊行走了二個小時。

Southwestern [ˌsauθˈwɛstən] *adj.* 西南部

例 Most of the **southwestern** United States is unsettled desert.
美國西南部的大部分是無人居住的沙漠。

Spacious [ˈspeʃəs] *adj.* 寬闊的

例 Our yard is **spacious** enough for a tennis court.
我們的院子很寬敞，足夠建一座網球場。

Stadium [ˈstedɪəm] *n.* 體育館

例 The **stadium** is being used for a match.
那個運動場正在進行一場比賽。

Underneath [ˌʌndəˈniθ] *prep.* 在底下

例 Working **underneath** the car is always a messy job.
在汽車底下工作是件髒汙的工作。

Verge [vɝdʒ] *n.* 範圍；邊緣

例 The country's financial crisis is on the **verge** of collapse.
這國家的財政危機已到了崩潰的邊緣。

Vertical [ˈvɝtɪk!] *adj.* 垂直的

例 He slowly climbed up a **vertical** wall of rock.
他慢慢爬上了陡直的石壁。

Village [ˈvɪlɪdʒ] *n.* 村莊

例 They lived in a remote **village** when they were young.
當他們小時後，他們都住在一個偏遠的小村莊裏。

Widespread [ˈwaɪdˌsprɛd] *adj.* 分佈廣的

例 The bomb had caused **widespread** devastation on the ground.
炸彈在地面上造成大面積破壞。

隨堂練習！

(   ) 1. His remains were interred in the _____ .
     (A) memorial   (B) cemetery
     (C) commemoration   (D) monument

(   ) 2. He claims that the laws are antiquated and have no _____ meaning.
     (A) contemporary   (B) constant   (C) contemplative (D) contest

(   ) 3. They have moved to a more _____ residence on a hill top.
     (A) reverse   (B) spacious   (C) widespread   (D) polar

(   ) 4. Tokyo is one of the largest _____ areas in the world.
     (A) mainland   (B) inland
     (C) remote   (D) metropolitan

(   ) 5. A: Excuse me, where is the entrance to the theater?
     B: _____ .
     A: It's nice of you, thank you !
     (A) Go straight, and you'll see the toilet.
     (B) It's just on the left corner along this corridor.
     (C) The theater is usually closed at this time.
     (D) It's completely slipped of my mind.

中譯解析

1. B；中譯：他的遺體葬在墓地。
  解析：(A) memorial 紀念館 (B) cemetery 墓地 (C) commemoration 紀念節日 (D) monument 紀念碑
  本題考名詞。inter（埋葬），遺體應葬在墓地（cemetery），所以答案為 (B)。

2. A；中譯：他聲稱這些法規過於陳舊，已沒有任何現代意義。
  解析：(A) contemporary 現代的 (B) constant 固定的 (C) contemplative 默想的 (D) contest 爭奪
  本題考形容詞。antiquated（陳舊的），因為他認為那是陳舊的法條，相對的就沒有現代的意義，所以選項中應用 contemporary（現代的），答案為 (A)。

3. B；中譯：他們已搬到山頂上一個比較寬敞的住宅去了。
  解析：(A) reverse 相反的 (B) spacious 寬廣的 (C) widespread 分佈廣的 (D) polar 極線的
  本題考名詞。residence（住所），形容居住的場所，選項中以 spacious（寬廣的）最適宜，所以答案為 (B)。

4. D；中譯：東京是世界上最大的大都會之一。
  解析：(A) mainland 大陸 (B) inland 內地 (C) remote 偏遠的 (D) metropolitan 大都會的
  東京是一個世界上的大城市，所以選項中用 metropolitan（大都會的）最適合，答案為 (D)。

5. B；中譯：A：請問劇院的入口在哪裡？
  B：_____ .A：你真是太好了，謝謝！
  (A) 直走過去，你就會看到廁所 (B) 沿著這條走廊的左邊就是了 (C) 戲院在這時候通常是關閉的 (D) 我完全忘記了。
  解析：A 問 B 說戲院入口在哪？B 回答後 A 很滿意並感謝他，表示A已明確告訴B了，所以選項中以 (B) 最適宜。

重要介系詞、連接詞

Aboard [ə`bord] *prep.* 上（車、船、飛機）

例 We were already **aboard** the ship at that time.
當時我們已經上船了。

Above [ə`bʌv] *prep.* 在…上面

例 The water came **above** our knees.
水淹過了我們的膝蓋。

According to [ə`kɔrdɪŋ][tu] *prep.* 依照

例 The books in the shelf are classified **according to** subject.
架子上的書按學科分類。

Across [ə`krɔs] *prep.* 橫過

例 The only access to the wooden cabin is **across** the fields.
去那小木屋的唯一通路是穿過田野。

Against [ə`gɛnst] *prep.* 反對；依靠

例 He was accused of conspiring **against** the king.
他被指控陰謀反對國王。

Along [ə`lɔŋ] *prep.* 沿著

例 He and his wife walked slowly **along** the road.
他與妻子沿公路慢慢走。

Among [ə`mʌŋ] *prep.* 在…之中

例 The great news caused great excitement **among** all her friends.
這好消息使她的朋友們興奮不已。

Around [ə`raʊnd] *prep.* 在…四處

例 Jenny travelled **around** Europe for a month.
珍妮在歐洲各地旅遊了一個月。

As a consequence *ph.* 結果

例 He missed his plane; **As a consequence**, he can't be in New York on Monday.
他錯過了它的班機，因此他不能在星期一抵達紐約。

As a result *ph.* 結果

例 The sergeant disobeied the order; **as a result**, he was punished.
這位陸軍中士違反規定，結果他被處罰了。

As soon as *ph.* 一…就

例 Come here **as soon as** you finish the work.
工作一結束你就到這裡來。

Aside from *ph.* 除…之外

例 **Aside from** a few abrasions, I'm OK.
除了幾處擦傷外，我安然無恙。

Behind [bɪ`haɪnd] *prep.* 在…之後

例 Who's the girl standing behind Jan?
站在珍身後的女孩是誰？

Beneath [bɪ`niθ] *prep.* 在…下方

例 Jan found pleasure in sitting **beneath** that tree.
珍喜歡坐在那棵樹下。

Beside [bɪ`saɪd] *prep.* 在…旁邊

例 There were sheeps grazing **beside** the river.
有些羊在河邊吃草。

Besides [bɪ`saɪdz] *prep.* 除…之外

例 **Besides** cancer, smoking can lead on to other diseases.
除了癌症外，吸煙還可引起其他疾病。

Between [bɪ`twin] *prep.* 介於…之間

例 She left the table to stand **between** the

two men.
她離開桌子站在了那兩個男人之間。

Beyond [bɪ`jɑnd] *prep.* 在…範圍之外

例 This is **beyond** the confines of my knowledge.
這超出了我的知識範圍。

Concerning [kən`sɝnɪŋ] *prep.* 就…而言

例 We enjoyed the great benefit of his assistan ceconcerning the matter.
在這一問題上他的幫助使我們受益匪淺。

Despite [dɪ`spaɪt] *prep.* 儘管；雖然

例 **Despite** being a super star, he's very approachable.
雖然是個大明星，他卻非常平易近人。

During [`djʊrɪŋ] *prep.* 在…期間

例 Plants need to be carefully looked after **during** bad weather.
天氣惡劣時要小心照顧好植物。

Either... or *conj.* 不是…就是

例 **Either** dye **or** paints can be used to colour cloth.
不論是染料還是顏料都可用來染布。

Except [ɪk`sɛpt] *prep.* 除…之外 *conj.* 除非

例 She wouldn't have accepted anything **except** a job in Asia.
除了到亞洲工作外，她本來什麼都不會接受。

例 The wooden cabin stayed empty, **except** when they came.
除非他們到來，要不然那間小木屋一直都是空的。

For that reason *ph.* 因此

例 It snowed for two days; **for that reason**, the highway was closed.
天氣已經下二天雪了，因此高速公路關閉了。

In fact *ph.* 事實上

例 There was considerable turbulence; **in fact**, it was the worst flight I had experienced.
那時有相當大的亂流，事實上那是我所經歷過最糟糕的飛行。

In addition *ph.* 此外

例 You need capital and time; **in addition**, you also need diligence.
你需要金錢和時間，此外你還需要努力。

In spite of *ph.* 不管；儘管

例 **In spite of** her disappointment, she kept a weak smile.
儘管她很失望，她還是保持一絲淡淡的微笑。

Inside [`ɪn`saɪd] *prep.* 在…內部

例 There is a public telephone **inside** the lobby.
大廳內有部公共電話。

Instead of *ph.* 而非

例 We should farm the land **instead of** letting it lay waste.
他們應當在這塊地務農，不要讓它荒廢了。

Like [laɪk] *prep.* 像 *conj.* 如同

例 He looks **like** Father Christmas.
他長得像聖誕老人。

例 On the train to Waterloo, I felt **like** I was going on an adventure.
坐在開往滑鐵盧的火車上，我覺得自己好像正踏上一趟冒險旅程。

Near [nɪr] *prep.* 靠近

例 Jenny bought it at the jeweller's **near** her office.
珍妮在辦公室附近珠寶店買的。

Otherwise [`ʌðɚˌwaɪz] *conj.* 否則；不然

例 You must stay, **otherwise** he will be

punished.
你必須留下來，否則他就要被處分。

Owing to *ph.* 因為

例 **Owing to** engine trouble, the plane had to make anemergent landing.
由於發動機出了毛病，飛機不得不進行緊急降落。

Provided that *ph.* 以…為條件

例 I will go, **provided that** you go, too.
你也去的話我就去。

Regarding [rɪˋɡɑrdɪŋ] *prep.* 關於

例 Jeffrey has said nothing **regarding** your request.
關於你的要求傑弗里什麼也沒說。

Since [sɪns] *prep.* 從…至今 *conj.* 自…以來

例 We haven not heardfromhim **since** last summer .
我們自去年暑假以來未曾收到過他的信。.

例 He's been in the depression ever **since** she left him.
自從她離開他以來，他一直很消沉。

Though [ðo] *conj.* 雖然；即使

例 She is the best teacher, even **though** she has the least experience.
她雖然經驗最少，卻是最出色的老師。

Through [θru] *prep.* 經過

例 Visitors usually enter the room **through** a side entrance.
遊客通常經過側門進入房間。

Under [ˋʌndɚ] *prep.* 在…之下方

例 They found a tunnel **under** the ground.
他們發現了一處迷宮似的地道。

Unless [ʌnˋlɛs] *conj.* 除非 *prep.* 除…之外

例 She won't get paid for time off **unless** she has a doctor's note.
除非她有醫生證明，否則她不上班便拿不到

工資。

例 **Unless** paying by credit card, you must pay in cash.
如果不用信用卡付帳，你就需付現金。

Unlike [ʌnˋlaɪk] *prep.* 不像

例 She was **unlike** her father in every way except for her coal black eyes.
除了那雙烏黑的眼睛外，她跟父親沒有一點兒相像。

Until [ənˋtɪl] *prep.* 直到…才 *conj.* 直到…才

例 The traffic laws don't take effect **until** the end of the year.
交通法要到年底才生效。

例 I didn't want to make an accusation **until** I had some evidence.
我直到有一些證據以後才提出控告。

Whereas [hwɛrˋæz] *conj.* 反過來；卻是

例 Some of the results show positive results, **whereas** others do not.
有一些研究結果令人滿意，然而其他的則不然。

While [hwaɪl] *conj.* 當…時候

例 She was playing with hercat **while** I called her last night.
我昨天晚上打電話給她時她正與她的貓在玩。

Within [wɪˋðɪn] *prep.* 在…之內

例 I completed the assignment **within** the time allotted.
我在限定的時間內完成了指派的任務。

Without [wɪˋðaʊt] *prep.* 沒有

例 We can not enter the security area **without** authorization.
我們未經批准不得進入警戒地區。

Yet [jɛt] *conj.* 但是；可是；*adv.* 但是；可是

例 He understands English, **yet** he can't speak it.
他懂英文，但他不會說。

隨堂練習！

( ) 1. The two opposing armies faced each other _____ the battlefield.
  (A) across   (B) in   (C) among   (D) against

( ) 2. She could see the muscles of his shoulders _____ his T-shirt.
  (A) of   (B) in   (C) on   (D) beneath

( ) 3. Her voice was shaking _____ all her efforts to control it.
  (A) though   (B) however   (C) despite   (D) because of

( ) 4. _____ she was badly frightened, she remained calm.
  (A) Though   (B) In spite of   (C) Despite   (D) Because

( ) 5. He was fiddling with his keys _____ he talked to me.
  (A) and   (B) while   (C) until   (D) because

中譯解析

1. A；中譯：敵對兩軍在戰場上嚴陣對峙。
   解析：本題考介系詞。opposing（對立的），二軍面對面橫跨在戰場上，故介系詞應用 across，故答案為 (A)。

2. D；中譯：她可以看到他T恤衫下肩部肌肉。
   解析：本題考介系詞。表示在他的 T-shirt 底下，介系詞應用 beneath（在…之下），故答案為 (D)。

3. C；中譯：儘管她竭盡全力控制自己，聲音仍然在顫抖。
   解析：空格後面為片語，所以此處應用介系詞。選項 (A) 與 (B) 同為副詞或連接詞，其餘可當介系詞用，(C) despite 儘管 (D) because of 因為，考量句中意義，應用 despite（儘管），故答案為 (C)。

4. A；中譯：她雖然非常害怕，但表面上依然很鎮靜。
   解析：空格後面為子句，所以此處應用連接詞。(B) (C) 均為介系詞，其餘為連接詞，其中 Though（雖然），Because（因為）。考量句中意義，應用 Though（雖然）較適宜，故答案為 (A)。

5. B；中譯：和我談話時他不停地擺弄鑰匙。
   解析：fiddle（玩弄）空格後面為子句，所以此處應用連接詞。四個選項均為連接詞，考量句中意義，表示有二個動作發生的當下，連接詞可用 while 較適宜，故答案為 (B)。

重要形容詞、副詞

Accordingly [ə`kɔrdɪŋlɪ] *adv.* 因此；相應地

例 We have to find out his plans and act **accordingly**.
我們得找出他的計畫照著辦。

Adequate [`ædəkwɪt] *adj.* 足夠地；充分地

例 Can vegetables obtain **adequate** nourishment from such poor soil?
土壤這樣貧瘠，蔬菜能獲得足夠的養分嗎？

Authentic [ɔ`θɛntɪk] *adj.* 可信的；真正的

例 All the data should be encrypted and verified as **authentic** and unmodified.
所有傳送的資料應要加密，並驗證為可信的且沒有被更改。

Available [ə`veləbl] *adj.* 可用的；有效的

例 All our products are **available** by mail order.
我們的商品都可以郵購。

Capable [`kepəbl] *adj.* 有才能的；有資格的

例 **Capable** workers are the most valuable resource of the business.
能幹的工人是工商企業最寶貴的資源。

Comprehensive [ˌkɑmprɪ`hɛnsɪv] *adj.* 全面的；廣泛的

例 The newspaper made a **comprehensive** report of his deeds.
報紙對他的行為做了內容廣泛的報導。

Consecutive [kən`sɛkjʊtɪv] *adj.* 連續的

例 Mary was absent for nine **consecutive** days.
瑪莉一連缺席了九天。

Considerable [kən`sɪdərəbl] *adj.* 重要的；相當的

例 There is **considerable** uncertainty about the company's further development.
這家公司的未來發展相當渺茫。

Considerably [kən`sɪdərəblɪ] *adv.* 相當地

例 The economic situation of this country has changed **considerably**.
這國家經濟形勢已發生了相當大的變化。

Consistently [kən`sɪstəntlɪ] *adv.* 一致地

例 This is a policy we have pursued **consistently**.
這是我們一貫奉行政策。

Constantly [`kɑnstəntlɪ] *adv.* 不斷地；持續地

例 The two companies have been contending **constantly** for years.
這兩公司多年來一直相互競爭。

Crucial [`kruʃəl] *adj.* 重要的；決定性的

例 It's a **crucial** decision for me.
這對我來說是個重要的決定。

Currently [`kɝəntlɪ] *adv.* 通常；現在

例 We **currently** have nine sales associates on our marketing team.
我們目前行銷團隊裏有九個人。

Dangerous [`dendʒərəs] *adj.* 危險的

例 The traffic here is very **dangerous** for children.
這裡的交通對孩子很危險。

Durable [`djʊrəbl] *adj.* 耐用的

例 All of our laptop computers come with a **durable** carrying case.
我們所有的筆記型電腦都有附贈耐用的攜行袋。

Edible [`ɛdəb!] *adj.* 可食用的

例 This kind of mushroom is **edible**, but others may not.
這種蘑菇可以吃，但其它的可能不能吃。

Effective [ɪ`fɛktɪv] *adj.* 有效的

例 This medicine that the doctor prescribes for me is **effective**.
這醫生開給我的藥是有效的。

Enthusiastically [ɪn͵θjuzɪ`æstɪk!ɪ] *adv.* 熱心地

例 The audience clapped **enthusiastically** and called for one more singing.
觀眾們熱烈鼓掌要求再來唱一曲。

Eventually [ɪ`vɛntʃʊəlɪ] *adv.* 最終地

例 It will **eventually** need to be modernized.
那最終還是需要現代化。

Express [ɪk`sprɛs] *adj.* 快速的；明確的；*n.* 快車

例 The **express** train is 30 minutes faster than the commuter one.
快車比通勤火車快上30分鐘。

Formidable [`fɔrmɪdəb!] *adj.* 可怕的；龐大的

例 In debate contest he was a **formidable** opponent.
在辯論賽中他是位可怕的對手。

Frequently [`frikwəntlɪ] *adv.* 常見地；時常地

例 Service problem of this kind occur **frequently** with this type of automobile.
這種維修問題時常發生在這種型車上。

General [`dʒɛnərəl] *adj.* 一般的；普遍的

例 In **general**, our events attract young people.
一般說來，我們的活動會吸引年輕人。

Hazardous [`hæzədəs] *adj.* 危險的；冒險的

例 These weather conditions are very **hazardous** for shipping.
這些天氣情況對航海非常不利。

Homogeneous [͵homə`dʒinɪəs] *adj.* 同質的；均勻的

例 America is not an ethnically **homogeneous** country.
美國不是個民族成分同質的國家。

Identical [aɪ`dɛntɪk!] *adj.* 同樣的；相同的

例 Their views on this problem are **identical**.
他們對於這個問題的看法是一致的。

Indispensable [͵ɪndɪs`pɛnsəb!] *adj.* 必須的；重要的

例 Water is **indispensable** for plants.
水是植物不可缺少的。

Innocent [`ɪnəsnt] *adj.* 無罪的；單純的

例 The accused was found **innocent**.
被告被判定無罪。

Notorious [no`torɪəs] *adj.* 聲名狼藉的

例 He was **notorious** as a gambler.
他是臭名昭著的賭徒。

Organic [ɔr`gænɪk] *adj.* 有機的；器官的

例 **Organic** farming is promptly expanding in the county.
有機農業正在這個郡中迅速發展起來。

Originally [ə`rɪdʒən!ɪ] *adv.* 原本的；獨創的

例 The school was **originally** very small.
這所學校原本是很小的。

Prevalent [`prɛvələnt] *adj.* 普遍的；流行的

例 The **prevalent** view of the people is that interest rates will fall.
人們普遍認為利率會下降。

Primarily [praɪˋmɛrəlɪ] adv. 首先；主要地

例 The president **primarily** concerned about the drop in sales over the last quarter.
總裁主要關心上季度銷售下滑的事。

Primitive [ˋprɪmətɪv] adj. 原始的；古老的

例 The construction of a **primitive** society may not be necessarily simple.
原始社會的結構可能未必簡單。

Provocative [prəˋvɑkətɪv] adj. 挑釁的；刺激的

例 His behavior and thinking was thought as **provocative** and antisocial.
他的思想及行為被認為是煽動性的和反社會的。

Remote [rɪˋmot] adj. 遙遠的；偏僻的

例 There are thousands of **remote** locations along this route.
沿著這條路線上有上千個偏遠的地區。

Sequentially [sɪˋkwɛnʃəlɪ] adv. 連續

例 Streets and buildings are numbered **sequentially**.
街道和建築物按順序編號。

Significantly [sɪgˋnɪfəkəntlɪ] adv. 有意義地；明顯地

例 There is not **significantly** different between the two sets of figures.
這兩組數字沒有明顯的差別。

Simultaneously [saɪməlˋtenɪəslɪ] adv. 同時地

例 Hundreds of fire works burst **simultaneously** in night sky.
成百上千朵煙花在夜空中同時綻放。

Specific [spɪˋsɪfɪk] adj. 特殊的；專門的

例 I gave him **specific** instructions.
我給過他明確的指示。

Suspicious [səˋspɪʃəs] adj. 可疑的；多疑的

例 The policeman was examining the **suspicious** man when I passed by.
我經過時員警正盤問那個可疑的人。

Sustainable [səˋstenəb!] adj. 可持續的

例 An efficient and **sustainable** transport system is critical to the long-term future of London.
一套高效穩定的交通體系對倫敦的長遠發展意義重大。

Tentative [ˋtɛntətɪv] adj. 暫時的；不確定的

例 We made a **tentative** engagement on Sunday.
我們暫定星期日見面。

Typically [ˋtɪpɪklɪ] adv. 典型地

例 The flu **typically** manifests itself in a high fever and sore throat.
流感的典型症狀是發高燒和喉嚨痛。

Various [ˋvɛrɪəs] adj. 不同的

例 Tents come in **various** shapes and sizes.
帳篷有各種各樣的形狀和大小。

Virtual [ˋvɝtʃʊəl] adj. 實際上的；虛像的

例 A firewall acts like a **virtual** security guarding for your network.
防火牆類似於一個虛擬的網路安全守衛。

Vulnerable [ˋvʌlnərəb!] n. 脆弱的，易受傷的

例 Jenny was left feeling exposed and **vulnerable**.
珍妮感到自己孤立無助，非常脆弱。

Weird [wɪrd] 怪誕的；不可思議的

例 Judging from his **weird** behaviour, he seems a bit of an oddity.
從他怪異的行為看來，他好像有古怪。

📝 隨堂練習！

( ) 1. He _____ found his niche in sports journalism.
　　(A) evenly　　　　　　　　(B) eventually
　　(C) considerably　　　　　(D) consequently

( ) 2. Two very clear and _____ handbooks are available.
　　(A) compressible　　　　　(B) convenient
　　(C) consistent　　　　　　(D) comprehensive

( ) 3. The _____ proposal approved by both sides.
　　(A) moderate　(B) prevalent　(C) apprehensive　(D) primitive

( ) 4. Everybody spoke _____ at the meeting. There were no awkward silences.
　　(A) simultaneously　　　　(B) enthusiastically
　　(C) consistently　　　　　(D) apprehensively

( ) 5. We've made a _____ plan for the vacation but haven't really decided yet.
　　(A) tentative　(B) effective　(C) alternative　(D) primitive

💬 中譯解析

1. B；中譯：最後他在體育新聞界找到了理想的工作。
　解析：(A) evenly 平順地 (B) eventually 最終地 (C) considerably 相當地 (D) consequently 必然地
　本題考副詞。niche 指適合個性的工作，journalism（新聞工作），選項中以 eventually（最終地）來形容動詞 found 最恰當，表示他最終才找到適合他的體育新聞工作，故答案為 (B)。

2. D；中譯：現有兩種清晰易懂內容全面的手冊供應。
　解析：(A) compressible 可壓縮的 (B) convenient便利的 (C) consistent一致的 (D) comprehensive 全面性的
　本題考形容詞。available（可用的），手冊內容要清晰及全面的，故用 comprehensive（全面性的）來形容，答案為 (D)。

3. A；中譯：這個穩健的提案得到雙方的認可。
　解析：(A) moderate 穩健的 (B) prevalent 普遍的 (C) apprehensive 擔憂的 (D) primitive 原始的
　本題考形容詞。proposal（提案，建議），對描述雙方都能認同的提案，依選項中以moderate（穩健的）最恰當，答案為 (A)。

4. B；中譯：會上大家發言很熱烈，沒有冷場。
　解析：(A) simultaneously 同時發生地 (B) enthusiastically 熱烈地 (C) consistently 一致地 (D) apprehensively憂慮地
　本題考副詞。awkward為笨拙的，不熟練的，awkward silences 解釋為冷場，沒有人討論。所以形容沒有冷場，討論熱烈的發言，依選項中以 enthusiastically（熱烈地）最恰當，答案為 (B)。

5. A；中譯：我們擬定了一個暫定度假計畫，但是沒有真正定下來。
　解析：(A) tentative 暫時性的 (B) effective 有效的 (C) alternative 替代的 (D) primitive 早期的
　本題考形容詞。說明還未決定的計畫應屬暫定性質的，依選項中以 tentative（暫時性的）最恰當，答案為 (A)。

重要動詞

Accredit [ə`krɛdɪt] v. 認可；委任

例 The president will **accredit** you as his assistant.
董事長將任命你做他的助理。

Adapt [ə`dæpt] v. 適應

例 We must constantly **adapt** and innovate to ensure success in the international market.
我們必須不時地適應並創新，以確保在國際市場中取得成功。

Anticipate [æn`tɪsə‚pet] v. 預測；預言

例 They don't **anticipate** any major problem.
他們預料不會發生什麼大問題。

Approach [ə`protʃ] v. 靠近；接近

例 The scout **approached** the enemy position stealthily.
偵察兵偷偷地靠近敵軍陣地。

Arrest [ə`rɛst] v. 逮捕

例 You can't **arrest** me in my own house.
在我的房子裡面你不能拘捕我。

Associate [ə`soʃɪt] v. 使聯合；交往

例 My wife always **associates** that song with our tour to Hawaii.
我太太總是把那首歌與我們的夏威夷之行聯想在一起。

Assume [ə`sjum] v. 假設；採取

例 We can safely **assume** that this ideal situation will continue.
我們可以有把握地認為這種理想的情況將持續下去。

Attach [ə`tætʃ] v. 附著；附上

例 Be sure to **attach** the coupon to the front of your letter.
切記要把優惠券附在信的正面。

Attribute [ə`trɪbjʊt] v. 歸因於

例 Most historians **attribute** such declines to wars and famine.
大多數的歷史學家把這樣的衰亡歸於戰爭和饑荒。

Breed [brid] v. 產子；下蛋

例 Most of the animals **breed** only at certain times of the year.
大多數動物只在一年的某些時候繁殖。

Capture [`kæptʃə] v. 捕獲

例 The guerrillas shot down a helicopter and **captured** the pilot.
遊擊隊擊落了一架直升機，並俘獲了飛行員。

Commit [kə`mɪt] v. 做（某事）；委託

例 She would not **commit** herself in any way.
她不願作任何承諾。

Communicate [kə`mjunə‚ket] v. 傳達；相通

例 We can only **communicate** by email.
我們只能互通電郵。

Compensate [`kampən‚set] v. 補償；賠償

例 Nothing in the world can **compensate** for the loss of a loved one.
世上沒有任何東西可補償失去心愛的人。

Comprise [kəm`praɪz] v. 由…構成

例 The medical emergency team **comprises** three doctors and two nurses.
緊急醫療團隊由三名醫生和兩名護士組成。

Concede [kən`sid] *v.* 承認；讓步

例 He **conceded** that I was right.
他承認我是對的。

Contend [kən`tɛnd] *v.* 主張；爭論

例 I would **contend** that the president's thinking is flawed on this point.
我認為董事長的想法在這一點上有漏洞。

Contradict [ˌkɑntrə`dɪkt] *v.* 反駁；抗辯

例 I think that children should never **contradict** what their parents say.
我認為孩子們絕對不應頂撞父母。

Convey [kən`ve] *v.* 輸送；表達

例 I was so sad that I could't **convey** my feelings in words.
我如此悲傷致於無法用言語來表達我的情感。

Corrupt [kə`rʌpt] *v.* 貪汙；腐敗

例 Power trends to corruptand absolute power **corrupts** absolutely.
權力使人腐化，絕對的權力使人絕對地腐化。

Deflate [dɪ`flet] *v.* 抽去；降低

例 I **deflate** the tyres to make it easier and safer to cross the desert.
我把輪胎放了氣，以便穿越沙漠時更容易且安全一些。

Devote [dɪ`vot] *v.* 貢獻於；致力於

例 I will **devote** all my life to the cause of education.
我願把畢生獻給教育事業。

Discipline [`dɪsəplɪn] *v.* 訓練，懲戒

例 She never **disciplines** her children and they become uncontrollable now.
她從不懲戒自己的孩子，因而他們都變得無法無天。

Disintegrate [dɪs`ɪntəgret] *v.* 分解；崩裂

例 The plane may **disintegrate** at that high speed.
飛機以那麼高速飛行可能會四分五裂。

Dispute [dɪ`spjut] *v.* 爭論；辯論

例 John often **dispute** againsthis friends.
約翰常和朋友們辯論。

Entrust [ɪn`trʌst] *v.* 託付

例 I couldn't **entrust** my children to strangers at any circumstance.
在任何情況下，我都不會把孩子交給陌生人照看。

Fasten [`fæsn] *v.* 繫緊；固定

例 **Fasten** your seatbelts, please.
請繫好安全帶。

Gaze [gez] *v.* 注視；寧視

例 Sitting in the wicker chair, she **gazed** reflectively at the fire.
她坐在籐椅上，若有所思地凝視著爐火。

Greet [grit] *v.* 向…致意

例 She rose to **greet** her guests in a hurry.
她匆忙地起身迎接客人。

Hasten [`hesn] *v.* 加緊

例 Jenny had to **hasten** her steps to keep pace with his.
珍妮得加快腳步才能趕得上他。

Heighten [`haɪtn] *v.* 升高

例 He made use of every opportunity to **heighten** racial tensions.
他利用一切機會加劇種族間的緊張關係。

Inaugurate [ɪn`ɔgjəˌret] *v.* 就職；就任

例 He will be **inaugurated** as president in January.
他將在一月就任總裁。

Infuse [ɪnˋfjuz] *v.* 注入;灌輸

例 The general's speech **infused** great courage into soldiers.
這位將軍的講話給士兵們灌輸了充足的勇氣。

Modify [ˋmɑdəˏfaɪ] *v.* 修改

例 We must **modify** our plan a little bit .
我們得對我們的計畫稍加修改。

Monitor [ˋmɑnətə] *v.* 監督;監控

例 If we know their frequency, we will **monitor** their communication.
如果我們知道他們的頻率,我們就能監聽他們的通訊。

Motivate [ˋmotəˏvet] *v.* 激發

例 I don't want to fail, and that **motivates** me to get up early every day.
我不想失敗,這促使我每天早起。

Operate [ˋɑpəˏret] *v.* 操作;起作用

例 Some of the students can **operate** the computer.
一些學生能操作電腦。

Overlap [ˏovəˋlæp] *v.* 交叉;重疊

例 His duties and mine **overlaped**.
他的任務和我的任務有重疊。

Pledge [plɛdʒ] *v.* 發誓;保證

例 I will **pledge** myself to this top secret.
我發誓保守這個極度機密。

Promote [prəˋmot] *v.* 增進

例 The enterprise **promotes** originality and encourages innovation.
這家企業提倡創意,鼓勵革新。

Provoke [prəˋvok] *v.* 觸怒;驅使

例 Don't **provoke** your father to anger.
別激怒你父親生氣。

Remind [rɪˋmaɪnd] *v.* 提醒

例 You should always **remind** youself that time and tide wait for no man.
你需總是提醒你自己歲月不等待人。

Reserve [rɪˋzɝv] *v.* 保留;保存

例 I'd like to **reserve** a table for three at eight o'clock.
我想預訂八點鐘供三人用餐的桌位。

Resolve [rɪˋzɑlv] *v.* 使下決心;決心

例 She **resolves** to study English.
她決定學英語。

Retain [rɪˋten] *v.* 保留

例 She has managed to **retain** most of her fortune.
她設法保存了大部分財產。

Submerge [səbˋmɝdʒ] *v.* 浸入水中

例 This new submarine can **submerge** into the sea very quickly.
這艘新潛艇能非常迅速地潛入海中。

Suspect [səˋspɛkt] *v.* 懷疑;覺得可疑

例 Police **suspect** there may be a link between the two robberies.
警方懷疑那兩樁搶案可能有關聯。

Transplant [trænsˋplænt] *v.* 移植;移居

例 It is very important that some plants do not **transplant** well.
知道有些植物不宜移植是很重要的。

Vanish [ˋvænɪʃ] *v.* 消失

例 She seemed to **vanish** into thin air.
她不留痕跡地消失了。

隨堂練習！

( ) 1. I _____ his arrival at four o'clock.
　　(A) accumulate　　(B) associate　　(C) anticipate　　(D) attribute
( ) 2. I _____ that point,but I still think you are wrong generally.
　　(A) concede　　(B) corrupt　　(C)comprise　　(D) contend
( ) 3. They _____ each other all the time.
　　(A) concede　　(B) comprise　　(C) convey　　(D) contradict
( ) 4. I _____ that by next year we will have the problem solved.
　　(A) provoke　　(B) compromise　　(C) pledge　　(D) dispute
( ) 5. A：I think Marry is _____ to comic too much.
　　 B：Yes, every time I want her to study, she always put it off.
　　(A) linked　　(B) attributed　　(C) addicted　　(D) fastened

中譯解析

1. C；中譯：我預期他 4 點鐘到達。
　解析：(A) accumulate 累積 (B) associate 使聯合 (C) anticipate 預期 (D) attribute 歸因於
　本題考動詞。他四點鐘要到來，動詞用選項中的 anticipate（預期）最適宜，答案為 (C)。
2. A；中譯：我承認那一點，不過我認為你還是錯的。
　解析：(A) concede 承認 (B) corrupt 腐蝕 (C) comprise 構成 (D) contend 爭奪
　本題考動詞。generally 在此解釋為一般說來，句中動詞用選項中 concede（承認）最適宜，表示承認某些論點，答案為 (A)。
3. D；中譯：他們總是相互抵觸。
　解析：(A) concede 承認 (B) comprise 構成 (C) convey 傳送 (D) contradict 與…抵觸
　本題考動詞。all the time（總是，時常），本句表是二者之間的關係（each other），動詞用選項中 contradict（與…抵觸）最適宜，答案為 (D)。
4. C；中譯：我保證明年之前我們將解決這個問題。
　解析：(A) provoke 觸怒 (B) compromise 妥協 (C) pledge 誓言 (D) dispute 爭論
　本題考動詞。have the problem solved（把這問題給解決），動詞依選項中以 pledge（誓言）最適宜，意思也就是發誓把問題解決，答案為 (C)。
5. C；中譯：A：我認為瑪莉太 _____ 於漫畫了。
　B：對，每一次我要她去念書，她總是拖拖拉啦。
　(A) 連結在一起 (B) 歸因於 (C) 沉溺 (D) 困住
　解析：put it off（拖延時間），對漫畫太過投入就是沉迷，用 be addicted to（沉溺於），所以答案為 (C)。

重要片語

Be out of 沒有…了

例 I have to go to the store. We're **out of** sugar.
我必須到店裏去,我們的糖用光了。

Be up on 精通

例 I'm not really **up on** modern art, and I enjoy looking at it.
我對現代藝術不在行,我只是欣賞藝術而以。

Call back 回電

例 If he calls while I'm gone, tell me and I'll **call** him **back**.
如果它在我不在的時候來電,告訴他我會回電。

Call down 斥責

例 His father **called** him **down** for staying out so late.
他因他待外面太晚回家而被他父親斥責。

Call for

1.接人

例 The movie starts at seven o'clock. I'll **call for** you at about six.
電影七點開始;我將在六點來接你。

2.需要

例 This is a problem that **calls for** immediate solution.
這是個迫切需要解決的問題。

Call in 請求

例 We **call** Jim **in** to help settle the argument.
我們請求吉姆幫忙停止那場紛爭。

Carry out 實現

例 They received the order, but they never **carried** them **out**.
他們獲得命令,但他從來沒有實現過。

Check up on 檢查某事物

例 The police are **checking up on** the recent activities of all four men.
警方正在查證這四個人近期的活動。

Cheer up 振作起來

例 **Cheer up!** It can't be as bad as you had thought.
振作起來!情況不會你想的那麼糟。

Come across 碰見

例 When I was cleaning out a drawer, I **came across** some interesting old photographs.
當我在清理抽屜時,我發現了一些有趣的老照片。

Do over

1. 把(某事)重新做一遍,完成

例 There are several spelling mistakes in this letter, but I'm too tried to **do** it **over**.
這邊有很多拼字上的錯誤,但我很累無法完成它。

2. 裝飾(房間、牆壁等)

例 We plane to **do over** our guest bedroom in time from Mary's visit.
我們計劃在瑪莉的來訪前將客房完成整修。

Drop in on 順道拜訪

例 Our neighbor **drops in on** us from time to time.
我們鄰居不時順道來拜訪我們。

Drop off

1. 讓…下車

例 I'll **drop** you **off** on the corner of Huston

and Texas Street.

我將讓你在休士頓及德州街口下車。

2.打盹兒；打瞌睡

例 I **dropped off** and missed the end of the film.

我打瞌睡，把影片的結尾給錯過了。

Get across 解釋清晰明白；使人瞭解

例 Your lecture wouldn't **get across** if you used too many technical terms in it.

如果你用了過多的專業術語，你的演講內容就不會被人理解。

Get along

1.相處

例 Jim is sincere and very easy to **get along** with.

吉姆為人誠懇，很好相處。

2.進展

例 How is he getting along with his studies ?

他學習上進展如何？

Get in 到達

例 The train didn't **get in** until midnight.

那火車依直到半夜才抵達。

Get on with 繼續某事

例 Let's **get on with** our math lesson!

我們來繼續我們的數學課程吧！

Get over 克服

例 We are certain that he will **get over** his illness.

我們相信他一定會戰勝病魔的。

Go on with 繼續做

例 **Go on with** your story. I'm enjoying it.

繼續你的故事，我很喜歡它們。

Go over 複習

例 Let's **go over** the last pages of the lesson again.

我們再來複習上次課程那頁。

Go through

1.經歷

例 That was the worst experience I ever **went through**.

那是我經歷過最糟糕的狀況。

2.討論

例 Let's **go through** the argument again .

讓我們再來討論一下這一論點。

Hand in 交出去

例 I'd finish my report, but I haven't **handed** it **in** yet.

我已經完成我的報告了，但我還沒交出去。

Look after 照顧

例 We have a baby sitter to **look after** our child when we want to go out.

當需要外出時，我們請一個保母來照顧我們的小孩

Look down on 輕視

例 She **looks down on** everyone who has less education than she does.

她看不起任何教育程度比她差的人。

Look out 小心

例 **Look out**, your cigarette's burning your coat.

當心!你的香菸快燒到你外套了。

Look over 檢查

例 I hope you would **look** them **over** and tell me what you think of them.

我希望你能檢查們並且告訴我你認為他們怎麼樣。

Look up

1.拜訪

例 If you visit Taipei, be sure to **look** me **up.**
如果你有來到台北，記得順道來看我。

2.查詢

例 If I'm not sure the meaning of a new word, I always **look** it **up** in the dictionary.
如果我不確定一個新字的意思，我總是查閱字典。

Pay back 還錢

例 I'll **pay** it **back** next week.
我下星期將還你錢。

Put aside 放一邊

例 Can you **put aside** what you're doing for a minute?
你可以先暫時放下手邊工作一下子嗎?

Run across 偶遇

例 We **ran across** some old friends at the theater last night.
昨天晚上我們在戲院巧遇一些老朋友。

Run out of 用光了

例 Coming back from Taipei, we **ran out of** gas.
從臺北回來後，我們汽油用光了。

Take after 相像；仿效

例 You must **take after** the best example.
你應該學習最好的榜樣。

Take off 起飛

例 Our plane **took off** at 10:30, and at 16:10 we were in Dallas.
我們的飛機10:30起飛，並且在16:10抵達達拉斯。

Take on 承擔

例 I'm up to my ears in work now, I can't **take** them **on** anymore.
我現在工作已經滿檔了，我無法再做更多了。

Talk over 討論

例 Let's **talk** it **over** a little more before we make up our mind.
再做決定前讓我們再好好討論一下。

Think up 想出

例 He is always **thinking up** ways to get rich quickly.
他總是想著快速致富的方法。

Try on 試衣

例 **Try** this hat **on** for size!
試看看這頂帽子的尺寸。

Turn down 拒絕

例 He applied for a job, but the boss **turned** him **down.**
他應徵一個工作，但老闆拒絕他。

Turn in 交出；歸還

例 Don't forget to **turn in** your homework before the deadline.
記得在截止日前要交家庭作業。

Turn over 翻轉

例 After the meat becomes brown, **turn** it **over** and cook it for ten more minutes.
在肉變成褐色以後，記得翻面並再煮十分鐘。

Turn up 出現

例 Don't worry about misplacing that letter. It will **turn up** the next time you clean house.
不要擔心那封遺失的信，下次你清理房子的時候就會出現了。

☑ 隨堂練習！

( ) 1. Please _____ a fast train to Leeds.
    (A) look for   (B) look up   (C) check up   (D) look over

( ) 2. It's easy to _____ in a crowd because he is very tall.
    (A) take him out   (B) look him up
    (C) check him up   (D) pick him out

( ) 3. How long will it take to _____ the book?
    (A) go through   (B) do over   (C) go on with   (D) come to

( ) 4. I've promised that the next time I go to Taipei I'll _____ .
    (A) look him up   (B) pick him up
    (C) call for him   (D) bring him back

( ) 5. A: I forgot to put my ID number in the form.
    B: Did you write your name?
    A: Yes, of course.
    B: No problem, then. We'll _____ your file easily.
    (A) lookat   (B) look over   (C) find out   (D) think out

---

💬 中譯解析

1. B；中譯：請查一下去里茲的快車。
  解析：(A) look for 期待 (B) look up 查看 (C) check up 核對 (D) look over 檢查
  本題考片語用法。句中意思應該是去查看火車時刻等，所以選項中用look up（查看），答案為 (B)。

2. D；中譯：很容易從人群中辨認出他，因為他個子很高。
  解析：(A) take him out 帶出他 (B) look him up 查看他 (C) check him up 核對他 (D) pick him out 認出他
  本題考片語用法。句中意思是從一堆人中認出他來，所以選項中用pick him out（認出他），答案為 (D)。

3. A；中譯：讀完這本書要多少時間？
  解析：(A) go through 完成 (B) do over 裝修 (C) go on with 繼續 (D) come to 醒來
  本題考片語用法。本句意思是指完成讀這本書，所以用 go through（完成），答案為 (A)。

4. A；中譯：我已經答應下次去台北，就去拜訪他。
  解析：(A) look him up 拜訪他 (B) pick him up 去載他 (C) call for him 要求他 (D) bring him back 想起他
  本題考片語用法。本句意思是到台北去拜訪他，所以用look up（拜訪），答案為 (A)。

5. C；中譯：A：我忘記在表格上填上身分證號碼。
  B：你有寫名字嗎？
  A：當然有。
  B：沒問題。我們很容易就可找出你的檔案。
  (A) look at 觀察 (B) look over 檢查 (C) find out 找出 (D) think out 想出
  解析：在最後一句中很明顯就是表示要找出 A 的檔案，所以要用 find out（找出），答案為 (C)。

03
CHAPTER

閱讀測驗
解題要領

UNIT 01 閱讀測驗答題技巧

　　鐵路特考的閱讀測驗字數；長度約介於200至250個字之間，其內容大致以自然科學及人文歷史及地理的描述居多，題目數一般為4-5個，如何在有限的時間內完成有效的答題就成為閱讀測驗拿高分的關鍵，以下提供幾個答題方法供各位讀者參考，只要熟練題型及技巧，相信必有好成績。

一、 先瀏覽題目再作答

　　先看閱測題目的意義在於先瞭解測驗的範圍，幫助掌握文章的重點。運氣好時，有些題目的問題甚至只需要依一般的邏輯或常識便可回答，這時就像將英文當成國文來考，翻譯出來即可迅速作答。

　　一般來說，鐵路特考閱讀測驗問題大致不出以下幾者，如本段文章的主旨、文章敘述何者為真（或為非）、有關文中人事物的細節、特定單字的意義…等，讀者可以先有心理準備。

二、快速概略性的閱讀

　　很快流覽完題目後，對所需要答題的方向有所了解，回過頭來即進行快速概略性的閱讀。重點在於以最快的速度瀏覽整篇文章，大致掌握文章的主題，即使遇到不知道意思的字彙也不要停頓，只要綜觀整篇文章的走向，應該就能推測出文章大致的意思。對於文章只需要了解各段落的大意與少部份的細節，基本上只需要讀每一段的前兩句話，因為那往往就是整段的討論主題，而考題也是依此方向來設計。其他部分則是衍生的論點，原則上只需快速瀏覽過就好（如果前兩句話還沒出現明確意義，只要繼續讀到有論點出現即可）。在最後一段，重點可能會改放在最後一句。在此同時，有些比較明確的答案的題目就可以直接作答了。

三、劃線、圈字、給代號

　　而對於詢問關鍵字描述的題目，除了在略讀時剛好碰到可以 將相關句子劃線或圈起來，以利後續回過頭來作答。如果碰到不懂的單字是以「主角」身份頻繁出現，而該單字或片語你無法以前後文來理解，可能影響理解文章時，應判斷該單字的屬性為何，試著給它一個代號（如A人、B物或C事等），不見得會妨礙該段主旨的理解。

以下再針對各類型題目提供答題技巧及要注意的地方供讀者參考：

（一）、本段文章的主旨為何？

　　這些答案應該都會在整篇文章的第一到第三句，或每段文章的開頭一句，通常是會重複強調事或物的關鍵字作為主旨，應不難答題。

（二）、下列關於本段文章敘述何者為真（或為非）？

　　這種題目一般先跳過，放到最後再來答，因為難度高，花的時間也長。解題方法就是，去文章裡找到所有選項裡的句子，如果運氣好的話，有些句子是完全一字沒改放進題目裡，其他就要靠耐心了。

（三）、有關文中人事物的細節，如所提到人物的角色，年代，數字等。

　　這類題目最明顯也最簡單，題目或選項裡面都會有數字（年份、百分比之類），在文章裡面找到相同的數字，答案就出來了，但也要注意如單位換算陷阱，如文章中以公分計，題目問公尺計等。

（四）、文章一段句中特定單字的意義與何者最相似？

　　遇這種問題除了多背單字外，就只好靠運氣了。文中的這個單字本身通常會有一到兩個意思，結果你就會在選項裡看到類似意思的字，或比較冷門的字。所以還是要回原文中確認該字的涵意。

（五）、針對文章中某人、事或某物的描述是正確（或不正確）？

　　該型題目與上述（二）類型題目有些類似，但差別是（二）類型題目一般需以全篇文章來找，範圍較大。此類題目範圍較小，僅需針對一小段，甚至一個句子便能答題，文章中通常會有關於該答案的一連串的敘述（如：…調查團成員中包含醫生、教授及專家學者…），只要跟隨著文章敘述，將不正確或沒提到的選項挑出即可。但需注意：文章中沒提到的，雖然認為合理，也算是錯的。

UNIT 02 閱讀測驗實戰練習

實戰練習一

South America is a place of striking beauty and wonderful. The heart of this continent is the Amazon River, a vast paradise, watered by one of the world's greatest river. Because of tremendous amount of oxygen produced in this area, it can be called "the lung of the world."

A team of scientists, teachers, and students, the Amazon Quest team, recently explored some of the wonders of the Amazon Rainforest. They canoed down river, hiked along muddy trails, and climbed into the forest to explore and learn. The following is a report by one of the team member.

"I watch a small piece of the Amazon Rainforest disappear today. This morning, two men from the village of Roaboia led us into the forest. For 20 minutes, we walked along a path tall weeds, banana tree, and low brush. Our destination was a 150-foot tall capirana tree, by far the biggest tree around. It would take 10 people holding hands surround the base of the trunk.

The man took an axis and an electric saw and start cutting into the tree's silky smooth skin. As beautiful as they are, people here chop down capirana tree for their lumber. With a loud roar, the saw cut into the 150-year tree. Then in about 30 minutes, the giant tree crashed down violently.

This, of course, is just one of the millions of tree that fall in this area each year. The authority estimates that in 1970's, 99 percent of the original Amazon Rainforest remained, but in 2000, only 85 percent. It is estimated that more than 33 million acres of Amazon Rainforest disappear ever year, which means 64 acres of rainforest is lost every minute."

(   ) 1. According to the paragraph,where is call "the lung the earth"?

    (A) South America   (B) Amazon River

    (C) Amazon Quest   (D) Roaboia

(   ) 2. What kind of people is not contained on the Amazon Quest team?

    (A) scientists   (B) students   (C) instructors   (D) technicians

(   ) 3. What is the optimal topic of this paragraph?

    (A) How to protect the Amazon Rainforest

    (B) The lung of the world

    (C) An explore to the Amazon Rainforest

    (D) The importance of rainforest.

(   ) 4. According to the paragraph, which of the following statement is not true?

    (A) Amazon River is one of the world's greatest rivers.

    (B) The Amazon Quest team used various ways to go the Amazon Rainforest.

    (C) One man from the village of Roaboia led the team into the forest.

    (D) In 1970's, almost all of the original Amazon Rainforest remained.

(   ) 5. Accoording to the report, about how many acres of the rainforest are lost every hour?

    (A) 64   (B) 85   (C) 2000   (D) 3800

中譯解析

　　南美洲是個令人驚艷和充滿奇蹟的地方，這塊大陸的心臟地帶是亞馬遜森林，它是一個被世界上最大河流之一所灌溉的天堂，因大量氣體都在這地方產生，所以它一直被稱為『地球之肺』。

　　一個由科學家、老師及學生所組成的團隊—亞馬遜尋秘隊，最近探索了亞馬遜雨林的奇觀。他們乘坐獨木舟沿河而下，沿著泥濘小徑步行，爬進森林裏探索和學習，以下是某位團隊成員的一篇報告：

　　「今天我親眼看見亞馬遜雨林的一小部份消失了。今早羅亞波雅村的兩名男子帶領我們進入森林。我們延著小徑走過長草，香蕉樹和矮樹叢，時間長達 20 分鐘。我們的目的地是一顆有 150 尺高的樹，這種樹稱為 capirana，是附近最大的一棵樹，它需要十人還抱才能把樹幹底部圍起來。

　　那人拿出斧頭和電鋸，開始切割那平滑如絲的樹皮。雖然它們很美，但這而的人為了木材還是會砍倒這些樹。伴隨著震耳欲聾的響聲，電鋸鋸進這顆 150 年的樹。接著，再砍了約 30 分鐘後，這顆巨樹猛然倒下，震動了我們腳底的地面。

　　當然，這只是每年在亞馬遜流域被砍倒的數百萬棵樹其中之一而已。當局估計，1970 年代有百分之 99 的亞馬遜雨林被保存下來。但到了 2000 年時，只剩百分之 85。估計每年約有 3 千 3 百萬英畝的亞馬遜雨林消失，這表示每分鐘我們會失去 64 英畝。」

1. B；中譯：依據本文，哪裡被稱為「地球之肺」？(A) 南美洲 (B) 亞馬遜河 (C) 亞馬遜探險 (D) 羅亞波雅

2. D；中譯：甚麼樣的人沒有在亞馬遜尋秘隊成員裏？(A) 科學家 (B) 學生 (C) 老師 (D) 技術人員。

3. C；中譯：何者是本文的最佳標題？(A) 如何保護亞馬遜雨林 (B) 世界之肺 (C) 亞馬遜雨林的探險 (D) 雨林的重要性。

　　解析：本文一開始就提到亞馬遜雨林是世界之肺，後面主要敘述一個由科學家、老師及學生等人組成的尋秘隊伍到雨林中的經過，並經由一位學員的報告，敘述整個活動的經過及看到的感想等，所以整篇著重在探險的經過，故標題應該是亞馬遜雨林的探險，答案為(C)。

4. C；中譯：依據本文，下列何者敘述不正確？(A) 亞馬遜河是世界上最大河流之一 (B) 亞馬遜尋秘隊使用各種方式進到亞馬遜雨林裏 (C) 一個來自於羅亞波雅村落的人帶領這團隊進入森林 (D) 在1970年代，幾乎所有原始亞馬遜雨林都還存在著。

　　解析：(A) 由…The heart of this continent is the Amazon River, a vast paradise, watered by one of the world's greatest river.之敘述為真 (B) 由They canoed down river, hiked along muddy trails, and climbed into the forest to explore and learn.知他們使用各種方式才能進到亞馬遜雨林，敘述為真 (C) 由…two men from the village of Roaboia led us into the forest.知有二個來自於羅亞波雅村落的人帶領這團隊進入森林，而非單獨一人，故敘述為非 (D) 由…1970's, 99 percent of the original Amazon Rainforest remained…知在 1970 年代幾乎所有原始亞馬遜雨林都還存在著，敘述為真。故答案為 (C)。

5. D；中譯：依據這份報告，每小時大約有多少英畝的雨林會消失？(A) 64 (B) 85 (C) 2000 (D) 3800

　　解析：由文中最後提到…which means 64 acres of rainforest is lost every minute.（每分鐘會有 64 英畝消失），所以每小時會有 60*64=3840 英畝消失，答案以 (D) 3800最接近。

實戰練習二

When astronauts return from space walks and remove their helmets, they are welcomed back with a specific smell, which is distinct and weird: something like seared steak, also like hot metal or welding smoke. Three-time spacewalker Thomas Jones has said, "Space carries a distinct odor of ozone. It is acrid and smells a little like gunpowder."

But how does it smell weird? It turns out that it is the atmosphere that gives space the special odor. According to a research, when astronauts move their bodies from space to the station, they bring some particles back inside. The odor they smell comes from the high-energy vibrations in these particles which mix with the air.

"Each time, when I pressed the airlock, opened the hatch and welcomed two tired workers inside, a peculiar smell tickled my nose," astronaut Don Pettit recalled. "At first I thought it must have come from the air channel. Then I noticed that this odor was on their suits, helmets, gloves, and tools. It was more obvious on cloth than on metal or plastic surfaces."

So NASA, now, is trying to reproduce that odor for training purposes—to help astronauts adapt better to the odor of the extra-atmospheric environment.

( ) 1. Where does the weird smell of space come from ?

(A) The atmosphere

(B) The suits, helmets, glovesof astronauts

(C) The body of the astronauts

(D) The air channel of the space station

( ) 2. Which of the following words is closest in meaning to "distinct" in paragraph 1?

(A) mysterious

(B) virtuous

(C) hazardous

(D) ambitious

( ) 3. According to the paragraph, which of the following statement is true?

(A) As astronauts return from space walks, they have a specific welcome.

(B) The atmosphere gives space the special odor.

(C) The space carries gunpowder, and smells acrid.

(D) The odor was more obvious on metal or plastic surfaces than on cloth.

( ) 4. Why does NASA try to reproduce that odor?

(A) They want to reproduce all the equipment for the astronauts.

(B) They want to help the astronauts to addict the odor.

(C) They want the astronauts to get used to the odor.

(D) They want the astronauts to conduct a new training.

中譯解析

當太空人從太空漫步回來並脫下它們的頭盔時，他們迎面而來的是一股獨特且怪異的特殊氣味：那像是燒焦的牛排，也像是火熱的金屬或是焊接煙味。有三次太空漫步經驗的約翰湯姆斯說：太空具有臭氧的獨特氣味，它是辛辣的且聞起來像是火藥味。

但它如何會聞起來很奇怪呢？原來是大氣給了太空中這種奇怪的味道。依據一個研究，當太空人從太空中移動身體回太空站，他們裏面也帶回一些粒子，它們聞到的味道就是來自於這些混合在空氣的中的粒子的高能量震動所造成的。

「每一次我壓下空氣鎖，打開艙口以迎接在裏面二位疲憊不堪的工作人員時，一股特殊的刺激氣味就會撲鼻而來。」太空人唐‧配帝回憶說道。「起初，我想那一定是從空氣管道來的，這時我注意到了這氣未來自於他們的服裝、頭盔、手套及工具等處。這味道在布面上會比在金屬或其它塑膠表面更明顯。」

所以為了訓練需要，NASA 現在正設法重現這種氣味---以幫助太空人更適應這種外太空環境的氣味。

1. A；中譯：這種太空中怪異的味道來自何處？(A) 大氣 (B) 太空人的服裝、頭盔、手套 (C) 太空人的身體 (D) 太空站的空氣管道

解析：由 It turns out that it is the atmosphere that gives space the special odor. 知這種獨特的氣味就是源自於大氣中，答案為 (A)。另 (B) 太空人的服裝、頭盔、手套只是沾染這種氣體，並非原自於該處 (C) 文中沒提到太空人的身體 (D) 太空站的空氣管道是原本懷疑的地方，但結果不是。

2. A；中譯：下列哪一個字的意義與第二行 "distinct" 這字最接近？

解析：distinct 中文為神秘的，怪異的，比較下列：(A) mysterious 神秘的 (B) virtuous 有道德的 (C) hazardous 有害的 (D) ambitious 有野心的。所以答案為 (A)。

3. B；中譯：依據本文，下列敘述何者為真？(A) 當太空人從太空漫步回來後，他們會有一個特殊的迎接 (B) 大氣給了太空特殊的味道 (C) 大氣中具有火藥，聞起來刺鼻 (D) 這種氣味在金屬或其它塑膠表面會比布面上更明顯。

解析：(A) …they are welcomed back with a specific smell…在此處 welcome 是當動詞，表示迎面而來的氣味，而非迎接他們，故敘述為非 (B) 由…it is the atmosphere that gives space the special odor. 知大氣給了太空特殊的味道，敘述為真 (C) 是大氣中的臭氧具有火藥味道，聞起來刺鼻，故敘述為非 (D) 這種氣味在布面上會比金屬或其它塑膠表面更明顯，故敘述為非。

4. A；中譯：NASA 為何要設法重現這種氣味？(A) 他們要為太空人重新生產設備 (B)他們要太空人沉溺於這種氣味 (C) 他們要太空人習慣於這種氣味 (D) 他們要太空人進行一項新的訓練。

解析：由…to help astronauts adapt better to the odor of the extra-atmospheric environment. 可知 NASA 是要幫助太空人更適應這種外太空環境的氣味，答案為 (C)。注意：addict（v.沉溺於）；get used to（習慣於）。

04
CHAPTER

近年考題與
中譯解析

98 年特種考試交通事業鐵路人員

等別：三等考試、高員三級
類科：警察、鐵路各類科別
科目：法學知識與英文（此節錄英文部分）

( ) 31. _____ in Taipei is becoming much more convenient with the newly built Mass Rapid Transit.

(A) Passenger (B) Traffic (C) Transportation (D) Vehicle

( ) 32. Native Americans have a cultural _____ that extends back over 1,000 years.

(A) average (B) heritage (C) exchange (D) visage

( ) 33. Do not expect John to apply for a visa. Too much paperwork can overload him.

(A) John might not be able to get a visa because he does not like to fill out many forms.

(B) John fails to get the visa because he forgets to bring the papers with him.

(C) John does not expect to have a good job because it is quite demanding.

(D) John is overwhelmed with the questions asked by the customs officer.

( ) 34. Microsoft's Windows are the computer software _____ that I am most familiar with.

(A) bandages (B) barrages (C) packages (D) personages

( ) 35. If a professor uses others' essays without documentation, he will be accused of _____ and expelled out of the academic community.

(A) burglary (B) counterfeit (C) ghostwriting (D) plagiarism

( ) 36. In his childhood, his family lived in an inner city where parents were _____ by bad housing and shortage of money.

(A) anticipated　　(B) backfired　　(C) committed　　(D) depressed

(　) 37. By learning to express _____ , to show thankfulness to people, people can become more satisfied with their daily lives.

(A) hostility　　(B) gratitude　　(C) intimacy　　(D) fantasy

(　) 38. Jenny is very kind to her next-door neighbor, _____ her neighbor is not easy to get along with.

(A) besides　　(B) except　　(C) even　　(D) even though

(　) 39. I'll go to the library later today, if I _____ the time.

(A) have　　(B) had　　(C) am having　　(D) will have

(　) 40. Fat people must be careful because obesity is on its way to _____ smoking as the number one killer in many countries.

(A) progressing　　(B) regressing　　(C) transacting　　(D) surpassing

(　) 41. _____ its cost, the office ladies still dream of owning a designer bag.

(A) Except　　(B) Despite　　(C) Even if　　(D) Owing to

(　) 42. For many people, there seemed to be no escape from poverty.

(A) It seemed that many people could not change their impoverished condition.

(B) Many people found little difficulty in getting rid of poverty.

(C) Many people were poor, and they found no way to get away from the rich.

(D) It seemed that many people found no way to help those poor people.

Someone in Hollywood should snap up the movie rights to the backstory of Falcarius utahensis, the 125 million-year-old dinosaur with 10-cm claws and spoon-shaped molars ____43____ last week. Scientists say it offers the first glimpse into how dinos made the ____44____ from small, agile meat eaters to elephant-size vegetarians. Falcarius, as it turns out, was dug up by a black-market fossil collector named Lawrence Walker, who found it on US government land in Utah while digging at night under a tarpaulin. Convinced he was onto something big, the poacher tipped ____45____ a paleontologist he knew, James Kirkland, and led him to the site. Kirkland tried to protect his source but, asked under oath how the dinosaur was discovered, reluctantly ____46____ Walker in. Kirkland got his 15 minutes of fame last week. Walker served five months in prison.

( ) 43. (A) concealed　　(B) unveiled　　(C) restored　　(D) explored
( ) 44. (A) movement　　(B) flowing　　(C) transition　　(D) gap
( ) 45. (A) off　　(B) over　　(C) up　　(D) into
( ) 46. (A) handed　　(B) told　　(C) took　　(D) turned

As little as thirty years ago, few people questioned the gender roles that had prevailed for centuries. The conventional wisdom was that a woman's place was in the home and that a man's main responsibility to his family was to put food on the table. In the 1970s and 1980s, however, greater numbers of working women meant that men were no longer the sole breadwinners. A father's emotional involvement with his family also became more important. Forty years ago, almost no husbands were present in the delivery room when their wives gave birth. Today, it is generally expected for male partners to attend childbirth classes, to be there for the delivery, and to take more responsibility for child rearing than their fathers or grandfathers did.

In addition to society's changing views of the role men play in relation to childcare, social scientists also found that the presence of the father in the home can contribute to lower juvenile crime rates, a decrease in child poverty, and lower rates of teenage pregnancy. Differences in parenting styles between men and women are also believed to contribute to children's ability to understand and communicate emotions in different ways. The research supports the claim that the absence of a father in the family is the single biggest problem in modern society.

( ) 47. Forty years ago, a father usually _____.
  (A) won bread for his family
  (B) attended childbirth classes
  (C) educated his children
  (D) stayed at home

( ) 48. The father's presence at home does NOT contribute to _____.
  (A) lower juvenile crime rates
  (B) more serious family violence
  (C) a decrease in child poverty
  (D) children's better development

( ) 49. Children under the care of both parents develop good ability to communicate emotions because _____.
  (A) there are more conflicts in the family
  (B) there are two breadwinners in the family
  (C) there are two parenting styles in the family
  (D) there are fathers and grandfathers in the family

( ) 50. The author would agree that _____.
  (A) the increased number of working women brings about serious problems in childcare
  (B) contemporary men take more responsibility for childcare than their fathers
  (C) a father's emotional involvement with his family is not as important as a mother's
  (D) a mother's emotional involvement with her family is not as important as a father's

98 年特種考試交通事業鐵路人員——高員級中譯解析

31. C；中譯：有了新建的捷運，台北的交通變得愈來愈方便了。

解析：(A) Passenger 乘客 (B) Traffic 交通 (C) Transportation 運輸 (D) Vehicle 車輛

本題考名詞。Mass Rapid Transit（捷運，MRT），transportation 強調運輸，如運輸人或物，而 traffic 指交通未必一定要運輸。本題應是指台北的交通運輸，所以應該用 transportation，故答案為 (C)。

32. B；中譯：美國的原住民有綿延超過 1,000 年的文化傳承。

解析：(A) average 平均 (B) heritage 傳承 (C) exchange 交換 (D) visage 外觀

本題考名詞。句中提到有綿延超過 1000 年的文化，選項中以 heritage（傳承）最適合，故答案為 (B)。

33. A；中譯：不要期待約翰會去申請簽證，太多的文件作業會超過他的負荷。

(A) 約翰可能不會得到簽證因為他不喜歡填很多表格。

(B) 約翰沒有得到簽證因為他忘記將文件帶在身上。

(C) 約翰不被期待會得到一個好工作因為他工作要求相當高。

(D) 約翰對海關所問的問題倒了。

解析：題目暗示約翰無法填太多文件（paperwork），故答案為 (A)。

34. C；中譯：微軟的視窗作業系統是我最熟悉的電腦套裝軟體。

解析：(A) bandages 繃帶 (B) barrages 阻塞 (C) package 套組 (D) personages 角色

本題考名詞。微軟的視窗作業系統是一種套裝軟體，所以用 package（套組）最適合，故答案為 (C)。

35. D；中譯：如果一個教授使用別人的論文而沒有列出參考文獻，他將被控瓢竊並被逐出學術界。

解析：本題考名詞。be accused of 是指被控訴，後面接名詞或動名詞，說明被控的事物。就本題而言 (A) burglar（竊盜）主要指偷竊一般物品 (B) counterfeit（仿冒品）(C) ghostwriting（代為撰寫）(D) plagiarism（盜用）指抄襲、瓢竊論文。依本題句意，答案應為 (D)。

36. D；中譯：在他孩童時期，他家住在一個內陸城市，而他雙親因不良的住屋環境及缺錢而意志消沉。

解析：(A) anticipated 預期 (B) backfired（引擎的）逆火 (C) committed 違犯 (D) depressed 消沉

本題考被動式。where 所引導的形容詞子句說明他住的城市，由題意來判斷應為被動語氣，故空格內須為動詞過去分詞，用 be depressed by（因某事而消沉）最符合題意，故答案為 (D)。

37. B；中譯：經由學習表達感激，或對人表現謝意，人們對他們日常生活會覺得更滿意。

解析：(A) hostility 敵意 (B) gratitude 感謝 (C) intimacy 親密 (D) fantasy 幻想

本題考名詞。後面同位語提到有關對人們的感謝（thankfulness to people），所以 gratitude（感謝）讓前後相呼應最符合題意，故答案為 (B)。

38. D；中譯：珍妮對門隔壁鄰居非常親切，儘管她的鄰居不好相處。

解析：空格前後為二個獨立完整的子句，所以要用連接詞，(A) beside 介系詞，在…旁邊 (B) except 連接詞，除了…以外 (C) even 副詞，甚至…連 (D) even though 連接詞，儘管。依題意二句表達轉折的語氣，所以應用 even though，答案為 (D)。

39. A；中譯：假如我有時間，我今天稍後要去圖書館。

解析：本題為對未來一般敘述性的語氣，if 子句用動詞簡單現在式即可，即if+現在式…，
S+will+V…，所以答案為 (A)。

40. D；中譯：肥胖的人必須小心因為肥胖在很多國家正趕上吸菸成為第一名的殺手。

解析：(A) progressing 前進 (B) regressing 回歸 (C) transacting 處理 (D) surpassing超越
本題考動詞。On its way to 為在…過程中，後面接 Ving，本句表示肥胖正趕過吸菸的意思，動詞用
progressing（前進）最恰當，所以答案為 (A)。

41. B；中譯：儘管它的價格（偏高），這位 OL 仍然夢想要有個設計師的包包。

解析：(A) Except 除了，介系詞；連接詞(B) Despite 儘管，介系詞(C) Even if 雖然，連接詞 (D) Owing to
由於，介系詞
本題考介系詞。該句表達雖然設計師的包包昂貴，但是 OL 仍想要有一個，所以選項中用Despite
（儘管）最符合，故答案為(B)。注意：Even if（雖然，連接詞）後面要接子句，故不能選。

42. A；中譯：對很多人來說，貧窮似乎是無可避免。

(A) 許多人似乎都無法改變他們困頓的情況。

(B) 許多人發現脫離貧窮沒甚麼困難。

(C) 許多人貧窮，而且它們發現無法逃離富人。

(D) 許多人似乎發現無法去幫助那些貧窮的人。

解析：注意以下用語：there seem(ed) to be （某事）…似乎是；It seem(ed) that+子句似乎（某事發
生）；get rid of 擺脫；get away from 脫逃。答案為 (A)。

43－46. 中譯：

　　有些在好萊塢的人應該會鍾情於有關猶他鑄鐮龍這角色的背景故事，這1億2500萬年前具有 10 公
分長爪以及湯匙形狀臼齒的恐龍在上星期揭露了。科學家說它對恐龍如何由小巧敏捷的肉食者，演變到
大象一般大小的素食者提供了第一手的資料。原來鑄鐮龍是由一位名為 Lawrence Walker 的黑市化石收
藏家所挖掘的，他有一晚在猶他州一塊美國政府擁有地上的一塊油帆布底下所挖掘到的。當他確信挖到
寶後，這個盜獵者向他一位認識的古生物學家 James Kirkland 透漏消息，並讓他進到現場。Kirkland 試
圖保護它的來源，但當被要求作證恐龍是如何發掘到的時，Walker 被不情願的說出來，結果 Kirkland
得到 15 分鐘的名氣，而 Walker 要在牢裡待5個月。

43. B；解析：(A) conceal 隱藏 (B) unveil 揭露 (C) restore 回復 (D) explore 探索
空格內應為省略的形容詞子句修飾名詞 dinosaur，也就是 dinosaur…molars（which is）…last week，
動詞應用過去分詞，依題意應選 unveiled（揭露），故答案為 (B)，意思是上週被揭露的恐龍。

44. C；解析：(A) movement 活動 (B) flowing 流動的 (C) transition 轉變 (D) gap 差距
該空格需填入名詞作為 made 的受詞，依前後句意表示由小巧敏捷的肉食者到大象一般大小的素食的
經過，所以transition（轉變）是最恰當的，故答案為 (C) make transition from 從…轉變成。

45. A；解析：(A) tip off 向…洩漏消息 (B) tip over 翻倒 (C) tip up 翻起的 (D) tip into 倒進

該空格需填入本句動詞，該句表示盜獵者告訴他一位認識的古生物學家這件事，所以選項中以 tip off （向…洩漏消息）最恰當的，故答案為 (A)。

46. D；解析：該空格需填入本句動詞，並考慮片語用法，(A) hand in 繳交出來，但通常用於交出報告之類 (C) took in 接受 (D) turn in 交出來，可以用於人或物，意味把 Walker 交出來，所以答案為 (D)。

47.—50. 中譯：

　　不過就在 30 年前，人們不會質疑已普遍流傳數世紀之久的性別角色問題。傳統觀念認為女人的角色是在家中，而男人對家庭的主要任務是把食物放到桌上。然而，在 1970 到 1980 年代，大量的職業婦女意味著男人已不再是唯一養家活口的人了，父親對家庭感情的投入變得更為重要。40 年前，幾乎沒有男人會在他的太太生產時出現在產房，今天，男人通常被期待要參加一些母親分娩的課程，出現在生產的當下，以及負擔比他們父執輩更多的育兒後備任務。

　　除了目前社會正在改變男人對有關育兒角色觀念，社會學家同時也發現父親出現在家中可降低青少年犯罪的發生率，減少兒童貧困及降低少女懷孕率。父母親之間照護方式的不同，也被認為可以增進孩子以不同的方式來了解並增進感情的能力。研究支持說父親在家庭中缺席是現代社會的最大單一問題。

47. A；中譯：40 年前，父親通常 (A) 為他的家庭賺取麵包 (B)參加分娩課程(C)教育他的小孩(D)待在家裡。

　　解析：由…a man's main responsibility to his family was to put food on the table.可知已前父親的角色就是提供家庭的溫飽，所以答案為 (A)。

48. B；中譯：父親出現在家庭對何項沒做出貢獻 (A) 降低青少年犯罪率 (B) 更嚴重的家庭暴力 (C) 降低兒童貧困 (D) 兒童更好的發展。

　　解析：由…social scientists also found that the presence of the father in the home cancontribute to lower juvenile crime rates, a decrease in child poverty, and lower rates of teenage pregnancy.可知 (A) 及 (C) 都有提到，另由 Differences …are also believed to contribute to children's ability to understand and communicate emotions in different ways.表示對兒童的處理溝通及感情的能力也有貢獻，所以能有更好發展，選項 (D) 也成立，只有 (B) 沒有提到且是負面，所以答案為 (B)。

49. C；中譯：在父母雙親的照顧下會發展良好溝通情緒能力是因為 (A) 在家庭中有更多衝突(B)在家庭中有二個養家的人 (C) 在家庭中有二種教養型態 (D) 父親及祖父在家中。

　　解析：由第2段倒數第4行 Differences in parenting styles between men and women are also believed to contributeto children's ability to understand and communicate emotions…，顯示父母雙親的照顧下會發展良好溝通情緒能力是因為父母親的二種不同教養型態，故答案為 (C)。注意原文文中是以 men and women 來代表父母親。

50. B；中譯：作者同意下列何者 (A) 職業婦女的增加引起嚴重的兒童照顧問題

　　(B) 現代男人比他們父執輩承擔更多照顧兒童的責任 (C) 父親對家庭的情感上的參與沒有像母親對家庭的那樣重要 (D) 母親對家庭的情感上的參與沒有像父親對家庭的那樣重要。

　　解析：(A) 由greater numbers of working women meant that men were no longer the sole breadwinners，可

知職業婦女的增加是改變家庭收入方式，並沒提到有引起嚴重的照顧問題。(B) 由…male partners to attend…for child rearing than their fathers or grandfathers did.可知男人比它們父執輩承擔更多照顧兒童的責任，本句為真。(C) 及 (D) 提到情緒是指藉由雙親不同教養方式的差異來增進孩子以不同的方式了解並溝通情緒的能力，沒有提到與父母親的情緒有關的內容，所以不能為答案。故本題答案為 (B)。

 NOTE

98 年特種考試交通事業鐵路人員

等別：四等考試、員級
類科：警察、鐵路各類科別
科目：法學知識與英文（此節錄英文部分）

( ) 31. Calm down! You can't think rationally when you are so _____ .

(A) emotional　　(B) pleasan　　(C) respectful　　(D) speechless

( ) 32. Cover the chicken with foil when you put it in the oven, _____ it will take a long time to cook.

(A) otherwise　　(B) whereas　　(C) while　　(D) until

( ) 33. He was _____ hit the jackpot and became a millionaire overnight.

(A) lucky as to　　　　　　　(B) such lucky to

(C) lucky enough to　　　　　(D) so lucky enough to

( ) 34. I can't see any differences between a real diamond and an artificial one. They look _____ to me.

(A) moderate　　(B) identical　　(C) hazardous　　(D) primitive

( ) 35. The old man tells his young grandson that life is tougher than he _____ .

(A) breeds　　(B) conveys　　(C) disputes　　(D) assumes

( ) 36. A cow _____ in a green meadow often represents the peace of a pastoral life.

(A) greeting　　(B) glancing　　(C) grazing　　(D) gazing

( ) 37. The island is hot and _____ in the summer. We feel uncomfortable because the air is wet.

(A) spicy　　(B) salty　　(C) humble　　(D) humid

( ) 38. The chairperson's speech was full of _____ . Many people thought her language was meant to be intentionally vague so as to please everybody.

(A) ambiguities　　(B) compensations　(C) disturbances　　(D) harassments

(   ) 39. He was a _____ player and never gave his opponent even the smallest chance.

(A) merciless   (B) virtuous   (C) curious   (D) generous

The food, eating, and nutrition practices and patterns of a society have been discussed in many ways, each of which offers different perspectives for analyses of social dynamics. *Foodways* is a term often used by _____40_____ who seek to portray the traditional food and eating patterns in a society. Foodways typically denote such traditional societal practices _____41_____ are informally transmitted and may be difficult to modify. More recently, the term food culture has been used to denote the components of a larger culture _____42_____ food, eating, and nutrition. Both foodways and food culture have specific connotations, with foodways having more specific historical and geographical referents _____43_____ food culture offers more universalistic and scientific connotations. To avoid the past images conjured up under foodways (and related terms such as food habits or cuisine), food culture will be used here to _____44_____ the food, eating, and nutrition-related categories, rules, and plans used in a particular society.

(   ) 40. (A) those   (B) one   (C) them   (D) he
(   ) 41. (A) they   (B) as   (C) like   (D) what
(   ) 42. (A) making up   (B) associated with (C) filled with   (D) bringing up
(   ) 43. (A) while   (B) despite   (C) if   (D) except
(   ) 44. (A) take as   (B) judge from   (C) refer to   (D) depend on
(   ) 45. Mr. Lin: I come to say sorry for what I did to you last week.

Mr. Chiang: I don't understand. What for?

Mr. Lin: I felt really bad about talking back to you.

Mr. Chiang:_____

Mr. Lin: So we're OK?

Mr. Chiang: Sure.

(A) Don't worry about that.

(B) No problem. You're always welcome.

(C)I'll be a good listener.

(D)It won't take too long.

( ) 46. Passenger 1: Can you tell me where I can change my money?

Passenger 2: _____

(A) Sorry, I don't have any change.

(B) No, it's rude of you to say so.

(C) I don't know where your money is.

(D) At most banks and hotels.

( ) 47. Andy: I'll mail the letter for you on my way to school.

James: You won't forget, will you?

Andy: Don't worry. _____

(A) Go ahead.   (B) I can't agree more.

(C) You can count on me.   (D) You can say that again.

The term Black English is a relatively "new" word in American English. During the Civil Rights Movement in the 1960s, the adjective "black" became popular. It replaced "Negro," which recalled the memories of slavery. Black was considered a more dignified word. Americans began speaking about Black English, Black studies, Black Power, Black History, and so forth.

The origins of Black English really go back to West Africa. The English slave traders were often unfamiliar with the various African languages. They needed a common language to deal with the slaves. The slaves, who came from many different tribes, needed a common language to communicate. This mixture of English and the various African languages was the foundation of Black English.

During the long trip to the New World, the slaves spoke this "new" language. They built new friendships through this common bond. More important still, they kept some of their African traditions and customs alive in this "new" language. Some of the slaves went to the West Indies. Today Caribbean English has its own grammar, vocabulary, and pronunciation. Despite the common origins, there are differences between the English of a Caribbean Black and an American Black.

(　) 48. According to this passage, why did people start using "black" to replace Negro?

(A) Because "black" was a relatively popular word.

(B) Because people wanted to remember the history of slavery.

(C) Because in the 1960s, people wanted to use a word that could show respect to the black people.

(D) Because the word "Negro" reminded people of the Civil Rights Movement.

(　) 49. According to this passage, which of the following is NOT true about the origins of Black English?

(A) The slaves, who came from different tribes, couldn't communicate with each other without a common language.

(B) The slave traders were not familiar with the various African languages, so they invented a whole new language.

(C) The birth of Black English has much to do with the slave trade in West Africa.

(D) Black English came from the mixture of English and African languages.

(　) 50. According to the passage, which of the following statements is true?

(A) The origins of Black English can be traced back to West Africa.

(B) With a "new" language, the slaves couldn't keep their old traditions and customs alive.

(C) Black people in different parts of the world speak the same language.

(D) Black English is derived from the one used in the West Indies.

98 年特種考試交通事業鐵路人員——員級中譯解析

31. A；中譯：冷靜下來，你在如此情緒的狀況下無法理性地思考。

解析：(A) emotional 情緒性的 (B) pleasant 愉快的 (C) respectful 尊敬的 (D) speechless 無言的

本題考形容詞。calm down（冷靜下來），so 為表程度的副詞，選項中以 emotional（情緒性的）最符合題意，故答案為 (A)。

32. A；中譯：當你把雞放進烤箱時要用錫箔紙包起來，否則將會煮很久。

解析：(A) otherwise 否則 (B) whereas 有鑑於 (C) while 當…的時候 (D) until 直到

二句具有因果關係（沒包就會煮很久），所以用 otherwise 最適合，故答案為 (A)。

33. C；中譯：他相當地幸運中了賭注而在一夜之間變成百萬富翁。

解析：本題考形容詞修飾語用法，用 enough 修飾形容詞時，要放在形容詞後面，所以要用 lucky enough to，故答案為 (C)。

34. B；中譯：我無法分辨真鑽石與人工鑽石的差別，他們對我來說看起來都是相同的。

解析：(A) moderate 溫和的 (B) identical 相同的 (C) hazardous 有害的 (D) primitive 原始的

本題考形容詞，無法分辨差別表示它們是很像的，所以用 identical（相同的）最適合句意，故答案為 (B)。

35. D；中譯：這位老人告訴他的小孫子生活比他想像來的艱困。

解析：(A) breeds 生產 (B) conveys 運輸 (C) disputes 爭論 (D) assumes 想像

本題考動詞。than 後面引導的副詞子句修飾比較級形容詞 tougher，表示生活比他認為來的辛苦，所以動詞用 assumes（想像）最符合，故答案為 (D)。

36. C；中譯：牛隻在青翠的草地上吃草通常代表著畜牧生活的寧靜。

解析：(A) greeting 問候 (B) glancing 瞥見 (C) grazing 吃草 (D) gazing 凝視

本題考分詞用法。空格為分詞當形容詞修飾主詞 cow，且因為主動，所以用現在分詞 grazing，表示牛在吃草，故答案為 (C)。

37. D；中譯：這座島在夏天炎熱且潮濕，我們對空氣潮濕感到不舒服。

解析：(A) spicy 辛辣的 (B) salty 鹹的 (C) humble 謙卑的 (D) humid 潮濕的

本題考形容詞。後面提到空氣潮濕，表示氣候炎熱潮濕，故答案為 (D)。

38. A；中譯：主席的言論充滿著模稜兩可，許多人認為她是故意含糊其詞來讓每個人滿意。

解析：(A) ambiguities 模稜兩可 (B) compensations 補償 (C) disturbances 動亂 (D) harassments 騷擾

本題考形容詞。be full of+名詞（充滿某事務），vague（含糊的）。後面提到她含糊其詞就表示講的不清不楚，故空格內用 ambiguities（模稜兩可）最恰當，故答案為 (A)。

39. A；中譯：他是一個無情的選手，而且從不給他的對手一點機會。

解析：(A) merciless 無情的 (B) virtuous 善良的 (C) curious 好奇的 (D) generous 大方的

本題考形容詞。opponent（對手），由他不給對手一點機會表示可能他是一位無情的選手，空格內用 merciless（無情的）最恰當，故答案為 (A)。

40－44 中譯：

　　食物、飲食、營養習慣及社會型態已經做了很多方面的討論了，而這每個面向都對分析社會動力學提供了不同的觀點。飲食方式是個常被那些試圖描述社會中傳統飲食及食物的人使用的名詞，飲食方式代表著那些從古沿用至今且可能不易改變傳統社會的飲食習慣，甚至在最近，飲食文化一詞已被用來代表與食物、飲食及營養有關的廣泛的文化內涵。飲食方式及飲食文化二者有特殊的關聯性，飲食方式比較有歷史上或地理上的概念，然而飲食文化則提供更多普遍及科學性的內涵。為了避免被誤認為是飲食方式過去的印象（相關的用語還有飲食習慣及烹飪），飲食文化在這裡將泛指食物、飲食及與營養有關的範疇，以及用在一個特定社會的各種範疇。

40. A；解析：空格 who 後面接一個形容詞子句，而且前面被動式的介系詞 by 後面須接一名詞或代名詞當受詞，選項中只有是 those 是指示代名詞，可以引導一形容詞子句，所以答案為 (A)。

41. B；解析：such…as與…相同的事物（或人），空格後面為動詞，須有關係代名詞引導關係子句，選項中只有是as可當關係代名詞使用，所以答案為(B)。

42. B；解析：空格後面有三個相關飲食的名詞來說明前面的culture，可以用分詞來修飾，所以選項(B)associated with 與…有關為本題答案。另本句亦可以用形容詞子句…culture（which is）associated with…來表示。

43. A；解析：由…with foodways having…food culture offers…可知這是在敘述二個不同的概念，須用轉折語氣，故本處應用連接詞 while（然而），答案為 (A)。

44. C；解析：(A) take as 當作是 (B) judge from 從…判斷 (C) refer to 關於 (D) depend on 依據
本處為一不定詞片語修飾here，文中提到飲食文化與食物、飲食及與營養有關的事，所以用答案用(C) 最洽當。

45. A；中譯：林先生：我來向你致歉對於上週我對你所做的事。
　　江先生：我不明白，為何要道歉？
　　林先生：我對於跟你頂嘴的事感到過意不去。
　　江先生：(A) 不要擔心 (B) 沒問題，歡迎你 (C) 我將是個好聽眾 (D) 那不會花太長時間。
　　林先生：所以，我們沒事啦？
　　江先生：當然。
　　解析：江先生表示不會在意，所以二人沒事了，所以答案為 (A)。

46. D；中譯：顧客 1：你可以告訴我哪邊可以換零錢嗎？
　　顧客 2：(A) 抱歉！我沒有零錢 (B) 不！你這樣說太魯莽了 (C) 我不知道你的錢在哪裡。(D)所有的銀行跟飯店。
　　解析：依據對方問的問題來切實回答即可，銀行及商店都可以是換零錢的地方，所以答案為 (D)。

47. C；中譯：安迪：我會在去學校的路上幫你寄這封信。
　　詹姆士：你該不會忘記，對吧？
　　安迪：不用擔心，(A) 去吧！(B)我非常同意。(C) 你可以信任我。(D) 說的好。
　　解析：安迪要他不用擔心，會幫他寄信的，故答案為 (C)。

48～50. 中譯：

　　「黑人英文」這個名詞在美式英文中是相當新的字。在 1960 年代人權運動時，黑色（black）這個形容詞變得很普遍，它取代了黑人（Negro）這個字，這字讓人回想起關於奴隸的不好回憶。黑色被認為是一個更尊貴的字，美國人開始談論著有關黑人英語、黑人研究、黑人勢力、黑人歷史等等。

　　黑人英文的源起真正要回到西非，英國的奴隸販子常常不熟悉各種不同的非洲語言，他們需要一種共通的語言來應付這些奴隸。而這些來自各個部落的奴隸也需要共同的語言來溝通，這種英語及各種不同非洲語言混合體就是黑人英文的基礎。

　　在前往新大陸的漫長旅途中，奴隸們講這種「新」的語言，他們經由這樣共同連結建立了新的友誼，更重要的事，他們保存了一些非洲生動的傳統及慣用語在這種新語言中。一些奴隸到西印度去，今天，加勒比英文有他自己的文法、字彙以及發音。雖然起源相同，還是有些差異存在於加勒比黑人英文與美式黑人英文。

48. C；中譯：依據本文，為何人們要用 black 取代 Negro 這個字？(A) 因為black是個相當受歡迎的字 (B) 因為人們要記住黑奴的歷史 (C) 因為在 1960 年代時，人們要用一個可以向黑人表達敬意的字(D) 因為 Negro 這個字使人想起人權運動。

解析：由…in the 1960s, the adjective "black" became popular. It replaced "Negro," which recalled the memories of slavery. Black was considered a more dignified word…可知在1960年代，black這個字開始流行，但會取代Negro是因為black這個字被認為比較高貴，所以可以用來表達對黑人的敬意，故答案為 (C)。

49. B；中譯：依據本文，關於黑人英文的源起哪一項是錯的？(A) 那些來自不同部落的奴隸沒有共同的語言而無法溝通(B)奴隸販子都不熟悉各種不同的非洲語言，所以他們創造了一種全新的語言 (C) 黑人語言的產生跟在西非的奴隸交易有很大的關聯 (D) 黑人語言來自於英語及非洲語言的混合。

解析：(A) 由The slaves, … needed a common language to communicate.可知一開始他們沒有溝通的語言，敘述為真 (B) 由The English slave traders were often unfamiliar with the various African languages可知奴隸販子不熟悉不同的非洲語言，但由The slaves, who…needed a common language to communicate. This mixture … was the foundation of Black English可知新語言不是單獨由奴隸販子創造的。敘述為非 (C) 由 The English slave traders were often unfamiliar with the various African languages. They needed a common language to deal with the slaves可知英國的奴隸販子常常不熟悉不同的非洲語言，他們需要一種共通的語言來應付這些奴隸，所以與奴隸交易有很大關聯，敘述為真。(D) 由This mixture of English and the various African languages was the foundation of Black English可知黑人語言來自於英語及非洲語言的混合體，敘述為真。故答案為 (B)。

50. A；中譯：依據本文，下列哪一項敘述是對的？(A) 黑人英文的源起可以被追溯到西非 (B) 有了新的語言，奴隸們就無法生動的保存他們老傳統及慣用語 (C) 黑人在世界不同的地區都講相同的語言 (D) 黑人英文是源起於西印度的一種語言。

解析：(A) 由The origins of Black English really go back to West Africa，敘述為真。

(B) 由 they kept some of their African traditions and customs alive in this "new" language可知奴隸們生動

的保存他們老傳統及慣用語在新的語言中，敘述為非。

(C) 由The slaves, who came from many different tribes, needed a common language to communicate…，可知黑人在世界不同的地區並非講同的語言，所以才要有一種共通語言來溝通，所以敘述為非(D)由This mixture of English and the various African languages was the foundation of Black English可知黑人英文為源起於英語及各種不同非洲語言，文中提到西印度只是說有些奴隸去了西印度，敘述為非。故答案為 (A)。

 NOTE

99 年特種考試交通事業鐵路人員

等別：三等考試、高員三級
類科：警察、鐵路各類科別
科目：法學知識與英文（此節錄英文部分）

( ) 31. I am always _____ to sign anything that I haven't read carefully.

(A) contingent　　(B) propelled　　(C) rejected　　(D) reluctant

( ) 32. The firewalkers of Fiji, Hawaii, and the Cook Islands walk over blazing hot coals without _____ .

(A) flinching　　(B) mercy　　(C) vindictiveness　(D) probation

( ) 33. Body language covers the infinite range of movements, including the _____ ways to smile, to walk, to manipulate your eyes, or to move your hands and arms.

(A) futile　　(B) myriad　　(C) garrulous　　(D) palatable

( ) 34. Overweight kids and their parents are _____ nutritionists to help them switch to healthier dining habits.

(A) referred to　　(B) engaged in　　(C) craved for　　(D) ascribed to

( ) 35. The airplane, which was _____ New York, crashed outside Paris.

(A) by way of　　(B) in terms of　　(C) en route to　　(D) in lieu of

( ) 36. The project would have failed even with Steven's help.

(A) The project failed because Steven didn't help.

(B) Steven helped, so the project did not fail.

(C) The project will fail without Steven's help.

(D) The project failed, and Steven did not help.

( ) 37. Men who eat a lot of tomatoes or pizza smothered with the stuff may be giving themselves a hedge against prostate cancer.

(A) Eating a large amount of tomatoes and pizza with a lot of tomato sauce may help men prevent prostate cancer.

(B) Tomatoes or pizza with a lot of tomatoes provide a good source of food for men to recover from prostate cancer.

(C) A lot of tomatoes and stuffed pizza are strong enough to stop the development of prostate cancer in most men.

(D) Men who eat a lot of pizza stuffed with tomatoes may end up fighting successfully against prostate cancer.

(　) 38. Heroes may come from all walks of life, but they all have this in common: they are just ordinary people who react in an extraordinary way to help others.

(A) Heroes, poor or rich, differ from general people in the way they look and the way they behave.

(B) All people with courage and justice are just common people offering help to others voluntarily.

(C) Heroes are just human beings who are particularly ordinary in their deeds.

(D) Anyone who helps people in a phenomenal way is considered a hero.

(　) 39. The problem of climate change has reached a level that threatens the planet.

(A) It is argued that change in weather can destroy the globe.

(B) It is problematic that change in climate will protect the earth.

(C) The degree of change in weather has signaled a menace to the globe.

(D) The problem brought forth by climate change will reach a level that no one can solve.

(　) 40. One of the reasons why casting a play is no easy task is that people who show up for tryouts mumble or speak in inaudible whispers.

(A) The only reason why casting a play is not easy is that people coming for tryouts would mumble or speak in inaudible whispers.

(B) Casting a play is quite difficult. For one thing, people who come to auditions are often inarticulate.

(C) Casting a play is not a hard task because lots of people who show up for tryouts speak loudly.

(D) Watching a play is hard because the audience that show up mumble or speak in inaudible whispers.

( ) 41. Countries that once thought they could escape fiscal upheavals that plagued the United States are now faltering, too.

(A) Countries that once thought they could fight off their own economic crisis are now, just like the United States, failing to do so.

(B) Countries that used to think they would do better than the United States in financial crisis control are now losing control, too.

(C) Countries that used to think they would not be like the United States suffering from the financial crisis are now in big trouble, too.

(D) Countries that once thought they could keep up their own economy are now suffering from the financial crisis of the United States.

( ) 42. It is the balancing out of sociological likenesses and psychological differences that seems to point the way for the most solid lifelong romance.

(A) The most stable kind of romance that lasts a lifetime seems to happen to couples who share similar social background while differing in innate nature.

(B) Without the balance between social similarity and psychological discrepancy, couples struggle to maintain a lifelong romantic relationship.

(C) The balance between similar social background and divergent personal characteristics does not guarantee a strong romantic relationship.

(D) Couples who share similar social experiences yet differ in physical features seem to love each other for a long time.

(　　) 43. The oil of the landlocked country does not flow easily as it is left isolated from global markets.

(A) The markets of the country are isolated and its oil becomes expensive.

(B) The country blocks the oil pipelines so that its oil would not flow to other countries.

(C) Due to geographic barriers, the country has difficulty transporting and selling its oil.

(D) The global trade organization isolates the country and forces it to lower the price of its oil.

(　　) 44. Often teachers demand that students perform skills without having observed an expert performance of those skills within a relevant task context.

(A) Students are frequently required by teachers to execute skills before they see demonstrations by the more experienced in real settings.

(B) It is reasonable to require students to carry out skills before they can observe expert performance of the skills.

(C) Many students believe that observing an expert performance of a certain skill is the best way to learn the skill.

(D) Students are oftentimes asked by teachers to demonstrate skills in a realistic context.

(　　) 45. There is no scarcity of opportunity to make a living at what you love; there's only a scarcity of resolve to make it happen.

(A) Determination is prior to opportunity in making a living at what you love.

(B) If you get scared, you won't be able to make a living at what you love.

(C) The opportunity for you to make a living at what you love is quite limited.

(D) To find an opportunity to make a living at what you love is most urgent.

The beavers at the Minnesota Zoo seem engaged in an unending task. Each week they fell scores of inch-thick young trees for their winter food supply. Each week zoo workers surreptitiously replace the downed trees, anchoring new ones in the iron holders so the animals can keep on cutting. Letting the beavers do what comes naturally has paid off: Minnesota is one of the few zoos to get them to reproduce in captivity. The chimps at the St. Louis Zoo also work for a living: they poke stiff pieces of hay into an anthill to scoop out the baby food and honey that curators hide inside. Instead of idly awaiting banana handouts, the chimps get to manipulate tools, just as they do in the wild. Last year, when 13 gorillas moved into Zoo Atlanta's new $4.5 million rain forest, they mated and formed families— a rarity among captives. "Zoos have changed from being mere menageries to being celebrations of life," says John Gwynne of the Bronx Zoo. "As the wild places get smaller, the role of zoos gets larger, which means intensifying the naturalness of the experience for both visitors and animals."

( ) 46. What do the beavers do at the Minnesota Zoo?

(A) They are engaged in a task to find baby food.

(B) They are busy making tools for their winter food.

(C) They keep cutting down young trees for their winter food.

(D) They do nothing but idly awaiting winter food.

( ) 47. What does "surreptitiously" mean in the passage?

(A) Secretly   (B) Carefully   (C) Considerately   (D) Hurriedly

( ) 48. According to the passage, how has the Minnesota Zoo benefited from their new project for the beavers?

(A) The Zoo has to hire more people to work for the beavers.

(B) The Zoo has more beaver families and baby beavers.

(C) The Zoo has to spend more money building houses for the beavers.

(D) The Zoo attracts more visitors to see the beavers.

(   ) 49. According to the passage, which of the following statements is NOT true?

    (A) The chimps at the St. Louis Zoo work for a living.

    (B) The chimps at the St. Louis Zoo try to get baby food themselves.

    (C) The chimps hide the baby food and honey inside anthills.

    (D) The chimps know how to make and use tools.

(   ) 50. What can we infer from the passage about the concept of new zoo management?

    (A) New zoos must be large enough to attract more visitors to make a profit.

    (B) New zoos must have more wild animals to mate with each other.

    (C) New zoos have to build more cages to keep their wild animals safe.

    (D) New zoos have to accommodate animals' natural ways of living.

99 年特種考試交通事業鐵路人員──高員級中譯解析

31. D；中譯：我總是不願意去簽我還沒有仔細看過的任何東西。

解析：(A) contingent 偶然的 (B) propelled 推進 (C) rejected 拒絕 (D) reluctant 不情願的

此題是考片語。對沒看過的東西不放心所以不想簽，be reluctant to 為不情願之意，最符合題意，答案為 (D)。

32. A；中譯：斐濟、夏威夷以及庫克島上的火行者走過熾熱火紅的煤炭上面而不畏縮。

解析：(A) flinching 畏縮（現在分詞）(B) mercy 仁慈（名詞）(C) probation 檢驗（名詞）(D) vindictiveness 懷恨在心（名詞）此題考的是單字。walk over（走在…之上），without（介係詞）後面需接名詞或現在分詞，選項中以 flinching 表示毫無退縮，最符合題意，答案為 (A)。

33. B；中譯：肢體語言涵蓋無限的活動範圍，包含了無數的笑、走、使眼色或移動手及手臂等的方式。

解析：(A) futile 無用的 (B) myriad 無數的 (C) garrulous 聒噪的 (D) palatable 可口的

此題考的是形容詞。manipulate youreyes 操控你的眼睛，也就是使眼色之意，including 引導的片語說明前面所提和為無限的活動範圍，所以選項中需選擇與數量等有關的形容詞，以 myriad（無數的）最符合題意，答案為 (A)。

34. A；中譯：體重過重的孩童及其雙親被交付給營養師來幫他們改變成較健康的飲食習慣。

解析：(A) referred to 交付 (B) engaged in 致力於 (C) craved for 懇求 (D) ascribed to 歸咎於

此題考的是片語。switch to 轉移；改變，選項中以 be referred to 表示被交付給…最符合題意，答案為 (A)。

35. C；中譯：這班飛往紐約途中的飛機墜毀在巴黎市郊。

解析：(A) by way of 經由 (B) in terms of 就…來說 (C) en route to 在…途中 (D) in lieu of 以…替代

此題考的是片語，en route to New York 表示飛往紐約的班機（還沒飛到），符合題意，答案為 (C)，注意：by way of 表示經由紐約，但沒說明飛往何處，故與墜毀巴黎沒有直接關連，所以不能選。

36. D；中譯：這計畫就算有史蒂芬的幫忙也會失敗。

解析：(A) 這計畫因為史蒂芬沒有幫忙而失敗 (B) 史蒂芬幫忙，這計畫沒有失敗 (C) 沒有史蒂芬的幫忙這計畫將會失敗 (D) 這計畫將會失敗了，且史蒂芬沒有幫忙。

此題考的是假設語語氣，even 即使，在這裡是當副詞使用，表示就算史蒂芬會幫忙也沒用，而事實上他也沒幫忙，與過去事實相反，所以用 would have failed，答案為 (D)。

37. A；中譯：男性吃大量的番茄或塗滿這種原料的披薩可能會讓他們可以防止前列腺癌。

解析：(A) 吃大量的番茄及裹著大量番茄醬的披薩可能幫助男性防止前列腺癌 (B) 番茄或有大量番茄醬的披薩提供了男人從前列腺癌康復的一種良好的食物來源 (C) 大部分男性來說，大量的番茄及厚片披薩就足夠強壯來阻止前列腺癌的發展 (D) 男性吃大量塞滿番茄的披薩可能最終能戰勝前列腺癌。

題目中，…smothered with the stuff…，stuff 物質是指番茄，另 a hedge against 指防護某物；題目主要表達是番茄所含的物質可以預防男人的前列腺癌，而吃披薩會塗有厚厚的番茄醬，所以也有相同功效。

38. D；中譯：英雄可能來自各行各業，但他們都有共通點：他們都只是一般人民，但能以非比尋常的方式來幫助其他人。

解析：(A) 不論貧窮或富有，英雄與一般人不同的地方在於他們看事的方式及他們表現的方式 (B) 所有具有勇氣與正義的人都只是自願幫忙其他人的一般人 (C) 英雄是就是行為特別正直的凡人 (D) 任何人以一種非凡的方式來幫助別人就可被認為是英雄。

題目中，all walks of life（各行各業），in common（共同）；題目主要表達只要是能以一般人做不到的方式來幫助人的人就是英雄，不論他出身為何，所以答案為 (D)。

39. C；中譯：氣候變遷的問題已經達到威脅地球的程度了。

解析：(A) 天氣的變化能夠摧毀地球是仍有爭議 (B) 氣候的變化將可以保護地球是有疑問的 (C) 天氣改變的程度已對地球發出警訊了 (D) 氣候變遷產生的問題將到達沒人可解決的程度。

題目中，It is argued… 是有爭議的；signaled a menace 發出威脅警訊；brought forth 產生，本題答案為 (C)。

40. B；中譯：選派一個角色不是個簡單工作的原因之一是因為來參加選拔的人說話含糊或是講話輕聲細語。

解析：(A) 選派一個角色不是個簡單任務的唯一原因是來參加選拔的人說話含糊或是講話輕聲細語 (B) 選派一個角色是相當困難的，有件事情就是，人們來試音時常常是口齒不清的 (C) 選派一個角色不難因為許多來參加選拔的人都大聲講話 (D) 觀賞一場表演是困難的，因為來參加的觀眾都說話含糊或是講話輕聲細語。

題目中，show up for 為…出現；inaudible whispers 發出幾乎聽不見的耳語，也就是講話輕聲細語；come to auditions 試音。題目主要表達選派一個角色很難的其中一個原因是很多來參加選拔的人根本是口齒不清，所以答案為 (B)。

41. C；中譯：那些曾經以為他們能免於那場肆虐美國金融海嘯的國家現在也搖搖欲墜了。

解析：(A) 那些曾經以為能打敗自己國家經濟危機的國家現在也即將失敗，就像美國一樣 (B) 那些過去認為他們可以在財政危機控管做得比美國好的國家現在也失控了 (C) 那些過去認為他們將不會像美國那樣遭受財政危機的國家現在也有大麻煩了 (D) 那些曾經認為他們可以維持他們經濟的國家現在也遭受美國財政危機之苦。

題目主要表達的是美國海嘯引起全世界經濟動盪，有些國家以為能逃得過，但大多事與願違，所以答案為 (D)。

42. A；中譯：社會化程度的相似與心理上的互補似乎就是能保證堅定且終身相伴的方式。

解析：(A) 最堅定而持續一生的浪漫似乎發生在那些具有相似的社會背景同時卻有著不同天生特質的夫妻 (B) 沒有在社會相似性及心理差異取得平衡，夫妻要維持終身浪漫關係就會很辛苦 (C) 相似的社會背景及差異的個人特質不保證一個強有力的浪漫關係 (D) 有相似的社會經驗但身體特質有差異的夫妻似乎會長時間相愛。

題目中，out of（離開）在此解釋為出自於…，本句主要表達的是夫妻或情侶要能堅守終身的浪漫關係必須在社會的相似性以及心理的差異間取得平衡，故本題答案為 (A)。

43. C；中譯：內陸國家的石油不容易輸出當它是被孤立於全球市場之外的時候。

解析：(A) 這國家的市場被孤立且它的油變得很貴 (B) 這國家阻斷了油管以致於油不能流到其他國家 (C) 由於地理上的阻隔，這國家在運輸及販賣他國家的油皆有困難 (D) 全球交易組織孤立了這國家並迫使它降低它石油價格。

landlocked country 內陸國家，沒出海口且四周都被其他國家包圍的國家；isolated from 阻隔於；本句主要表達的是內陸國家的石油不容易輸出，很容易被其他因素所影響。

44. A；中譯：在一個適當的場合下，通常老師會要求學生先動手做一些技藝，而不要事先看過專業示範。

解析：(A) 學生常被老師要求在他們可以看更有經驗的人在實際情況的示範之前，動手做一些技藝 (B) 在他們可以觀察這些專業技巧的示範前，要求學生去演練這些技巧是合理的 (C) 許多學生相信觀察這些技巧的專業示範是學習這種技巧最好的方法 (D) 學生們常常被老師要求在實際的情況下展示一些技巧。

relevant task context 適當的工作情況；本句主要表達在適當的情況下，通常老師會要求學生先動手做過後，再讓有經驗的人事如何做，藉此來增加學習。

45. A；中譯：依你喜歡做的事來過生活是不缺機會的，缺的只是讓它發生的決心。

解析：(A) 要依你喜歡做的事來過生活上，決心是比機會更重要 (B) 如果你不敢，你將無法依你喜歡做的事來過生活 (C) 依你喜歡做的事來過生活的機會是很低的 (D) 尋求一個依你喜歡做的事來過生活的機會是非常重要的。

what you love 你所想要的；be priorto 優先於；make a living 過生活、養家活口；本句主要表達如果要完全依你的興趣來過生活，那需要下定很強的決心，否則只是不切實際。

46.–50. 中譯：

明尼蘇達動物園的海狸似乎忙於無止盡的工作，每周他們砍倒 20 幾個約一英吋粗的幼齡樹木當作它們冬天的食物補給，而每周動物園工作人員也暗地裡更新這些被啃倒的樹木，他們把新的樹木固定支撐在鐵架上讓海狸可以繼續啃食。讓這些海狸展現他們的本能已經有了回饋：明尼蘇達動物園是少數之一能在圈養環境中繁殖海狸的動物園。聖路易士動物園的黑猩猩也依樣忙碌過活，他們把硬乾草梗戳入螞蟻土丘來挖出研究人員藏在裡面的嬰兒食物及蜜汁，他們不會閒著等待香蕉遞過來，就如同在野外一樣，他們會動手製造工具。而當 13 隻大猩猩搬進亞特蘭大動物園耗資 450 萬美金的新雨林後，他們配對並組成家庭，這在圈養動物中非常罕見。「動物園已經由單純的圈養進步到對生命的慶祝」，Bronz 動物園的 John Gwynne 說「當野外棲息地變小，動物園的角色就變大，這意味著會加強遊客及動物們對自然狀態的體驗…」。

46. C；中譯：明尼蘇達動物園的海狸做些甚麼呢？(A) 他們忙著尋找寶寶的食物 (B) 他們為他們冬季的食物準備工具 (C) 他們持續砍倒小樹來準備冬天的食物 (D) 他們甚麼都沒做只是懶惰地等待冬天的食物。

解析：由 Each week they fell scores of inch-thick young trees for their winter food supply…這段話可知答案為 (C)（當作冬天食物的補充）。

47. A；中譯：　"surreptitiously" 這個字在文章中的意義為何？(A) Secretly 秘密地 (B) Carefully 小心地 (C) Considerately 體諒地 (D) Hurriedly 倉促地

解析：Surreptitiously（秘密地），由選項中所以答案應為 (A)。

48. B；中譯：依據本文，明尼蘇達動物園如何由他們對海狸的新計畫中獲得好處？(A) 動物園雇用更多人員照顧海狸(B)動物園有更多海狸家族及小海狸(C)動物園必須花更多錢來為海狸蓋房子(D)動物園吸引更多遊客來看海狸。

解析：由第四行中：Letting the beavers do what comes naturally has paid off Minnesota is one of the few zoos to get them to reproduce in captivity 這段話，明白表示好處是動物園可以繁殖(reproduce) 海狸，所以答案 (B) 動物園會有更多的海狸家庭與海狸寶寶是最適切的答案，其他選項在文中都沒提到。

49. C；中譯：根據文章中所述，下列何者為非？(A) 聖路易士動物園的黑猩猩忙碌過活 (B) 聖路易士動物園的黑猩猩自己設法獲取嬰兒食物 (C) 黑猩猩把嬰兒食物藏在蟻丘裡面 (D) 黑猩猩知道如何製造及使用工具。

解析：(A) 由The chimps at the St.Louis Zoo also work for a living. ，本句為真(B) 由…they poke stiff pieces of hay into an anthill to scoop out the baby food... ，可知黑猩猩會自己獲取食物，本句為真 (C) 由…they poke stiff pieces of hay into an anthill to scoop out the baby food and honey that curators hide inside.可知藏東西的是研究人員(curators)，而不是黑猩猩自己，本句為非 (D) 由…the chimps get to manipulate tools, just as they do in the wild，知本句為真。故答案為 (C)。

50. D；中譯：從文章我們可以推論新的動物園管理的理念是甚麼？(A) 新的動物園必須夠大才能吸引更引遊客及創造利潤 (B) 新的動物園必須有更多的動物來互相配對 (C) 新的動物園必須建更多獸欄來維護動物安全 (D) 新的動物園必須提供動物自然生活的方式。

解析：由本文章最後一段：…Zoos have changed from being mere menageries to being celebrations of life,… which means intensifying the naturalness of the experience for both visitors and animals.可知動物園應不只圈養動物，而且應該尊重生命，並要加強動物及遊客對自然狀態的體驗，所以答案為 (D)。其他答案：(A) 文章中提到是指角色更大(the role of zoos gets larger)，非動物園要更大。(B) 文章中提到在仿自然的雨林環境中黑猩猩會自然配對，並沒提到要找更多動物來配對 (C) 完全沒提到。

99 年特種考試交通事業鐵路人員考試試題

等別：四等考試、員級
類科：警察、鐵路各類科別
科目：法學知識與英文（此節錄英文部分）

( ) 31. By visiting international websites, we can have direct _____ with the whole world.

(A) contract   (B) access   (C) contact   (D) admission

( ) 32. The conference was initially _____ to take place on August 8th, but due to the typhoon, it was canceled at the last minute.

(A) scheduled   (B) signaled   (C) surveyed   (D) schemed

( ) 33. I think he was just _____ me. His compliment on my big success didn't sound sincere.

(A) assisting   (B) blaming   (C) engaging   (D) flattering

( ) 34. To _____ the risk of heart disease, you should start reducing your daily intake of oil and salt.

(A) capture   (B) hasten   (C) lessen   (D) reserve

( ) 35. His parents died when he was very young, so his uncle _____ him.

(A) adapted   (B) attached   (C) arrested   (D) adopted

( ) 36. He proudly states that having a happy family and obtaining a Ph.D. degree top his list of _____ .

(A) accomplishments   (B) developments

(C) illustrations   (D) probations

( ) 37. If more money is not _____ , we will have to shut down the factory.

(A) fulfilling   (B) forthcoming   (C) propelling   (D) enhancing

（　）38. I wish I _____ that Anne was ill. I would have gone to see her.

(A) knew　　　　(B) would know　　(C) have known　　(D) had known

（　）39. The passage mainly discusses the plight of _____ species.

(A) endangered　　　　　　(B) endangering

(C) is endangered　　　　　(D) being endangering

　　When we talk about "communication," most of us probably think about verbal communication—that is, the words we use when talking. However, there is another important aspect to communication: non-verbal communication, which is communication done by using our bodies, gestures, and tones of voice—simply everything ___40___ the actual words we use. Actually, non-verbal communication is a rather recent field of study. Originally, scientists called this field kinesics, which is the scientific study of body movements used in communication. Movements ___41___ gestures, facial expressions, and posture. In addition to these movements, we also communicate with our speech rate and the volume of our speech. Non-verbal communication includes a wide range of actions. The field of kinesics ___42___ a great deal to one man: Raymond Birdwhistle. Birdwhistle was a very famous American anthropologist. He predicted that about 70 percent of what is communicated in a conversation is non-verbal. It was Birdwhistle's belief that the meaning of non-verbal behavior depended on the ___43___ in which it occurred. Because of this belief, he was very ___44___ looking at the whole context of non-verbal behavior—how and where certain types of non-verbal behavior appeared, not just the particular behavior alone.

（　）40. (A) as well as　(B) besides　　(C) except　　(D) exclusive

（　）41. (A) point out　　(B) refer to　　(C) show up　　(D) boast of

（　）42. (A) provides　　(B) contributes　(C) grants　　(D) owes

（　）43. (A) context　　　(B) atmosphere　(C) consequence　(D) influence

（　）44. (A) considerate of　(B) concerned with　(C) conformed to　(D) confined by

(　　) 45. Ticket Agent: May I help you?

Woman: Yes. I have this ticket for next Saturday's train to Tainan. _____

Ticket Agent: Do you want to go somewhere else?

Woman: No. I'm still going to Tainan, but I need to go today. My sister had her baby early!

(A) I need to buy a ticket to Taipei.

(B) I don't know if it's on time or not.

(C) I want to know when it will arrive.

(D) I need to exchange it.

To toot, to cut the cheese, or to pass gas. These are all funny ways to talk about something that everyone does: Farts! A normal person passes about half a liter of gas a day. That equals about 14 farts per day.

Then where do farts come from? There are several sources of fart gas. We get fart gas from the air we swallow. Gas also goes into our intestines from our blood. In addition, gas is also produced from chemical reactions and bacteria living in our intestines. Nervous people usually have more gas. This is because they swallow more air. Besides, food goes through their digestive systems faster. This means oxygen cannot be absorbed from the food in time. It turns into fart gas.

People's diet affects the stinkiness of farts. The smell has to do with the sulphur in foods such as eggs, meat, and cauliflower. Beans cause a lot of farts, but these farts aren't usually really stinky. Beans are not high in sulphur, but the sugar in them produces gas in the intestines.

Finally, people wonder, "Where do farts go when you hold them in?" Well, these farts will not poison you. However, you may get a bad stomachache from the pressure. Farts you hold in are neither released nor absorbed. They will come out sooner or later.

(　　) 46. What is this passage mainly about?

      (A) The way to reduce farts.   (B) Facts to know about farts.

      (C) How to have a healthy diet.   (D) The dangers of holding in farts.

(　　) 47. Which of the following is NOT a way we call "fart"?

      (A)To cut the cheese.   (B)To toot.

      (C)To pass gas.   (D)To empty bowels.

(　　) 48. Why do nervous people have more farts?

      (A) They eat too many beans.

      (B) They do not have enough sleep.

      (C) Their blood pressure is too high.

      (D) The food they eat is not well digested.

(　　) 49. According to this passage, which of the following foods is likely to cause the stinkiest farts?

      (A) Beans.   (B) Steak.   (C) Bread.   (D) Pasta.

(　　) 50. When we hold in a fart, where does it go?

      (A) It is absorbed by the intestines.

      (B) It is released from the mouth or nose.

      (C) It is just delayed and will come out later.

      (D) It goes back to the stomach and helps with digestion.

99 年特種考試交通事業鐵路人員——員級中譯解析

31. C；中譯：藉由瀏覽國際間的網站，我們可以與整個世界有直接的接觸。

解析：(A) contract 契約 (B) access 進入 (C) contact 接觸 (D) admission 許可

此題考的是名詞。該句表達我們可以透過網路來與世界連結，所以選項中以contact（接觸）最適宜，答案為 (C)。

32. A；中譯：這研討會最初要在8月8日舉行，但由於颱風的緣故在最後一刻被取消。

解析：(A) scheduled 計畫 (B) signaled 簽署 (C) surveyed 審視 (D) schemed 策劃

此題考的是動詞。Take place（舉行）；at the last minute（最後一刻）。會議是被舉行的，本句用被動式，空格前看到was initially動詞要用過去分詞。schedule一般跟時間安排有關，scheme主要指擬定計劃本身，所以在此用 scheduled，表達在某日期被預定舉行之意，所以答案為 (A)。

33. D；中譯：我認為他只是奉承我而已，他對我成就的恭維聽來不誠懇。

解析：(A) assisting 幫助 (B) blaming 責難 (C) engaging 吸引 (D) flattering 奉承

我想他只是奉承我而已，因為是過去才剛發生的事所以可用過去進行式。由該句後面表達對我的恭維聽來不誠懇研判，選項中用 flattering（奉承）最合題意，答案為 (D)。

34. C；中譯：為了減少心臟疾病的風險，你應該開始減少每日的油與鹽的攝取。

解析：(A) capture 獲得 (B) hasten 催促 (C) lessen 減少 (D) reserve 儲存

此題考的是動詞。要減少每日的油與鹽的攝取應是為要減少疾病的風險，選項中以 lessen（減少）最符合，故答案為 (C)。

35. D；中譯：他的雙親在他很小的時候就過世了，所以他的伯父收養他。

解析：(A) adapted 適應 (B) attached 使附屬 (C) arrested 逮捕 (D) adopted 收養

本題純粹考過去式動詞單字。題意為雙親在他很小的時候就過世所以由伯父來照料之意，選項中以 adopted（收養）最符合，故答案為 (D)。

36. A；中譯：他驕傲地陳述有個快樂的家庭以及獲得博士學位是他最大的成就。

解析：(A) accomplishments 成就 (B) developments 發展 (C) illustrations 說明 (D) probations 檢驗

本題考名詞。to top his list of（把…列為首位）。題目提到有關她的一些事蹟均為表示成就之意，故選項中應用 accomplishments（成就），答案為 (A)。

37. B；中譯：如果錢再沒有進來，我們將必須把工廠關掉。

解析：(A) fulfilling 實現抱負的 (B) forthcoming 將出現的 (C) propelling 推進（現在分詞）(D) enhancing 增強（現在分詞）

if 子句中以現在式代表示未來時間。題意是指錢沒有出現，工廠就要關，故選項中應用 forthcoming（將出現的）最符合，答案為 (B)。

38. D；中譯：我希望我那時候能知道安妮生病了，我就會去看她。

解析：由 wish 可推斷本句是與事實相反的假設句，在由後面用 would+完成式，可知與過去事實相反，所以空格內假設句用過去完成式，故動詞用 had known，答案為 (D)。

39. A；中譯：這個通過案主要是討論瀕臨絕種物種的誓言。

解析：本題考分詞用法。plight（誓約），分詞可當形容詞用修飾名詞，瀕臨絕種物種表示物種是被消滅的，所以用過去分詞，也就是 endangered species，故答案為 (A)。

40～44 中譯：

當我們談到溝通時，我們大部分可能想到關於言語溝通，也就是說當我們講話時所用的語言。然而，還有有一種重要的溝通形式：非語言的溝通，那是一種用我們身體、手勢以及聲音的語調來作的溝通一純粹除了我們說的話以的外任何東西。一開始，非語言的溝通是相當新的一個研究領域，科學家稱這個領域叫做人體動作學，這是一種研究身體的動作運用於溝通的一門科學研究。動作是指手勢、臉部表情以及站姿。除了以上這些動作外，我們也用我們說話的速度及音量來溝通。非言語的溝通包含很大範圍的動作。

人體動作學領域中要感激一個人：Raymond Birdwhistle。Birdwhistle是個非常有名的美國人類學者，他預測在會話中，有百分之七十的所謂溝通是非言語的溝通，他相信非言語的溝通的行為決定於它發生時的背景，因為這個信念，他非常關心整個非言語的溝通行為的來龍去脈一一些非言語的溝通行為會如何以及在何處出現，而不只有特定行為本身。

40. C；(A) as well as而且（連接詞）(B) besides在…之外還有（介係詞）(C) except除…之外其他都…（介係詞）(D) exclusive 除外的（形容詞）

解析：空格內應填入介係詞，來說明前面的 anything，依文中意義應為語言以外的任何東西，故答案為 (C)。

41. B；(A) point out 指出 (B) refer to 意指 (C) show up 出現 (D) boast of 吹噓

解析：本題考動詞片語。文中意思為動作是指姿態、臉部表情以及態度等等，故答案應該選 (B)。

42. D；(A) provides 提供 (B) contributes 貢獻 (C) grants 授予 (D) owes 虧欠

解析：本題考動詞。owe a great deal of 指應該感謝，與文中需表達的意義最合適，表示該門學科應該感謝某人的意思，故答案應選 (D)。

43. A；(A) context 背景 (B) atmosphere 氣氛 (C) consequence結果 (D) influence 影響

解析：本題考名詞。依文意溝通的行為決定於它發生時的情況，選項中以 context（背景）最恰當，表示依不同情況有不同的肢體語言，故答案為 (A)。

44. B；(A) considerate of 體諒 (B) concerned with 關心 (C) conformed to 符合 (D) confined by 限制

解析：本題考片語字意。由他認為非語言溝通佔溝通很大的比重，所以他應該會非常關心觀察整個非言語的溝通行為的來龍去脈，故答案應該選(B)。

45. D；中譯：票務員：我能為你服務嗎？

女士：是的，我有一張下星期六到台南的火車票 (A) 我要買一張去台北的票 (B) 我不知道它是否會準時？(C) 我要知道它何時會到達？(D) 我要把它換掉。

票務員：你要到其他地方嗎？

女士：不，我仍然要到台南，但我要今天去，我姊姊小孩提早出生了。

解析：她手上有下星期到台南的票，但她今天要提早到台南因為姊姊的小孩提早出生了，所以選項(D)

把它換掉為正確。

46－50. 中譯：

　　按喇叭，切起司，或排氣，這些談的都是關於每人都會做的玩笑話：放屁。一個正常人每天排放半公升的氣體，相當於每天放屁 14 次。

　　那屁從何而來呢？屁有幾種來源，屁從我們吞進去的空氣而來，氣體也會經由我們的血液進入腸道中。除此之外，氣體也會經由化學反應及由在腸道中的細菌而產生，緊張的人通常比較多氣體，這是因為它們會吞進去叫多空氣，此外，食物也會較快速通過他們的消化系統，這意味著食物中的氧氣無法及時被人體吸收，結果變成屁。

　　人們的飲食影響屁的臭味，屁的味道與食物中的硫有關，例如雞蛋、肉類以及花椰菜等。大豆會產生許多屁，但這些屁不會真的很臭，大豆沒有含太多硫，但內含的糖分會在腸道內產生氣體。

　　最後，人們會問：當你忍住不放時屁去了哪裡？這些屁不會讓你中毒，然而，你可能因為壓力而肚子痛，你忍住的屁不會消失或吸收掉，它們早晚會排出來的。

46. B；中譯：這篇主要談到甚麼？(A) 減少屁的方式 (B) 認識放屁 (C) 如何吃得健康 (D) 屁忍住不放的危險。

　　解析：本篇由一開始談到屁的來源，再談到味道及最後忍住不放屁的情形來判斷，都是談到對於屁的認識，所以答案應該選(B)認識放屁最為恰當。

47. D；中譯：下列何者不是我們稱「放屁」的說法？(A) 切起司 (B) 按喇叭 (C) 排氣 (D) 清腸胃

　　解析：由首句 To toot, to cut the cheese, or to pass gas. These are all funny ways to talk about something that everyone does: Farts! 得知按喇叭，切起司，或排氣，這些指的都是關於放屁的話語，只有 (D) 清腸胃沒提到，所以答案為 (D)。

48. D；中譯：為何緊張的人有較多的屁？(A) 他們吃太多的大豆 (B) 他們沒有足夠的睡眠 (C) 他們血壓太高 (D) 他們吃的食物沒有好好消化。

　　解析：由 Nervous people usually have more gas.⋯Besides, food goes through their digestive systems faster. This means oxygen cannot be absorbed from the food in time⋯，可知緊張的人會讓食物較快速通過他們的消化系統，所以氧氣無法從食物中及時由被吸收而變成屁，也就是說食物沒經過完全消化吸收造成較多的屁，所以答案為 (D)。

49. B；中譯：依據本文，下列哪種食物可能導致臭屁？(A) 大豆 (B) 牛排 (C) 麵包 (D) 披薩。

　　解析：由文中提到 People's diet affects the stinkiness of farts. The smell has to do with the sulphur in foods such as eggs, meat, and cauliflower⋯可知雞蛋、肉類以及花椰菜等會產生臭屁，對照答案選項，應為同屬肉類的牛排，所以答案為 (B)。

50. C；中譯：當我們把屁忍住時，它到哪裡去了？(A) 它們被腸子吸收了 (B) 它們從嘴巴或鼻子排出來 (C) 它們只是被延後且以後會排出來 (D) 它們回到胃裡去且可以促進消化。

　　解析：由最後一句 Farts you hold in are neither released nor absorbed. They will come out sooner or later. 得知，忍住的屁不會消失或吸收掉，它們早晚會排出來，所以答案為 (C)。

NOTE

📋 99 年特種考試交通事業鐵路人員考試試題

等別：佐級
類科：鐵路各類科別
科目：公民與英文（此節錄英文部分）

( ) 36. Knives and guns are dangerous _____ that can kill people.

(A) fighters　　　(B) weapons　　　(C) projects　　　(D) exercises

( ) 37. It is _____ surprising that Frank flunked English. He never paid any attention in class.

(A) hardly　　　(B) simply　　　(C) nearly　　　(D) really

( ) 38. _____ a new house on the beach was his life-long dream.

(A) Have　　　(B) Has　　　(C) Had　　　(D) To have

( ) 39. Daniel would have married that girl if only her parents _____ .

(A) agreed　　　　　　　　(B) have agreed

(C) would have agreed　　　(D) had agreed

( ) 40. Lucy: Would you mind if we discuss our plan for next week immediately?

Brenda: _____ .

Lucy: O.K. I suggest that we visit Sam to talk about the experiment on Monday morning.

(A) Of course, Sam has come, too.

(B) No problem. Let's do it tomorrow night.

(C) Not at all, let's do it right now.

(D) Yes, I will talk to you in a minute.

In our busy modern world, doctors do not always take the time to explain illness and possible remedies to their patients. Doctors may even not give any scientific details in words that are easy to ____41____ , either. For this reason, many hopeful people ____42____ advantage of Internet resources to find the facts they need for good medical decisions. On the subject of physical and medical research, there are thousands of amazing websites ____43____ people can get information. Some people believe that the great amount of medical information ____44____ on the Internet can improve their health, while others claim that these facts and opinions may be inaccurate and therefore dangerous. Indeed, to find out the best ways to ____45____ difficult health problems, we may still need to seek advice from doctors.

( ) 41. (A) heal   (B) understand   (C) cope   (D) look
( ) 42. (A) take   (B) make   (C) bring   (D) receive
( ) 43. (A) what   (B) which   (C) where   (D) whose
( ) 44. (A) portable   (B) capable   (C) movable   (D) available
( ) 45. (A) solve   (B) deal   (C) respond   (D) lead

Catherine sells houses for a company. A man has agreed to buy a house for $450,000, but then he changes his mind. Her boss calls her into his office. He is so angry that he speaks rudely to her. She knows it is not her fault, and she bursts into tears.

Having just finished dinner, Jim is talking in the backyard with his wife and children. The phone rings. It is Jim's mother calling from another city. Jim's father has just had a heart attack and died. Jim starts crying as he tells his mother he will come as soon as possible.

How do people feel about crying? Catherine was embarrassed and very angry with herself. Jim felt better after he let out his feelings.

Chemists have been studying why people cry. They say the body produces two kinds of tears. One kind cleans out the eye if it gets dirt in it. But when people cry because of their feelings, these tears have poison chemicals in them. The body is getting rid of chemicals produced by strong feelings.

(　　) 46. Catherine's boss speaks rudely to her because_____ .

(A) he thinks that she didn't do her job well

(B) she sold the house at a lower price

(C) she was late for the appointment with the buyer

(D) she refused to listen to his advice

(　　) 47. Which of the following statements is true about Jim?

(A) He cried because he had a heart problem.

(B) He did not cry, because he hated his father.

(C) He felt better after he cried.

(D) He felt relieved on hearing the news of his father's death.

(　　) 48. According to the passage, Jim and his mother are living_____ .

(A) together   (B) in different cities

(C) in the same neighborhood   (D) with Jim's grandparents

(　　) 49. Which of the following statements is true about the passage?

(A) Catherine sells cars.

(B) Jim learned from his mother's letter that his father died.

(C) Crying is a way of removing chemicals from the body.

(D) People cry only when they feel very sad.

(　　) 50. Which of the following is the best title for the passage?

(A) Business.   (B) Feeling.   (C) Anger.   (D) Crying.

99 年特種考試交通事業鐵路人員──佐級中譯解析

36. B；中譯：刀和槍都是可以殺人的危險武器。

　　解析：(A) fighters 戰士 (B) weapons 武器 (C) exercises 練習 (D) projects 計畫

　　此題考的是名詞。刀和槍都屬於武器，所以選用 weapon，答案為 (B)。

37. A；中譯：福蘭克英語考試沒過沒有甚麼好驚訝的，他從來沒在課堂上專心。

　　解析：(A) hardly 幾乎不 (B) simply 簡單地 (C) nearly 接近地 (D) really 真正地

　　此題考的是副詞。flunk（不及格）；It is+adj.+that+子句，真正主詞為後面 that 子句，表示某事是如何，所以空格需填依副詞修飾形容詞surprising，且題意為否定的涵意，所以應選 hardly 幾乎不，答案為 (A)。

38. D；中譯：在海邊有一間新房子是他畢生的夢想。

　　解析：此題考的是不定詞。選項中只有 To have 不定詞當名詞用， To have a new house 是這句主詞，所以答案為 (D)。注意：本題意可用動名詞表示：having a new house…

39. D；中譯：假如她的父母親同意，丹尼爾本來要與那女來結婚。

　　解析：本題為假設句題型，由主要子句用 would have+p.p. 得知是與過去事實相反的假設句，if子句要用過去完成式，所以動詞用 had agreed，答案為 (D)。

40. C；中譯：璐西：你介意我們立刻來討論我們下禮拜的計畫嗎？

　　布蘭達：(A) 當然，山姆也已經來了 (B) 沒問題，我們明天晚上再做吧 (C) 一點也不，我們現在馬上做 (D) 是的，我馬上跟你談。

　　璐西：好，沒問題，我建議我們禮拜一上午去拜訪山姆討論那個實驗。

　　解析：對話中顯示璐西要討論下周二人的一些工作計畫，布蘭達立刻答應，所以說一點也不(沒問題之意)，答案為 (C)。

41.－45. 中譯：

　　在現代忙碌的社會中，醫生不會總是花時間為病人解釋病情以及可能的醫療方式，醫生甚至也不會用易懂的字眼來說明任何科學細節。因為這個原因，許多抱持希望的民眾利用網路資源來發掘他們所需知道的真相來做正確醫療決定。在生理及醫藥研究的主題方面，有數以千計令人驚訝的網站讓民眾可以得到訊息。一些民眾相信在網路上大量隨手可得的資訊可以增進他們的健康，然而其他人認為這些事實何意見也許並不正確且因此會有危險。確實如此，為了要尋求最好的方式來解決困難的醫療難題，我們仍然須尋求醫生的意見。

41. B；(A) heal 治療 (B) understand 了解 (C) cope 應付 (D) look 觀看

　　解析：空格內需填入動詞，與 to 形成不定詞片語，修飾前面 easy，表示容易理解的文字，所以選項中應用 understand（了解），答案為 (B)。

42. A；解析：本處考片語。take advantage of 利用…來，表示人們利用網路資源來做甚麼事，答案為(A)。

43. C；解析：空格前面為名詞 websites，後面有一子句，所以空格內應填入關係詞，並考量該處是指出自某處，所以用代表地方的關係副詞 where，故答案為 (C)。

44. D；(A) portable 便於攜帶的 (B) capable 有能力的 (C) movable 可移動的 (D) available 有用的
解析：此處應填入形容詞片語修飾前面的名詞說明information，句意為人們認為在網路上有大量有用的資訊，所以選項中以 available（有用的）最洽當，故答案為(D)。

45. A；(A) solve 解決 (B) deal 處理 (C) respond 回應 (D) lead 引導
解析：此處空格內應為原形動詞，與 to 形成不定詞片語修飾前面 the best way，依據文中所述要尋求最好的方式來解決困難的醫療難題，所以應選solve（解決）最洽當，故答案為 (A)。

46-50. 中譯：
　　凱瑟琳為公司賣房子，有一個人已經同意用 450,000 元買房子，但最後他反悔了。她的老闆把她叫進辦公室，他是如此生氣以至於用粗暴的口氣對她說話，她知道那不是自己的錯而且大哭一場。

　　就在剛用完晚餐後，傑姆在後院與他的妻兒聊天，這時電話響起，那是傑姆母親從另一座城市打來的，傑姆的父親剛因心臟病發而死，傑姆邊哭邊告訴她母親他會盡速趕過去。

　　人們對於哭泣的感受如何？凱瑟琳非常愧疚並且很氣她自己，傑姆在發洩情感後覺得好多了。

　　化學家一直在研究人們為何要哭，他們說人體會產生二種眼淚，一種是當眼睛有髒汙時用來清潔眼睛，但當人們是因為感情而哭的時候，這些眼淚中含有有毒化學成分，身體藉由強烈情感而排出化學物質。

46. A；中譯：凱瑟琳的老闆粗暴地對她說話是因為 (A) 他認為她沒有把工作做好 (B)她以低價賣了她的房子 (C) 她與她買主的約會遲到 (D) 她拒絕聽他的勸告。
解析：由A man has agreed to buy a house for $450,000, but then he changes his mind…可推斷他老闆認為她沒有將買主掌握好，以致於無法成交房子，所以她沒有把工作做好，故答案為(A)，其他選項文中都沒提到。

47. C；中譯：下列何項關於傑姆的敘述是正確的？(A) 他哭是因為他心臟有問題
(B) 他沒哭，因為他恨他的父親 (C) 他哭完後覺得好一點了 (D) 他聽到他父親去世的消息後覺得鬆了一口氣。
解析：(A) 由…Jim's father has just had a heart attack and died.是他父親心臟有問題，該敘述不正確。(B)文章中並沒提及他恨父親，該敘述不正確。(C) 由Jim felt better after he let out his feelings.可知哭完後覺得好一點了，此處用let out his feelings發洩完情緒來代表哭的意思，該敘述正確。(D) 文中沒有提到，該敘述不正確。所以答案為 (C)。

48. B；中譯：依據文章中，傑姆與他的母親居住在 (A) 一起 (B) 不同城市 (C) 鄰近 (D) 與傑姆的祖父母
解析：由 The phone rings. It is Jim's mother calling from an other city.，可知傑姆的母親居住在另一個城市，所以本題答案為 (B)。

49. C；中譯：下列有關本文何項敘述是正確的？(A) 凱薩琳賣汽車 (B) 傑姆從他母親信中得知他父親的死 (C) 哭是一種將化學物質自身體移除的方式 (D) 人們只有在非常悲傷時才會哭。

解析：(A) 由Catherine sells houses for a company.可知她是賣房子，不是汽車，敘述為非。

(B) 由…Jim's mother calling from another city. Jim's father has just had a heart attack and died.可知母親電話通知他父親的死，敘述為非。

(C) 由The body is getting rid of chemicals produced by strong feelings.此處用 strong feelings 來代表哭的意思，敘述正確。

(D) 由 Catherine was embarrassed and very angry with herself. 可知會哭的原因不只有悲傷，還有憤怒等等情緒，敘述為非。所以本題答案為 (C)。

50. D；中譯：下列何者是本篇文章最佳的標題 (A) 商業 (B) 感情 (C) 生氣 (D) 哭泣

解析：由本篇中一開始提到凱瑟琳為公司賣房子受老闆責罵而哭泣，到傑姆從他母親得知他父親的死而哭泣，再提到哭泣對人體的影響等，均圍繞這哭泣這個主題，所以本篇標題應為 crying 哭泣，所以答案為 (D)。

 NOTE

📋 100 年特種考試交通事業鐵路人員考試試題

等別：三等一般警察人員考試、高員三級
類科：各類科
科目：法學知識與英文（此節錄英文部分）

( ) 31. In 1983, researchers first _____ HIV, the virus responsible for AIDS.

(A) generated   (B) identified   (C) minimized   (D) validated

( ) 32. The police cannot break the law in order to _____ it.

(A) convene   (B) enforce   (C) entrust   (D) promote

( ) 33. The government official said, "I hereby request that the attached application _____ under 35 USC 122(b)."

(A) not be published   (B) cannot be published

(C) may not be published   (D) will not be published

( ) 34. It is believed that chewing helps to _____ your facial muscles.

(A) pile up   (B) tone up   (C) tune up   (D) wrap up

( ) 35. American presidents are not selected directly by the people. Instead, presidential candidates compete for Electoral _____ votes by winning the popular vote in each state.

(A) Body   (B) College   (C) Committee   (D) Apparatus

( ) 36. Ignoring educational experts' professional advice last year, the government _____ facing a national embarrassment of educational reform failure.

(A) called for   (B) lasted for   (C) ended up   (D) made up

( ) 37. We do have choice with our lives since we have got two lives—one we are given and the other one we make.

(A) Whatever choice we make for our lives, we should try to give and make our lives at the same time.

(B) Although we cannot choose where we come from in our lives, we can choose how to live.

(C) We certainly have choice with our two lives—one for our own and the other one for our children's.

(D) We can choose our lifestyles because we have two lives—one in our minds and the other one for real.

( ) 38. As an experienced director, he knows how to bring all these risk management skills to bear in guiding a corporation to success.

(A) As an experienced director, he learns to risk applying these skills to lead a company to success.

(B) As an experienced director, he takes it as his own burden to lead a company to its success.

(C) As an experienced director, he applies all these skills purposefully to lead a company to success.

(D) As an experienced director, he endures risks to cultivate in himself these skills so that he may lead a company to success.

( ) 39. Jack Lang, who is renowned for his protectionist views, despises American culture as "pure entertainment."

(A) Jack Lang is very protective of American culture, which he regards as "pure entertainment."

(B) Jack Lang, due to his protectionism, looks down upon American culture as "pure entertainment."

(C) Jack Lang wants to protect American culture from "pure entertainment."

(D) Jack Lang, despite his protectionist view on American culture, is known for his distaste toward "pure entertainment."

(　) 40. Everyone is born with dual citizenship, in the kingdom of the well and in the kingdom of the sick; illness is the night-side of life, a more onerous citizenship.

(A) All people live with the well and the sick throughout their lives, and living with the sick is the more depressing of the two.

(B) All living people are bound to have their healthy days and sick days; people are in a gloomy and annoying mood at night.

(C) All people born with dual citizenship, though sometimes lead a healthy life, see more of the dark side of life, feeling helpless.

(D) All living people go through their lives by both living in health and suffering from illness, and being sick is the less desirable of the two.

(　) 41. Oprah Winfrey's father had concerns about his daughter making the best of her life, and would not accept anything less than what he thought was her best.

(A) Oprah Winfrey's father only accepted the things of best quality his daughter bought him.

(B) Oprah Winfrey's father believed in his daughter's ability and demanded the best from her.

(C) Oprah Winfrey could make a successful career because her father always gave her the best.

(D) Oprah Winfrey had best concerns for her father, who was the most valuable treasure in her life.

(　) 42. Any public _____ of this scandal would do great damage to this movie star.

(A) proposal　　(B) enclosure　　(C) disclosure　　(D) refusal

(　) 43. Underemployment is _____; a physicist working in a customs house is a symbol of national stagnation, not advancement.

(A) ambiguous　　(B) demoralizing　　(C) optimistic　　(D) invaluable

(   ) 44. Forgiveness seems its own form of revenge since it is like we have risen above what happened to us and above people who should be blamed.

(A) Forgiveness and revenge share something in common since both involve what happened to us and people who should be blamed.

(B) In a way forgiveness can be seen as revenge since it sends a message that we are somewhat superior.

(C) Both forgiveness and revenge need us to show that we are able to rise above what happened to us and above people to be blamed.

(D) Only by showing that what happened to us has had little influence on us can we claim that forgiveness is its own form of revenge.

(   ) 45. The idea of good character sounds old-fashioned and patronizing, but it may be the key to some of our most entrenched social problems.

(A) To solve some of our deep-rooted social problems, we may need to resort to the traditional and somewhat condescending idea of good character.

(B) To talk about the old but fashionable idea of good character may sound patriotic, but it is the only sure way to solve some of our most cumbersome social problems.

(C) The concept of good character may have been there for a long time, but it may be the key to opening the Pandora's Box of our society.

(D) Good character, though out-dated and rare, may be the only weapon to attack some of our most ingrained social problems.

(   ) 46. What is a weed? A plant whose virtue has not been discovered.

(A) A weed will always be a weed, no matter how long it takes.

(B) A weed is called a weed becausewe are blind to its virtues.

(C) Once some virtues are discovered, a weed will change.

(D) We should not call a weed a weed.

請回答第47題至第50題：

Male-female conversation is cross-cultural communication. ____47____ And women and men have different past experiences. From the time they are born, they are treated differently, talked to differently, and talk differently as a result. ____48____ And when they become adults, they travel in different worlds, reinforcing patterns established in childhood. These cultural differences include different expectations about the role of talk in relationships.

Everyone knows that as a relationship becomes long-term, its terms change. ____49____ Many women feel, "After all this time, you should know what I want without my telling you." Many men feel, "After all this time, we should be able to tell each other what we want."

These incongruent expectations capture one of the key differences between men and women. ____50____ Though everyone has both these needs, women often have a relatively greater need for involvement, and men a relatively greater need for independence. Being understood without saying what you mean gives a payoff in involvement, and that is why women value it so highly.

(　　) 47.

(A) But women and men often differ in how they expect them to change.

(B) Boys and girls grow up in different worlds, even if they grow up in the same house.

(C) Culture is simply a network of habits and patterns gleaned from past experience.

(D) Different habits have repercussions when men and women talk about their relationship.

(　　) 48.

(A) Culture is simply a network of habits and patterns gleaned from past experience.

(B) Boys and girls grow up in different worlds, even if they grow up in the same house.

(C) Communication is always a matter of balancing conflicting needs for involvement and independence.

(D) Different habits have repercussions when men and women talk about their relationship.

(　) 49.

(A) But women and men often differ in how they expect them to change.

(B) Culture is simply a network of habits and patterns gleaned from past experience.

(C) Boys and girls grow up in different worlds, even if they grow up in the same house.

(D) It is difficult to straighten out such misunderstandings because each one feels convinced of his or her points.

(　) 50.

(A) Boys and girls grow up in different worlds, even if they grow up in the same house.

(B) Communication is always a matter of balancing conflicting needs for involvement and independence.

(C) Different habits have repercussions when the man and the woman are talking about their relationship.

(D) It is difficult to straighten out such misunderstandings because each one feels convinced of his or her points.

100年特種考試交通事業鐵路人員——高員級中譯解析

31. B;中譯:在1983年,研究人員首度確認HIV,造成AIDS的病毒。

解析:(A) generated 產生 (B) identified 確認 (C) minimized 最小化 (D) validated 承認

此題考的是動詞。表示要確認 HIV 是造成 AIDS 的病毒,選項中 identify(確認)即視為同一事物之意,最符合題意,答案為 (B)。

32. B;中譯:為了要執法,警察不可不守法。

解析:(A) convene 集合 (B) enforce 推行 (C) entrust 託付 (D) promote 促進

此題考的是動詞,break the law 犯法,in order to 為了要。執法自己要先守法,執法可以用 enforce(推行),答案為 (B)。

33. A;中譯:政府官員說:依據 35 USC122(b) 條款,我在此要求附加的申請不能被公佈。

解析:(A) not be published 不被公佈 (B) cannot be published 不能被公佈 (C) may not be published 可能不被公佈 (D) will not be published 將不被公佈。

此題考的是動詞時態用法。hereby 在此,request(要求)後面要接原形動詞,且此處要用被動式,故用 not be published,答案為 (A)。

34. B;中譯:咀嚼被認為可以幫助強化臉部肌肉。

解析:(A) pile up 累積 (B) tone up 強化 (C) tune up 調整 (D) wrap up 包起來

此題考的是片語用法。it is believed that 被認為是…,咀嚼可以幫助臉部肌肉運動,用選項中 tone up(強化)最符合題意,表示強化臉部肌肉,所以答案為 (B)。

35. B;中譯:美國總統不是由人民直接選出的,相反地,總統候選人需競相贏得各州普通選舉的選舉人票。

解析:此題考的是專有名詞的用法。Electoral College選舉人團,所以答案為 (B)。

36. C;中譯:由於去年政府忽略教育專家的專業建議,政府最後面臨教育改革失敗的窘境。

解析:(A) called for 需求 (B) lasted for 持續 (C) ended up 最後 (D) made up 虛構的

此題考的是片語用法。政府忽略教育專家的專業建議,但最終還是要面臨失敗的結果,選項中以 ended up(最後)最符合句意,表示最後面臨的狀況,所以答案 (C)。

37. B;中譯:我們可以選擇我們的生命因為我們的生命有二種,一種是我們被給予,另一種是我們施予。(A)不管我們生命的選擇為何,我們應該設法同時間過著給與及施與的生命 (B) 雖然我們沒辦法選擇我們生命來自何處,我們可以選擇如何過生活 (C) 我們確實在生命中有二種選擇:一種為我們自己的,另一種為我們孩子的 (D) 我們可以選擇我們的生活型態因為我們有二種生命——一種在心靈上,另一種在實際上。

解析:our lives 是我們的生命,our life 是我們的生活,life 作為抽象名詞生活無複數,作為生命意思時才有複數;given 及 make 就是給予及創造,也就是施與受。題目主要是說生命有二種意義,就是施捨與接受二種,我們可以選擇你要過的是哪種生命方式。本題答案為 (B)。

38. C;中譯:他身為老經驗的指揮者,知道如何有效運用所有這些危機處理的技巧來引導公司邁向成功

(A) 作為一個有經驗的指揮者，他學會冒險應用這些技巧以引導公司走向成功(B)作為一個有經驗的指揮者，他把帶領一家公司邁向成功當作是他自己的責任 (C) 作為一個有經驗的指揮者，他運用所有技巧有目的地來引導公司走向成功 (D) 作為一個有經驗的指揮者，他忍受風險去培養自己學會這些技巧，然後他才可以引導公司走向成功。

解析：bring…to bear 等於to bring into operation or effect運用…來做事。題目主要是說這個指揮者有很多危機處理的經驗，而運用這些經驗可以讓一家公司安然度過危機，邁向成功，本題答案為 (C)。

39. B；中譯：Jack Lang以他的貿易保護者的觀點而有名望，他藐視美國文化是純粹的娛樂。(A) Jack Lang 非常保護那個他認為是純粹娛樂的美國文化 (B) 由於Jack Lang他的貿易保護主義，輕視美國文化並認為是純粹的娛樂 (C) Jack Lang要去保護美國文化從純粹娛樂角度 (D) Jack Lang，不單以貿易保護者的觀點看待美國文化，以厭惡純粹娛樂而聞名。

解析：renowned for（以…聞名），protectionist（貿易保護者），despises（看不起）。本句是指 Jack Lang 是個貿易保護者，而且他藐視美國文化，本題答案為 (B)。

40. D；中譯：每人生來有二種身份，在健康的國度及生病的國度，疾病是生命的黑暗面，那是一個更為沉重的身分。(A) 所有人們終其一生都需與健康及生病共處，而與病痛相處是較二者更令人沮喪的 (B) 所有活著的人們都必定有健康及生病的日子，人們在夜間會覺得沮喪及煩悶的心情 (C) 每人生來有二種公民權，雖然有時有健康生活，看了更多生命的黑暗面後，會感到不快樂。(D) 所有活著的人們終其一生都與健康生活及生病痛苦共存，而生病是這二者中更不願見到的。

解析：born with（與生俱來），onerous（繁重的）。本句是指人的一生不是健康就是生病，而當疾病纏身時那是另外一種不可承受的痛，本題答案為 (D)。

41. B；中譯：歐普拉‧溫芙蕾的父親關切的是她是否充分利用她的人生，並且不會接受任何低於他認為應該還可以做的更好的事情。(A) 歐普拉‧溫芙蕾的父親只接受她女兒買給他最高品質的東西 (B) 歐普拉‧溫芙蕾的父親信任她女兒的能力，並要求她到最好 (C) 歐普拉‧溫芙蕾有成功的事業因為她父親總是給她最好的 (D) 歐普拉‧溫芙蕾對她父親非常關心，而她父親是她人生中最有價值的資產。

解析：have concern about（關心），make the best of（充分利用），less than（少於）；本句是指歐普拉的父親非常關心她女兒的未來發展，所以對她的要求及期望都很高，本題答案為(B)

42. C；中譯：任何公開的揭露這種醜聞將對這位影星造成極大傷害。

解析：(A) proposal 提案 (B) enclosure 包圍 (C) disclosure 揭露 (D) refusal 拒絕
此題考的是單字名詞，do great damage to 對…造成傷害，依題意答案為 (C)。

43. B；中譯：失業是令人沮喪的，一個物理學家在海關工作是一個國家停滯的象徵，而非進步。

解析：(A) ambiguous 模糊的 (B) demoralizing 令人洩氣的 (C) optimistic 樂觀的 (D) invaluable 無價的
此題考的是形容詞，失業造成述物理學家學非所用是國家的停滯，所以是令人洩氣的，答案為 (B)。

44. B；中譯：寬恕似乎是本身就是報復的形式，因為它就像我們已經超越了發生在我們身上的事以及那些應該被責難的人。(A) 寬恕與報復有著一些相同的東西因為二者都牽涉到那些發生在我們身上的事以及那些應該被責難的人 (B) 在某方面寬恕可以被視為報復因為它發出一個我們是稍微高尚一點的訊

號 (C) 寬恕與報復二者都需要我們來表現出我們能夠超越發生在我們身上的事以及那些應該被責難的人 (D) 只有表現出發生在我們身上的事對我們沒有太多影響我們才能聲稱寬恕是報復的自我形式

解析：rise above（超越）；本句是指寬恕就是由超越自己及別人時己經得到精神的回報了，依題意答案為 (B)。

45. A；中譯：好品德的觀念聽來似乎是老氣且傲慢的，但它可能是對我們一些最根深地固社會問題的解決之道。(A) 為了解決我們一些最根深地固社會問題，我們可能需要倚靠傳統且有些高傲的道德觀念 (B) 談論古老但流行的道德觀念可能聽來是愛國的，但它是解決一些我們最惱人的社會問題的唯一確定方式(C) 品德的觀念可能已存在好長一段時間了，但它可能是打開我們社會潘朵拉盒子的鑰匙 (D) 道德，雖然過時且稀有，可能是解決一些我們最根深地固社會問題的唯一武器。

解析：patronizing（傲慢的），entrench（固定）；本句是指道德觀念雖然是老生常談，卻是解決現代社會根本問題的好方法，答案為 (A)。

46. B；中譯：甚麼是雜草？一棵價值沒有被發現的植物。

解析：(A) 雜草中就是雜草，不管它長多高 (B) 雜草被稱為雜草是因為我們沒有看到它的價值 (C) 當價值被發現後，雜草就會改變 (D) 我們不該稱雜草為雜草。

解析：本句是指雜草就是它背後的價值沒有被發現的植物，答案為 (B)。

47.－50. 中譯：

男女間的談話是一種跨文化的溝通，文化單純只是一種由過去的經驗獲得的習慣與生活型態形成的網絡，且男人與女人有過去不同的經驗。從出生開始，他們就被不同地對待，被不同地要求，到最後說話也不同，男孩和女孩生長在不同的世界，縱使它們成長在同個屋簷下。當他們長大成人後他們各自在不同的世界旅行，持續增強他們在孩童時期所被塑造的型態。這些文化的差異包括了在男女關係的對談話角色有不同的期待。

每個人都應該知道當關係變成長久以後，它本質會改變的，但男女之間對彼此改變的期待時常不同，許多女人認為：「過了這段期間後，我不需要說話你就應該知道我要甚麼。許多男人覺得：我們應該能告訴對方我們需要甚麼。」

這些不一致的期待是造成男人與女人關鍵性差異的其中之一。溝通時常是為了包容與獨立之間的衝突而做的平衡。雖然每個人都有這些需求，但女人通常具有相當多被關懷的需要，而男人有較多的獨立自主需求，不需要說出口就能被了解就是一種滿足的回報，而那就是女人為何如此看重它。

47. C；中譯：(A) 但男女之間對彼此改變的期待時常不同 (B) 男孩和女孩生長在不同的世界，縱使他們成長在同個屋簷下 (C) 文化單純只是一種由過去的經驗獲得的習慣與生活型態形成的網絡(D)在男人與女人談到他們之間的關係時，各種不同的習慣會有影響。

解析：解題時，將前後段有提到的關鍵字找出，即可輕易帶入找出答案。空格前面一句提到cross-cultural communication（跨文化的溝通），後面提到different past experiences（不同的過去經驗），四個選項中以 (C) 有提到這二者，並帶入本文後句意通順，所以答案為 (C)。

48. B；中譯：(A) 文化單純只是一種由過去的經驗獲得的習慣與生活型態形成的網絡 (B) 男孩和女孩生長在不同的世界，縱使它們成長在同個屋簷下 (C) 溝通時常是一種為了包容及獨立之間的衝突而做的平

衡 (D) 在男人與女人談到他們之間的關係時，各種不同的習慣會有影響。

解析：空格前面一句提到 From the time they are born…，後面提到when they become adults…，表示空格內應為說明男孩與女孩的成長有關的事，四個選項中 (B) 帶入本文後句意通順，所以答案為 (B)。

49. A；中譯：(A) 但男女之間對彼此改變的期待時常不同 (B) 文化單純只是一種由過去的經驗獲得的習慣與生活型態形成的網絡 (C) 男孩和女孩生長在不同的世界，縱使它們成長在同個屋簷下 (D) 要改正這樣的誤解是很困難的，因為雙方都堅信他（或她）自己的觀點。

解析：空格前面一句提到its terms change…，後面提到男人與女人的感受大不同，所以表示空格內應為男女間的想法改變有關的事，四個選項中(A)帶入本文後句意通順，所以答案為 (A)。

50. B；中譯：(A) 男孩和女孩生長在不同的世界，縱使它們成長在同個屋簷下 (B) 溝通時常是為了包容與獨立之間的衝突而做的平衡 (C) 在男人與女人談到他們之間的關係時，各種不同的習慣會有影響。(D) 要改正這樣的誤解是很困難的，因為雙方都堅信他（或她）自己的觀點

解析：空格前面一句提到 These incongruent expectations…（這些不一致的期待），暗示空格內應為男女間有關不同需求討論的事，四個選項中 (B) 帶入本文後句意通順，所以答案為 (B)。

 NOTE

📋 100 年特種考試交通事業鐵路人員考試試題

等別：員級鐵路人員考試
類科：各類科
科目：法學知識與英文（此節錄英文部分）

( ) 31. Geniuses don't follow what they are taught. They often come up with _____ ideas.

(A) unconventional (B) uncomfortable (C) unconscious (D) unconditional

( ) 32. When traveling in the mountains, we had better carry a _____ with us; otherwise, it is very likely that we will get lost.

(A) bandage (B) tent (C) compass (D) cord

( ) 33. The city government met with strong _____ from residents about its proposal to build a nuclear plant in this area. In the end, the government had to drop the plan.

(A) recreation (B) reliance (C) resignation (D) resistance

( ) 34. The _____ sale will start tomorrow because this department store is going out of business.

(A) delegation (B) inflation (C) clearance (D) budget

( ) 35. Rock climbing can be an exciting but _____ sport, so it's important to be careful.

(A) dangerous (B) energetic (C) inferior (D) mysterious

( ) 36. It required a big effort to make the house _____ . The heating system had to be replaced, several windows repaired, and one bathroom rebuilt.

(A) habitable (B) hospitable (C) inevitable (D) imaginative

( ) 37. During wartime, people often suffer terrible _____ , such as not enough food or fuel to keep them warm.

(A) hardship (B) leadership (C) partnership (D) relationship

(　　) 38. Ken: I'm going to study in the library for several hours tonight.

Wendy: _____ .

Ken: Around 9:00 p.m. If anyone calls, take a message for me. Would you?

(A) Which library will you go?　　(B) Where are you going?

(C) What are you going to study?　　(D) When will you return home?

(　　) 39. Peter: Would you like to stay in the Capsule Inn in Japan?

Jerry: _____ I think it would be very uncomfortable.

Peter: But it sounds like a fantastic experience.

(A) For fun!　　(B) By all means!　　(C) No way!　　(D) In no time!

(　　) 40. Amy: I'm frustrated. I failed my math test.

Anne: _____ This is not the end of the world.

Amy: Thank you.

(A) You can count on it.　　(B) You deserve it.

(C) Get out!　　(D) Cheer up!

　　Nanotechnology is moving closer to our daily life. Researchers from the University of New South Wales, Australia, are developing a coating that may make cleaning bathrooms _____41_____ of a chore. The leading researchers, Professors Rose Amal and Michael Brungs, are hoping to apply a tiny coating of titanium dioxide to keep the toilets clean. Currently titanium dioxide is being used on outdoor items _____42_____ self-cleaning windows.

　　To further keep the bathroom clean, nanoparticles kill the germs and remove organic compounds. _____43_____ , the coating prevents liquid droplets from forming on the surface. It makes the liquid run off, _____44_____ the toilet in the process.

　　Exciting as this research project is, at this time it is currently only in development. The researchers _____45_____ it will take about a year before it can be seen on the market. It would certainly be great to have a clean bathroom that would clean itself.

( ) 41. (A) hardly   (B) never   (C) anymore   (D) less

( ) 42. (A) by   (B) as   (C) like   (D) and

( ) 43. (A) Instead   (B) Besides   (C) However   (D) Therefore

( ) 44. (A) wash   (B) washed   (C) washing   (D) washes

( ) 45. (A) estimate   (B) demand   (C) criticize   (D) summarize

      The tower of Pisa is the bell tower of the cathedral of Pisa in Tuscany, Italy. It leans because when the building was half completed, the soil under one half of the circular structure began to subside and the tower tipped.

      Work on the tower was begun in 1173, but was discontinued for a century after the subsidence. However, in 1275, architects devised a plan to compensate for the tilt. Two stories, the third and the fifth, were built out of line with the others and closer to the vertical in an effort to alter the tower's center of gravity.

      But the leaning has continued to increase gradually throughout the centuries. Pumping to keep water away from the surrounding ground and the injection of cement grout into the foundations and the surrounding subsoil have been tried in recent years, but without success.

      The tower, which is one of the most unusual in existence, is Romanesque in style and made of white marble. It is cylindrical in shape and has eight stories.

      The tilt is about 17 feet, or more than five degrees, from the perpendicular. The tower continues to increase its tilt by about a quarter of an inch each year.

( ) 46. What is the main idea of this passage?

    (A) Of all the tourist attractions in Italy, the tower of Pisa is undoubtedly the most popular.

    (B) The collaboration of the Italian government and people has made the tower of Pisa become famous.

    (C) The best way to study Italian culture is to visit the tower of Pisa.

(D) Despite the effort over the past years, the tower of Pisa still keeps tipping.

(　) 47. According to the passage, which of the following is true about the tower of Pisa?

(A) It is made of cement.

(B) It looks like a cylinder in appearance.

(C) It is a Gothic cathedral.

(D) It is a five-story building.

(　) 48. In four years' time, how many inches will the tower of Pisa increase its tilt?

(A) one　　　　(B) two　　　　(C) three　　　　(D) four

(　) 49. Which of the following words is closest in meaning to "subside" in paragraph 1?

(A) collapse　　(B) float　　　(C) ascend　　　(D) sink

(　) 50. Which of the following statements is NOT true about the tower of Pisa?

(A) Its construction began in the twelfth century.

(B) It was not until 1275 that a plan was put forward to solve the problem of its tilt.

(C) Substituting water for cement was adopted to prevent the tower from leaning further.

(D) The third and fifth floors were built out of line with the others.

100 年特種考試交通事業鐵路人員──員級中譯解析

31. A；中譯：天才不會依循他們所教的東西，他們通常會有不尋常的點子。

解析：(A) unconventional 不尋常的 (B) uncomfortable 不舒適的 (C) unconscious 無意識的 (D) unconditional 無條件的

本題考形容詞。come up with 想出，天才通常與眾不同，所以能想出不尋常的主意，選項中以 unconventional（不尋常的）最符合，故答案為 (A)。

32. C；中譯：當在山中遊走時，我們最好隨身攜帶指南針，否則我們很有可能會迷路。

解析：(A) bandage 繃帶 (B) tent 帳篷 (C) compass 指南針 (D) cord 繩索

本題考名詞。carry something with（隨身攜帶），get lost（迷路）。登山中要隨身攜帶的預防迷路的指南針，所以答案為 (C)。

33. D；中譯：在關於要在這個區域興建一座核電廠的計畫上，市政府遇到居民強烈的反抗。

解析：(A) recreation 娛樂 (B) reliance 信任 (C) resignation 辭職 (D) resistance 反抗

本題考名詞。met with（遇到）。興建核電廠是一項有爭議性的計畫，所以會遇到居民強烈的反應，選項中以 resistance（反抗）最符合，所以答案為 (D)。

34. C；中譯：清倉特賣將於明天開始因為這家百貨公司將結束營業。

解析：(A) delegation 委任 (B) inflation 膨脹 (C) clearance 清除 (D) budget 預算

本題考名詞，go out of business（快關門大吉）。句中提到百貨公司將不再營業，結束前會有清倉的特賣，所以答案為 (C)。

35. A；中譯：攀岩可以是一項刺激但危險的運動，所以小心謹慎是重要的。

解析：(A) dangerous 危險的 (B) energetic 有活力的 (C) inferior 低劣的 (D) mysterious 神秘的

本題考形容詞，句中提到攀岩可以要小心謹慎，代表該項活動具有危險性，所以選項中用 dangerous（危險的）最符合，故答案為 (A)。

36. A；中譯：讓這間房子變成適合居住要費一番努力，暖器系統必須更新，好幾個窗戶要更換且浴室要重建。

解析：(A) habitable 適宜居住的 (B) hospitable 好客的 (C) inevitable 必然的 (D) imaginative 想像的

本題考形容詞。a big effort（一番努力）。句中提到房子有很多地方都要翻修，應該是讓房子可以住人，所以選項中用 habitable（適宜居住的）最符合，故答案為 (A)。

37. A；中譯：在戰爭期間，人們時常遭逢可怕的艱苦，像是沒有足夠的食物或燃料來保持溫暖。

解析：(A) hardship 艱苦 (B) leadership 領導力 (C) partnership 夥伴關係 (D) relationship 關係

本題考名詞，suffer（動詞，遭受）。由於句中所題無足夠的食物或燃料來保持溫暖代表艱困的環境，所以選項中用 hardship（艱苦）最符合，故答案為 (A)。

38. D；中譯：肯：今天晚上我要到圖書館幾個小時去念書。

溫蒂：(A) 你要去哪個圖書館？(B) 你要去哪？(C) 你要去念甚麼？(D) 你何時要回家？

肯：大約下午九點，如果有任何人找我，先幫我留話好嗎？

解析：由肯回答說他大約下午九點，暗示溫蒂有提到時間的問題，所以溫蒂最有可能問他何時回來，故答案為 (D)。

39. C；中譯：彼得：你想要去住日本的膠囊旅館嗎？

傑利：(A) 開玩笑！(B) 當然可以！(C) 一點也不！(D) 馬上去！我想那將會很不舒服

彼得：但那聽起來像是個很吸引人的經驗。

解析：由傑利有提到說那將會很不舒服，暗示他不想去住那種地方，彼得最後只能自我安慰說那聽起來還不錯，故答案為 (C)。

40. D；中譯：艾咪：我很受挫，我數學測驗不及格。

安妮：(A) 你可以相信它 (B) 你活該 (C) 滾開！(D) 振作起來！這不是世界末日

艾咪：謝謝你。

解析：安妮聽到艾咪說考試成績不好，正常反應會說些鼓勵他的話，來對他加油打氣，所以答案為 (D)。

41.－45. 中譯：

奈米科技正逐漸接近我們日常生活中。澳洲新南威爾斯大學的研究人員正在發展一種塗料讓清潔浴廁不再是苦差事。二位領導研究者，羅斯教授及米契爾教授，正設法運用一種二氧化鈦微粒的塗層來使廁所保持乾淨。目前二氧化鈦正被使用於戶外的項目，像是自潔的窗戶。

為了更進一步讓浴室保持乾淨，奈米粒子可以殺死細菌及移除有機複合物，除此之外，塗層可以讓液體滴粒免於在表面上形成，它讓液體流走，在這過程中洗淨馬桶。跟這項研究一樣令人振奮的是目前它仍僅在研究發展階段，研究人員估計大概還要約一年後才可以在市面上看到它，有一間可以自潔的乾淨浴室確實是很棒的事。

41. D；解析：chore 是雜事，討厭的工作之意，less of a chore（少一件苦差事）最符合前後文意，且選項中只有 less 可作為名詞使用，其他均為副詞，後面不可接 of，故答案為 (D)。

42. C；解析：空格內要用介系詞，表示像甚麼用途的介系詞應用 like，故答案為 (C)。

43. B；解析：空格置於句首要用副詞，前句提到奈米粒子可以殺死細菌及移除有機複合物，本句說塗層還可以讓液體滴粒免於在表面上形成⋯，表示二句為相加成的語氣，所以選項中應用 Besides（除此之外）最恰當，故答案為 (B)。

44. C；解析：該句為表示附加狀況的分詞構句，故空格處用現在分詞 washing，指這些液體因滑落而在過程中幫馬桶清潔，所以故答案為 (C)。

45. A；(A) estimate 估計 (B) demand 要求 (C) criticize 批判 (D) summarize 總結

解析：空格處應用現在式動詞，由於提到時間約要一年，故選項中 estimate（估計）最符合，故答案為 (A)。

46-50. 中譯：

比薩塔是位於義大利塔斯卡尼比薩教堂的一座鐘樓，他會傾斜是因為當這座建築概到一半時，在它圓形結構一邊的地底土壤開始下沉且塔變傾斜。

這座塔於 1173 年開始建造，但在下沉發生後被迫停工長達一個世紀，然而於 1275 年時，建築師擬定一個計劃來補償傾斜情況。第三層級第五層這兩層樓建在與其他樓層不同一線上，並且比較靠垂直線，以設法改變塔的重心。

但傾斜仍持續增加並且持續一個世紀之久，近幾年試過抽地表周圍的水及灌水泥將到地基及其周圍，但仍然不成功。

這座難得一見仍存在的塔是一座羅馬式建築並以白色大理石建造，形狀為圓柱形並有八層樓高。

從垂直面算起，它傾斜 17 英呎，傾斜約超過五度，這座塔每年仍繼續增加傾斜約四分之一英吋。

46. D；中譯：本文主旨為何？(A) 在義大利的旅遊景點中，比薩斜塔無疑是最受歡迎的 (B) 義大利政府及居民的合作讓比薩斜塔變得有名 (C) 要研究義大利最好的方式是去參觀比薩斜塔 (D) 雖然經過多年的努力，比薩斜塔仍繼續傾斜。

解析：本文開始提到比薩塔一開始建造就因地質因素傾斜，後來停工長達一世紀後再設法補救，但仍繼續傾斜，故答案為 (D)。

47. B；中譯：依據本文，下列何項關於比薩斜塔是真的？(A) 它是用水泥蓋的(B)它看起來像個圓柱體 (C) 由他是一座哥德式的教堂 (D) 他是座五層樓建築。

解析：(A) 由…is Romanesque in style and made of white marble.它是用白色大理石蓋的，敘述為非 (B) 由 It is cylindrical in shape …它像個圓柱體，敘述為真 (C) 由The tower of Pisais the bell tower of the cathedral…知它是一座教堂的鐘樓，敘述為非；且是羅馬式的建築風格 (D) 由It is cylindrical in shape and has eight stories知它是座八層樓建築，敘述為非。故答案為 (B)。

48. A；中譯：四年時間內，比薩斜塔將增加它的傾斜幾英吋？(A) 1 (B) 2 (C) 3 (D) 4。

解析：由The tower continues to increase its tilt by about a quarter of an inch each year.，知這座塔每年仍繼續增加傾斜約四分之一英吋，四年增加一英吋，故答案為 (A)。

49. D；中譯：下列哪一個字與在第一段的 "subside" 這個字的意思相近？(A) collapse 倒塌 (B) float 浮起 (C) ascend 上升 (D) sink 下沉

解析：subside 意思是沉下去，故答案為 (D)。

50. C；中譯：下列何項關於比薩斜塔的敘述不是真的？(A)它的建造開始於十二世紀世紀(B)直到1275年有一個計畫才被提出來解決它傾斜的問題(C)用水來替代水泥的方法被採用來防止塔更加傾斜(D)第三和第五樓被建在與其他樓不同線上。

解析：(A) 由Work on the tower was begun in 1173…知該塔建於十二世紀，敘述為真 (B) 由…in 1275, architects devised a plan to compensate for the tilt.知敘述為真 (C) 由Pumping to keep water away from the surrounding ground and the injection of cement grout into the foundations…知敘述為非 (D) 由…the third and the fifth, were built out of line with the others…知敘述為真。

NOTE

📋 100年特種考試交通事業鐵路人員考試試題

等別：佐級鐵路人員考試
類科：各類科
科目：公民與英文（此節錄英文部分）

( ) 36. Dad told Mary to _____ the phone in five minutes because she had been talking on the phone for an hour.

    (A) hang up   (B) put down   (C) turn off   (D) chat with

( ) 37. John doesn't smoke, yet his older brother is a _____ smoker.

    (A) second-hand   (B) non   (C) chain   (D) strong

( ) 38. I hate comments. I cannot stand people who always criticize.

    (A) negative   (B) positive   (C) ideal   (D) kind

( ) 39. Of all the board games, this one is _____ difficult to play.

    (A) least   (B) less than   (C) the less   (D) the least

( ) 40. The goal of our meetings is to make the directors _____ our problem.

    (A) be understanding   (B) understand

    (C) understood   (D) understanding

( ) 41. Mark is one of our best employees and _____ working in the company for two years.

    (A) has   (B) has been   (C) is   (D) will

42 - 46.

When I was a kid, I did not like to play the piano. My parents asked me to practice the piano every day, but I just ____42____ to go out and play with my classmates. I was so bored with practicing the same piece of music for hours that I almost gave it ____43____ . When I was ten years old, I began my piano lessons with an ____44____ teacher, Beth, who allowed me to choose the piece I would like to play and urged me to play for the pleasure of the music. Instead of criticizing me, she encouraged me and taught me to have self confidence. I also learned from Beth that the beauty of music comes from passion rather than from techniques. I am grateful to her ____45____ introducing me to the wonderful world of music.

Now I enjoy playing the piano. I practice not for my parents but for ____46____ . Playing the piano can be a lot of fun.

(　) 42. (A) want 　　　　(B) wants 　　　　(C) wanted 　　　　(D) wanting

(　) 43. (A) up 　　　　　(B) out 　　　　　(C) off 　　　　　(D) back

(　) 44. (A) angry 　　　　(B) inspiring 　　　　(C) intensive 　　　　(D) absent

(　) 45. (A) for 　　　　　(B) at 　　　　　　(C) with 　　　　　(D) by

(　) 46. (A) I 　　　　　　(B) we 　　　　　　(C) myself 　　　　　(D) they

(　) 47. John: How often does Bus 625 run every day?

Jean: _____ .

(A) It runs on weekends too 　　　　(B) It runs every 30 minutes

(C) It runs very fast 　　　　　　　(D) It comes so slow

48－50.

　　Sam, who was born in Canada, moved to Taipei with his family last year. Now he is studying Chinese in a language school. The teachers and students there are very friendly to him. In the school, Sam not only studies Chinese but gets to learn about Chinese culture. He is also learning to eat with chopsticks and write with brushes.

　　For Sam, Taipei is a city full of excitement. There are food stalls everywhere and they offer him a variety of meal choices. Besides, Sam also finds the Shih-lin Night Market very convenient for it sells everything that Sam wants to buy. Sam loves to wander around from one vendor to another vendor. He is overwhelmed by the variety of products he finds at the night market.

　　On weekends, Sam usually goes to the movies and goes jogging in the park. And he also loves to go to Beitou to enjoy the hot spring in winter. In summer, Sam likes to go surfing in Fu Long. Sam really loves his life in Taipei.

(　　) 48. Where is Sam studying now?

　　　　(A) A senior high school.

　　　　(B) A college.

　　　　(C) A language school.

　　　　(D) A junior high school.

(　) 49. According to the passage, what is Sam's impression of Taipei?

　　(A) Taipei is an ugly city.

　　(B) There are many bad people in Taipei.

　　(C) People in Taipei know how to use chopsticks.

　　(D) Taipei is an exciting city.

(　) 50. According to the passage, what does Sam usually do on weekends?

　　(A) He goes to the movies only.

　　(B) He goes to the movies and goes jogging.

　　(C) He goes jogging.

　　(D) He goes diving.

100 年特種考試交通事業鐵路人員——佐級中譯解析

36. A；中譯：父親告訴瑪莉五分鐘內掛斷電話因為她已經講了一小時電話。

解析：(A) hang up 掛斷 (B) put down 放下 (C) turn off 關掉 (D) chat with 跟某人聊天

本題考片語用法。已經講電話一小時，表示父親認為講太久了，所以應該是要她停止講電話，故答案為 (A)。

37. C；中譯：約翰不喜歡抽菸，然而他的哥哥是菸不離口。

解析：(A) second-hand 二手 (B) non(adv.)不 (D) strong(adj.)強烈的

本題考慣用語。前面說約翰不喜歡抽菸，後面語氣轉折所以用 yet，表示他哥哥恰巧相反，應該用 chain smoker（菸不離口），所以答案為 (C)。

38. A；中譯：我不喜歡負面的評語，我不能忍受總是喜歡批評的人。

解析：(A) negative 負面的 (B) positive 正面的 (C) ideal 理想的 (D) kind 仁慈的

本題考慣用語。comment 評語、評價。後面提到不能忍受愛批評的人，推論他應該是不喜歡被批評的人，所以選項中用 negative（負面的）最恰當，答案為 (A)。

39. D；中譯：在所有棋盤遊戲中，這一種是最不難玩的。

解析：本題考比較句用法。little（少的）比較級是 less，最高級 least。空格中可用比較級或最高級，用比較級時用法為 less difficult…，用最高級時用法為 the least difficult…，故本題答案為 (D)。

40. B；中譯：我們會議的目的在於使老闆知道我們的問題。

解析：本題考使役動詞用法。have、 make 及 let 三個使役動詞後面要接原形動詞，答案為 (B)。

41. B；中譯：馬克是我們其中一位最好的員工，且已經在公司工作二年了。

解析：本題考動詞時態。由句中知馬克已經從二年前工作到現在，從過去一段時間到現在並可能持續到未來，時態可用現在完成式或完成進行式，句中動詞已經用 working，表示是用完成進行式，故應為 has been working…，答案為 (B)。

42－46 中譯：

　　當我還是小孩時，我不喜歡彈鋼琴。我爸媽要求我每天練習，但我只想出去與同學玩。我厭煩於花好幾個鐘頭練習一段音樂以至於我幾乎想放棄它。當我十歲時，我開始跟一位啟發我很多的貝絲老師練習，她允許我挑選我喜歡的片段來練習，並鼓勵我為音樂的樂趣而彈琴。她鼓勵我並教我要有自信心，而不是責罵我，而我也從她那學到音樂的美在於發自於熱情而不是出於技巧，我感謝她帶領我進入音樂的美好世界。

　　現在我享受彈琴，我彈琴不是為了我爸媽而是為我自己，彈琴是很大的享受。

42. C；解析：該處空格需填入動詞，因為該句敘述一段過去事情，所以用簡單過去式即可，want（想要）的過去式為 wanted，所以答案為 (C)。

43. A；解析：該句前面提到因為厭煩幾個鐘頭練習一段音樂以至於想…，所以此處用 give it up（放棄它）最適合，故答案為 (A)。

44. B；(A) angry 生氣的 (B) inspiring 啟發的 (C) intensive 加強的 (D) absent 缺席的

解析：該處空格需填入形容詞來形容該位新老師，由後面有關這位老師的一些敘述，如挑選喜歡的片段來練習，鼓勵為音樂的樂趣而彈琴，選項中以inspiring（啟發的）最符合這位老師的形容，故答案為 (B)。

45. A；解析：該處空格需填入介系詞，表示他感謝這位老師的原因，表示為某原因或為了某事，介係詞用for，故答案為 (A)。

46. C；解析：該處空格需填入名詞或代名詞，作為 for 的受詞，由該句意思應該是現在彈琴目的不是為了雙親而是為自己，故 for 的受詞就是主詞自己，應用反身代名詞，所以用 myself，故答案為(C)。

47. B；中譯：約翰：625 路公車每天多久來一次？

傑利：(A) 它周末也有開 (B) 每 30 分鐘一班 (C) 它開很快 (D) 它都很慢到

解析：Howoften 多久來一次的意思，所以直接回答多久時間即可，故答案為 (B)。

48－50. 中譯：

出生於加拿大的山姆去年與他的家人搬到台北，目前他在一間語言學校學習中文，那裏的老師及學生們對他都很友善。在學校中，他不僅學習中文，也學習相關中國文化，他也學著用筷子吃飯及用毛筆寫字。

對山姆來說，台北是一個充滿驚奇的城市，到處都有小吃店可提供多樣的餐飲選擇；除此之外，山姆也認為士林夜市很方便，因為有賣山姆想買的任何東西，山姆喜歡一攤一攤的逛，他被夜市裡琳瑯滿目的東西給征服了。

在周末的時候，山姆通常去看電影並且在公園慢跑，冬天的時候他也喜歡去北投享受溫泉，夏天時他也喜歡到福隆衝浪，山姆真的很喜歡在台北的生活。

48. C；中譯：山姆現在在哪裡念書？(A) 一所高中 (B) 一所大學 (C) 一所語言學校(D)一所國中。

解析：由Now he is studying Chinese in a language school.知他是在一所語言學校念書，故答案為 (C)。

49. D；中譯：依據本文，甚麼是山姆對台北的印象？(A) 台北是個醜陋的城市 (B) 台北有許多壞人 (C) 台北人知道如何使用筷子 (D) 台北是一個驚奇的城市。

解析：由For Sam, Taipei is a city full of excitement.，知他認為台北是一個驚奇的城市，故答案為 (D)。

50. B；中譯：依據本文，山姆通常在周末做甚麼？(A) 他只有去看電影(B)他去看電影及慢跑 (C) 他去慢跑 (D) 他去潛水。

解析：由 On weekends, Sam usually goes to the movies and goes jogging in the park.，知他周末去看電影及慢跑，故答案為 (B)。

101年特種考試交通事業鐵路人員考試試題

等別：三等一般警察人員考試、高員三級鐵路人員考試
類科：各類科
科目：法學知識與英文（此節錄英文部分）

( ) 31. Shu-yu is highly _____ to succeed in her career, so she works fourteen hours every day.

(A) mortified   (B) motivated   (C) monitored   (D) modified

( ) 32. Traditional Chinese medicine plays an important role in treating cancer and managing pain, where the effectiveness of Western _____ is limited.

(A) benefits   (B) commodities   (C) disciplines   (D)remedies

( ) 33. The galaxy to which our solar system belongs is so _____ that is takes between 60,000 to 100,000 years at light speed to cross it.

(A) abundant   (B) enormous   (C) imaginable   (D) various

( ) 34. In 1995, Beth plucked up the courage and went to the United States to further _____ her singing skill. A year later, she participated in a Canadian contest for vocalists.

(A) hint   (B) hone   (C) hijack   (D) hibernate

( ) 35. After its engine failed, the small boat _____ with the current.

(A) drifted   (B) washed   (C) launched   (D) waved

( ) 36. The environmentalist movement, a reaction against industrial pollution of air and water, grew up in the 1960s.

(A) Industrialization received negative response but still grew up in the 1960s.

(B) Environmentalists finally won the fight against industry in the 1960s.

(C) The environmental movement triggered the industrial revolution in the 1960s.

(D) Aware of the damage brought by industrialization, people began to protect the environment in the 1960s.

( ) 37. One similar attribute of all science fictions is that the main character is usually taken on a fantastic journey.

(A) Most science fictions involve the main character in an exciting and imaginary journey.

(B) Most science fictions involve the main character in a fun and enjoyable journey.

(C) If the main character is not on a journey, the story cannot be classified as science fiction.

(D) Science fictions attribute their success to the fantastic journey the main character takes.

( ) 38. While they are not immune to the hot and cold winds of politics, artists have become adept at taking shelter from them most of the time.

(A) Though they can hardly turn a deaf ear to politics, artists have become better at working for politicians.

(B) Though they can hardly remain politically impassive, artists have learned better to take a political stance.

(C) Though they may suffer from the drastic change of politics, artists have been able to adapt such change into their creations.

(D) Though they may suffer from the drastic change of politics, artists have become skillful in surviving such change.

( ) 39. Experience is not what happens to you; it is what you do with what happens to you.

(A) An experience is not a good one if you simply let it happen and do nothing about it.

(B) It is not what happens to you but the lesson you learn from it that is called experience.

(C) What happens to you is part of your experience; it is complete with a follow-up action.

(D) Experience is more than what happens to you; you need to take some action afterwards.

( ) 40. Capitalism has improved the lives of billions of people, but it has left out billions more.

(A) The prevalent adoption of capitalism has resulted in prosperity to millions of people.

(B) Free enterprise is welcome among the rich but not the poor because of its inequitable nature.

(C) The promotion of private enterprise has not only made poor people's lives easier but also made the rich more well off.

(D) A substantial amount of people have gained benefits from capitalism and lived a better life; nevertheless, more have not.

( ) 41. This cutting-edge equipment is state-of-the-art.

(A) These powered knives and saws are very good for arts and crafts.

(B) This cutlery is designed only for use in art.

(C) This modern, hi-tech tool is designed especially for art.

(D) This equipment is the newest and most advanced of its kind.

請回答第42題至第45題：

　　One of the most important features that distinguish man from animals is the ability to laugh. People who have investigated the phenomenon have offered many theories to explain human laughter. Scholars in the field of psychology, for example, have done ____42____ on the subject of what makes people laugh. But, as usually happens, the experts disagree, and there is much ____43____ in the field. Some people claim that human beings laugh at things which are strange to their experience. Others feel that people laugh at what they secretly believe to be their own weaknesses. It is _____44_____ that all people do not laugh at the same things. Sometimes people laugh at what they see; sometimes they laugh at what they hear. Humor often _____45_____ on a knowledge of certain words or even on an understanding of a particular cultural background. There are, of course, many different sources of humor, but the important fact is that all people share the great pleasure of laughter.

(　) 42. (A) efforts　　(B) explanation　(C) issues　　(D) research

(　) 43. (A) applause　(B) controversy　(C) failure　　(D) objection

(　) 44. (A) clear　　(B) dubious　　(C) impossible　(D) relevant

(　) 45. (A) depends　(B) keeps　　(C) looks　　(D) stays

請回答第46題至第50題：

It is easy to understand why the Greeks found geocentric cosmology so appealing. Night after night, we see celestial objects moving across the sky from east to west. Wouldn't it be natural to assume that the Earth lies motionless at the center of the universe and that the Sun, the moon, planets, and stars revolve around it? In the 4th century B.C., Plato postulated a world system with the stationary Earth as its hub and a huge outer space that carried the planets and stars in its daily revolution. But his two-sphere configuration could not account for a particular motion of certain planets. As a rule, the planets and stars traveled together across the sky every night from east to west. But now and then, inexplicably, some planets seemed to drift backwards. Today we know that retrograde motion is an illusion caused by the fact that we observe planetary motion from a planet that is itself in motion. It never entered the mind of Eudoxus, a young contemporary of Plato's, that the Earth could actually move. But he did try to accommodate planetary retrogression to the motionless earth by developing from the two-sphere Platonic system a model with twenty-seven spheres, one for every known planet; each was attached to another sphere whose rotation, combined with the rotation of the other planetary spheres, explained the "reversed" direction of certain heavenly bodies.

( ) 46. According to Greek cosmology, which of the following did NOT move?

(A) The Earth　　　(B) The Moon　　　(C) Mars　　　(D) The Sun

( ) 47. According to the passage, what did Plato's world system look like?

(A) A river　　　(B) A spoon　　　(C) A tent　　　(D) A wheel

( ) 48. Which movement of some planets can NOT be explained in Plato's system?

(A) Backward　　　(B) Forward　　　(C) Upward　　　(D) Downward

( ) 49. Why do all planets seem NOT to move in the same direction?

(A) The Sun does not move.　　　(B) All planets move sideways.

(C) The Earth is in motion.　　　(D) All planets move backwards.

( ) 50. Which of the following statements is true about Eudoxus?

(A) He was born two centuries after Plato.

(B) He believed that the Earth was stationary.

(C) He proposed that the planetary retrogression was an illusion.

(D) His cosmological structure was smaller in scale than Plato's.

101 年特種考試交通事業鐵路人員──高員級中譯解析

31. B；中譯：Shu-yu 有強烈的動機在她職場能成功，所以她每天工作 14 小時。

解析：(A) mortified 抑制 (B) motivated 動機 (C) monitored 監控 (D) modified 修改

此題考的是動詞單字。be highly motivated to 在某方面有強烈動機最符合題意，答案為 (B)。

32. D；中譯：傳統中醫在治療癌症及處理疼痛方面扮演一個重要角色，而這種效果是西式療法有所不足的。

解析：(A) benefits 益處 (B) commodities 日常用品 (C) disciplines 訓練；紀律 (D) remedies 療法

33. B；中譯：我們太陽系所處的銀河系是如此巨大，以致於光速要花 60,000 到 100,000 年才能橫越銀河系。

解析：(A) abundant 豐富的 (B) enormous 巨大的 (C) imaginable 可想像的 (D) various 各種的

34. B；中譯：1995 年時，貝絲鼓起勇氣到美國去進一步磨練她的歌藝，一年後，她參加一場加拿大的聲樂家比賽。

解析：(A) hint 暗示 (B) hone 磨練 (C) hijack 劫持 (D) hibernate 冬眠

35. A；中譯：在引擎失效後，這艘小艇隨波逐流。

解析：(A) drifted 漂流 (B) washed 洗滌 (C) launched 發射 (D) waved 波動

36. D；中譯：環境保護運動興起於 1960 年代，是一項對抗水及空氣工業汙染的反制運動。(A) 工業化雖有負面的反應但仍然成長於 1960 年代 (B) 環境保護者最後在 1960 年代贏得這場對抗工業的戰爭 (C) 環境運動在 1960 年代引發了工業革命 (D) 瞭解了工業化帶來的危害後，人們在 1960 年代開始來保護環境

解析：grow up 發展，成長；答案為 (D)。

37. A；中譯：所有科幻小說的其中一個共通點是主角通常經歷一場奇幻的旅程的冒險。(A) 大部分的科幻小說都會使主角參與一場刺激又充滿奇幻的旅程 (B) 大部分的科幻小說都會使主角參與一場好玩又快樂的旅程 (C) 假如主角不是在一個旅程中，這故事就不能被歸類成科幻小說 (D) 科幻小說的成功歸功於主角經歷的奇幻旅程。

解析：attribute something to 將某事歸功於，take on 具有；題目是指科幻小說的主角都會經歷一段奇幻旅程，答案為 (A)。

38. D；中譯：當他們無法免於政治的冷熱無常的同時，大多數情況下藝術家已經變得擅於自保了。(A) 雖然他們不能對政治置若罔聞，藝術家們會變得很會為政治服務 (B) 雖然他們很難保持對政治冷感，藝術家們已變得比較會站在政治的立場 (C) 雖然他們可能遭受政治劇烈變化之苦，藝術家們已經可以將這樣的變化融入他們創作中 (D) 雖然它們可能遭受政治劇烈變化之苦，藝術家們已經可以靈活地生存在這樣的變化中。

解析：be immune to 免疫於，adept at 擅長於，take shelter 安身；題目是指藝術家已經可以在變化無常的政治環境中，找出自保免於政治干擾的方式，答案為 (D)。

39. B；中譯：經驗不是發生在你身上的事，而是發生在你身上時你怎麼應對。(A) 一個經驗不會是個好經

驗如果你只是讓它發生而沒有做任何事 (B) 不是只有發生在你身上的事,而是你從中學到教訓的事才叫做經驗 (C) 發生在你身上的事是你的經驗的一部分,包含緊跟而來的動作 (D) 經驗不只是發生在你身上的事,你需要在事後做更多動作。

解析:what happens to you 是指發生在你身上的事,what you do 是指你做了甚麼事;題目意思是指經驗不只是指發生過的事,而是要從中學到東西才能稱為經驗,答案為 (B)。

40. D;中譯:資本主義制度已改善數百萬人生活,但它另外也遺棄了數百萬人。(A) 資本主義的盛行已經造成數百萬人民的富裕(B)自由企業在富人圈中是受歡迎的,但由於窮人們不公平的出身所以沒有被窮人所擁戴(C)私有企業的發展不僅使得窮人的生活更加容易些且讓富人更富有 (D) 有相當多的人已經從資本主義得到好處且過的更好的生活,然而更多人沒有。

解析:left out 遺忘;題目意思是指資本主義造成一些人得到好處,但更多人沒有受惠,答案為 (D)。

41. D;中譯:這個尖端科技的設備是一流的產品。(A) 這些有動力的刀和鋸對藝術和工藝都是很好的 (B) 這刀具被設計只用在藝術上 (C) 這現代且高科技的工具被特別設計用在藝術上 (D) 這個設備是最新且在這類產品中是最進步的。

42.－45. 中譯

要分辨人與動物的其中一個最大的不同點就是笑的能力,研究這種現象的學者已提出很多論點來解釋人類的笑聲。例如,心理學領域的學者做了到底是甚麼使人們會笑的研究,但就像通常的情況,專家們並不同意,並且在這方面還有很多爭議。有些人認為人類會對就他們經驗中感到稀奇古怪的事而笑,其他人則認為人們會對暗地裡承認是自己弱點的事物而笑。很清楚地,不會所有人都會笑相同的事情,有時候,人們會笑他們看到的東西,有時人們會笑他們聽到的事。幽默通常基於對某些言語的認知,或於對一些特定文化背景的了解。當然,幽默出於許多不同的原因,但重要的是所有人們都可得到歡笑的極大愉悅。

42. D;(A) efforts 努力 (B) explanation 解釋 (C) issues 論點 (D) research 研究

解析:空格前面是完成式 have done 所以應該要填入適當名詞作為 done 的受詞。空格後面提到心理學家要知道是甚麼造成人們會笑,所以空格應選 (D),即科學家做一個研究。

43. B;(A) applause 喝采 (B) controversy 爭議 (C) failure 失敗 (D) objection 反對

解析:空格前面是 there is much,應該要填入一適當名詞作為主詞補語,文中提到專家不同意這種說法,也就是這種說法有爭議,所以空格應選 (B)。

44. A;(A) clear 清楚的 (B) dubious 半信半疑的;可疑的 (C) impossible 不可能的 (D) relevant 有關的

解析:It is…that表示這件事情是如何…,由空格後面一句Sometimes people laugh at what they see; sometimes they laugh at what they hear,知人們笑的東西不一樣,所以空格應選 (A),也就是說:不會所有人都笑相同的事情這件事是很清楚的。

45. A;(A) depends on 取決於 (B) keeps on 繼續 (C) looks on 觀望 (D) stays on 保留

解析:本處考片語,依句意應選 (A),也就是說:幽默通常取決於對某些言語的認知。

46.－50. 中譯

希臘人創立以地球為中心的宇宙論會如此吸引人的原因是很容易理解的。夜復一夜,我們看到星體由東向西移動跨過天空，而認為地球是靜止在宇宙的中心，太陽、月亮、行星及其他星體都繞地球轉的假設是不是應該很正常呢？西元前四世紀時，柏拉圖提出一個世界說，他以不動的地球做為世界的中心，以及一個帶有很多行星及其他星體的巨大外太空每日運行。但它雙球構造並無法解釋某些行星的特殊的運行。通常，行星與星體每晚一起從東向西跨過天空，但有時候，有些行星似乎莫名其妙地倒退移動，今天我們知道這樣倒退移動是一種幻覺，而它的原因在於我們是在一個本身就在移動的行星上面觀察行星的移動。歐多斯克是個與柏拉圖同時代的年輕人，他也不認為地球會移動，但他嘗試調合天體逆行及地心學說（以地球為中心），將源自於柏拉圖的雙球學說發展成為二十七球，每球都代表一個已知的行星，每個球都被連接到其他的球，而這些球的旋轉再配合其他行星的旋轉，就可解釋某些星體逆行的現象。

46. A；中譯：依據希臘的宇宙論，下列何者不會移動：(A) 地球 (B) 月亮 (C) 火星 (D) 太陽。

解析：由 Night after night, we see celestial objects moving across the sky … assume that the Earth lies motionless at the center of the universe…可知當時人們認為地球是靜止的，其他星體繞地球轉，所以答案為 (A) 地球。

47. D；中譯：依據句本文，柏拉圖的世界系統看起來像甚麼？(A) 河流 (B) 湯匙 (C) 帳篷 (D) 車輪。

解析：由 Plato postulated a world system with the stationary Earth as its hub and a huge outer space that carried the planets…可知他把地球當成輪子的中心不動，其他星球像巨大的外圓，所以答案為 (D) 車輪。

48. A；中譯：一些行星的哪種運動不能被柏拉圖的系統所解釋？(A) 後退 (B) 前進 (C) 向上 (D) 向下。

解析：由 But his two-sphere configuration could not account for a particular motion of certain planets. …, some planets seemed to drift backwards…可知依柏拉圖的模型，所有星體都是由西向東走，但實際上有些行星似乎是倒退走的，而所以答案為 (A)。

49. C；中譯：為何所有行星似乎不是在相同方向運行？(A) 太陽沒有移動 (B) 行星從側邊移動 (C) 地球是在移動 (D) 行星向後移動。

解析：由 … retrograde motion is an illusion caused by the fact that we observe planetary motion from a planet that is itself in motion…，可知倒退移動是一種幻覺，而它的原因在於我們是在一個本身就在移動的行星上面觀察行星的移動，而所以答案為(C)。

50. B；中譯：下列哪一項關於歐多斯克的敘述是正確的？(A) 他比柏拉圖晚二個世紀出生 (B) 他相信地球是靜止不動的 (C) 他提出行星的倒退是一種幻覺(D) 他的宇宙構造在尺寸上比柏拉圖的小。

解析：(A) 由…Eudoxus, a young contemporary of Plato's,…可知他和柏拉圖是同時期的人，contemporary 同時代的人，本項敘述為非(B)由It never entered the mind of Eudoxus…that the Earth could actually move…可知他也不認為地球會移動，也就是認為地球是靜止的，本項敘述為真 (C) 文中提到 Today we know that retrograde motion is an illusion caused by…，那是後來的人才知道倒退移動是一種幻覺，不是Eudoxus 提出的，所以本項敘述為非 (D) 文中只提到他將源自於柏拉圖的雙球學說發展成二十七球，每球都代表一個已知的行星，但沒提到尺寸問題，且常理判斷應該會大於柏拉圖的模型構造，所以本項敘述為非。答案為 (B)。

101年特種考試交通事業鐵路人員考試試題

等別：員級鐵路人員考試
類科：各類科
科目：法學知識與英文（此節錄英文部分）

請回答第31題至第35題：

　　Are you into skiing? Is winter your favorite time of year? If you like snow and ice, maybe you should stay at the Ice Hotel in Quebec, Canada. But, you can only check in at this hotel during the winter. Why? Because this hotel is only made of ice and snow! This amazing hotel is built every December. It has 32 rooms and 80 people can stay there each night. The hotel even has a movie theater, art gallery, and church. Of course, all of these parts of the hotel are made of ice. In fact, all the furniture, art, lights, and even plates and drinking glasses are made out of ice.

　　Because this hotel is so unusual, it is becoming very popular. People from all over the world come to the Ice Hotel to look at the fantastic ice art, drink and eat from designer ice dishes, and experience the unique atmosphere. Some couples have even gotten married in the hotel's ice church. But all these guests keep their winter coats on! Because of all the ice, the temperature inside the hotel is always between -2℃and -5℃. Surprisingly, sleeping is not a problem in the freezing cold hotel rooms. Every guest gets a special cold-weather sleeping bag and some fur blankets. These keep them cozy and warm until morning.

(　) 31. What is this passage mainly about?

(A) What makes the Ice Hotel so special.

(B) How you keep warm in a cold place.

(C) Why the Ice Hotel is located in Quebec.

(D) How hard it is to build the hotel.

(　) 32. According to the passage, what kind of people are likely to pay a visit to the Ice Hotel?

(A) People who like swimming.

(B) People whose favorite season is winter.

(C) People who enjoy the tropical climate.

(D) People who appreciate wooden carving.

(　) 33. Many activities are provided in the Ice Hotel. Which of the following is NOT included?

(A) Designing coats.　　　　　　(B) Watching a movie.

(C) Getting married.　　　　　　(D) Having interesting meals.

(　) 34. Which of the following is true?

(A) All parts of the hotel, except beds, are made of ice.

(B) The hotel uses some special heater to keep guests warm in the room.

(C) Only a small number of tourists are attracted to the Ice Hotel.

(D) One of the features of the hotel is that it exists in winter only.

(　) 35. This passage is probably extracted from a(n)

(A) editorial in the newspapers　　(B) science fiction

(C) magazine on traveling　　　　(D) cook book

(　) 36. Carrie: I've got a job interview tomorrow.

Karen: Are you ready?

Carrie: Yes. Although I get nervous easily, _____ .

Karen: Good luck to you.

(A) I'll try it on　　　　　　　　(B) I'll take a look at it

(C) I'll make it up (D) I'll give it my best shot

( ) 37. Mary: I want to go shopping this weekend. Want to join me?

Jane: Well, _____ .

Mary: On what?

Jane: If you want to shop in a department store, then I'll go with you.

(A) it depends (B) no problem

(C) that sounds great (D) I have no idea

( ) 38. Daniel: Kevin, do you have the time?

Kevin: _____

Daniel: That's OK. Thanks anyway.

(A) Sorry, I forgot to wear my watch today.

(B) Sure, what can I do for you?

(C) Yes, it's a quarter to ten.

(D) Sorry, but my watch gains five minutes a day.

請回答第39題至第40題：

A: Did you enjoy the conference last week?

B: _____39_____

A: You don't seem very sure.

B: Generally it went well, _____40_____ .

( ) 39. (A) Very much. (B) Not at all. (C) Sort of. (D) No more.

( ) 40. (A) if it was held in the morning (B) so it was slightly to my surprise

(C) and it was very interesting (D) but it was a bit too long

請回答第41題至第44題：

Thanks to the Internet, a quiet revolution of e-commerce is taking place. More and more people are using their computers as shopping carts. Slowly but surely, shoppers are leaving real stores and going instead to _____41_____ ones.

Let's take going to the movies for example. Have you ever rushed to a theater _____42_____ find the tickets were sold out? I bet you have. Now you can solve this problem by ordering your tickets online. _____43_____ , there are trade-offs in everything. Not being able to talk with clerks in person is a big _____44_____ for e-commerce. At the online grocery store, you won't see the friendly neighborhood manager who knows you prefer ham to turkey, and you won't see any familiar faces smiling to you, either. Is it worthwhile to shop online? It's all up to you.

( ) 41. (A) fake   (B) convenient   (C) virtual   (D) legal

( ) 42. (A) so as to   (B) only to   (C) about to   (D) in order to

( ) 43. (A) Therefore   (B) What's more   (C) Otherwise   (D) However

( ) 44. (A) limitation   (B) advantage   (C) virus   (D) dilemma

( ) 45. Many Internet users like to _____ interesting messages to their friends because it can be done with just a click.

    (A) confirm   (B) forward   (C) reward   (D) reflect

( ) 46. Lina learned everything about the Grand Palace from an _____ tour guide.

    (A) optional   (B) informative   (C) adequate   (D) elastic

( ) 47. The police did not believe the suspect because his story was not _____ .

    (A) competitive   (B) complex   (C) consistent   (D) continuous

( ) 48. He used credit cards whenever he went shopping and _____ got into serious debt.

    (A) personally   (B) previously   (C) consequently   (D) sequentially

( ) 49. German measles is a highly _____ disease. In order to stop the spread, students who get this disease are asked to stay at home.

    (A) provocative   (B) universal   (C) infectious   (D) poisonous

( ) 50. Steve loves watching TV. Without TV, he may be bored to death. In fact, he is hopelessly _____ to TV.

    (A) addicted   (B) contributed   (C) obsessed   (D) attributed

101 年特種考試交通事業鐵路人員──員級中譯解析

31.－35. 中譯：

你對滑雪有興趣嗎？冬天是你一年中最喜歡的季節嗎？如果你喜歡雪和冰的話，你可能該到加拿大魁北克的冰屋旅館暫住，但是你只能在冬天入住，為什麼？因為這家飯店是由冰雪建造的！這家令人嘆為觀止的飯店每年十二月建造，飯店有32 個房間，且每晚只能有80人住在裡面。飯店甚至設有電影院、藝廊以及教堂，當然，所有這些部分也是用冰雪建造的。事實上，全部傢俱、藝品、燈、甚至盤子及飲料杯也是冰做成的。

正因為這家飯店如此與眾不同，它也變成非常熱門。世界各地的人們到冰屋旅館來欣賞奇幻的冰塊藝術，享用冰盤設計美食，並且體驗這獨特的氣氛。有些佳偶甚至在飯店的冰塊教堂中舉辦婚禮。但這些賓客們都要把冬天的大衣穿上！由於全都是冰，飯店內部溫度總是介於 -2℃到 -5℃之間。令人驚訝的是，在這樣冰凍寒冷的房間中睡覺不成問題，每位房客都有一個特殊的防寒睡袋以及一些羽毛毯，這些物品可以讓他們溫暖且舒適的一覺到天亮。

31. A；中譯：本篇主要是有關於 (A) 甚麼讓冰塊旅館如此特殊(B)在冰冷的地方你如何保持溫暖 (C) 為何冰塊旅館位魁北克 (D) 建造這旅館有多辛苦。

解析：本文談到這家飯店全是由冰雪建造的，包括用品及餐具等，人們到旅館來欣賞奇幻的冰塊藝術，享用冰盤設計美食，並且體驗這獨特的氣氛，都是講冰屋旅館的特殊之處，所以答案為 (A)。

32. B；中譯：依據本文，甚麼樣的人可能造訪冰屋旅館 (A) 喜歡游泳的人 (B) 最喜歡的季節是冬季的人 (C) 喜歡熱帶氣候的人 (D) 喜歡木雕作品的人。

解析：由If you like snow and ice, maybe you should stay at the Ice Hotel…，可知喜歡冬天冰雪的人會喜歡這家飯店，所以答案為 (B)。

33. A；中譯：冰塊旅館提供許多活動，下列何者不包括？(A) 設計外套 (B) 看電影 (C) 結婚 (D) 享用有趣的餐點。

解析：由文中之旅館有電影院可看電影，有提到新人辦結婚，沒提到設計外套，所以答案為 (A)。

34. D；中譯：下列敘述何者為真？(A) 除了床以外，旅館所有部分都是冰做的 (B) 旅館使用特殊加熱器讓賓客在房內保持溫暖 (C) 只有一小部分觀光客被吸引到冰屋飯店 (D) 旅館的其中一項特色是它只在冬天存在。

解析：(A) 旅館所有部分都是冰做的，床也不例外，敘述為非 (B) 賓客在房內防寒睡袋以及羽毛毯保持溫暖，敘述為非 (C) 冰屋旅館只能容納有限人數，並非只有少數觀光客被吸引，敘述為非 (D) 旅館的其中一項特色是它只在冬天存在，敘述為真，所以答案為 (D)。

35. C；中譯：這篇文章可能從何處摘錄 (A) 報紙的社論 (B) 科幻小說 (C) 旅遊雜誌 (D) 烹飪書籍

解析：由文中講旅館的特色、設施及各項活動的介紹均與旅遊有密切關係，所以可能由旅遊雜誌而來，答案為 (C)。

36. D；中譯：卡麗：我明天要參加一個工作面談。

克倫：你準備好了嗎？

卡麗：是的，雖然我有點緊張，(A) 我會試穿 (B) 我會看一看 (C) 我會彌補 (D) 我會盡力的。

克倫：祝你幸運！

解析：本題考一些日常會話用語，答案為 (D) 最符合，表示它雖然會緊張，但將會努力完成面試。

37. A；中譯：瑪麗：我這周末要去買東西，要跟我去嗎？

珍：嗯，(A) 那得看情形 (B) 沒問題 (C) 聽起來不錯 (D) 我不知道。

瑪麗：什麼情形?

珍：如果你要去百貨公司購物，我就跟你去。

解析：由瑪麗說 on what，此處 on 其實是前一句珍所講的話的省略字，也就是珍講說it depends(on)，在平常的談話，往往會省掉前面的 on 字，所以答案為 (A)。

38. A；中譯：丹尼爾：凱文，現在幾點了？

凱文：(A) 抱歉，我今天忘了帶錶 (B) 沒問題，我可以幫你甚麼？(C) 是的，現在是 9 點 45 分 (D) 抱歉，但我的錶每天快五分鐘。

丹尼爾：那沒關係！不論如何謝謝你。

解析：Thanks anyway 用於請別人幫忙，可是別人沒辦法幫的情況，凱文表示也無法知道現在時間，所以凱文說他也忘了帶錶是最合理，答案為 (A)。

39.40. C,D；中譯：A：你喜歡上週的研討會嗎？

B：(A) 非常 (B) 一點也不 (C) 有點 (D) 不再有。

A：你看起來沒有很確定。

B：一般來說它進行順利，(A) 假如它是早上舉行 (B) 所以它讓我有點驚訝 (C) 而且它非常有趣 (D) 但它太冗長了。

解析：首先 A 問 B 對研討會的想法，B 回答完後，A 認為 B 沒有很確定他喜不喜歡這場會議，表示 B 的回答可能是模擬兩可，由選項中 (A) 及 (B) 都非常確定，(D) 沒意義，(C) 表示有點喜歡符合前後句意，所以 39 題答案為 (C)。再由 B 認為研討會一般說來還順利，後面表示應該還有美中不足之處，(A) 講到會議時間在早上會更好雖然算是一項理由，但與會議進行較沒關係，(B) 及 (C) 不符前後意思，(D) 說會議太冗長符合前後關係及邏輯，故 40 題答案為 (D)。

41－44 中譯：

托網際網路的福，一種相當革命性的電子商務正在發展。愈來愈多人正把電腦當購物車使用，雖然緩慢但可確定的是，購物者將離開實體店面而進入虛擬商店。

我們舉一個進戲院看電影為例，你曾有過衝進一家戲院才發現票已經賣完的經驗嗎？我想一定有。現在，你可以透過網路購票就可以解決這個問題。然而，每件事都有得有失，無法當面跟店員交談對電子商務來說是一大限制，在網路商城裏，你將不會看到和善的鄰家經理，他知道你喜歡火腿而不喜歡火雞，也看不到任何熟悉且對你微笑的人。那還值得在網上消費嗎？一切看你了。

41. C；(A) fake 假的 (B) convenient 便利的 (C) virtual 虛擬的 (D) legal 合法的

解析：空格內要填入形容詞，形容後面何種類型的商店，從文中得知購物者正離開實體店面而進入網路經營的商店，所以空格處用 virtual（虛擬的），表示虛擬的商店最恰當，故答案為 (C)。

42. B；(A) so as to 為了 (B) only to 沒想到 (C) about to 正要 (D) in order to 為了要

解析：空格內要填入不定詞片語當受詞補語。本句說衝進一家戲院然後發現票已賣完，所以此處應該用 only to（沒想到）最符合句意，故答案為 (B)。

43. D；(A) Therefore 因此 (B) What's more 更有甚者 (C) Otherwise 否則 (D) However 然而

解析：空格內要填入副詞。前面說透過網路可以很方便購物，後面提到每件事都有得失，是一種轉折語氣，所以副詞應用However，故答案為 (D)。

44. A；(A) limitation 限制 (B) advantage好處 (C) virus 病毒 (D) dilemma 進退兩難

解析：空格內要填入名詞，相較於傳統商店可以面對面交談，電子商務無法當面跟店員交談對來說算是一大限制，故答案為 (A)。

45. B；中譯：許多網路使用者喜歡去轉寄有趣的訊息給他們的朋友，因為那只要點一下就能做得到。

解析：(A) confirm 確認 (B) forward 轉交 (C) reward 報答 (D) reflect 反射

本題考動詞。由題目前後文亦可推知空格要表達的是指將訊息轉寄之意，信件轉寄用 forward，所以答案為 (B)。

46. B；中譯：琳達從一本資料豐富的旅遊指引認識到有關大皇宮的每件事。

解析：(A) optional 選擇的 (B) informative 增進知識的 (C) adequate 足夠的 (D) elastic有彈性的

本題考形容詞。要形容一本詳盡講述關大皇宮的每件事的書，選項中(B) informative（增進知識的）最恰當，所以答案為 (B)。

47. C；中譯：警方不相信嫌犯因為他的說法不一致。

解析：(A) competitive 競爭的 (B) complex 複雜的 (C)consistent 一致的 (D) continuous 連續的

本題考形容詞。story 在這邊是指嫌犯的講法，而非他的故事，要表示警方會不相信嫌犯說法的原因，選項中以not consistent(不一致的)最合理，表示說法前後不一，所以答案為 (C)。

48. C；中譯：不管甚麼時候他消費時都用信用卡，而必然地陷入嚴重的債務危機。

解析：(A) personally 親自地 (B) previously 先前地 (C) consequently 必然地 (D) sequentially 繼續地

本題考副詞。消費使用信用卡而不節制，就會陷入卡債危機可能，所以選項中以consequently（必然地）最恰當，答案為 (C)。

49. C；中譯：德國麻疹是一種高度傳染性的疾病，為了防止散播，得到這種病的學生被要求待在家中。

解析：(A)provocative挑釁的(B)universal全體的；宇宙的(C)infectious傳染性的(D)poisonous有毒的

本題考形容詞。德國麻疹是一種傳染病，傳染病為infectious disease，所以答案為(C)。

50. A；中譯：史蒂芬喜歡看電視，沒有電視，他可能無聊到死。事實上，他對電視是無可救藥。

解析：(A) addicted 使沉溺 (B) contributed 貢獻 (C) obsessed 使迷住 (D) attributed 歸因於

本題考動詞用法，句中意思是他對電視入迷，應用 is addicted，也就是沉溺於電視，故答案為 (A)。

NOTE

101年特種考試交通事業鐵路人員考試試題

等別：佐級鐵路人員考試
類科：事務管理、材料管理、運輸營業
科目：公民與英文（此節錄英文部分）

( ) 36. Mr. Johnson is a successful manager. He can handle any situation _____.

    (A) movably   (B) puzzlingly   (C) skillfully   (D) trembly

( ) 37. When Bess couldn't locate her motorcycle for eight hours, she thought she had lost it for _____.

    (A) good   (B) best   (C) better   (D) well

( ) 38. Your article is good _____ the spelling.

    (A) in addition   (B) instead of   (C) in case of   (D) except for

( ) 39. The tree is 150 feet _____ .

    (A) high   (B) story   (C) polluted   (D) tall

( ) 40. Wiliam, you _____ for three hours already. It's time you go out with some friends to relax.

    (A) are studying   (B) studied

    (C) had studied   (D) have been studying

( ) 41. The knives are _____ the kitchen counter.

    (A) at   (B) in   (C) on   (D) across

( ) 42. The train went _____ through the mountains than on the plains.

    (A) slow down   (B) slow   (C) more slowly   (D) slowing

( ) 43. Michelle _____ to make a birthday cake and write a song for Charles, but she ran out of time.

    (A) intends   (B) has intended   (C) is intending   (D) had intended

請回答第44題至第48題：

　　Headphones seem to be getting smaller and smaller. But are the ones that sit inside you ears ____44____ for you than traditional ones that sit over you ears?

　　They can be, ____45____ your music is too loud. Earphones pushed into the ear are going to deliver a greater sound pressure level compared ____46____ normal ones. And this could increase the risk of damage.

　　If you hear ringing in your ears or things sound muffled ____47____ listening, you've overdone it. Usually the problem subsides, but listening to loud music regularly, with any type of headset, could ____48____ permanent hearing loss. Recent research suggests limiting use to an hour or less per day at no more than 60% volume for over-the-ear styles－and even less for ear-buds. Never sleep with them on.

(　) 44. (A) bad　　　　(B) worse　　　(C) best　　　　(D) worst
(　) 45. (A) or　　　　　(B) as　　　　　(C) if　　　　　(D) so
(　) 46. (A) with　　　　(B) at　　　　　(C) by　　　　　(D) for
(　) 47. (A) at　　　　　(B) since　　　　(C) without　　　(D) after
(　) 48. (A) fall in　　　(B) start over　　(C) lead to　　　(D) come up
(　) 49. Luke: Do you mind if I smoke?

　　　　　Lucy: _____ You can't smoke in the building. You have to go outside.

　　　　　Luke: Oh, OK.

　　　　　(A) It's OK.　　(B) Go ahead.　　(C) I'm sorry.　　(D) Not at all.

(　) 50. Candy: Have you been to that restaurant before?

　　　　　Alicia: _____

　　　　　Candy: Enjoy your dinner.

　　　　　(A) Yes. I will call and find out.　　(B) Yes. That's a good idea.

　　　　　(C) No. Not at all.　　　　　　　(D) No. I'm going for the first time

254 鐵路特考英文高分特快車
Railway Special Examination

101 年特種考試交通事業鐵路人員——佐級（專務管理等）中譯解析

36. C；中譯：強生先生是一位成功的經理人，他可以熟練地處理任何事情。

　　解析：(A) movably 可動 (B) puzzlingly費解地 (C) skillfully 熟練地 (D) trembly 顫抖的
本題考副詞（修飾動詞）。選項中 (D) trembly 為形容詞外，其餘均為副詞。由前句提到他是成功的
經理人，所以處理事情應該是很幹練的，所以副詞用skillfully最恰當，故答案為 (C)。

37. A；中譯：當貝絲經過八小時仍找不到她的摩托車，她想她已經永遠遺失它了。

　　解析：本題考副詞片語，修飾動詞 lost，其中 for good 永遠；for best 最好；for better 變好；for well
無此用法，所以選項中用 for good 最恰當，故答案為 (A)。

38. D；中譯：你的文章是良好的，除了拼字外。

　　解析：(A) in addition 除此之外 (B) instead of 而不是 (C) in case of 如果 (D) except for 除了…以外
本題考介係詞片語。由題意知用 exceptfor（除了…以外）最恰當，表示除拼字問題之外文章內容都
是好的，故答案為 (D)。注意：in addition（除此之外）與 except for（除了…以外）二者是完全相反
的意思，應分辨清楚使用時機。

39. D／A；中譯：這棵樹有 150 英呎高。

　　解析：本題考物體高度的用法，表示人、動物或樹木的主要用 tall，此題放寬用法 (A) high 與 (D) tall
皆可以。

40. D；中譯：威廉，你已持續念書三個小時了，你是該與朋友出去放鬆一下了。

　　解析：本題考動詞時態用法，It's time(that) 現在該是…的時候了。要表示從過去到現在一段持續的時
間（持續念書三個小時），動詞時態可用現在完成式或現在完成進行式，選項中(D)為現在完成進行
式，故答案為(D)。

41. C；中譯：刀子放在廚房的檯子上。

　　解析：本題考介系詞用法，kitchen counter 是廚房的檯子（流理臺）。東西放在某個物品（如桌子）
的平面上，介係詞用 on，如 The cup is on the table.，故答案為 (C)。

42. C；中譯：火車經過山區時比在平地時速度慢下來。

　　解析：此題考副詞的比較級。

43. D；中譯：米歇爾想要作一個生日蛋糕及寫一首歌給查爾斯，但她沒時間了。

　　解析：本題考動詞時態。由…but she ran out of time.（她時間用完了，也就是沒時間了）知發生時間
為過去，且現在已經結束了，所以動詞可用過去式或過去完成式，選項中 (D) 為過去完成式，故答案
為 (D)。

44－48 中譯：

　　耳機似乎愈來愈小，但是在你耳朵裡面的那種比起傳統那種在你耳朵上的對你來說比較不好嗎？

　　也許是，因為你的音樂太大聲了。比較起正常耳機而言，塞入耳內的耳機將會傳送較大程度的聲
壓，而這可能增加造成傷害的風險。

　　如果你在耳內聽到嗡嗡聲，或常聽到像是被蓋住的聲音，你已經過度使用它了。通常這個問題會

消退，但太常聽大聲的音樂，就算是用任何形式耳機，都可能導致永久聽力喪失。最近研究建議限制每日使用一小時或更少時間，耳掛式以不超過60%的音量－甚至耳內式要更低。不要戴著耳機睡覺。

44. B；解析：空格內要填入形容詞的比較級或最高級，本句提到耳內式與傳統耳掛式的比較，如果用最高級，形容詞前必須加 the，但在選項及題目中均沒出現，故只能用比較級，worse 是 bed 的比較級，故答案為 (B)。

45. C；解析：選 (B) if 如果最貼切文意。

46. A；解析：空格內要用配合動詞 (compare) 的介系詞，compare with 與…相較之下，故答案為 (A)。

47. D；解析：用耳機聽音樂之後的後遺症。故選 (D)。

48. C；解析：(A) fall in 陷入 (B) start over 從新開始 (C) lead to 導致於 (D) come up 出現
空格內填入適當動詞片語。句中提到聽太大聲的音樂與暫時性聽力喪失的情形，選項中以 lead to（導致於）最適合，表示聽太大聲的音樂會導致暫時性聽力喪失，故答案為 (C)。

49. C；中譯：盧克：你介意我抽菸嗎？
露西：(A) 那沒問題 (B) 請繼續 (C) 很抱歉 (D) 一點也不，你不能在這裏，你要到外面去。
盧克：噢！沒問題。
解析：露西明白表示他不能在這邊抽菸，先用 I'm sorry 表示禮貌性的回絕最適宜，所以答案為 (C)。

50. D；中譯：肯蒂：你以前去過那家餐廳嗎？
麗莉西雅：(A) 是的，我將打電話並找出來(B)是的，它是一家好餐廳 (C) 不，一點也不 (D) 不，我將第一次去。
肯蒂：祝你晚餐用餐愉快。
解析：肯蒂問麗莉西雅是否去過那餐廳，後來祝他用餐愉快，表示麗莉西雅有說他沒去過，所以答案為 (D)。

101年特種考試交通事業鐵路人員考試試題

等別：佐級鐵路人員考試
類科：車輛調度、土木工程、機械工程、機檢工程、電力工程、電子工程、養路工程
科目：公民與英文（此節錄英文部分）

( ) 36. The river is _____ , so it is not clean.

(A) flowing   (B) destroyed   (C) polluted   (D) lying

( ) 37. He always faces all kinds of difficulties in a highly _____ way. He will never run away from them.

(A) pessimistic   (B) materialistic   (C) experimental   (D) optimistic

( ) 38. What Mr. Jones said is _____ ; he doesn't tell lies.

(A) crazy   (B) real   (C) true   (D) story

( ) 39. Most Americans will _____ their homes for Christmas.

(A) deny   (B) contain   (C) decorate   (D) complain

( ) 40. Today I am _____ than I was yesterday.

(A) happy   (B) happier   (C) more happy   (D) more happier

( ) 41. These are _____ hats.

(A) women   (B) women's   (C) woman   (D) womans

( ) 42. What kind of food _____ their company produce?

(A) is   (B) does   (C) have   (D) has

( ) 43. The construction company must pay to have archeologists _____ the historical sites.

(A) study   (B) studied   (C) studying   (D) to study

請回答第44題至第48題：

One of the easiest ways to help your health is just to sleep eight hours or more every night. ＿＿＿44＿＿＿ , more and more people in the world are not sleeping enough. According to the World Health Organization, over half the people in the world may be sleep-deprived. The result of this is not just a lot of tired people; in the United States alone, sleepy drivers ＿＿＿45＿＿＿ at least 100,000 car crashes and 1500 deaths a year.

According to experts, sleep is like ＿＿＿46＿＿＿ If you sleep only five hours a day, you don't "get used to it," but instead, build up a "sleep deficit." "It's like a credit card," says Dr. Mass. "You are only ＿＿＿47＿＿＿ time. You always have to pay it back." The more hours you don't sleep, ＿＿＿48＿＿＿ you should sleep to "pay back" the hours on your "sleep credit card."

( ) 44. (A) Moreover   (B) However   (C) Therefore   (D) Because

( ) 45. (A) cause   (B) result   (C) make   (D) lead

( ) 46. (A) time   (B) trick   (C) money   (D) medicine

( ) 47. (A) lending   (B) using   (C) collecting   (D) borrowing

( ) 48. (A) the more hours   (B) the better

      (C) all the more   (D) the better hours

( ) 49. Waiter: May I take your order now, sir?

      Steven: Yes, ＿＿＿＿＿＿ .

      (A) let's go Dutch   (B) keep the change

      (C) a soup and a steak   (D) the food tastes really good

( ) 50. Stacia: I'm getting married.

      Linda: ＿＿＿＿＿＿ .

      Stacia: Thank you! Neil and I would like to invite you to our wedding.

      (A) What a crazy idea!   (B) Congratulations!

      (C) I'm sorry.   (D) Excuse me?

101 年特種考試交通事業鐵路人員——佐級（車輛調度等）中譯解析

36. C；**中譯**：這條河流被汙染了，所以它不乾淨。

解析：(A) flowing 流動 (B) destroyed 摧毀 (C) polluted 汙染 (D) lying 躺臥

本題考被動式。河流不乾淨是因為被汙染，所以用被動式，空格內用過去分詞，故答案為 (C)。

37. D；**中譯**：他總是用高度樂觀方式來面對各種困境，他從不逃避它們。

解析：(A) pessimistic 悲觀的 (B) materialistic 唯物主義的 (C) experimental 實驗的 (D) optimistic 樂觀的

本題考形容詞。run away 逃走，由句中意思是他對事情都樂觀看待且不逃避，所以應該是 in a highly optimistic way，也就用高度樂觀的方式，答案為 (D)。

38. C；**中譯**：瓊斯先生說的是真的，他沒有說謊。

解析：(A) crazy 瘋狂的 (B) real 實際的 (C) true 真實的 (D) story 故事

本題考主詞補語用法，be 動詞的主詞補語可使用形容詞或名詞，四個選項中，(A) (B) (C) 均為形容詞，(D) story 為名詞。由句中後面提到他沒說謊，表示他所說的是真實的，(D) story 不能選，因為與前後句意不和，所以答案為 (C)。注意：real 與 true 意義很像，但 real 主要指物體的特性的真實，如 real man，而 true 主要指事情的真實性。

39. C；**中譯**：大部分美國人為耶誕節而裝飾他們的房子。

解析：(A) deny 拒絕 (B) contain 包含 (C) decorate 裝飾 (D) complain 抱怨

本題考動詞。西方人耶誕節時要佈置它們房子，選項中以 decorate（裝飾）最符合，所以答案為 (C)。

40. B；**中譯**：今天的我比昨天的我更快樂。

解析：本題考比較句中的形容詞比較級。happy（快樂的）比較級為 happier，所以答案為 (B)。

41. B；**中譯**：這些都是女人的帽子。

解析：本題考所有格用法。空格內需用所有格來表示這些帽子的擁有者，woman（單數為 woman）的所有格為 women's，所以答案為 (B)。

42. B；**中譯**：他們公司生產哪類的食品？

解析：本題考疑問句用法。句中主詞為 food（單數名詞），動詞 produce（生產）為原形，所以空格內需用助動詞用 does，所以答案為 (B)。

43. A；**中譯**：這家建設公司必須付錢請考古學家研究這歷史遺跡。

解析：本題考使役動詞。句中動詞為 pay（付錢），pay to have…表示付錢做某事，其中 have 為使役動詞，所以後面接的動詞需用原型，故答案為 (A)。注意：使役動詞：have, make, let

44－48 **中譯**：

促進健康其中一種最簡單的方式就是只要每晚睡超過八個鐘頭或以上，然而，世上愈來愈多人沒有足夠睡眠。依據世界衛生組織統計，世界上超過一半的人可能睡眠不足，這個後果不只是許多疲倦的人，單是在美國，每年因開車打瞌睡造成 100,000 件車禍以及 1500 人喪生。

專家表示，睡眠就像金錢，假如你一天只睡五小時，你不會「習慣它」，相反的，會形成「睡眠赤字」。「那就像一張信用卡」，瑪斯博士說道：「你只是在借時間，你總有一天要還回去」。你不睡覺的時數愈多，你要從你的「睡眠信用卡」中「還回」睡覺的時數就愈多。

44. B；(A) Moreover 況且 (B) However 然而 (C) Therefore 因此 (D) Because 因為

解析：空格內要填入副詞，選項中前三者均可用做副詞，(D) Because 只能當連接詞用。前句提到睡眠很重要，後面說很多人睡眠不足，所以二句之間是轉折語氣，副詞用 however 最恰當，故答案為 (B)。

45. A；(A) cause 引起 (B) result 導致 (C) make 製造 (D) lead 引導

解析：空格內要填入動詞，本句敘述每年因開車打瞌睡造成的車禍以及傷亡，引起車禍動詞要用 cause，故答案為 (A)。

46. C；(A) time 時間 (B) trick 詭計 (C) money 金錢 (D) medicine 醫藥

解析：空格內要填入名詞作為主詞sleep的補語，說明睡覺就像甚麼東西。由後面的敘述談到睡眠與信用卡及赤字等與金錢有關用語，判斷應是用金錢來比喻睡眠，故答案為 (C)。

47. D；(A) lending 借出 (B) using 使用 (C) collecting 收集 (D) borrowing 借入

解析：選項中均為動詞現在分詞，本句為現在進行式。因為睡眠就像金錢，本句後半段說你總是要還回去，推斷前面是說借入（時間），所以動詞用 borrowing，故答案為 (D)。

48. A；解析：本句為 the more…, the more…的比較句型。所以前句用 The more hours…，後句用the more hours…即可，故答案為 (A)。

49. C；中譯：服務生：先生，您要點餐了嗎？

史帝芬：是的，(A)我們各付各的 (B) 不用找零錢 (C) 一碗湯跟一份牛排 (D) 食物嚐起來相當美味。

解析：顧客說是的表示要點餐了，所以回答內容一定是與點餐有關，選項中以 (C) 最符合。

50. B；中譯：史塔夏：我要結婚了

琳達：(A) 這是多麼瘋狂的點子！(B) 恭喜你！(C) 很抱歉！(D) 請問？

史塔夏：謝謝你！尼爾跟我想邀請你參加我們的婚禮。

解析：聽到別人像你說他要結婚了，應該是馬上恭喜他，所以答案為 (B)。

📋 102 年特種考試交通事業鐵路人員考試試題

等別：三等一般警察人員考試、高員三級鐵路人員考試
類科：各類別、各類科
科目：法學知識與英文（此節錄英文部分）

( ) 31. To _____ foreign cultures into language curriculum, teachers would introduce particular activities of festivals or celebrations to their students.
(A) concede   (B) devote   (C) infuse   (D) transplant

( ) 32. The authorities concerned investigate banks and brokers _____ of discriminating against minority applicants whoneed loans to buy houses.
(A) comprised   (B) deprived   (C) reminded   (D) suspected

( ) 33. Starting January 1, 2012, one of the _____ Taipei City Government uses to encourage childbirth is to offerfamilies a one-time payment of NT$20,000 per child.
(A) formulas   (B) guidelines   (C) measures   (D) provisions

( ) 34. Screening does not reduce cancer-related mortality. In fact, it may increase mortality by increasing the number of _____ medical procedures carried out.
(A) interventional   (B) invasive   (C) panicked   (D) panoramic

(　) 35. The ambassador's offensive remarks have _____ widespread criticism and storms of protests in the country.

(A) corrupted　　(B) deflated　　(C) languished　　(D) provoked

(　) 36. The presidential candidate avoided talking much about _____ issues related to national health insurance and tax increase.

(A) concomitant　(B) hedonistic　　(C) provocative　　(D) subliminal

(　) 37. Tourism is a dynamic and competitive industry that requires the ability to constantly _____ to customers'changing needs and desires.

(A) adapt　　　　(B) addict　　　(C) apply　　　　(D) attach

(　) 38. Melissa is very into politics. In fact, she has had _____ to become the first female prime minister of the countrysince she was a little girl.

(A) alienation　　(B) annihilation　(C) aspirations　　(D) assumptions

請回答第39題至第42題：

Evaluating job applicants on the basis of embedded life interests is a useful macro approach to matching job candidates with jobs they excel at. People with a life interest in the application of technology ____39____ howthings work and are curious about finding better ways to use technology to solve business problems. People with ____40____ analysis background excel at running the numbers and see it as the best way to figure out business solutions. Theory and concept people enjoy thinking and talking about abstract ideas. People with a life interest in creative production are imaginative thinkers, comfortable and engaged during brainstorming sessions. Many of them have an interest in the arts and ____41____ creative industries such as entertainment. Individuals with a life interest in coaching and mentoring like to teach. Many like feeling useful to others; some genuinely take satisfaction from the success of those they counsel. Individuals with a life interest in enterprise control like to be in charge. They are happiest when they have authority over their little piece of universe in decision-making. They ask for as much responsibility as possible in any work situation. Because many people have more than one interest, these classifications of life interests may ____42____ in an individual. So do not try to pigeonhole individuals too narrowly.

( ) 39. (A) are afflicted with   (B) are intrigued by

       (C) are fed up with   (D) are ignorant of

( ) 40. (A) subjective   (B) superlative   (C) qualitative   (D) quantitative

( ) 41. (A) gravitate toward   (B) refrain from

       (C) discriminate against   (D) conflict with

( ) 42. (A) disintegrate   (B) overlap   (C) submerge   (D) vanish

( ) 43. The US is not a homogeneous country, and each state has a different appetite for different things, which poses a challenge for other countries that wish to target the US market.

(A) The US is particularly challenging for foreign businesses that are unaware of the homogeneous taste of the US market.

(B) Countries that prefer regional differences will have greater success in the US market because it is not a homogeneous country.

(C) The US market shows that foreign businesses that are not familiar with regional preferences can be successful in a homogeneous counrty.

(D) Other countries that are not familiar with US regional preferences find it challenging to target the US market due to its non-homogeneous nature.

( ) 44. Jonny is _____ for being lazy and late to work. He always postpones his work, slowing down the team's work.

(A) formidable　　(B) notorious　　(C) remarkable　　(D) ambitious

( ) 45. The paper presents the hypothesis that human emotion originates biochemically without scanting the likelihood that cultural influences are almost equally important.

(A) In the paper, it is contended that human emotion is created by biochemical processes of the human body rather than by cultural factors.

(B) The paper asserts that human emotion is the result of biochemical processes which are in turn shaped by cultural influences.

(C) The paper hypothesizes that there is a biochemical foundation for human emotion, while admitting that cultural influences cannot be neglected.

(D) It is hypothesized in the paper that human emotion has a biochemical origin and is exempted from cultural influences.

請回答第46題至第50題：

The Saisiyat people—one of Taiwan's officially recognized aboriginal groups—have a unique ritual ceremony called Pas-ta'al. That ceremony is said to have been carried out for as many as 400 years. Today, it takes place every two years. And every ten years, it is larger and takes on added significance. The most recent ten-year ceremony was held in 2006 at two complementary and overlapping sites in northern Taiwan during the full moon of the 10th lunar month.

Thousands gathered for the first day of the ceremony in Wufeng, Hsinchu County. Tourists from all over the island joined the local villagers in the elaborate ceremony in an open field. Men and women were dancing and singing, arms crossed, hand-in-hand, and moving in and out of a huge circle. Native Saisiyat people all wore bright red and white traditional costumes with intricate weaving and beading. Some had ornate decorations at the back, from which hung mirrors, beads, and bells that rang and clanged as the dancers moved. Tourists were welcome but were asked to stay away from particular areas where secret rituals were performed by village elders. They were also advised to tie Japanese silver grass around their arms, cameras, and recorders.

(　　) 46. What is Pas-ta'al?

(A) It is an annual ritual ceremony of the Saisiyat people.

(B) It is a Saisiyat wedding ceremony in which people sing and dance.

(C) It is a Saisiyat ceremony in which Japanese silver grass is used as sacrifice.

(D) It is a Saisiyat ceremony that has a history as long as four hundred years.

(　　) 47. When or where is Pas-ta'al normally held?

(A) It is held in October every two years.

(B) It takes place in two major sites in northern Taiwan.

(C) It is held only when the Japanese silver grass is fully grown.

(D) It takes place only at Wufeng, Hsinchu County.

(　) 48. Which of the following statements is NOT true about the ceremony?

(A) Tourists are welcome, and they can join the elders in secret rituals.

(B) Local villagers wear traditional red and white costumes.

(C) Tourists and villagers dance in a big circle in an open field.

(D) Tourists are advised to tie Japanese silver grass around their arms and cameras.

(　) 49. According to the passage, which of the following statements is true?

(A) Pas-ta'al is a common ceremony among the officially-recognized aboringinal peoples in Taiwan.

(B) Pas-ta'al is a ceremony unique to the Saisiyat people.

(C) Japanese tourists are invited to the big ceremony every ten years.

(D) Pas-ta'al takes place in mid-October every year.

(　) 50. Which of the following statements can be inferred from the passage?

(A) Each of the officially-recognized aboriginal peoples has its own unique tribal ceremony.

(B) Japanese silver grass is worn by tourists to indicate their non-native identity.

(C) The Saisiyat people use beads, bells, and mirrors as decorations in their daily clothing.

(D) Pas-ta'al is only partially open to the public.

102 年特種考試交通事業鐵路人員——高員級中譯解析

31. C；中譯：為了注入外國文化到語言課程，老師們會介紹節慶或慶祝的特定活動給學生們。

解析：(A) concede 承認 (B) devote 致力於 (C) infuse 注入 (D) transplant 移植

此題考的是動詞 To＋動詞等於in order to為了要…之意，依題意為了要讓外國文化進到課程中，選項以 infuse（注入）最符合題意，答案為(C)。

32. D；中譯：有關當局關切調查銀行及中間人涉嫌歧視少數需要貸款買房的申請者。

解析：(A) comprised 包括 (B) deprived 剝奪 (C) reminded 提醒 (D) suspected 懷疑

此題考的是片語。discriminating against（歧視），The authorities concerned (that) banks and…，該名詞子句的主詞是 banks and brokers，空格中的動詞與後面接的介系詞 of 形成動詞片語，且為過去式。依題意應為：涉嫌歧視少數需要貸款買房的申請者，答案為 (D)。

33. C；中譯：從2012年1月1日開始，台北市政府用來鼓勵生育的其中一個方案就是提供每個小孩一次性的 20,000 元補助給其家庭。

解析：(A) formulas 公式 (B) guidelines 指導方針 (C) measures 方案 (D) provisions 條款

本題考的是名詞。空格後的 Taipei City Government uses to encourage childbirth為形容詞子句來修飾前面的名詞。用來鼓勵生育應為一種方案，選項以 measures（方案）最符合，故答案為 (C)。注意：(D) provisions（條款）主要用在表示法律的規定方面，不宜用在此處。

34. B；中譯：大規模的篩檢並不能減少癌症相關得致死率，事實上，它還可能因為侵入性的醫療程序造成致死率的增加。

解析：(A) interventional 介入的 (B) invasive 侵略性的 (C) panicked 恐慌的 (D) panoramic 全景的

本題考的是形容詞。Carried out 執行，此處以invasive medical procedures 侵入性的醫療程序，為最符合句中含意，所以答案為 (B)。

35. D；中譯：這位大使冒犯的言論已經在這個國家引起全面的批評及抗議浪潮。

解析：(A) corrupted 貪汙 (B) deflated 降低 (C) languished 減少 (D) provoked 引起

本題考的是完成式動詞。widespread（全面性的），冒犯的言論會造成全面的批評及抗議浪潮，選項 provoked（引起）最恰當，所以答案為 (D)。

36. C；中譯：這位總統候選人避免談論太多有關於國民健康保險及增稅等引起爭論的議題。

解析：(A) concomitant 附隨的 (B) hedonistic 享樂主義的 (C) provocative 引起爭論的 (D) subliminal 潛意識的

本題考的是形容詞。Avoid talking something about…避免談到有關…，所以此處提到有關國民健保及增稅等在選舉中都屬於敏感且具有爭議性的議題，本題空格內用 provocative 為最符合題意，所以答案為 (C)。

37. A；中譯：旅遊是一項動態且競爭的產業，它需要有不斷地適應顧客的需求及期望的能力。

解析：(A) adapt 使適應 (B) addict 使沉溺 (C) apply 運用於 (D) attach 使附屬

本題考的是動詞。the ability to+V 作（某方面）的能力，此處提到有顧客的需求及期望等方面，空格內用 adapt，即不斷地適應顧客的需求等為最符合題意，所以答案為 (A)。

38. C；中譯：蒙莉莎非常投入政治，事實上，從她小時候起，她就以已經有成為這個國家首位女首相的願望。

解析：(A) alienation 疏遠 (B) annihilation 消滅 (C) aspirations 願望(D) assumptions 假設

本題考的是名詞。be very into 對（某方面）很有興趣，後面提到成為首位女首相等就是說明空格內的名詞，所以空格內用 aspirations（願望），表示這個是她從小的願望為最符合題意，所以答案為 (C)。

39.－42. 中譯：

以求職者與生俱來的生活興趣為基礎來評斷是一種很有用的方法，來依求職者的專長媒合他們的工作。一個在運用科技有興趣的人對事情如何運作會感到興趣，並會好奇如何用科技來解決商業問題。具數據分析背景的人對運用數字具有優勢，並且認為數字是找出解決事情的最好方式。理論及觀念派的人喜歡思考並談論一些抽象的觀念。具備以創造產品為樂趣的人是具想像力的思考者，尤其在需要腦力激盪的場合他們會非常投入並感到愉快。他們許多人都對藝術有興趣並被吸引投入創造性的產業，例如娛樂業。對輔導或指導有興趣的人喜歡教學，許多人喜歡讓人覺得自己是有用的，一些人對他們指導的人能成功就能得到滿足。對事業經營有興趣的人喜歡被賦予責任，當他們在管理一小群團體而能有決定權時是最快樂的事，在做任何工作時，他們盡可能要求更多的責任賦予。因為許多人擁有不只一個興趣，對每個人的這些生活興趣的分類可能會重疊，所以不要太狹隘的歸類每個人。

39. B；(A) are afflicted with 被…困擾(B)are intrigued by對…著迷(C) are fed up with 對…感到厭煩 (D) are ignorant 是無知的。

解析：依據上下文題意知選項 (B) 最合理，表示在對科技有興趣的人會對事情如何運作會感到著迷。

40. D；(A) subjective 主觀的 (B) superlative最高的 (C) qualitative 品質的 (D) quantitative 數量的

解析：with…background 具有…的背景，由後面…excel at running the numbers（運用數字具有優勢），知空格內應指對數據分析的背景，所以答案為 (D)。注意：qualitative 是指品質上的，quantitative 是指數量上的。

41. A；(A) gravitate toward 被吸引到 (B) refrain from 戒除 (C) discriminate against 歧視 (D) conflict with 與衝突

解析：空格前的 and 為對等連接詞，表示前面對藝術有興趣及後面創造性的產業有正面相關聯，所以選項 (A) 最為合理。

42. B；(A) disintegrate 使瓦解 (B) overlap 重疊 (C) submerge 淹沒 (D) vanish 消失

解析：前面提到人的興趣可能是雙重的，故分類時可能會有重複的現象，所以選項 (B) 最為合理。

43. D；中譯：美國不是一個同質性的國家，每一州對不同的事情各有不同的嗜好，這對有志於美國市場的國家造成一項挑戰 (A) 美國正挑戰那些沒有察覺到美國市場同質性口味的外國企業 (B) 那些喜歡區域性差異的國家在美國會成功，因為它不是個同質性的國家 (C) 美國市場顯示出那些不熟悉區域喜好的外國企業在一個同質性的國家是會成功的 (D) 不了解美國區域性喜好的其他國家發現要把美國市場當標的物是不容易的。

解析：題目主要表示美國各州都有不同的嗜好，要進軍美國市場的國家需瞭解這種差異性，否則將容易失敗，本題答案為 (D)。

44. B；中譯：強尼因懶惰及工作遲到而惡名昭彰，他總是拖延工作因此拖累他的工作團隊。

解析：(A) formidable 可怕的 (B) notorious 惡名的 (C) remarkable 卓越的 (D) ambitious 有野心的
本題考的是形容詞。本句後面提到他拖延他的工作因此拖累他的工作團隊等，表示他是一個表現不好的人，所以選項中以notorious（惡名的）為最符合題意，答案為 (B)。be notorious for 因…而惡名昭彰。

45. C；中譯：這篇文章發表假設認為人們感情起源是生化性地，而也沒有忽略文化影響也幾乎相同重要的可能性 (A) 這篇文章中，主張人們的感情是經由人體生化過程而不是由文化因素而產生 (B) 這篇文章假設人們的感情是有生化過程的結果，而它又再被文化因素加深 (C) 這篇文章假設人們的感情是有生化基礎，同時承認文化影響不能被忽視 (D) 這篇文章假設人們的感情有生化起源且排除文化影響。

解析：題目主要表示文章認為人們感情起源雖然主要是來自於生化反應，但文化影響也應該佔很大的比例，所以本題答案為 (C)

46－50. 中譯：

　　西拉雅族是台灣官方承認的原住民族群之一，它有一個獨特的宗教儀式叫做 Pas-ta'al這個儀式據說已經實施有四百年之久了，現在，它每二年舉辦一次，每隔十年它會較為盛大並賦予意義，最近一次的十年儀式在 2006 年農曆十月的滿月的日子裡在北台灣二個相補的地點同時舉辦。

　　儀式的第一天，數以千計的人聚集在新竹縣五峰鄉。從島內各地的觀光客在空曠的場地中參加當地村民精心策劃的儀式。男男女女唱歌跳舞，手牽手，手臂交叉，一起在一個大圓圈中來回移動。西拉雅原住民都穿上鮮豔的紅白相間，且編織精細及具有串珠的傳統服裝，有些人在背後也有華麗的裝飾品，而當舞者移動時，這些掛鏡、串珠以及鈴鐺就會敲擊並發出響聲。觀光客是可以參觀的，但他們被要求待在村內長老進行的神秘儀式的特定區域之外，觀光客也被勸告在手臂、照相機及錄音機等處繫上芒草。

46. D；中譯：何謂Pas-ta'al？(A) 它是西拉雅族的每年一度的宗教慶典 (B) 它是西拉雅族的一個唱歌跳舞的結婚儀式 (C) 它是西拉雅族的一個用芒草來祭獻的儀式 (D) 它是西拉雅族的一個有四百年歷史的儀式。

解析：(A) 由一開始The Saisiyat people…have a unique ritual ceremony called Pas-ta'al，及Today, it takes place every two years…可知 Pas-ta'al是一個宗教慶典名稱，但每二年舉辦一次 (B) 內容沒提到(C)由 They were also advised to tie Japanese silvergrass around their arms, cameras, and recorders.，文中唯一提到芒草（Japanese silver）不是用來祭祀，而是穿戴在身上（避邪用）(D) 由That ceremony is said to have been carried out for as manyas 400 years.知該儀式有四百年了，所以答案為 (D)。

47. B；中譯：通常Pas-ta'al在何時或何處舉行？(A) 它每二年的十月舉行 (B) 它在台灣北部的二個主要地點舉行 (C) 當芒草長得茂密的時候舉行 (D) 它只有在新竹五峰舉行。

解析：由The most recent ten-year ceremony was held in 2006 at two complementary and overlapping sites in northern Taiwan during…，所以答案為 (B)，(A) 不能選因為文中只說舉行時間為農曆十月的滿月的

日子，不一定是十月份。

48. A；中譯：關於這個儀式，下列哪項敘述是錯誤的？(A) 觀光客可以參加長老的神祕儀式 (B) 當地村民穿著傳統紅白相間的服裝 (C) 觀光客與村民在空曠場地圍成圓圈跳舞 (D) 觀光客被勸告在手臂及照相機繫上芒草。

解析：由 Tourists were welcome but were asked to stay away from particular areas where secret rituals were performed by village elders,…可知觀光客不可參加長老的儀式，所以 (A) 敘述為非，其餘正確。

49. B；中譯：依據本文，下列哪項敘述為真？(A) Pas-ta'al在台灣是一個官方認可的原住民共通性的儀式 (B) Pas-ta'al是西拉雅族的一個特有儀式 (C) 日本觀光客每十年獲邀參加這盛大的儀式 (D) Pas-ta'al每年十月中旬舉行。

解析：(A)西拉雅族是官方承認的原住民族群，而Pas-ta'al是西拉雅族一個獨特的宗教儀式 (B) 敘述正確 (C) 沒提到日本觀光客 (D) Pas-ta'al每二年舉行一次，所以答案為 (B)。

50. D；中譯：下列哪項敘述可從文章中得知？(A) 每一個官方認可的原住民族有自己的部落儀式 (B) 觀光客穿戴芒草來表示他們非本地人的象徵 (C) 西拉雅族用串珠、鈴鐺以及掛鏡來做為日常衣物的裝飾 (D) Pas-ta'al只有部分開放給大眾參觀。

解析：(A) 文中提及西拉雅族是官方承認的原住民族群，沒說每個都有自己的部落儀式 (B) 只有提及觀光客穿戴芒草，沒說用途 (C) 這些衣飾只有慶典使用，非日常服裝 (D) Pas-ta'al 不開放長老的儀式，可推論儀式只有部分開放，所以答案為 (D)。

 NOTE

102年特種考試交通事業鐵路人員考試試題

等別：員級鐵路人員考試
類科：各類科
科目：法學知識與英文（此節錄英文部分）

請回答第31題至第33題：

　　If knowledge is power, then literacy is the key to the kingdom. For centuries, the ability to read and write has given power to those who possessed it, although access to book learning—indeed, to books themselves—was often limited to a privileged minority. Today, by contrast, we inhabit a digital age in which written texts are more widely and democratically available than ever before. A prerequisite for access, however, is still the ability to comprehend and appraise those texts. Individuals who lack strong skills for finding, understanding, and evaluating written information cannot easily arm themselves with that information or use it to advance the causes they value. And because a free society depends on an informed and autonomous citizenry, the loss is not theirs alone. As we confront some of the great questions of our time—about war and diplomacy, immigration and citizenship, health care and human rights, and fair access to education and employment—literacy liberates us from dependence on received wisdom and allows us to find and weigh the evidence ourselves. Simply put, literacy is <u>cornerstone</u> of our freedom.

(　　) 31. What is the passage mainly about?

(A) The importance of literacy today.

(B) Freedom in a digital age.

(C) The autonomous citizenry in a free society.

(D) The relationship of knowledge, power, and corruption.

(　　) 32. Traditionally, who had access to literacy?

(A) Internet hackers.　　　　　　(B) Computer programmers.

(C) The privileged minority.　　　(D) Every individual eager to learn.

(　　) 33. What does the word "cornerstone" mean?

(A) Foundation.　(B) Ceremony.　(C) Procedure.　(D) Etiquette.

請回答第34 題至第37題：

All that you will need to decorate your birdhouse are a few simple tools you probably already have at home. You also need some paint. When painting the birdhouse, make sure the paint is safe for the birds as well as ____34____ enough for an outdoor setting. Exterior latex paint is ideal. But this type of paint tends to be sold in large quantities and can be costly if you are using a ____35____ of colors. Many craft stores now carry small containers of exterior latex or exterior acrylic craft paints in a ____36____ spectrum of colors. These paints will ____37____ ____ your birdhouse project well. Use white and black or dark brown paints to lighten or darken your colors. Finding all the supplies you will need and preparing your work space before you begin to paint will make decorating the birdhouse more pleasant and cleanup easier.

(　　) 34. (A) durable　　　(B) edible　　　(C) sociable　　　(D) portable

(　　) 35. (A) dynasty　　　(B) facility　　　(C) majesty　　　(D) variety

(　　) 36. (A) high　　　　(B) long　　　　(C) tall　　　　(D) wide

(　　) 37. (A) build　　　　(B) reserve　　　(C) serve　　　(D) describe

請回答第38題至第42題：

In 1368, a Buddhist monk called Chu Yuan-chang led a revolt in China against the Mongols, who ruled China at that time. His revolt succeeded and Chu Yuan-chang _____38_____ a new family of Chinese rulers called the Ming Dynasty. The early Ming rulers extended the Great Wall of China, which had _____39_____ been built to keep the Mongols out. They also brought the province of Yunnan _____40_____ their control and forced Korea to pay a tribute to China. Soon, the Chinese decided to _____41_____ from foreign contacts altogether. They were _____42_____ and did not want anything from abroad. They regarded foreigners as barbaric, uncivilized people.

(　) 38. (A) found 　　(B) founded 　　(C) had found 　　(D) was founding

(　) 39. (A) originally 　　　　　　(B) psychologically
　　　　 (C) rhetorically 　　　　　 (D) voluntarily

(　) 40. (A) beyond 　　(B) over 　　(C) under 　　(D) without

(　) 41. (A) prevent 　　(B) expand 　　(C) stem 　　(D) withdraw

(　) 42. (A) ready-made 　　　　　　(B) family-oriented
　　　　 (C) self-sufficient 　　　　　(D) counter-balanced

(　) 43. To fight against the inflation, the US government takes every measure to maintain the _____ of the dollar on the world's money markets.
　　　　 (A) stability 　　(B) innovation 　　(C) routine 　　(D) triumph

(　) 44. _____ in English is a key to effective communication in the global market.
　　　　 (A) Pride 　　(B) Fluency 　　(C) Frequency 　　(D) Prejudice

(　) 45. The poor girl knew that her dream of going to law school was as _____ as walking on the moon.
　　　　 (A) furious 　　(B) transparent 　　(C) superstitious 　　(D) unattainable

(　) 46. We should watch out for the change in weather to _____ ourselves from getting a cold.

(A) preserve　　　(B) prevent　　　(C) forbid　　　(D) force

(　　) 47. When you collect some wild plants to cook, you had better make sure they

are _____ in the first place.

(A) edible　　　(B) visible　　　(C) greasy　　　(D) sticky

(　　) 48. At first, he tried amphetamine and other drugs just out of curiosity, but

within a very short time, he developed an _____ .

(A) addiction　　　(B) eruption　　　(C) innovation　　　(D) oppression

(　　) 49. Soy milk, in some societies, has been commonly used as a milk

_____ .

(A) supplement　　　(B) substitute　　　(C) nutrient　　　(D) recipe

(　　) 50. Harry Potter, the hero created by J. K. Rowling, is the most famous

_____ in modern English literature.

(A) actor　　　(B) character　　　(C) director　　　(D) writer

102 年特種考試交通事業鐵路人員——員級中譯解析

31.－33. 中譯：

假如說知識就力量，那識字能力就是通往這個國度的鑰匙。幾世紀以來，讀寫字的能力給了那些擁有這能力的人力量，雖然真正進到課本學習─確實地到書本本身─仍時常限於享有特權的少數人。現在，相反地，我們生活在一個文字比起以前更加廣泛及更普及的數位時代。然而，進入的先決條件仍然是對文字領悟及評價的能力。對那些缺乏良好的搜尋、了解以及評估這些文章的人來說，他們就無法輕易的經由資訊來完備他們自己，或用它們來增強對他們有價值的事物。且因為一個自由的社會有賴於明理且自主的公民，損失的不只有他們的而已。當我們面對我們時代的一些大的問題時，如關於戰爭與外交，移民與公民權，健康保險與人權，公平的受教與雇用等，識字能力讓我們擺脫大眾信以為真的謬誤，並讓我們可以自己去發掘及評量自我。簡單來說，識字能力就是讓我們能自由的基礎。

31. A；中譯： 本篇主要是有關於 (A) 今日識字能力的重要性 (B) 在數位時代的自由 (C) 在自由社會的自主公民 (D) 知識、力量及貪汙的關係。

解析： 本文一開始就談到識字能力就是通往這知識國度的鑰匙，再來談到缺乏文字運用能力的人在現今的資訊化社會無法增加自己的能力等，所以都是在談識字能力的重要性，答案為 (A)。

32. C；中譯： 傳統上，誰可以識字？(A) 網路駭客 (B) 電腦程式設計者 (C) 享有特權的少數人 (D) 每個渴望學習的人。

解析： 由 For centuries, the ability to read and write …was often limited to a privileged minority，所以知以前識字是屬於享有特權的少數人，故答案為 (C)。

33. A；中譯： "cornerstone" 這個字的意思是 (A) Foundation 基礎 (B) Ceremony 儀式 (C) Procedure 程序 (D) Etiquette 禮節

34.－37. 中譯：

所有要裝修你的鳥舍所需用的一些簡單工具可能在你家中都已經有了。你同樣需要一些油漆，當你油漆鳥舍時，確認你的油漆對鳥兒是安全的且在室外能夠耐久使用。室外的乳膠漆是理想的，但這種塗料常常以大包裝販售且價格不斐，如果你要用好幾種顏色的話。許多工藝店現在有賣小包裝的室外乳膠漆，或室外的丙烯酸工藝塗料等多種顏色的塗料，這些塗料將對你的鳥舍工程有所助益。用白色與黑色或暗褐色來增亮或加深你的顏色，在你開始油漆之前，先準備好所需要用的東西並準備好你的工作場所，這將使裝修鳥舍會更愉快並更容易清理。

34. A； (A) durable 耐用的 (B) edible 可食用的 (C) sociable 社交性的 (D) portable 手提式的。

35. D； (A) dynasty 朝代 (B) facility 設備 (C) majesty 威嚴 (D) variety 多樣化

解析： 空格內是要敘述顏色的名詞，要用 a variety of（各樣的）最恰當，故答案為 (D)。

36. D；解析： 空格內要填入形容詞來形容後面 spectrum of colors（顏色的頻譜，在此簡單化為顏色種類），選項中以 wide（寬廣的）最適宜，表示許多種類的顏色，故答案為 (D)。

37. C； (A) build 建造 (B) reserve 保留 (C) serve 服務 (D) describe 敘述

解析： 空格內要填入動詞，serve 有對…有用之意，即對鳥舍工程有所助益，故答案為 (C)。

38－42.

　　1368 年時，一個佛教和尚名字叫朱元璋，在中國率兵起義對抗那時統治中國的蒙古人，他起義成功並且建立了漢人統治的一個新王朝稱為明朝。明朝早期統治者擴張原建造來阻絕蒙古人的萬里長城，他們同時也將雲南省納入版圖並要求高麗對中國朝貢。不久，中國決定全部撤回與外國的接觸，他們自給自足且不要任何國外的東西，他們把外國人認為都是野蠻且未開化的人。

38. B；解析：空格內要填入動詞，本句表示過去時間，且對等連接詞前動詞 succeeded 為過去式，所以空格內亦需用過去式動詞，故答案為 (B)。

39. A；(A) originally 原本地 (B) psychologically 心理上地 (C) rhetorically 修辭上地 (D) voluntarily 自願地

40. C；解析：空格內要填入介係詞形成片語修飾前面先行詞 province of Yunnan，選項中 under…control（為…所控制）最符合前後文句意義，表示將雲南省納入控制（版圖），故答案為 (C)。

41. D；(A) prevent 阻擋 (B) expand 擴張 (C) stem 反抗 (D) withdraw 縮回
　　解析：空格內要填入動詞形成不定詞片語。由後面文章中看出中國以後不與外國人接觸，所以用 withdraw（縮回）最適合，故答案為(D)。

42. C；(A) ready-made 現成 (B) family-oriented 家庭導向 (C) self-sufficient 自給自足 (D) counter-balanced 平衡

43. A；中譯：為了對抗通膨，美國政府極盡一切手段去維持美元在世界貨幣市場的穩定。
　　解析：(A) stability 穩定 (B) innovation 創新 (C) routine 例行事務 (D) triumph 勝利

44. B；中譯：英文流利是在全球市場有效溝通的關鍵。
　　解析：(A) Pride 驕傲 (B) Fluency 流利 (C) Frequency 頻率 (D) Prejudice 偏見

45. D；中譯：這位可憐的女孩知道她要念法律學院的夢想是與月球漫步一樣難完成的。
　　解析：(A) furious 狂暴的 (B) transparent 透明的 (C) superstitious 迷信的 (D) unattainable 難達到的
　　本題考形容詞，as+形容詞＋as（與…一樣…），月球漫步對一般人是很難達成的，本句中應用 as unattainable as（與…一樣難達成）最符合題意，所以答案為(D)。

46. B；中譯：我們應該留意天氣的變化以防我們自己感冒。
　　解析：(A) preserve 保留 (B) prevent 阻止 (C) forbid 禁止 (D) force 迫使
　　本題考動詞片語用法，避免遭受傷害或其它事物用 prevent…from，所以答案為 (B)。

47. A；中譯：當你採集一些野生植物來煮食，你最好一開始就確定它們是可食用的。
　　解析：(A) edible 可食用的 (B) visible 可看見的 (C) greasy 油脂的 (D) sticky 黏性的

48. A；中譯：一開始，他只是出於好奇心而嘗試安非他命及其他藥物，但一段短時間後，他成癮了。
　　解析：(A) addiction 沉溺 (B) eruption 爆發 (C) innovation 創新 (D) oppression 壓迫

49. B；中譯：在一些社會裏，豆漿已經廣泛的被當成一種牛奶替代品了。
　　解析：(A) supplement 補給品 (B) substitute 代用品 (C) nutrient 營養品 (D) recipe 處方

50. B；中譯：哈利波特，羅琳創造的英雄，是近代英國文學最有名的人物角色。
　　解析：(A) actor 演員 (B) character 角色 (C) director 導演 (D) writer 作家

📋 102 年特種考試交通事業鐵路人員考試試題

等別：佐級鐵路人員考試
類科：事務管理、機械工程、機檢工程、電力工程、電子工程、養路工程
科目：公民與英文（此節錄英文部分）

( ) 36. Cashier: The total is $2,500. Will this be cash or charge?

Mary: _____ .

Cashier: No, I'm afraid not.

(A) How will you like it?　　(B) Do you take JCB Card?

(C) Do you have change?　　(D) Should I write you a check?

( ) 37. Diane: You'll never believe this!

Jane: _____ ?

Diane: I got an A on my math test.

Jane: That's great. Congratulations!

(A) How's it going?　　(B) How've you been?

(C) What happened?　　(D) Why not?

( ) 38. Jason is very busy. He does not have _____ time reading newspapers or watching TV.

(A) lots　　(B) several　　(C) much　　(D) some

( ) 39. Jeff has a _____ cookbook with him, so he knows what to cook for his family.

(A) handy　　(B) delicious　　(C) juicy　　(D) scary

( ) 40. He went to the library and _____ a book.

(A) made　　(B) bought　　(C) lent　　(D) borrowed

請回答第41題至第45題：

Many people cannot tell the difference between the lotus and the water lily because the flowers and leaves have a similar appearance and both kinds of flowers grow in quiet ponds or lakes. In some ways, however, these flowers are very different. First of all, lotus flowers usually reach up out of the water, while the water lily rests on the floating leaves. Secondly, the pads or ridged leaves of the lotus flowers are completely rounded while those of the water lily have a split in them from the outer edge to the center. Finally, the lotus flower has the religious significance of purity in Asia while the water lily is mostly associated with feminine beauty and nymphs (water spirits), as in Greek culture. Although they have different characteristics and meanings, both the lotus and the water lily are highly appreciated in various cultures.

(　　) 41. The common natural habitat for the water lily and the lotus is _____ .

(A) on the bank of a river.　　　(B) in a pond or a lake.

(C) above a waterfall.　　　(D) in a fast-running brook.

(　　) 42. Which statement is NOT true?

(A) The leaves of the water lily float on the water.

(B) The leaves of the water lily are completely round.

(C) The leaves of the water lily have ridges.

(D) The leaves of the water lily are also called pads.

(　　) 43. According to the paragraph, the lotus flower is mostly known to be

(A) a flower found at weddings.　　　(B) a religious symbol.

(C) an extinct plant.　　　(D) a poisonous flower.

(　　) 44. In the West, the water lily is associated with

(A) beautiful water spirits.　　　(B) purity of mind and body.

(C) female fertility.　　　(D) everlasting love.

( ) 45. This paragraph is mainly a _____.

(A) story about the lives of plants.

(B) debate about religions.

(C) comparison of two kinds of flowers.

(D) plea for conservation of nature.

請回答第46題至第50題：

　　The appearance of smartphones has changed people's life to a large degree. Not only can people use them to make and receive phone calls, they can ___46___ use them to surf on the Internet, send and receive emails, communicate with each other through video and make new friends. They have helped make human contact become easier and more ___47___ than before. Besides helping people to connect ___48___ each other, smartphones allow people to have fun. People can watch videos and movies online as well as play many different online games either with themselves or with others. Using the camera function ___49___ by smartphones, people can take pictures of themselves, their family and friends and even things that interest them. Now smartphones have also been used as a kind of credit card. ___50___ , people can use them to pay for their grocery shopping without taking the money with them.

( ) 46. (A) also   (B) but   (C) again   (D) never

( ) 47. (A) helpful   (B) general   (C) confusing   (D) frequent

( ) 48. (A) from   (B) for   (C) with   (D) about

( ) 49. (A) provide   (B) provided   (C) providing   (D) to provide

( ) 50. (A) As well   (B) Such as   (C) For instance   (D) As if

102 年特種考試交通事業鐵路人員──佐級（事務管理等）中譯解析

36. B；中譯：收銀台店員：一共是為 $ 2,500 元，你要付現或刷卡？

　　瑪莉：(A) 你覺得它如何？(B) 你們接受 JBC 卡嗎？(C) 你有零錢嗎？(D) 我可以給你支票嗎？

　　店員：不！恐怕不能。

　　解析：店員已問是要刷卡或付現，則要依問題回答，選項中只有所 (B) 是回答到相關問題，所以為正確答案，雖然店員是拒絕她用 JBC 卡（但可以用其他卡），其它回答不符題意。

37. C；中譯：黛安：你不會相信這件事！

　　珍：(A) 你好嗎？(B) 你好嗎？(C) 發生甚麼事？(D) 為何不？

　　黛安：我數學考是得到一個 A。

　　珍：那很好，恭喜！

　　解析：由前後文知黛安是要告訴珍一個她料想不到的事，所以開頭就說你一定不相信，所以珍順勢說發 (C) 發生甚麼事？是符合邏輯且自然的反應，其它回答不符邏輯。

38. C；中譯：傑森非常忙，他沒有太多時間看電視或報紙。

　　解析：本題考有關數量形容詞用法。時間為不可數名詞，所以只能用 much 來形容 time，故答案為 (C)。

39. A；中譯：傑佛擁有一本實用的食譜，所以他知道煮什麼給家人吃。

　　解析：(A) handy 便利的 (B) delicious 美味的 (C) juicy 多汁的 (D) scary 膽怯的

　　本題考的是形容詞。have（has）something with somebody某人擁有某物，依句意應該用 (A) handy便利的，表示是一本方便容易使用的食譜。

40. D；中譯：他到圖書館借一本書。

　　解析：本題考的是動詞。當圖書館應該是借書，而不是買書，另外 lend 是指借出，borrow 才是指借入，所以本題答案為 (D)

41.－45. 中譯：

　　很多人沒有辦法分辨蓮花（荷花）與睡蓮的差別，因為兩者的花與葉都有相似的外表，且都生長在靜謐的池塘或湖泊中。然而，從某些地方來看這兩種花有很大不同，首先，蓮花的花通常會突出水面，而睡蓮會在水面的浮葉長在一起。再來，蓮花的浮葉或葉脊是完整的圓形，而睡蓮的葉子是從葉子外圍到中心點有條分開的縫。最後，在亞洲蓮花在宗教上具有純淨的意涵，然而就像在希臘文化中，睡蓮大部分是跟女性美以及精靈（水中仙子）有關。雖然蓮花與睡蓮具有不同的象徵與意義，在各種文化裡兩者仍然是被高度讚賞。

41. B；中譯：睡蓮與蓮花共同在自然界的生長環境是 (A) 在河邊 (B) 在水塘或湖中 (C) 在瀑布上面 (D) 在小溪的激流。

　　解析：由…both kinds of flowers grow in quiet ponds or lakes…知是長在水塘或湖中，答案為 (B)。

42. B；中譯：下列何項敘述是錯誤的 (A) 睡蓮的葉子浮在水面上 (B) 睡蓮的葉子是完整的圓形 (C) 睡蓮的葉子有背脊 (D) 睡蓮的葉子同時也被稱為大浮葉。

解析：(A) 由…the water lily rests on the floating leaves …，敘述為真 (B) 蓮花的葉子才是完整的圓形，故敘述為非。(C)、(D)因將蓮花與睡蓮的浮葉與葉脊一同比較，可知睡蓮也有浮葉與葉脊。

43. B；中譯：依據本篇文章，蓮花最為人所知的是 (A) 婚禮上看到的花 (B) 宗教的象徵 (C) 已滅絕的植物 (D) 一種有毒植物。

解析：由…the lotus flower has the religious significance of purity in Asia…知在亞洲蓮花在宗教上具有純淨的意涵，故本題答案為 (B)。

44. A；中譯：在西方，睡蓮與何者有關 (A) 美麗的水中仙子 (B) 心靈與身體的純淨 (C) 女性的生產力 (D) 永恆的愛

解析：由…the water lily is mostly associated with feminine beauty and nymphs（water spirits），as in Greek culture…知在西方睡蓮大部分是跟女性美以及精靈（水中仙子）有關，故本題答案為 (A)。

45. C；中譯：本篇文章主要是一個 (A) 關於植物生命的故事 (B) 有關宗教的爭論 (C) 二種植物的比較 (D)自然保育的懇求。

解析：由一開始提到二種植物的差別，到後面說明二種植物在東西方文化代表的意涵，都是在比較這二種植物，故本題答案為 (C)。

46.－50. 中譯：

智慧型手機的出現已經大幅度的改變人們的生活，人們不僅能用手機撥打及接電話，也可以用手機上網，收發電子郵件，與其他人用視訊通話及交朋友。手機已讓人類的溝通變得比以往更容易且更頻繁，智慧型手機除了可讓人們互相聯繫外，也讓人有更多樂趣。人們可以在線上看影片或電影，也可以自己或跟其他人玩各式線上遊戲。經由智慧型手機上提供的照相機功能，人們可以拍攝他們自己，他們的朋友及家人，以及他們認為有趣的事物。現在智慧型手機已經被當成信用卡使用，例如說，人們可以用它來支付買家用品的消費而不需隨身帶現金。

46. A；解析：本句為 Not only…（but） also（不僅…而且）的句型，所以答案為 (A)，表示人們不僅能用手機撥打及接電話，而且也可以用手機上網。

47. D；(A) helpful 有用的 (B) general 一般的 (C) confusing 令人混淆的 (D) frequent 時常的
解析：本處需填入一個被more修飾的形容詞，前面提到手機已讓人類的溝通變得比以往更容易且更如何，選項中以 frequent（時常的）最符合上下文意思，答案為(D)。

48. C；解析：connect with 與…聯絡，所以答案為 (C)，表示手機可讓人們互相聯繫。

49. B；解析：本處考分詞用法，用動詞過去分詞當形容詞用，修飾前面的名詞 function，所以答案為 (B)。另本句亦可看作：Using the camera function（which is） provided by smartphones,…，也就是用關係代名詞引導形容詞子句，並省略which is。

50. C；(A) As well 同樣地 (B) Such as 像是 (C) For instance 例如說 (D) As if 好像
解析：本處需填入一個副詞片語，說明後面的舉例，所以用 (C) Forinstance 最恰當，另也可用 for example，但不能用 such as，雖然意思很像，但因為形容詞片語，後面要加修飾的名詞。

📋 102 年特種考試交通事業鐵路人員考試試題

等別：佐級鐵路人員考試
類科：材料管理、運輸營業、車輛調度
科目：公民與英文（此節錄英文部分）

( ) 36. The children _____ TV in the living room while their parents prepared dinner in the kitchen.
   (A) have been watching (B) were watching
   (C) had watched (D) watch

( ) 37. Waiter: Are you ready to order?
   Leo: Ahh…not yet.
   Waiter: OK. _____ . Just call me when you are ready.
   (A) See you later (B) Wait a minute (C) Enjoy yourself (D) Take your time

( ) 38. Nick cannot _____ to buy a new wallet for himself because he has used up all of his money.
   (A) admit (B) accept (C) afford (D) alarm

( ) 39. Mike: May I speak with Lee?
   Lucy: I'm sorry. But he's not in. _____ .
   Mike: This is Mike. I'll call him later.
   (A) Do you have notes? (B) Is he there?
   (C) May I tell him? (D) Who's speaking please?

( ) 40. People usually buy bread from the _____ .
   (A) dentist's (B) butcher's (C) lawyer's (D) baker's

請回答第41 題至第45題：

Dr. Heidi Larson
Larson Veterinary Clinic
9179 Highbury Ave.
Flagstaff, AZ 86001-3862

Dear Dr. Larson:

Your accountant, Rusty Silhacek, is my neighbor. He mentioned that your office stays very busy, so I wondered if youcould use some extra help. I would like to apply for a position as a part-time veterinary assistant.

As far as animal care goes, I'm experienced in feeding, bathing, exercising, and cleaning up after small and large animals. I truly love animals and have always given them special attention and care. I would be available to help after school and onweekends.

I would be happy to come in for an interview at your convenience. You can contact me any weekday after 3:00 p.m. at 523-4418. Thank you for considering my application.

Sincerely,
Andrea Rodriguez

(　) 41. Who wrote this letter?

(A) Heidi Larson　　　　　　(B) Andrea Rodriguez

(C) Rusty Silhacek　　　　　(D) Elm Flagstaff

(　) 42. What is the purpose of this letter?

(A) to seek medical help　　　(B) to offer medical advice

(C) to contact a neighbor　　　(D) to apply for a job

(　) 43. A veterinary is a doctor who takes care of _____.

(A) accountants　(B) assistants　(C) animals　(D) women

(　) 44. Which of the following is true about the author of the letter?

(A) The author is a doctor.

(B) The author is an accountant.

(C) The author is not available for job interviews.

(D) The author is experienced in taking care of animals.

(　) 45. Which of the following is a suitable time to contact the author by phone?

(A) 4:00 p.m. on Monday　　　(B) 8:00 a.m. on Thursday

(C) 5:00 p.m. on Sunday　　　(D) 2:00 p.m. on Wednesday

請回答第46 題至第50題：

Emily Dickinson was born in Amherst, Massachusetts, in 1830.
____46____ her life, she seldom left her house. The peoplewith whom she did
come in ____47____ , however, had a great impact on her thoughts and poetry.
She was particularly stirred by Charles Wadsworth, whom she met ____48____ a
trip to Philadelphia. He left for the West Coast shortly after a visit to her home in
1860, ____49____ some people believe that she started to write sad poems in the
years that followed. ____50____ it is certain that he was an important figure in
her life, it is not certain that she fell in love with him. For she onlycalled him "my
closest earthly friend."

( ) 46. (A) Under   (B) Around   (C) Throughout   (D) Until
( ) 47. (A) charge   (B) contact   (C) action   (D) fever
( ) 48. (A) with   (B) as   (C) between   (D) on
( ) 49. (A) and   (B) because   (C) since   (D) which
( ) 50. (A) But   (B) Therefore   (C) Besides   (D) While

102年特種考試交通事業鐵路人員－佐級（車輛調度等）中譯解析

36. B；中譯：當他們的雙親在廚房準備晚餐時，小孩們正在客廳看電視。

解析：本題考有關動詞時態。while (conj.)當…的時候，本句表示一個過去時間，所以主要子句用過去進行式或過去式都是合理的，故答案為 (A)。

37. D；中譯：服務生：您要點菜了嗎？

利奧：哦……還沒有。

服務生：好的！(A) 待會見 (A) 等一下 (C) 請自便 (D) 請別急。當你準備好隨時叫我。

解析：由對話中可知服務生知道顧客還沒準備好，可能會不知所措，所以要顧客準備好再叫他，所以空格選項以(D)要顧客別急，慢慢來之意最恰當。

38. C；中譯：尼克買不起一個新的皮夾給自己因為他已花光他全部的錢。

解析：(A) admit承認 (A) accept 接受 (C) afford 受得起 (D) alarm 警告

本題考有關動詞片語。used up 花光了，買東西給自己可以用 can afford to，就是買得起、負擔的起之意，故答案為 (C)。

39. D；中譯：麥克：請問李先生在嗎？

露西：抱歉，他不在，(A)你需要留言嗎? (A) 他在那裏嗎？(C) 我要告訴他嗎？(D) 您是哪位？

麥克：我是麥克，我晚一點再找他。

解析：因為李先生不在，露西有必要知道誰要找他，且麥克後面接著說他是麥克，所以推論應該露西有問是誰要找李先生，所以答案為 (D)。

40. D；中譯：人們通常去麵包店買麵包。

解析：本題考所有格的省略用法，dentist's 等於 dentist's clinic，同理，butcher's 等於 butcher's shop 等，所以本題買麵包應到麵包店為 baker's，等於 baker's shop 故答案為 (D)。

40.－40. 中譯：

> Heidi Larson醫生
>
> Larson Veterinary診所
>
> 9179 Highbury Ave. Flagstaff, AZ 86001-3862
>
> 你的出納，也就是 Rusty Silhacek，他是我的鄰居，他提到你的公事非常忙碌，所以我不曉得你是否可以幫個額外的忙，我想應徵一個計時的獸醫助理的工作。
>
> 就動物照顧來說，我有飼養、洗澡、訓練、以及清潔大小動物的經驗，我真正愛動物且總是給牠們特別的關心與照顧，我會在放學後及周末有空去幫忙。
>
> 我很樂意在你方便的時候去接受面試，你可以在任何平日的下午三點過後以電話 523-4418 聯絡我，感謝你能考慮我的申請。
>
> 誠摯地
>
> Andrea Rodriguez

41. B；中譯：誰寫這封信？(A) Heidi Larson (A) Andrea Rodriguez (C) Rusty Silhacek (D) Elm Flagstaff

解析：由信尾署名即可知寫信者為 (A) Andrea Rodriguez；Heidi Larson 是診所醫生，Rusty Silhacek 是 Andrea Rodriguez 的鄰居，Flagstaff 是地名。

42. D；中譯：這封信的目的為何？(A) 尋求醫療協助 (A) 提供醫療指導 (C) 聯絡鄰居 (D) 找工作。

解析：由 Iwouldlikeapplyfora positionasa part-timeveterinaryassistant.可知這封信是要申請一項獸醫助理的工作，本題答案為 (D)。

43. C；中譯：獸醫是一個照顧 (A) 出納 (A) 助理 (C) 動物 (D) 女人的醫生。

解析：veterinary 獸醫，是指照顧動物的醫生，所以本題答案為 (C)。

44. D；中譯：下列有關這封信的作者何者是正確的 (A) 作者是位醫生(A) 作者是位出納 (C) 作者沒有空面談 (D) 作者對照顧動物是有經驗的。

解析：(A) 作者是位求職者 (A) 出納是作者的鄰居 (C) 作者說很樂意在醫生方便的時候去接受面試 (D) 作者有飼養、洗澡、訓練、以及清潔大小動物等照顧動物的經驗，所以本題答案為(D)。

45. A；中譯：下列何項是打電話聯絡作者的適合時間 (A) 星期一下午四點 (A) 星期四上午八點 (C) 星期天下午五點(D)星期三下午二點

解析：由You can contact me any weekday after 3:00 p.m. at…知道方便聯絡時間是平日（星期一到星期五）的下午三點過後，所以本題答案為 (A)。

46－50. 中譯：

艾蜜莉‧狄克森於 1830 年生於麻州的阿莫斯特，終其一生，她很少離開她的房子。然而，跟她有真正接觸的人對她的想法及詩作有重大的影響，她特別被查爾斯‧沃茲沃思所感動，一個她在到費城的旅程中遇到的人。在 1860 年他到她家拜訪後在西岸短暫停留，且有些人認為這是她在其後幾年開始寫悲傷詩。儘管他確定在她的生命中具有一個重要的角色，但她是否與他戀愛仍是不確定的，因為她只是稱呼他為：「我最親愛朋友。」

46. C；(A) Under 在…之下 (A) Around 在…四處 (C) Throughout 自始至終 (D) Until 直到…為止

解析：本處需填入介系詞，四個選項都可當介系詞用，依前後句意知，此處用 throughout 最適宜，表示終其一生，她很少離開她的房子，所以答案為 (C)。

47. B；解析：本處需填入名詞作為介系詞 in 的受詞，形成介系詞片語，其中 in charge照顧；in contact 與…有聯繫；in action 運轉；in a fever 狂熱，依前後句意知，此處用 in contact 與…有聯繫最適宜，所以答案為 (A)。

48. D；解析：本處需填入介系詞，空格後面是 a trip to Philadelphia，表到費城的旅程中，指一件事，所以介系詞用應用 on，答案為 (D)。

49. A；解析：此處前後敘述二件事，即查爾斯到她家拜訪，有些人認為這是她在其後幾年開始寫悲傷詩，所以用對等連接詞連接 and，答案為 (A)。

50. D；解析：本處需填入連接詞引導的副詞子句，來說明後面主要子句，由句意中得知，既確定在她的生命為一個重要的角色，但她是否與他戀愛仍是未知，所以用 while（雖然）最洽當，所以答案為 (D)。

📋 100 交通事業鐵路、公路、港務人員 升資考試試題

等別：佐級晉員級
類科：鐵路、公路、港務各類別
科目：法學知識與英文（此節錄英文部分）

( ) 31. The kids ate their lunch _____ and rushed out to play soccer.

    (A) on occasion   (B) by and large   (C) little by little   (D) in no time

( ) 32. A democratic country grants basic human rights and freedoms to the people she _____ .

    (A) governs   (B) invades   (C) overlooks   (D) enforces

( ) 33. Paul has been unemployed for a month. His _____ for a job has never paid off.

    (A) arrest   (B) charge   (C) respect   (D) search

( ) 34. Many developing countries have debts that are too _____ for them to handle.

    (A) huge   (B) minimal   (C) tiny   (D) flourishing

( ) 35. The _____ amount you may withdraw per day has been lowered to $30,000. If you need more money, you will have to come back tomorrow.

    (A) negligible   (B) maximum   (C) plentiful   (D) considerable

( ) 36. Nowadays few employees are _____ to their company. If another company offers higher salaries, they will quit the current job soon.

    (A) sensitive   (B) loyal   (C) liberal   (D) stable

( ) 37. Do you know how to _____ the coffee stain? I want to make my shirt clean.

    (A) recover   (B) rub   (C) release   (D) remove

( ) 38. You have to work harder; _____ you won't be able to keep your job.

    (A) whereby   (B) likewise   (C) whereas   (D) otherwise

請依下文回答第39～41題

    I wasn't born and raised to be a Kyoto geisha. I wasn't ___39___ born in Kyoto. I am a fisherman's daughter from a little town called Yoroido on the Sea of Japan. In all my life I have never told more than a handful of people anything at all about Yoroido, or about the house ___40___ I grew up, or about my father and mother, or my older sister. I certainly have not told anybody about how I became a geisha or ___41___ it was like to be one. Most people would rather carry on their fantasies that my mother and grandmother were geishas and that I began my training in dance when I weaned from the breast, and so on.

( ) 39. (A) still   (B) even   (C) ever   (D) been

( ) 40. (A) which   (B) in which   (C) of which   (D) that

( ) 41. (A) how   (B) that   (C) which   (D) what

( ) 42. A: _____ Your drums are driving me crazy.

    B: Sorry, I wasn't aware of the noise.

    A: That's OK.

    (A) Could you foot my bill?   (B) Could you keep me posted?

    (C) Could you knock it off?   (D) Could you eat your words?

( ) 43. Man: Would you tell me where the train station is?

Woman: _____ .

Man: It's OK. Thanks anyway.

(A) Go straight, and turn right at the second traffic light.

(B) It's within walking distance.

(C) The train just left. You have to wait for another fifty minutes.

(D) Sorry, I am a tourist, too.

( ) 44. A: Do you know what time it is?

B: It's ten to five.

A: _____ I'm supposed to pick up my kids at 5:00.

(A) Count on me.   (B) It is worthwhile.

(C) Oh, I'd better go.   (D) It is never too late.

( ) 45. Alex: I wonder what's keeping Steve?

Winnie: Oh, I forgot to tell you. He is not going to show up. He called just before we left.

Alex: What kind of excuse did he give you this time?

Winnie: Something about his car broken again.

Alex: _____ He doesn't even have a car. He commutes everywhere by bike. The man is totally unreliable.

(A) I believe his story.   (B) We should take pity on him.

(C) What nonsense!   (D) Honesty is the best policy.

請依下文回答第46～50題

　　Many US bird populations are in decline, some of which are even on the brink of extinction. Of the 800 species of birds in the United States, 67 are listed as endangered or threatened; another 184 are listed as "species of conservation concern" because they have small distribution, are facing high threats or have a declining population. Hawaiian birds and ocean birds appear most at risk. More than one-third of all US bird species are in Hawaii. However, 71 Hawaiian species have gone extinct since A.D. 300 and about 10 species have not been seen in the past 40 years. The declines of US bird populations can be traced to a variety of factors, including agriculture, climate change, unplanned urban development, and overfishing. In the grasslands, for example, intensified agricultural practices have hurt bird populations. Grassland cannot support many birds if it is overused or burned too frequently. Besides, public lands and parks are mowed too frequently and the grass is too short to provide a habitat for birds.

　　While many bird species are in decline, some other species are thriving. Research shows that wetland bird species began to increase in the late 1970s, which reflects the importance of the artificial habitats to the survival of many bird populations. The results prove that investment in wetlands has paid off and that it is now necessary to invest similarly in other neglected habitats where birds are undergoing steepest declines.

（　　）46. What is this passage mainly about?

　　　(A) Variety of bird species in Hawaii.

　　　(B) The decline of bird species in the US.

　　　(C) The habitat of bird species in the US.

　　　(D) The need for stricter bird protection laws.

(　) 47. Which of the following is NOT mentioned as a reason for the decline of the bird population?
(A) Agriculture. 　　　　　　　(B) Climate change.
(C) Harmful chemicals. 　　　　(D) Overfishing.

(　) 48. How many bird species inhabit Hawaii?
(A) About 70. 　(B) About 120. 　(C) About 180. 　(D) About 270.

(　) 49. According to the passage, which measure can effectively protect bird species?
(A) To monitor bird migration.
(B) To increase and preserve wetlands.
(C) To promote education in bird conservation.
(D) To develop medicine that can help birds live longer.

(　) 50. Which of the following statements is true?
(A) All of the US bird species are declining.
(B) Long grass provides ideal habitats for birds.
(C) Mowing can help birds to build their nests.
(D) In Hawaii 71 bird species have disappeared for three decades.

100 年鐵路人員升資考試（佐級晉員級）中譯解析

31. D；中譯：：小孩子們很快吃完他們的午餐然後衝出去玩足球。

解析：(A) on occasion 偶爾 (B) by and large一般而言 (C) little by little 一點一點地 (D) in no time 很快

本題考片語（當副詞修飾動詞ate）。小孩們會急著跑去玩球表示午餐應該是吃很快，選項中以in no time（很快）最恰當，故答案為 (D)。

32. A；中譯：一個民主的國家賦與他統治下人民基本的人權及自由。

解析：(A) governs 統治 (B) invades 入侵 (C) overlooks 眺望 (D) enforces 強制

本題考動詞。該句提到民主國家賦與人基本人權及自由，這些人民是指國家治理下的人，選項中用governs（統治）最恰當，所以答案為 (A)。

33. D；中譯：保羅已經失業一個月了，他找的工作都尚未有回應。

解析：(A) arrest 逮捕 (B) charge 索價 (C) respect 尊重 (D) search 尋求

本題考名詞，當所有格His的受詞。該句提到保羅失業一個月了，所以他應該是要找個工作，找工作可以用 to search for a job來表示，所以答案為 (D)。

34. A；中譯：許多發展中國家有著大到他們無法處理的債務。

解析：(A) huge 龐大的 (B) minimal 最小的 (C) tiny 極小的 (D) flourishing 茂盛的

本題考形容詞。too+形容詞+to+V 表示太…以致於。該句提到債務問題會到無法解決，表示債務是很大的，所以由選項中用 huge（龐大的）最恰當，故答案為 (A)。

35. B；中譯：你每天可提領的最大額度已經被限制低於 $ 30,000，如果你需要更多錢，你必須明天再來。

解析：(A) negligible 微不足道的 (B) maximum 最大的 (C) plentiful 豐富的 (D) considerable 重要的

本題考形容詞。句中提到額度被限制低於 $ 30,000，表示 $ 30,000 是最高的額度，由選項中用maximum（最大的）最恰當，故答案為 (B)。

36. B；中譯：現今很少員工對他們的公司忠誠，假如別家公司提供較高薪資，他們將很快辭掉現有工作。

解析：(A) sensitive 敏感的 (B) loyal 忠誠的 (C) liberal 自由的 (D) stable 安定的

本題考形容詞，表示對公司的態度。句中提到別家公司提供較高薪資，他們就會離開原公司，表示對公司不忠心，選項中用 loyal（忠誠的）最恰當，故答案為 (B)。

37. D；中譯：你知道如何去除咖啡汙漬嗎？我要把我的襯衫弄乾淨。

解析：(A) recover 恢復 (B) rub 擦去 (C) release 釋放 (D) remove 移除

本題考動詞。要把咖啡汙漬洗掉，選項中以 remove（移除）最恰當，故答案為 (D)。

38. D；中譯：你必須努力工作，否則你將不能保有你的工作。

解析：(A) whereby 由此 (B) likewise 同樣地 (C) whereas 其實 (D) otherwise 否則

本題考副詞用法，置於句首表示語氣的變化。如果工作不努力，則工作不保，二者是有前後因果關係，所以選項中以 otherwise（否則）最符合這種關係，故答案為 (D)。

39. -41. 中譯：

　　我並不是生來就是要成為京都藝妓，我甚至不是在京都出生的。我來自於日本海的一個叫做 Yoroido 小鎮的一個漁夫女兒。在我人生中，我從來根本沒有告訴太多人有關 Yoroido，或我長大的那房子，或我父親及母親，或我大姊的任何事情。我確定沒有告訴任何人有關我如何成為一個藝妓，或成為一個藝妓會如何。大部份的人寧願發揮他們的想像，認為我母親及祖母都是藝妓，以及當我斷奶以後，我就開始舞蹈訓練等等。

39. B；解析：前面說她不是生來就是要成為京都藝妓，後面再說他根本不是在京都出生，所以空格內需填入表示加強語氣的副詞，選項中以 even(甚至於) 最恰當，故答案為 (B)。

40. B；解析：空格處需填入關係詞，引導形容詞子句修飾先行詞 house，表地方的關係詞應用 where 或 in which，所以答案為 (B)。

41. D；解析：由…how I became a geisha or…，依句子的對稱結構及句意判斷空格處需填入疑問詞，本句應該表示是成為一個藝妓會發生甚麼事…，故疑問詞應用 what，所以答案為 (D)。

42. C；中譯：(A) 你能付我帳單嗎？(B) 你能讓我掌握狀況嗎？(C) 你能不要吵了嗎？(D) 你能把話收回去嗎？你的鼓聲快令我抓狂了。

　　B：抱歉，我沒有注意到那聲響。

　　A：那沒關係。

　　解析：由 A 的後段話知是 B 的鼓聲讓他受不了，應該會要求他不要吵了，所以答案為 (C)。

43. D；中譯：男人：你可以告訴我火車站在哪嗎？

　　女士：(A) 往前走，在第二個紅綠燈右轉 (B) 那是步行可到的 (C) 火車剛過，你要再多等15分鐘 (D) 抱歉，我也是個觀光客。

　　男人：沒關係。還是謝謝你。

　　解析：本題答案以合理性判斷，(B) 及 (C) 文不對題所以不可能，(A) 常用於問路，較不適宜問地點，(D) 是有可能發生於實際情況，所以答案為 (D)。

44. C；中譯：A：你知道現在幾點嗎？

　　B：現在四點五十分。

　　A：(A) 信任我 (B) 那是值得的 (C) 我必須要離開了 (D) 從不會太晚。我應該要在五點鐘去接我小孩。

　　解析：由於現在時間是四點五十分，且 A 說他五點鐘要接小孩，所以合理推斷 A 會說必須要離開了，所以答案為 (C)。

45. C；中譯：亞力克斯：我在想甚麼事耽擱了史蒂芬？

　　溫妮：啊！我忘了跟你說，他不會來的，在我們離開前他有打電話。

　　亞力克斯：這個時候了他跟你講甚麼理由？

　　溫妮：一些關於他汽車又壞掉了的事。

　　A：(A) 我相信這故事 (B) 真為他感到同情 (C) 真是荒唐啊！(D) 誠實是最上策。他沒有汽車，他到每個地方都騎腳踏車，這個人完全都靠不住。

　　解析：由對話中知亞力克斯知道史蒂芬在騙他們，他不高興所以會有較情緒性的反應，故答案為 (C)

46-50中譯：

　　許多美國鳥類族群正在減少，其中一些甚至已瀕臨絕種。在美國的 800 種鳥類中，67 種被列為受危急或受威脅，其它 184 種列為「有保護顧慮的物種」因為牠們分佈稀少、正遭受高度威脅或族群減少趨勢。夏威夷的鳥類及海鷗似乎是最為危急的，全美國超過三分之一鳥的種類是在夏威夷，然而，71 種夏威夷鳥類自從西元 300 年來已經消失了，且大約 10 個種類在過去 40 年沒有再被見到過。美國鳥類族群減少可被追溯於各種因素，包含農業、氣候變遷、無規劃的城市發展、以及過度漁撈。例如，在牧場上密集的農業耕作已經危害到鳥類族群，如果牧場被過度使用或太常放火燒，牧場就無法支撐許多鳥類。除此之外，公共道路及公園太常除草，而草也太短而無法供給鳥類棲息。

　　當許多鳥類減少的同時，一些其他種類的鳥正在成長茁壯。研究顯示沼澤地的鳥類自1970年代後期起開始增加，這反映出人造棲息地對許多鳥類群生存的重要性。這結果驗證了在沼澤地的投資已有回報，且類似地投資到其它鳥類數量正急速下降的那些被忽略的棲息地是必要的。

46. B；中譯：本文主旨是甚麼？(A) 在夏威夷的各種鳥類 (B) 美國鳥類的減少 (C) 美國鳥類的棲息環境 (D) 更嚴格的鳥類保護法需求。

解析：由一開始就說美國鳥類正在減少，然後說明鳥類減少的可能原因等，都是談到有關美國境內鳥類減少的事，故答案為 (B)。

47. C；中譯：下列何者沒有被提到是鳥類族群減少的原因？(A) 農業 (B) 氣候變遷 (C) 有害的化學物質 (D) 過度捕撈。

解析：由The declines of US bird populations can be traced to a variety of factors, including agriculture, climate change, unplanned urban development, and overfishing…知文中提到農業、氣候變遷、無計畫的城市發展、以及過度漁撈，沒提到化學物質，故答案為 (C)。

48. D；中譯：夏威夷有幾種鳥類棲息？(A) 約 70 種 (B) 約 120 種 (C) 約 180 種 (D) 約 270 種。

解析：文中提到全美有約800種鳥類，有三分之一是在夏威夷，所以約有 270 種，答案為 (D)。

49. B；中譯：依據本文，哪一項方法可以有效地保護鳥類？(A)監測鳥的遷移 (B) 增加保護濕地 (C) 提高鳥類保護教育 (D) 發展能讓鳥活得更久的藥。

解析：由 Research shows that wetland bird species began to increase in the late 1970s, which reflects the importance of the artificial habitats to the survival of many bird populations…知保護濕地已被確認是有效的方式，其它選項文中未提到，故答案為 (B)。

50. B；中譯：下列何項敘述為真？(A) 全部美國的鳥類都在減少 (B) 長草地提供鳥類理想的棲息地 (C) 割草可以幫助鳥類築牠們的巢 (D) 在夏威夷有71種鳥類已經消失了三世紀之久。

解析：由 (A) 文中提到許多美國鳥類族群正在減少，但後面有提到有部分(沼澤地的鳥類)正在增加，故非全部美國的鳥類都在減少，敘述錯誤 (B) 文中提到草也太短無法供給鳥類棲息，故推論長草地提供鳥類理想的棲息地，敘述正確 (C) 文中提到公園太常除草，無法供給鳥類棲息，所以割草無法幫助鳥類築巢，敘述錯誤 (D) 文中提到 71 種夏威夷鳥類自從西元 300 年來已經消失了，非消失了三世紀，敘述錯誤。故答案為 (B)。

📋 100 交通事業鐵路、公路、港務人員 升資考試試題

等別：員級晉高員級
類科：鐵路、公路、港務各類別
科目：法學知識與英文（此節錄英文部分）

( ) 31. Academic achievement certainly isn't the only _____ to reading. If one has developed a habit of reading, one will find the pure joy of reading itself.

(A) gratitude　　(B) incentive　　(C) implement　　(D) manual

( ) 32. My doctor suggested I stop eating junk food but eat foods full of vitamins, minerals, and other _____ .

(A) detriments　　(B) ingredients　　(C) merriments　　(D) nutrients

( ) 33. The city government is determined to _____ on soliciting. Those who are involved in exchanging money for sex will be arrested and prosecuted.

(A) crack down　　(B) get a move　　(C) put stress　　(D) take up

( ) 34. I have _____ for the child who lost both parents in this accident.

(A) apology　　(B) antipathy　　(C) solitude　　(D) sympathy

( ) 35. There is a debate in Turkey _____ whether or not to allow Muslim women to wear head scarves in public buildings.

(A) with　　(B) for　　(C) against　　(D) over

請依下文回答第36～40題

　　Few things play as central a role in our everyday lives as language. It is our most important tool in communicating our thoughts and feelings to each other. Infants cry and laugh, and their facial expressions surely give their parents some notion of the kinds of emotions they are experiencing, but it is

_____36_____ children are able to articulate speech that we gain much understanding of their private thoughts.

As we grow, language comes to serve other functions as well. Most young people develop _____37_____ that is more meaningful to those of the same age than to older or younger individuals. Such specialized language serves to bind us more closely with our peers while _____38_____ excluding those who are not our peers. Language becomes a badge of sorts, a means of identifying whether a person is within a social group.

Over time, for many of us language becomes not merely a means to an end but an end _____39_____ itself. We come to love words and word play. So we turn to writing poetry or short stories, or to playing word games. A tool that is _____40_____ for communicating our basic needs and wants has also become a source of leisurely pleasure.

(　) 36. (A) in fact　　　(B) not until　　　(C) as if　　　(D) no doubt

(　) 37. (A) potential　　(B) opinion　　　(C) jargon　　　(D) character

(　) 38. (A) in a word　　　　　　　　(B) at the same time

　　　　 (C) on the one hand　　　　　(D) for the same reason

(　) 39. (A) by　　　　　(B) with　　　　　(C) for　　　　　(D) in

(　) 40. (A) visible　　　(B) virtual　　　(C) vital　　　　(D) visual

(　) 41. Great leaps in scientific understanding are mostly driven by refutation, not confirmation.

　　　　 (A) Important progresses in science often result from confrontation rather than support of opinions.

　　　　 (B) Scientific knowledge that makes great leaps in human history is frequently opposed, not confirmed.

　　　　 (C) Debate breeds scientific truth and agreement leads to social harmony.

　　　　 (D) Great discoveries in science are often made by renowned scientists, not obscure ones.

請依下文回答第42～46題

Author Michael Crichton's follow-up to his best-selling novel was less a continuation of the original than a rewrite. It provided just two notions that excited Spielberg: the existence of a secret island where the DNA dinos had been created, and a set piece where a T. Rex tries pushing a trailer off a cliff after its babies are threatened by scientists. So Spielberg and David Koepp, a screenwriter on *Jurassic Park*, fashioned a new story. The novelist was never consulted about the sequel, nor was he sent a script until he held back approval of certain merchandising rights. But Crichton now sounds <u>sanguine</u>. "When I write," he says, "I have to have the book be exactly the way I want it to be, and that's that. The film will be exactly the way the director wants it to be. And that's that."

Spielberg came up with the theme of *The Lost World* at the end of a meeting with Koepp. Spielberg said, "I've got it! This movie is about hunters vs. gatherers." Out of that epiphany unfolded the story's central conflict about rogue businessmen who are breeding dinosaurs for their San Diego theme park—a most dangerous game that backfires. Spielberg suggested that Koepp watch the 1925 film of Sir Arthur Conan Doyle's *The Lost World*, which tells of an expedition to a South American jungle habitat where dinosaurs still roam, and Howard Hawks' *Hatari!*, starring John Wayne as a safari hunter on a game preserve. Says Koepp "*Hatari!* probably influenced us more than any dinosaur movie did."

(　　) 42. According to the passage, who is the director of *The Lost World*?

    (A) Michael Crichton　　　　　(B) Steven Spielberg

    (C) David Koepp　　　　　　　(D) Sir Arthur Conan Doyle

(　　) 43. According to the passage, who is the screenwriter on Jurassic Park?

    (A) Michael Crichton　　　　　(B) Steven Spielberg

    (C) David Koepp　　　　　　　(D) Sir Arthur Conan Doyle

(　　) 44. What is the theme of The Lost World?

    (A) Dinosaurs vs. human beings　　(B) Hunters vs. gatherers

(C) Science vs. archeology　　　　(D) Nature vs. human beings

(　) 45. Which of the following movies is NOT about dinosaurs?

(A) *Dinosaurs*　　　　　　　　(B) *The Lost World*

(C) *Hatari!*　　　　　　　　　(D) *Jurassic Park*

(　) 46. The word "sanguine" is closest in meaning to _____.

(A) fond of bloodshed　　　　　(B) healthy in mind

(C) optimistic　　　　　　　　(D) reasonable

請依下文回答第47～50題，各題答案內容不重複

That so many bacteria have become drug-resistant is testimony to the microbes' toughness. However, here is tougher: some bacteria actually eat antibiotics for breakfast. ____47____

To study bacteria with varying degrees of prior exposure to artificial antibiotics, a research team sampled dirt from eleven disparate locations. ____48____ All eleven soil types sheltered bacteria that could grow on antibiotics—including commonly prescribed ones—as their only source of carbon. ____49____

To be able to eat antibiotics, those bacteria must obviously have a high degree of resistance. Indeed, they tolerate antibiotics at an extremely concentrated level. The poison-munching bacteria are not harmful to people. ____50____ Because bacteria swap genes freely, scientists warn that the soil dwellers might be able to transfer the genes for super-resistance to their infective cousins.

(　) 47. (A) Others can be easily destroyed by antibiotics.

(B) Fortunately, not many can be found in the soil.

(C) Nevertheless, some of them have close relatives that are harmful to people.

(D) Moreover, such super-tough bacteria are naturally widespread in the soil.

(　) 48. (A) Others can be easily destroyed by antibiotics.

　　　(B) Surprisingly, not all the bacteria are drug-resistant.

　　　(C) Then they exposed the samples to eighteen antibiotics.

　　　(D) What is more, all but one of the antibiotics became food for bacteria in most soil types.

(　) 49. (A) Fortunately, not many can be found in the soil.

　　　(B) Then they exposed the samples to eighteen antibiotics.

　　　(C) Also, the antibiotics can be natural ones like penicillin.

　　　(D) What is more, all but one of the antibiotics became food for bacteria in most soil types.

(　) 50. (A) They can even be used for medical purposes.

　　　(B) Surprisingly, not all the bacteria are drug-resistant.

　　　(C) Nevertheless, some of them have close relatives that are harmful to people.

　　　(D) Moreover, such super-tough bacteria are naturally widespread in the soil.

100 年鐵路人員升資考試（員級晉高員級）中譯解析

31. B；中譯：學術成就當然不是讀書唯一的動機，如果一個人已養成讀書的習慣，他將會發現閱讀本身的樂趣。

　　解析：(A) gratitude 感謝 (B) incentive 動機 (C) implement 工具 (D) manual 手冊

32. D；中譯：我的醫生建議我停止吃垃圾食物而要吃富含維他命、礦物質及其他營養食物。

　　解析：(A) detriments 損害 (B) ingredients 成分 (C) merriments 歡樂 (D) nutrients 營養

33. A；中譯：市政府決定要制裁嫖妓，那些涉入以金錢來換取性的人將被逮捕並起訴。

　　解析：(A) crack down 制裁 (B) get a move 加緊 (C) put stress 施壓 (D) take up 接受

34. D；中譯：我對那位在車禍中失去雙親的孩子感到同情。

　　解析：(B) apology 抱歉 (B) antipathy 反感 (C) solitude 孤獨 (D) sympathy 同情

　　此題考的是名詞。對…感到同情要用 have sympathy for…，故答案為 (D)。

35. D；中譯：在土耳其有一個爭論就是是否要讓穆斯林婦女在公共建築中戴著頭巾。

36－40. 中譯

　　在我們生活中沒有甚麼事情像語言一樣扮演中心角色，它是我們在溝通想法及感情最重要的工具，嬰兒的哭和笑以及他們臉部表情的確給他們的雙親一些關於他們情緒上的提示，直到小孩子能夠開口講話我們才能知道更多他們自己的想法。

　　當我們長大後，語言同樣用來做為其他功能。大部分年輕人發展出的特殊用語（行話），那些話對他們相同年紀的人來說是比對他們年長或年輕的人是更有意義的，這樣的特殊用語用來讓我們與同夥更加緊密，而同時排除那些不是同夥的人，語言變成一種類型的徽章，一種識別是否一個人在一個社會群體的方法。

　　隨著時間演進，對我們許多人而言，語言變成不僅是一種達到目的手段，而是本身即是一種重要的事，我們最終還是會喜愛文字及文字的樂趣，所以以我們轉向寫詩或短篇故事，或玩文字遊戲。語言作為一種用來溝通基本需求的重要工具也已經成為平常休閒娛樂的源頭。

36. B；(A) in fact 事實上 (B) not until 直到…才 (C) as if 似乎 (D) no doubt 無疑問的

　　解析：本句句型為 it is…that…，真正主詞為 that 後面的子句，句中提到我們能了解小孩真正的想法是在他們長大可以講話後，所以有時間前後關聯性，故應用 (B) not until，才能表現這種時間順序關係。

37. C；(A) potential 潛在的 (B) opinion 意見 (C) jargon 行話 (D) character 性格

38. B；(A) in a word 總之 (B) at the same time 同時 (C) on the one hand 一方面 (D) for the same reason 同理

　　解析：前面提到用行話讓同夥更加緊密，而連接詞while「和…同時」，後面談到排除不是同夥的人，所以二件事同時並行，所以應以 (B) at the same time（同時）最符合題意。

39. D；解析：本處單純考片語用法。to an end 達到目的，an endin itself本身即是很重要的事，所以本題答案為 (D)。

40. C；(A) visible 可看見的 (B) virtual實際上的 (C) vital 必要的 (D) visual 視覺的

41. A；中譯：科學認知的重大躍進大部分是被駁斥所驅動，而不是認可。(A) 科學重大的進步時常由質疑
而產生而不是支持意見 (B) 在人類史上造成大躍進的科學知識常被反對，不是被肯定 (C) 爭論產生科
學真理而達成共識致使社會融和 (D) 科學重大的發現時常是有名望的科學家做的，而非默默無聞的科
學家。

解析：題目主要說明重大科學進展一開始提出時常都是招致質疑的，經過辯論驗證後才會產生進步。
所以答案為 (A)。

42 – 46. 中譯：

麥克‧克萊頓接續他最暢銷小說的後續是一部比改寫作品更不持續原路線的作品，史匹柏只對
他的兩個點子有興趣：一座恐龍 DNA 已被創造出的神祕島嶼出現及一段暴龍在牠的寶寶被科學家威脅
後，想把一輛拖掛車推下山崖。所以史匹柏與〈侏羅紀公園〉編劇大衛柯普創造出一個新故事。這位小
說家既沒有被徵詢相關結局，也沒有收到腳本，一直到他撤回某些商業所有權。但克萊頓現在看來充滿
自信的說：「當我寫書時，我必須使書看起來就像是我要的一樣，就是這樣。影片將會是像導演所要的
一樣，就是這樣了。」

史匹柏後來在與柯普會面結束之前想出了〈失落的世界〉的主題，史匹柏說：「我想到了，這部
電影是有關於獵人及採集者」，戲劇張力發自關於無賴的商人為聖地牙哥主題公園繁殖恐龍作為故事核
心衝突─這最危險的計劃招自慘烈的後果。史匹柏建議柯普去看1925年阿瑟‧柯南‧道先生的〈失落的
世界〉，它談到一個南美洲叢林保護區的探險，在那裏還存有恐龍悠遊其中，以及霍華‧霍克斯的
〈獵獸奇觀〉，它由約翰偉恩主演敘述在獵獸計畫（幫動物園抓動物抽取酬勞）中作為一個遠征隊獵人
的故事，柯普說：「〈獵獸奇觀〉可能對我們的影響比任何恐龍的電影來得多」。

42. B；中譯：依據本文，誰是〈失落的世界〉導演？(A) 麥克‧克萊頓 (B) 史匹柏 (C) 大衛柯普 (D) 阿瑟‧
柯南‧道先生。

解析：由 Spielberg came up with the theme of *The Lost World* at the end of a meeting with Koepp⋯表示是
史蒂芬想出整個故事的主要架構，後面提到指導柯普去看其他電影，所以導演是史蒂芬。

43. C；中譯：依據本文，誰是〈侏羅紀公園〉的編劇？(A) 麥克‧克萊頓 (B) 史匹柏 (C) 大衛柯普 (D) 阿
瑟‧柯南‧道先生。

解析：由⋯Spielberg and David Koepp, a screenwriter on *Jurassic Park*, fashioned a new story⋯可看出大
衛柯普是〈侏羅紀公園〉的編劇。

44. B；中譯：〈失落的世界〉主題為何？(A) 恐龍和人類 (B) 獵人與採集者 (C) 科學與考古 (D) 自然與人
類。

解析：由Spielberg came up with the theme of *The Lost World*⋯"I've got it! This movie is about hunters vs.
gatherers."⋯可看出〈失落的世界〉主題是獵人與採集者。

45. C；中譯：下列哪一部電影與恐龍無關？(A)〈恐龍〉(B)〈失落的世界〉(C)〈獵獸奇觀〉(D)〈侏儸紀公
園〉。

解析：(A) 文中沒有提到〈恐龍〉這部電影，但合理判斷與恐龍有關 (B) 本文主要談〈失落的世界〉中
相關恐龍情節 (C) 文中提到*Hatari!*, starring John Wayne as a safari hunter on a game preserve⋯並沒有提

到本片與恐龍有關，後面提到〈獵獸奇觀〉對恐龍電影的影響是它的探險劇情 (D) 由文中推知〈侏儸紀公園〉為〈失落的世界〉前部，而〈失落的世界〉講述恐龍，所以〈侏儸紀公園〉必與恐龍有關。

46. C；中譯："sanguine"這個字的意思與下列何者相近？

解析：文中 sanguine 充滿自信的，(A) fond of blood shed 嗜殺 (B) healthy in mind 心靈健康 (C) optimistic 樂觀的 (D) reasonable 有理的；與 (C) optimistic 樂觀比較相近。

46－50. 中譯：

有許多細菌已經變得有抗藥性這件事證明了微生物的強韌性，然而還有更強的。一些細菌甚至將抗生素當早餐吃，更有甚者，這些超級細菌已自然地散佈在土壤中了。

為了進行細菌在曝露於人造抗生素之各種不同程度的研究，研究團隊從分散的11個地點採土壤取樣，這時他們將這些樣本曝露於 18 種抗生素中，全部 11 個土壤樣本都含有細菌且可以用抗生素來做實驗而這些細菌把抗生素當碳的唯一來源而存活，這些抗生素包括一些常被開處方籤的，更有甚者，在大部分土壤樣本中，除了一個抗生素外其他抗生素全成了細菌的食物。

為了要能夠吃抗生素，這些細菌顯然必須有高度的抵抗性。確實它們能忍受極度濃縮的抗生素，這些能吃毒的細菌不會危害人類，然而它們的有些近親會危害人類，因為細菌隨地地交換基因，科學家警告這些居住土壤裏的細菌可能有能力將超級抗藥基因傳遞給他們的那些易於感染人的同類。

47. D；中譯：(A) 其它可以很容易被抗生素摧毀 (B) 幸運地，沒有很多在土壤裡被發現 (C) 然而，它們有些近親會危害人類 (D) 更有甚者，這些超級細菌已自然地散佈在土壤中了。

解析：注意本段提到的用語，由However, here is tougher some bacteria actually…開頭說細菌有抗藥性，再來說有更強的，所以可期待後面可能還有更令人驚訝的事會出現，選項中以 (D) 最合適，且帶入文章中符合邏輯。

48. C；中譯：(A) 其它可以很容易被抗生素摧毀 (B) 令人驚訝的是，不是所有細菌都有抗藥性 (C) 這時他們將這些樣本曝露於 18 種抗生素中 (D) 更有甚者，在大部分土壤樣本中，除了一個抗生素外其他抗生素全成了細菌的食物。

解析：空格前提到取樣的方式，後面是加入抗生素的結果，所以依流程應該有說明加入的方式等，所以選項 (C) 最合適，且帶入文章中符合邏輯。

49. D；中譯：(A) 幸運地，沒有很多在土壤裡被發現 (B) 這時他們將這些樣品曝露於 18 種抗生素中 (C) 而且這些抗生素還有像是天然的盤尼西林 (D) 更有甚者，在大部分土壤樣本中，除了一個抗生素外其他抗生素全成了細菌的食物。

解析：本段主要在說土壤中的細菌與抗生素間的關係，空格前提到細菌把抗生素當碳的唯一來源而存活，故用實驗的情況來說明結尾是合理的，所以選項 (D) 最合適，且帶入文章中符合邏輯。

50. C；中譯：(A) 它們甚至可以被用來做藥物使用 (B) 令人驚訝的是，不是所有細菌都有抗藥性 (C) 然而，它們有些近親會危害人類 (D) 更有甚者，這些超級細菌已自然地散佈在土壤中了。

解析：空格前提到這些可以吃毒的細菌不會危害人類，後面提到有可能會透過基因交換而改變，所以談的都是細菌與人類的關係，所以選項 (C) 說有些細菌的親戚是會危害人類的是最合適的答案。

📋 102 公務人員普通考試試題

類科：各類別
科目：法學知識與英文（此節錄英文部分）

( ) 31. The woman sued her company for gender _____ because she was laid off for her pregnancy.

    (A) distinction   (B) discrimination (C) inspection   (D) examination

( ) 32. It is a _____ that the kid fell from the tenth floor and survived with only some abrasions.

    (A) misery   (B) muscle   (C) medal   (D) miracle

( ) 33. Many people took _____ surgery to make themselves look prettier.

    (A) electric   (B) historic   (C) realistic   (D) plastic

( ) 34. It is customary that Chinese _____ red color with good luck.

    (A) associate   (B) communicate (C) operate   (D) resolve

( ) 35. Although the company did not make profits this season, the manager is still _____ about the prospect.

    (A) imaginative   (B) optimistic   (C) realistic   (D) objective

( ) 36. Jewish teaching says that at death the body returns to God, so funerals take place within 24 hours to get the _____ there all the quicker.

    (A) adherent   (B) deceased   (C) eccentric   (D) veteran

請依下文回答第37題至第40題：

    Robert Frost (1874-1963) is one of the most well-known 20th century American poets. People like to talk about his nature poems, which seem to show a spontaneous love of nature and simple little pleasures in life. But little do most people know about the ___37___ side of the great poet's life. Robert Frost lost his first son and second daughter when theywere little. And in his sixties, two years after his beloved wife's death, his son, long _____38_____ from depression and suspiciousness, committed suicide with a deer hunting rifle. In his last years, _____39_____ still keeping a terribly busy and active public life, he was tortured by pneumonia, cancer, and embolism. Having learned about the _____40_____ of the poet,we can finally fully appreciate the death wish shown in one of his famous poems of his last years, "Stopping by Woodson a Snowy Evening."

(　) 37. (A) organic 　　(B) optimistic 　　(C) symbolic 　　(D) traumatic
(　) 38. (A) refraining 　　(B) issuing 　　(C) suffering 　　(D) coming
(　) 39. (A) as 　　(B) while 　　(C) yet 　　(D) because of
(　) 40. (A) myths 　　(B) morals 　　(C) misfortunes 　　(D) mistakes

請依下文回答第41 題至第45 題：

　　Many people feel jealous from time to time. Jealousy is easy to deal with, once you understand what it's teaching you. Here are some pointers on working through your feelings of jealousy.

　　First of all, you should understand your emotions. Jealousy is a combination of fear and anger; a fear of losing something, and anger that someone is "moving in on" something that you feel belongs only to you. When you start feeling jealous, ask yourself: is it more fear based, or more anger based? If you feel a dropping or clutching sensation in your stomach, it's probably fear. If you feel a burning, tight sensation in your shoulders and jaw, then you're likely feeling anger. You might also feel a combination of those sensations.

　　Secondly, understand that jealousy can alert you to what you want, and what is important to you. If you're jealous of someone talking to a friend of yours, personal relationships may be important to you. If you're jealous about money, you may have an underlying need for security. When you begin to understand what makes you jealous, you can begin to take positive steps to maintain those things, without the cloud of negative emotion that accompanies jealousy.

( ) 41. What is the best title for this passage?

(A) The Consequences of Jealousy

(B) How to Better Understand Jealousy

(C) The Importance of Personal Relationships

(D) Understanding What You Want

( ) 42. Which of the following is true about jealousy?

(A) Fear is the primary reason for jealousy.

(B) Jealousy can cause stomachache.

(C) It is not possible to figure out why we are jealous.

(D) People are jealous about the things they dislike.

( ) 43. What is a symptom of anger-based jealousy?

(A) Coldness in the stomach.   (B) A burning heart.

(C) Lack of appetite.   (D) Tightness in the shoulders.

( ) 44. What does the author suggest for dealing with jealousy?

(A) Earn more money to be secure.

(B) Talk to an important friend about your jealousy.

(C) Take medicine to deal with fear-based jealousy.

(D) Understand what contributes to your jealousy.

( ) 45. If you are jealous of someone talking to your good friends, which of the following statements may be true?

(A) You value this relationship greatly.

(B) You do not have financial security.

(C) You are not sociable.

(D) You do not understand your emotions.

請依下文回答第46 題至第50 題：

　　A young woman went to her mother and told her how life was so hard for her. She did not know how she was going to make it and wanted to give up. Her mother took her to the kitchen. She filled three pots with water and placed each on a high fire. Soon the pots came to boil. In the first she placed carrots, in the second she placed eggs, and in the last she placed ground coffee beans. She let them sit and boil. In about twenty minutes she turned off the burners. She ladled out the carrots, the eggs, and the coffee and placed each in a bowl. Turning to her daughter, she asked, "Tell me what you see." "Carrots, eggs, and coffee," she replied.

　　Her mother brought her closer and asked her to feel the carrots. She noted that they were soft. The mother then asked the daughter to take an egg and break it. After pulling off the shell, she observed the hard boiled egg. Finally, the mother asked the daughter to sip the coffee. The daughter smiled as she tasted its rich aroma. The daughter then asked, "What does it mean, mother?"

　　Her mother explained that each of these objects had faced the same adversity: boiling water. Each reacted differently. The carrot went in strong, hard, and unrelenting. However, after being subjected to the boiling water, it softened and became weak. The egg had been fragile. Its thin outer shell had protected its liquid interior, but after sitting through the boiling water, its inside became hardened. The ground coffee beans were unique, however. After they were in the boiling water, they had changed the water.

　　"Which are you?" she asked her daughter. "When adversity knocks on your door, how do you respond? Are you acarrot, an egg, or a coffee bean?"

(　　) 46. What is this story mainly about?

(A) How to cook carrots, eggs, and coffee beans.

(B) The importance of cooking for a woman.

(C) A mother's affection for her daughter.

(D) Different attitudes when facing difficulties.

(　　) 47. How did the mother cook carrots, eggs, and coffee beans?

(A) She mixed and boiled them in one pot.

(B) With a pot, she cooked each in order.

(C) She boiled them in separate pots.

(D) She placed them directly above the oven.

(　　) 48. What lesson would the daughter learn from the eggs?

(A) Birds of a feather flock together.

(B) God helps those who help themselves.

(C) The harder the life is, the stronger one becomes.

(D) Don't bite off more than you can chew.

(　　) 49. According to the story, which of the following is NOT true?

(A) Like the carrots, one may surrender in a tough situation.

(B) Like the eggs, one may be still as fragile as the shell even after struggling for a long time.

(C) Like the ground coffee beans, one may change the circumstance that brings the pain.

(D) Like the carrots, one may become weaker after a series of adversities.

(　　) 50. What does "adversity" mean in the third paragraph?

(A) Hardship.　　(B) Value.　　(C) Failure.　　(D) Luck.

102 年公務人員普通考試中譯解析

31. B；中譯：這位婦女告她的公司性別歧視，因為她被公司以懷孕的理由解雇。

　　解析：(A) distinction 區別 (B) discrimination 歧視 (C) inspection 檢查 (D) examination 考試

32. D；中譯：那個小孩從十樓摔下還能活著且只有一些擦傷真是一個奇蹟。

　　解析：(A) misery 痛苦 (B) muscle 肌肉 (C) medal 勳章 (D) miracle 奇蹟

33. D；中譯：許多人去做整形手術讓他們自己看來更漂亮。

　　解析：(A) electric 電動的 (B) historic 歷史的 (C) realistic 現實的 (D) plastic 塑料的

34. A；中譯：中國人把紅色與好運連結在一起是慣例。

　　解析：(A) associate 使聯結 (B) communicate 傳達 (C) operate 操作 (D) resolve 決定

　　本題考動詞用法，It is…that 指（某事）是如何的…，中國人常把紅色與好運的想法連結在一起，故答案為 (A)。

35. B；中譯：雖然公司在這季沒有賺錢，經理仍然對未來展望感到樂觀。

　　解析：(A) imaginative 想像的 (B) optimistic 樂觀的 (C) realistic 現實的 (D) objective 目標的

36. B；中譯：猶太的說法認為人死後身體回歸上帝，所以喪禮在 24 小時內舉行以讓死者盡快到那裏。

　　解析：(A) adherent 黏附的 (B) deceased 已死的 (C) eccentric 古怪的 (D) veteran 老練的

　　本題考形容詞單字及慣用語 to get somebody there 讓某人到那裏；all the quicker 盡快。本題重點為 the+形容詞表示那種人，例如：the poor（窮人），依據題意本處指死掉的人，也就是 the deceased（死者），所以答案為 (B)。

37.－40. 中譯：

　　羅伯佛斯特（1874-1963）是 20 世紀美國最有名的詩人之一，人們喜愛談到有他有關田園的詩，那些似乎顯示出對自然自發的愛以及生活中的小確幸，但大部分人不知道這位偉大詩人生命中受創傷的一面。羅伯佛斯特的小孩還很小的時候就相繼失去大兒子與二女兒，在他六十歲時，就在他摯愛的妻子過逝後二年，他長期為憂鬱症及恐懼症所苦的兒子，用一隻獵鹿獵槍自殺了。在他的最後幾年，當他仍然持續非常忙碌及積極參與群眾生活時候，他被肺炎、癌症及栓塞所折磨。我們在知道這位詩人的不幸後，我們終於可以完全體會在他晚年一首有名的詩句中說的死的期許：「雪夜暫停於林外」。

37. D；(A) organic 器官的 (B) optimistic 樂觀的 (C) symbolic 象徵的 (D) traumatic 創傷的

　　解析：本處需填入形容詞，來說明他生命中的狀況，由後面幾句話得知他其實是有很多不幸，所以選項中以 (D) traumatic（創傷的）最為符合。

38. C；(A) refraining 忍住 (B) issuing 發行 (C) suffering 遭受 (D) coming 前來

　　解析：本處需填入一動名詞，由後面 from depression and suspiciousness…得知應該用 suffering from（為…所苦），所以答案為 (C)。

39. B；解析：本處需填入連接詞引導的副詞片語，說明他生命後面幾年的情況，也就是說當他仍然持續各項工作時，他被肺炎等疾病所苦。所以在此用 while（當…同時），答案為 (B)。

40. C；(A) myths 神話 (B) morals 道德 (C) misfortunes 不幸 (D) mistakes 錯誤

41.－45. 中譯：

　　許多人不時感到忌妒，忌妒是容易處理的，當你一旦瞭解它在教你甚麼時，這邊是一些要點來處理你忌妒的感覺。

　　首先，你應該了解你的情緒。忌妒是一種恐懼及憤怒的組合，一種害怕失去，對某人正對你認為該屬於自己東西步步逼進而來感到生氣。當你開始感到忌妒，問問自己：那是基於恐懼，或比較基於生氣。如果在你腹部有一種落下或緊握的感覺，那可能是害怕；如果你感覺到在你的肩部及下顎有燃燒、緊緊的感覺，這時你可能正感到生氣。你可能也會覺得有這些感覺的混合。

　　再來，瞭解忌妒可以提醒你要的是甚麼，以及甚麼對你是重要的。如果你是忌妒某人跟你朋友講話，人際關係可能對你是重要的，如果你忌妒金錢，你可能有安全的潛在需求。當你開始去瞭解甚麼東西讓你感到忌妒，你就可以開始採取正向的步驟來處理這些事情，而沒有伴隨忌妒而來負面情緒的陰霾。

41. B；中譯：下列何者是本文最適當的題目 (A) 忌妒的後果 (B) 如何更了解忌妒 (C) 人際關係的重要性 (D) 瞭解你要甚麼。

　　解析：本篇一開始談到產生忌妒的由來，再談到忌妒的感覺，最後說忌妒代表的意涵，讓人更了解忌妒，所以本題答案為 (B)。

42. B；中譯：下列何項關於忌妒是真的 (A) 恐懼是忌妒最主要原因 (B) 忌妒會引起胃痛 (C) 知道我們自己為什麼忌妒是不可能的 (D) 人們對他不喜歡的東西會忌妒

　　解析：(A) 由…Jealousy is a combination of fear and anger…知恐懼及生氣才是忌妒最主要原因，敘述為非 (B) 由If you feel a dropping or clutching sensation in your stomach, it's probably fear…，這種因害怕產生的忌妒症狀，引申出忌妒會引起胃痛，敘述正確 (C) 文中已有指出忌妒是一種恐懼及憤怒的組合，敘述為非 (D) 由…that jealousy can alert you to what you want, and what is important to you…知人對想要的東西及重要的東西才會忌妒，敘述為非。所以本題答案為 (B)。

43. D；中譯：下列何項症狀是起因於生氣的忌妒 (A) 胃部冷冷的 (B) 心像火在燒 (C) 沒食慾 (D) 肩膀緊緊的

　　解析：由…If you feel a burning, tight sensation in your shoulders and jaw, then you're likely feeling anger，可知因生氣引起的忌妒的症狀是肩部及下顎有燃燒、緊緊的感覺，所以答案為 (D)。

44. D；中譯：作者建議如何處理忌妒 (A) 賺更多錢以策安全 (B) 向重要的朋友談你的忌妒 (C) 吃藥來處理有關因害怕引起的忌妒 (D) 瞭解是甚麼造成你的忌妒

　　解析：由…When you begin to understand what makes you jealous, you can begin to take positive steps to…，可知去瞭解甚麼東西讓你感到忌妒，你就可以處理忌妒的問題，所以答案為 (D)。

45. A；中譯：如果你忌妒某人跟你好朋友講話，下列何像敘述為真？(A) 你很重視這個關係 (B) 你沒有財務安全 (C) 你不擅長於社交 (D) 你不了解你的情緒。

　　解析：由…If you're jealous of someone talking to a friend of yours, personal relationships may be important to you…，可知如果是忌妒某人跟你朋友講話，人際關係可能對你是重要的，所以答案為(A)。

46.－50. 中譯：

　　一個年輕女子去見她媽媽並告訴她對她來說生活是如此辛苦。她並不知道她要如何克服且想要放棄，她母親帶她到廚房。她倒滿三個鍋子的水並將每個鍋子放在大火上煮，不久鍋子開始沸騰，第一個她放進紅蘿蔔，第二個她放蛋，在最後一個她放咖啡粉，她讓它們大火快煮，約二十分鐘後她關掉爐火，她撈出紅蘿蔔，雞蛋及咖啡，並將每個放進一個碗內，她轉身對著她女兒問說：「告訴我你看到甚麼」，「紅蘿蔔、蛋、及咖啡」，她回答。

她母親帶她靠近一點並且要求她去摸紅蘿蔔，她發現它們都變軟了，母親這時要求女兒去拿一個蛋並打破它，在撥開蛋殼後，她觀察到變硬的熟蛋，最後，母親要求女兒啜飲咖啡，當她嚐到咖啡豐富的風味後女兒笑了，女兒這時問她：「母親，這是甚麼意思？」

她母親解釋說這些東西每一樣都已歷經相同的苦難：滾燙的水。每個反應都不同，紅蘿蔔進去的時候強壯堅硬且不屈不撓，然而，在滾水中煮後它變軟化並柔弱，雞蛋原來是易脆的，它的薄外殼原本保護它液態的內部，但經由待在滾水中，它的內部變成硬化了。咖啡粉原來都是獨特單一的，在它們與開水加在一起之後，它們已經改變了水。

「你是哪一個？」，她問她的女兒，「當逆境敲你門時，你如何回應，你是紅蘿蔔、雞蛋或是一個咖啡粉？」

46. D；中譯：這故事主要談到甚麼？(A) 如何煮紅蘿蔔、雞蛋及咖啡 (B) 烹飪對女人的重要性 (C) 一個母親對女兒的影響 (D) 當面臨困境的不同態度

解析：本篇主要講述一個母親用三種食物煮過後不同的結果，讓女兒了解不同的東西經過相同的苦難後每個反應都不同，所以本題答案為 (D)。

47. C；中譯：這位母親如何煮紅蘿蔔、雞蛋及咖啡？(A) 她把它們混在一鍋煮 (B) 用一個鍋子依序來煮(C) 她把它們在不同的鍋子煮 (D) 她把它們直接在放在爐子上

解析：由…She filled three pots with water and placed each on a high fire…，知她把三樣東西分開放三個鍋子來煮，所以本題答案為 (C)。

48. C；中譯：女兒從雞蛋中會學到甚麼？(A) 物以類聚 (B) 人助自助者 (C) 生活愈艱困，人就愈堅強 (D) 不要貪得無厭。

解析：由文中提到雞蛋受到滾水煮過後，原來柔弱的內部變成硬化了，意指外在環境困難會讓原本柔弱的東西變堅強，所以選項 (C) 最符合。

49. B；中譯：依據這故事，下列何者為非？(A) 就像紅蘿蔔，人可能在艱苦環境中投降 (B) 就像雞蛋，經過長時間的掙扎後，人可能仍然跟蛋殼一樣易碎 (C) 就像咖啡粉，人可能把帶給他痛苦的環境給改變了 (D) 就像紅蘿蔔，在一連串的苦難後，人可能變得更軟弱

解析：(A) 紅蘿蔔原來堅硬，煮過後變軟，就像在艱苦環境中投降，敘述正確 (B) 雞蛋煮過後內部變硬，但沒提到蛋殼變化，敘述為非 (C) 咖啡粉煮後與開水混合後，變得風味更好，就像把帶給它痛苦的環境給改變了，敘述正確 (D) 紅蘿蔔原來堅硬，煮過後變軟，就像在一連串的苦難後把人變得更軟弱，敘述正確。故答案為 (B)。

50. A；中譯：在第三段"adversity"這個字意義是麼？(A) Hardship 艱難 (B) Value 價值 (C) Failure 缺乏 (D) Luck 幸運

解析：adversity 意思是苦難，與 (A) Hardship 艱難意義最相近。

📋 102 公務人員高等考試三級考試試題

類科：各類科
科目：法學知識與英文（此節錄英文部分）

( ) 31. The land is a storehouse of _____ for all kinds of plants, and its reserve of nutrients is essential to any successful agriculture.

(A) facilities   (B) fertility   (C) nuance   (D) pesticides

( ) 32. The United States is _____ with an energy, a can-do ambition and an entrepreneurial spirit that can only be described as distinctly American.

(A) invested   (B) compatible   (C) consistent   (D) infused

( ) 33. The movie was recommended for mature audiences only because there were many scenes of intense violence which would be too _____ for children.

(A) authentic   (B) contagious   (C) disturbing   (D) embarrassing

( ) 34. The restaurant's advertisement was a bit _____ . It said all of the drinks were free, but actually wines were not included.

(A) cautious   (B) pretending   (C) suspicious   (D) misleading

( ) 35. Smartphones seem to have a _____ market since they are getting more and more popular around the world.

(A) burgeoning   (B) languishing   (C) perplexing   (D) squandering

( ) 36. The Colosseum in Rome and sites in the historic walled town of Urbino have suffered damage due to _____ snow-fall.

(A) indispensable   (B) minuscule   (C) picturesque   (D) unprecedented

( ) 37. Basic _____ like greeting people and saying please to show politeness are becoming less common among the youth.

(A) customs   (B) courtesies   (C) gestures   (D) situations

(　) 38. The first comprehensive system for nationwide _____ was instituted by France for the Napoleonic wars that followed the French Revolution.

(A) conscription　　(B) description　　(C) inscription　　(D) prescription

請依下文回答第39 題至43 題：

　　A study at the University of New South Wales in Sydney found that around a quarter of people have a ___39___ sense of taste, making foods like broccoli taste bitter and rich foods ___40___ . These "supertasters" tend to be slim and have a lower risk of heart disease. To determine if you are a supertaster, ___41___ a dot of blue food coloring on your tongue and look in the mirror. If you see a densely spotted area, there is a good chance you are a supertaster. If the spots are ___42___ distributed, you are not. The study also found 15 percent of people, ___43___ men, were "non-tasters"—they will devour anything put in front of them. They get the benefits of a broad diet, but risk overdoing it.

(　) 39. (A) heightened　　(B) enlightened　　(C) fastened　　(D) lengthened
(　) 40. (A) unperceptive　　(B) unpredictable　　(C) unpalatable　　(D) unparalleled
(　) 41. (A) notice　　(B) delete　　(C) put　　(D) remove
(　) 42. (A) succinctly　　(B) sparsely　　(C) diminutively　　(D) trivially
(　) 43. (A) innocently　　(B) mostly　　(C) arrogantly　　(D) currently

(　) 44. A study has shown that a messy environment could make people long for order and inspire them to hastily simplify and classify things in their minds, which could often lead to discrimination.

(A) Eliminating discrimination can be done by living with a simple and neat mind.

(B) Inspiring simplicity and order is the key to preventing discrimination from happening.

(C) Discriminating against the people living in a messy environment could inspire them to improve.

(D) Rushing to create order in a messy environment could sometimes lead to discrimination.

( ) 45. Investors and the public are demanding increasingly detailed information on nonfinancial metrics that define sustainability.

(A) In terms of financial metrics, investors and the public are never satisfied with the sustainable business.

(B) Detailed information on monetary metrics plays a more important role for sustainable investors and the public.

(C) Other than financial reports, investors and the public are asking for more details about factors indicating sustainability.

(D) Investors and the public keep inquiring detailed information on nonfinancial metrics to sustain the validity of the contract.

( ) 46. What great horror movies do is that they show us our fears and make them so beautiful that we can't take our eyes off the screen.

(A) Great horror movies catch our eyes by showing us our fears in an irresistibly beautiful way on the screen.

(B) Great horror movies force us to examine our fears through frightening but beautiful scenes on the screen.

(C) Great horror movies amaze us by showing us frightening scenes about our beauty on the screen.

(D) Great horror movies allow us to transform our fears in an irresistible way into beautiful scenes on the screen.

請依下文回答第47題至第50題：

In 1349 it resumed in Paris, spread to Picardy, Flanders, and the Low Countries, and from England to Scotland and Ireland as well as to Norway, where a ghost ship with a cargo of wool and a dead crew drifted offshore until it ran aground near Bergen. From there the plague passed into Sweden, Denmark,

Prussia, Iceland, and as far as Greenland. Leaving a strange pocket of immunity in Bohemia and Russia unattacked until 1351, it had passed from most of Europe by the mid-1350s. Although the mortality rate was erratic, ranging from one-fifth in some places to nine-tenths or almost total elimination in others, the overall estimate of modern demographers has settled—for the area extending from India to Iceland—around the same figure expressed in Froissart's casual words: "A third of the world dies." His estimate, the common one at the time, was not an inspired guess but a borrowing of St. John's figure for mortality from the plague in Revelation, the favorite guide to human affairs of the Middle Ages.

(　) 47. What does the underlined "it" in the first line refer to?

(A) The ghost ship　　　　　　(B) The mortality

(C) The immunity　　　　　　(D) The plague

(　) 48. Which of the following countries was NOT affected by the disease at first?

(A) Denmark　　　　　　(B) France

(C) Russia　　　　　　(D) United Kingdom

(　) 49. According to the passage, which of the following statements is true?

(A) The number of deaths given by Froissart is not reliable.

(B) The disease described in the passage broke out first in 1349.

(C) The mortality rates of the affected countries differ greatly.

(D) An infected ship landing on Bergen started the spread of the disease in Norway.

(　) 50. What is the sequence in which the plague reached the countries or cities?

(A) Paris—Bergen—Iceland—Russia

(B) Picardy—Iceland—Greenland—Flanders

(C) The Low Countries—Prussia—England—India

(D) Russia—Picardy—the Low Countries—Norway

102年公務人員高等考試中譯解析

31. B；中譯：這塊地對所有植物來說是一塊肥沃的寶地，且它所含有的養份對任何成功的農耕都是必需的。

解析：(A) facilities 設施 (B) fertility 肥沃 (C) nuance 細微差別 (D) pesticides 農藥
本題考名詞。storehouse 寶庫，一塊適合種植的寶地應該是很肥沃的，所以選項中以 fertility（肥沃）最適合，也就是 a storehouse of fertility 一個肥沃的寶庫，所以答案為 (B)。

32. D；中譯：美國是充滿了活力、樂觀進取心及創業者精神，而這只能用獨特的美國人來形容。

解析：(A) invested 投資 (p.p.) (B) compatible 相容的 (C) consistent 前後一致的 (D) infused 注入 (p.p.)
本題考被動用法。美國有三種不同特質，也就是三種特質注入形成美國文化，觀念上是被動語氣，所以選項中用 infused（注入），即 be infused with，故答案為 (D)。

33. C；中譯：這部電影只適合成年人因為裡面有許多殘暴的場景會太驚擾到小孩子。

解析：(A) authentic 可信的 (B) contagious 傳染的 (C) disturbing 驚擾的 (D) embarrassing 令人為難的
本題考形容詞。too+adj for…對…來說，本句提到電影暴力會對孩子的影響，所以選項中用disturbing（驚擾的）最符合題意，故答案為(C)。

34. D；中譯：餐廳的廣告有點誤導人，它說所有飲料都免費，但事實上酒類不包括。

解析：(A) cautious 小心的 (B) pretending 假裝的 (C) suspicious 可疑的 (D) misleading 令人誤解的
本題考形容詞。句中提到酒類並非免費，有誤導之嫌，所以此處用 misleading（誤導）最符合題意，故答案為 (D)。

35. A；中譯：智慧型手機自從它們在全世界愈來愈流行後似乎有急速成長的市場。

解析：(A) burgeoning 急速成長的 (B) languishing 衰弱的 (C) perplexing 麻煩的 (D) squandering 揮霍（現在分詞）
本題考形容詞。句中提到智慧型手機是愈來愈風行，所以市場應該是蓬勃發展，所以選項中以 burgeoning（急速成長的）最符合題意，故答案為 (A)。

36. D；中譯：古羅馬競技場及在Urbino具歷史的城牆遺址由於空前的降雪已遭受損壞。

解析：(A) indispensable 不可或缺的 (B) minuscule 微小的 (C) picturesque 圖畫般美麗的 (D) unprecedented 空前的
本題考形容詞用法，due to 由於（原因），句中提到古蹟損壞的原因是有關降雪（snow-fall），所以選項中以 unprecedented（空前的）最符合題意，表示因空前的降雪導致古蹟損壞，故答案為 (D)。

37. B；中譯：基本的禮貌，像是問候別人及說聲請來表示有禮的，在年輕人間變得愈來愈少。

解析：(A) customs 習慣 (B) courtesies 禮貌 (C) gestures 姿態 (D) situations 位置
本題考名詞。由句子中提到的一些行為都是跟禮貌有關，表示這些都是基本的禮貌，故答案為 (B)。

38. A；中譯：第一次全國性的兵役徵用系統是由法國創立為了在法國大革命後拿破崙的戰爭。

解析：(A) conscription 徵兵 (B) description 敘述 (C) inscription 記載 (D) prescription 處方
本題考名詞，be instituted by由…所創立，句子中提到拿破崙戰爭，所以選項中以conscription徵兵最符合題意，故答案為 (A)。

39.－43. 中譯：

　　一項雪梨新南威爾斯大學的研究發現，四分之一的人有高度的味覺，使一些食物像是花椰菜嚐起來更苦且油膩的食品味道不好。這些超級味覺者比較瘦且有較低的心臟疾病風險。為了確認你是否是個超級味覺者，放一滴的藍色食物染料在你舌頭上並照鏡子看，假如你看到一個濃稠的點狀範圍，你有很大的機會是超級味覺者。假如點成稀疏分佈，那你就不是。這項研究也發現有15%的人，大部分是男人，是沒有味覺的，它們將吃光放在它們前面的任何東西，他們有好食慾的優點，但有過度的風險。

39. A；(A) heightened 增高 (B) enlightened 開導 (C) fastened 固定 (D) lengthened 拉長

解析：空格中需填入形容詞，選項中均為動詞過去分詞，可當形容詞用，由後面 making foods…知該段是講有關味覺比一般敏感的人，所以選項中以 heightened 增高來形容味覺最符合，故答案為 (A)。

40. C；(A) unperceptive 無知覺的 (B) unpredictable 無法預測的 (C) unpalatable 不好吃的 (D) unparalleled 空前的

解析：空格中需填入形容詞，說明油膩的食物這些人口中的感覺，所以選項中以unpalatable不好吃最符合，並可與前面…broccoli taste bitter…（花椰菜嚐起來更苦）相對應，故答案為 (C)。

41. C；解析：本句為祈使句結構，所以空格中需填入動詞原形，由…a dot of blue food coloring on your tongue…，知要將一滴染料放進舌頭上，所以動詞用 put，故答案為 (C)。

42. B；(A) succinctly 簡潔地 (B) sparsely 稀疏地 (C) diminutively 小地 (D) trivially 瑣細地

解析：空格中需填入副詞修飾後面動詞，由前面提到染料放進超級味覺者舌頭上，會呈濃稠狀，對比非超級味覺者應該相反，所以用sparsely稀疏地，故答案為 (B)。

43. B；(A) innocently 無辜地 (B) mostly 大部分 (C) arrogantly 自大地 (D) currently 現在

解析：選項中均為副詞，用mostly大部分，表示這些人大部分是男性，故答案為(B)。

44. D；中譯：一項研究顯示，一個混亂環境會讓人民渴望秩序，且激發他們輕率地依照他們心中的想法來分類事情，這時常導致歧視。(A) 生活在簡單及純淨的心境中可以消彌歧視 (B) 激發單純化及秩序是避免歧視不要發生的關鍵 (C) 歧視生活在一個混亂環境人民可以激發他們進步 (D) 在混亂的環境貿然建立秩序有時會導致歧視。

解析：…make people long for…make使役動詞，後面long是當動詞用，指渴望。本句主要意思式表達混亂的環境會讓人失去理性判斷的能力，並導致歧視，所以答案為 (D)。

45. C；中譯：投資者及大眾正逐漸地要求提供可做為持續性指標的非財務度量的明確資訊。(A)有關於財務度量，投資者及大眾從來不滿意可持續的事務 (B) 對可持續的投資者及大眾而言，詳細的財務度量資訊扮演一個更重要的角色 (C) 除了財政報告，投資者及大眾正要求更多有關顯示持續性因素的細節 (D) 投資者及大眾持續要求在非財務度量的詳細資訊以維持合約的正當性

解析：題目重點為要求非財務度量（nonfinancial metrics）投資者會關心這些詳細資訊。所以答案為 (C)。

46. A；中譯：好的恐怖電影就是它們能顯現出我們的恐懼，且讓它們變得如此美好的以致於我們的眼睛離不開螢幕。(A) 好的恐怖電影可以在螢幕上以一個無法抗拒的美好方式以顯現我們的恐懼來引起我們的注意 (B) 好的恐怖電影迫使我們經由螢幕上驚嚇但美好的場面來檢視我們的恐懼 (C) 好的恐怖電影經由螢幕上表現出關於我們美好的驚嚇場面來讓我們感到驚奇 (D) 好的恐怖電影讓我們能以一個無法抵擋的方式轉移我們的恐懼成為螢幕上美好的場景

解析：show us our fears 顯現給我們關於我們恐懼的事，該句重點為恐怖電影要能吸引人的注意力使眼睛離不開螢幕，雖然人們是恐懼的，所以答案為 (A)。

47.－50. 中譯：

在 1349 年，它由巴黎重新開始，傳播到皮卡第，佛蘭德，以及低地國家，且從英格蘭到蘇格蘭及愛爾蘭和挪威，在那裏一條鬼船帶著一船的原木及死掉的船員們漂浮在外海直到它在靠近卑爾根擱淺。瘟疫從那裏傳進瑞典、丹麥、普魯士、冰島且最遠到格林蘭。剩下一小部份不可思議免疫的地區如波西米亞及俄羅斯沒有受到攻擊直到 1351 年，在 1350 年代中期時它經過大部份的歐洲。雖然致命率是不固定的，某些國家範圍從1/5到9/10或在其他地區幾乎完全滅絕，現代人口統計學家全面估算已經確定了一從印度延伸到冰島的這個區域─這數值大約與 Froissart 隨意說的一樣：「死了世界上三分之一的人。」他的估算，在當時是個一般的估算，不是一個有根據的推測，而是借由約翰啟示錄上的瘟疫的致死率圖表，這在中世紀對人類事件最喜愛的指引。

47. D；中譯：在地一行的 "it" 是指 (A) 鬼船 (B) 致死率 (C) 免疫力 (D) 瘟疫

解析：In 1349 it resumed in Paris, spread to Picardy…，由該句動詞為 spread（傳播）知該 it 應是指瘟疫，而非鬼船，鬼船只是指那時在靠近卑爾根擱淺的一條神祕的船，所以答案為 (D) 瘟疫。

48. C；中譯：下列國家哪個最初沒有被這疾病影響 (A) 丹麥 (B) 法國 (C) 俄羅斯 (D) 英國

解析：由…Leaving a strange pocket of immunity in Bohemia and Russia unattacked until 1351…，知俄羅斯沒被影響，所以答案為 (C)。

49. C；中譯：依據本篇文章，下列哪像敘述為真 (A) Froissart 所給的死亡數目是不可靠的 (B) 文章中敘述的疾病最初爆發於 1349 年 (C) 被感染國家的致死率差異很大 (D) 一艘被感染的船在卑爾根登陸開啟了在挪威這種疾病的傳播

解析：(A) 由 the overall estimate of modern demographers has settled…around the same figure expressed in Froissart's casual words: "A third of the world dies." 知他所給的數目是大致吻合的，敘述為非 (B) 由 In 1349 it resumed in Paris…表示它由法國巴黎重新開始，但不是最初爆發，敘述為非 (C) 由 the mortality rate was erratic, ranging from one-fifth in some places to nine-tenths or almost total elimination …知致死率差異極大，敘述為真 (D) 文內有提到船在卑爾根擱淺，而進入挪威但沒說船上有被感傳染，敘述為非。所以答案為 (C)。

50. A；中譯：以下何者為瘟疫到達的國家或地區的順序 (A) 巴黎─卑爾根─冰島─俄羅斯 (B) 皮卡第─冰島─格林蘭─佛蘭德 (C) 低地國家─普魯士─英國─印度 (D) 俄羅斯─皮卡第─低地國家─挪威

解析：文中提到：由巴黎重新開始，傳播到皮卡第，佛蘭德，以及低地國家，從英格蘭到蘇格蘭及愛爾蘭和挪威，…靠近卑爾根…傳進瑞典、丹麥、普魯士、冰島且最遠到格林蘭…再到不可思議的免疫地區波西米亞及俄羅斯…，故 (A) 巴黎─卑爾根─冰島─俄羅斯的順序正確。

📋 102 公務人員初等考試考試試題

等別：初等考試
類科：一般行政
科目：公民與英文（此節錄英文部分）

( ) 36. I need some _____ to pay for the parking.

    (A) change   (B) checks

    (C) charge   (D) currency

( ) 37. Many people have died of liver cancer because it is difficult to _____ it in its early stages.

    (A) choose   (B) detect

    (C) prefer   (D) repeat

( ) 38. He gets very _____ with his job as a doorman.

    (A) bore   (B) boring

    (C) bores   (D) bored

( ) 39. It is a shame that the error was noticed only after Ms. Perng _____ the project proposal.

    (A) sends in   (B) has sent in

    (C) had sent in   (D) is sending in

( ) 40. William found the movie _____ because he loves the story about humans and animals.

    (A) to interest   (B) interest

    (C) interested   (D) interesting

( ) 41. David: I'm planning to go camping next weekend with my friends. Would you like to come with us?

    Doris: _____ .

    David: Are you sure you don't want to go? It should be a lot of fun.

(A) Oh, I'd like to, but I already have other plans.

(B) Where will you go?

(C) That sounds wonderful.

(D) Thanks for inviting me.

(　) 42. Waiter: Are you ready to order?

Tommy: Yes. Can I have the steak, please?

Waiter: _____ .

Tommy: Medium.

(A) How would you like it cooked?

(B) Which part would you like?

(C) How fast should we serve you?

(D) Do you prefer your steak well done?

Advertisements are everywhere. In order to draw our attention, advertisements have been _____43_____ in different mediums and forms. They have been shown in buses and cars to _____44_____ that people can see them wherever they go. They can also be seen in balloons floating up in the air. On the Internet, advertisements will pop up on the _____45_____ so that people cannot avoid them. Although most people might feel excited when first seeing them, they can still _____46_____ them away whenever they like. But people can do almost nothing about it if pop-up ads _____47_____ on television. It can really affect people and most people aren't happy to see them.

(　) 43. (A) suffered   (B) removed   (C) explained   (D) displayed

(　) 44. (A) take care   (B) make sure   (C) pay off   (D) act out

(　) 45. (A) screen   (B) keyboard   (C) mouse   (D) printer

(　) 46. (A) smile   (B) take   (C) click   (D) wipe

(　) 47. (A) perform   (B) watch   (C) appear   (D) sing

The thieves struck on the morning of August 22, 2004, not long after the Munch Museum had opened. The Sunday peace was broken by the shouting of the two men storming into the exhibition area. Using a gun to force the guards to the ground, they took two paintings off the wall and left. The whole thing took less than 5 minutes. The crime was seen as a shame to Norway, which regards Munch's paintings as among its most valued cultural treasures. One and a half years on, six men were charged and their trial began February 14, 2006. The police may catch the thieves, but they don't have the paintings. In the first place, the police took so long to arrive. By the time they did, the original witnesses were gone and the crime scene had been changed with other visitors. The only evidence they got was an unclear photo of two guys taken by the security camera. The police began to make some arrest 8 months later. As for the museum, it closed after the robbery and reopened 10 months later, after adding $6 million security equipment.

(　) 48. On what day did the robbery happen?

    (A) Monday.

    (B) Friday.

    (C) Saturday.

    (D) Sunday.

(　) 49. When did the Museum reopen?

    (A) April 2005.

    (B) June 2005.

    (C) February 2006.

    (D) December 2006.

(　) 50. Why did the late arrival of the police make it more difficult to find the paintings?

    (A) The guards had been seriously injured.

    (B) The security camera had been broken.

    (C) Some evidence might have been lost.

    (D) The visitors had been scared away

102年公務初等（一般行政）中譯解析

36. A；中譯：我需要一些零錢去付停車費。

解析：(A) change 零錢 (B)checks 支票 (C) charge 索價 (D) currency 貨幣

本題考名詞。停車費用零錢支付即可，所以答案所為 (A)。

37. B；中譯：許多人因肺癌而死亡，因為要早期發現它是很困難的。

解析：(A) choose 選擇 (B) detect 偵測 (C) prefer 寧可 (D) repeat 反覆

本題考動詞。die of（from）…因…而死亡，診斷出疾病動詞應用 detect，所以答案所為(B)。

38. D；中譯：他對成為一個看門人的工作感到無趣。

解析：本題空格要填入形容詞，作為主詞補語。因主詞（He）為人，應用動詞過去分詞當形容詞，也就是讓他感到無聊，所以答案所為 (D)。(C) 是令人感到無聊的。

39. C；中譯：這個錯誤直到彭先生呈交這份計畫書後才發現真是可恥。

解析：本題考動詞時態用法。It is a shame that…（那事）一件可恥的事；send in 呈送；依時間順序，二個動作在過去先後發生時，先發生者用過去完成式，後發生者用過去式。本題是 Ms.Perng 先送出計畫書，要用過去完成式，所以答案為 (C)。

40. D；中譯：威廉發現電影是有趣的，因為他喜歡有關人類與動物的故事。

解析：本題考分詞用法，空格內需填入形容詞當動詞受詞the movie的補語，因電影屬於「物」，要用現在分詞當形容詞，所以答案為 (D)。

41. A；中譯：大衛：我正計畫下個周末與我朋友去露營，你想要跟我們一塊去嗎？

桃莉絲：(A) 歐！我想去，但我已經有其它計畫了(B) 你要去哪裡？(C) 那聽起來不錯 (D) 感謝你邀請我。

大衛：你確定你不去？那將會很好玩的。

解析：本題由大衛最後一句問說：你確定不去？可見桃莉絲已有明白表示無法去的意思，所以答案為(A)。

42. A；中譯：服務生：你要點餐了嗎？

湯米：我想要牛排可以嗎？

服務生：(A) 你要幾分熟？(B) 你要哪個部位？(C) 你要多快上菜？(D) 你要全熟的牛排嗎？

湯米：五分熟。

解析：本題由湯米最後說要五分熟（medium），可見服務生有問要幾分熟的牛排，所以答案為(A)。

43.－47. 中譯：

　　廣告到處充斥，為了要吸引我們注意，廣告已經以各種不同媒體及型式呈現。他們已出現於巴士及車輛，以確定人們不論到哪都能看到它們。它們也可以在飄揚空中的氣球上被看見。在網路中，廣告會在螢幕中跳出來，讓人們無法迴避它們，雖然大部分民眾第一次看到它們時會感到興奮，人們仍可以隨時將他們按掉。但是假如彈跳式廣告是出現在電視上，人們幾乎對它們莫可奈何，它們確實影響到民眾，且大部分民眾並不樂意見到它們。

43. D；(A) suffered 遭受 (B) removed 移開 (C) explained 解釋 (D) displayed 展示

解析：空格中需填入動詞過去分詞，成為一個現在完成式的句子。由本句提到廣告要吸引人，所以合理推斷要出現在不同媒體及方式，故答案為 (D)。

44. B；(A) take care 照顧 (B) make sure 確認 (C) pay off 回報 (D) act out 表現出

解析：空格中需填入動詞片語，由上下文知本句要表達廣告出現在車輛上是為了人們都能看見它，所以空格內用 make sure（確認），故答案為 (B)。

45. A；(A) screen 螢幕 (B) keyboard 鍵盤 (C) mouse 滑鼠 (D) printer 印表機

解析：空格中需填入資訊設備名詞，pop up 是彈跳出來，由 advertisements will pop up on…表示廣告會以彈跳方式出現，所以廣告是出現在螢幕上，故答案為 (A)。

46. C；(A) smile 微笑 (B) take 拿 (C) click 按滑鼠 (D) wipe 擦去

解析：空格中需填入動詞，句中提人們隨時可以讓他們消失（away），所以合理推斷是按滑鼠讓廣告消失，故答案為 (C)。

47. C；(A) perform 表演 (B) watch 看 (C) appear 出現 (D) sing 唱歌

解析：空格中需填入動詞，句中提人們不喜歡在電視上看到彈跳式廣告，所以該處是指彈跳式廣告出現在電視上，故答案為 (C)。

48－50. 中譯：

　　竊賊於 2004 年 8 月 22 日上午闖入，就在孟克美術館開門後不久。星期天早上的寧靜就被闖入展覽區域的二名男性的叫囂聲中破壞了。在用槍逼迫警衛趴在地上後，他們從牆上帶走二幅畫作後離開，全程花不到五分鐘。對把孟克美術館的畫視為最有價值文化寶藏的挪威而言，這起犯罪被視為一個恥辱。一年半過去了，2006 年 2 月 14 日，六個人被起訴且審判開始。警方也許抓到了竊賊，但他們沒有找到畫作。在案發現場，警方花了一些時間才趕到，當他們到達時，原始目擊者已經離開且犯罪現場已經被其他參觀者破壞了。警方唯一的證據是一張由保全攝影機拍攝的模糊照片，警方於八個月後展開逮捕。至於美術館方面，搶案發生後關閉，並在加裝 6 百萬元的安全裝備後，於 10 個月後重新開放。

48. D；中譯：搶案是哪天發生的 (A) 星期一 (B) 星期五 (C) 星期六 (D) 星期日

解析：由 The Sunday peace was broken by the shouting of the two men storming into the exhibition area…，知搶案是星期日發生的，答案為(D)。

49. B；中譯：美術館何時重新開放 (A) 2005年四月 (B) 2005 年六月 (C) 2006 年二月 (D) 2006 年十二月

解析：由文章知：搶案發生於 2004 年 8 月，隨後立即關閉，於10個月後重新開放，故時間應為 2005 年六月，答案為 (B)。

50. C；中譯：為何警方晚抵達現場使得要尋回畫作更加困難？(A) 因警衛受傷嚴重 (B) 保全攝影機已經壞掉了 (C) 一些證據可能已經遺失了 (D) 訪客已經被驚嚇逃離了。

解析：由 By the time they did, the original witnesses were gone and the crime scene had been changed with other visitors，知原始目擊者已經離開，且犯罪現場已經被其他參觀者破壞了，可能造成證據被破壞或遺失，故答案為 (C)。

102 公務人員初等考試試題

等別：初等考試

類科：社會行政、人事行政、教育行政、財稅行政、 融保險、統計、會計、經建行政、
地政、圖書資訊管 、廉政、交通行政、電子工程

科目：公民與英文（此節錄英文部分）

( ) 36. I need to go to the _____ to exchange my new basketball shoes.

    (A) clinic   (B) mall   (C) coffee shop   (D) restaurant

( ) 37. Eating breakfast every morning is very important for students. It enables them to have enough _____ to learn new things.

    (A) interest   (B) energy   (C) dream   (D) fun

( ) 38. The endings of the modern movies are often open, _____ the viewers in doubt as to the final outcome of the characters.

    (A) left   (B) leaves   (C) left to   (D) leaving

( ) 39. This luggage is three times as heavy _____ that.

    (A) for   (B) as   (C) of   (D) than

( ) 40. Some people like football and _____ like basketball.

    (A) other   (B) others   (C) another   (D) the other

( ) 41. John: Hello, is Mark there?

    Mary: Yes.

    John: _____ .

    Mary: Well, he's busy right now.

    (A) Where is he?

    (B) May I speak to him?

    (C) I'll call again later.

    (D) This is John speaking.

(　) 42. Lisa: I'm going to the supermarket. Do you need anything?

　　　John: _____ .

　　　Lisa: Sure. Anything else?

　　　(A) Yes. It's great.

　　　(B) May I take your order?

　　　(C) Yes, please do.

　　　(D) Could you buy some bread for me?

　　　Online learning is also called distance education. Many American colleges and universities have been offering it for years. Online classes are usually taught by ___43___ who have been trained in online teaching. These classes can be highly interactive, ___44___ students communicate with each other and their teachers. Some classes require students to all log in at the same time so they can ___45___ live lectures by a professor. Students can also ask questions and work together on team projects. Many schools offer online education. Students should be especially careful of programs that offer a degree ___46___ for little or no work. These are known as diploma mills, and are illegal in the United States. Educational advisers also say that before you enter any program, make sure the work will ___47___ in your country.

(　) 43. (A) technicians　　(B) colleagues　　(C) professors　　(D) nurses

(　) 44. (A) where　　(B) which　　(C) that　　(D) when

(　) 45. (A) join　　(B) participate　　(C) make　　(D) listen

(　) 45. (A) exchange　　(B) in return　　(C) require　　(D) in need

(　) 47. (A) regard　　(B) be regarded　　(C) recognize　　(D) be recognized

In 1888, Vincent Van Gogh moved to Arles, a town in southern France. The artist Paul Gauguin moved there too, and they became good friends. The weather was beautiful, and they were both inspired by the colorful countryside. They painted daily and talked about art, but they didn't have much money. Van Gogh often became sad and couldn't paint. One day he became very angry and argued with Gauguin. Gauguin left Arles, and shortly after, Van Gogh cut off a piece of his own ear.

After a while, Van Gogh began to paint again. He sent some paintings to Paris but couldn't sell them. Then, in 1890, early on a Sunday evening, Van Gogh went out to the countryside with his paints. He took out a gun and shot himself in the chest. His brother Theo traveled from Paris to be with him. Two days later, Van Gogh died.

In his short, sad life, Van Gogh painted 200 paintings. He sold only one of them. In 1990, one of his paintings was sold for 82.5 million U.S. dollars.

( ) 48. This passage is mainly about _____.

(A) a short friendship between Van Gogh and Gauguin

(B) the reason why Van Gogh cut off his own ear

(C) Van Gogh's life in Arles as an unknown painter

(D) Theo's brotherly love for Vincent Van Gogh

( ) 49. Which of the following statements is correct?

(A) Van Gogh could not paint any more after his crazy act.

(B) Van Gogh did not attempt to kill himself.

(C) Theo came from Paris to attend Van Gogh's funeral.

(D) Van Gogh killed himself in the countryside.

( ) 50. One of Van Gogh's paintings was sold for 82.5 million U.S. dollars about _____ years after his death.

(A) 50

(B) 100

(C) 150

(D) 200

102年公務初等（人事行政等）中譯解析

36. B；中譯：我要到購物中心去換我新的籃球鞋。

解析：(A) clinic 診所 (B) mall 購物中心 (C) coffee shop 咖啡店 (D) restaurant 餐廳

本題考名詞。籃球鞋應該到購物商店去換，所以答案所為 (B)。

37. B；中譯：每天早晨吃早餐對學生是很重要的，它讓他們有足夠的體力去學新的東西。

解析：(A) interest 興趣 (B) energy 體力 (C) dream 夢想 (D) fun 歡樂

本題考名詞單字，吃早餐才會有體力，學習也需要體力，所以答案所為 (B)。

38. D；中譯：現代電影的結尾時常是開放的，留下觀眾對主角們最後的結局感到不確定。

解析：本題考分詞構句用法，形容詞子句簡化成分詞片語，此處用 leaving the viewers…，所以答案為 (D)。

39. B；中譯：這行李比那個重三倍。

解析：本題考比較句用法。A 比 B 重三倍可以用 A is three times as heavy as B，或 A is three times heavier than B，本題用第一種用法，所以答案所為 (B)。

40. B；中譯：一些人喜歡足球其他人喜歡籃球。

解析：本題考限定及不定代名詞用法，other指不特定的其他人、物，後面接名詞；others 表複數不特定的其他人、物，可當主詞；another 指特定的其他人、物，後面接名詞，the other 指二者以上的特定對象，可當主詞。所以此處應用 others，表示其它不特定的多數人，答案所為 (B)。

41. B；中譯：約翰：Hello，馬克在這邊嗎？

瑪莉：是的。

約翰：(A) 他在哪裡？(B) 我可以跟他談話嗎？(C) 我晚一點再打(D) 我是約翰（電話中說）。

瑪莉：嗯，他現在正在忙。

解析：本題由瑪莉說他正在忙，表示約翰有要求找馬克或想跟談話，所以選項 (B) 最適合。

42. D；中譯：麗莎：我要到超市去，你有要買甚麼嗎？

約翰：(A) 是的，那很好 (B) 準備好點甚麼了嗎？(C) 是的，請自便 (D) 你可以幫我買些麵包嗎？

麗莎：沒問題，還有甚麼嗎？

解析：由麗莎問說有沒要買甚麼，約翰只需針對問題來回答，所以答案為 (D)。

43.－47. 中譯：

　　線上學習又稱為遠距教學，許多美國大學院校已行之多年。線上課程通常由那些已受過線上教學訓練的教授來上課，這些課程式是可以有高度互動的，學生可以與其他學生及教師溝通。有些課程會要求學生在同一時間登錄進去，如此他們就可以參與教授的即時講座。學生們也可以發問以及一起參與團隊計畫，許多學校都有提供線上教學，學生們需特別注意這些很少或是根本無須作業負擔課程的學位，這些被稱為文憑工廠，且在美國是非法的。教育顧問們也說在你參加任何課程前，先確認這證書在你的國家是有被認可的。

43. C；(A) technicians 技師 (B) colleagues 同事 (C) professors 教授 (D) nurses 護士

解析：空格中需填入有關職業的名詞，由上下文提到這事有關大學線上學習的課程，合理推斷應該是由教授來教導，故答案為 (C)。

44. A；解析：空格中需填入關係詞，由上下文知道該子句是修飾前面主要子句講有關在課堂的事，所以關係副詞要用 where，表處所的關係詞，故答案為 (A)。

45. A；(A) join 參加 (B) participate 參與 (C) make 做 (D) listen 傾聽

解析：空格中需填入有關參加語課程的動詞，參與課程的動詞可用 join 或 participate in，故答案為 (A)。

46. B；(A) exchange 交流 (B) in return 交換 (C) require 要求 (D) in need 在窮困的

解析：本處形容詞子句已有動詞offer，所以 (A) 與 (C) 是動詞不能選的，經考量上下文含意，應以in return 符合文中意思，也就是說：以很少或是根本無須作業來換取學位⋯故答案為 (B)。

47. D；解析：空格中需填入該子句的動詞，因學位是被承認的，所以該動詞應該用被動式來表示，承認學位用 recognize，所以答案為 (D)。regard 認為。

48 – 50. 中譯：

在 1888 年，梵谷移居到一個法國南方小鎮亞爾，藝術家高更也搬到那裏去，且他們變成好朋友。那邊天氣好極了，且他們都被五彩繽紛的鄉間所啟發，他們每天作畫並且談論藝術，然而他們沒有錢，梵谷時常感到悲傷且無法作畫。有一天他發怒並與高更吵架，高更離開亞爾，而那不久之後，梵谷割下他自己的一隻耳朵。

過一段時間後，梵谷又開始作畫，他送了一些畫作到巴黎，但這些畫都賣不掉。這時，在1890年一個星期日的下午，梵谷帶著他的顏料外出到了鄉間，他拿出一把手槍朝自己胸口射擊，他的哥哥泰奧從巴黎趕來陪伴他，二天後，梵谷過世了。

梵谷在他短暫且悲慘的一生中共畫了200幅畫，他只有賣掉其中一幅。在1990年時，他的其中一幅畫被以 8 千 2 百 5 拾萬美金賣掉。

48. C；中譯：這篇文章主要是有關 (A) 梵谷與高更短暫的友情 (B) 為何梵谷割掉他的耳朵 (C) 梵谷在亞爾做為一個不知名畫家的生活 (D) 泰奧對梵谷的兄弟之愛。

解析：本篇文章一開始就提到梵谷般到亞爾後被那裏風景所吸引，然後在那邊遇到高更和他一起作畫，最後也在那邊自殺，所以都是描述有關於他在亞爾的生活，故答案為 (C)。

49. D；中譯：下列何項敘述為真 (A) 梵谷在他瘋狂的行為後再也不能作畫 (B) 梵谷沒有試圖要自殺 (C) 泰奧從巴黎趕來參加梵谷的葬禮 (D) 梵谷在鄉間自殺。

解析：(A) 梵谷在他割掉一隻耳朵後不久繼續作畫，敘述為非 (B) 梵谷拿著槍抵著胸口自殺，敘述為非 (C) 泰奧從巴黎趕來是陪伴梵谷，不是要參加葬禮，敘述為非 (D) 梵谷在外出鄉間作畫時舉槍自盡，敘述正確。故答案為 (D)。

50. B；中譯：梵谷的其中一幅畫被以8千2百5拾萬美金賣掉約在他過世後幾年 (A) 50 (B) 100 (C) 150 (D) 200

解析：文章提到他 1890 年自殺，那幅畫於 1990 年賣出，所以是過逝後 100 年，故答案為 (B)。

05
CHAPTER

模擬考題
與中譯解析

⚠ 模擬考題 第一回

請回答第1題至第5題：

Acid rain is one of the biggest environmental problems today. It has many long-term effects, like damage to trees and buildings. It can lead to skin and breathing problems. It can also cause animals to become extinct.

Acid rain is caused by air pollution from cars and factories. These machines burn fuel for energy. When fuel burns, it produces smoke and invisible gases that mix with couds. These dark clouds rain harmful chemicals onto the earth. Although the rain is not acidic enough to <u>corrode</u> skin, it coats tree leaves, buildings,and the ground with toxic water.

Acid rain has actually been around since the mid-1800s. It was discoveredby Robert Angus Smith. Smith found a relationship between acid rain and air pollution. However, scientists did not start studying acid rain seriously until the 1950s. Acid rain can be prevented by burning less dangerous fuels. Factories have also experimented with special filters that remove harmful chemicals from the smoke. These are good solutions, but governments have to act fast. If they wait, the damage may be unstoppable.

(　　) 1. What is the main idea of the passage?

　　(A) The cause and environmental disaster of acid rain.

　　(B) The dangerous forms of airpollution.

　　(C) The environment in the mid-1800s.

　　(D) The discovery of acid rain by Robert Angus Smith.

(　　) 2. According to the passage, which of the following is NOT correct?

　　(A) Acid rain is a serious problem these days.

　　(B) Acid rain may cause the climatic change.

　　(C) Cars and factories are main reasons for acid rain.

(D) Acid rain has been known for more than 150 years.

(　) 3. Which of the following is correct about acid rain?

(A) It can cause humans to become extinct.

(B) Toxic water from cars and factories causes acid rain.

(C) Serious research on acid rain only started around 60 years ago.

(D) It can make people get lung cancer.

(　) 4. Who should act fast to prevent the acid rain?

(A) Scientists　　　　　　　　(B) Robert Angus Smith

(C) Governments　　　　　　　(D) Factories

(　) 5. Which of the following words is closest in meaning to "corrode" in paragraph 2?

(A) comfort　　　　　　　　　(B) convict

(C) convert　　　　　　　　　(D) corrupt

請回答第6題至第10題：

　In the United States, preparing students to read and write fluently has long been a central ___6___ of the public schools, and the emphasis that No Child Left Behind places on students' reading performance has only increased the centrality of literacy instruction. ___7___, schools have historically organized their curricula around academic disciplines, ___8___ rely heavily on texts to store and communicate knowledge. The consequence is that reading and writing ___9___ are critical determinants of students' overall success in school. In truth, sophisticated reading and writing skills may ___10___ among disciplines: Gleaning insight from a mathematical treatise is different, after all, from analyzing Borges.

(　) 6. (A) responsibility　　　　　(B) profitability

(C) adversity　　　　　　　(D) commodity

(　) 7. (A) Otherwise　　　　　　(B) However

(C) Whereas　　　　　　　(D) Moreover

(　) 8. (A) what　　　　　　　　　(B) which

　　　　(C) whom　　　　　　　　(D) where

(　) 9. (A) efficiency　　　　　　　(B) proficiency

　　　　(C) enthusiasm　　　　　　(D) antipathy

(　) 10. (A) adapt　　　　　　　　　(B) provoke

　　　　(C) change　　　　　　　　(D) vary

(　) 11. They have move _____ of this house because they want to replace them.

　　　　(A) the furnitures　(B) furnitures　　(C) the furniture　　(D) a furniture

(　) 12. He is a man who is always _____ . No wonder everyone dislike talking with him.

　　　　(A) cautious　　(B) captious　　(C) considerate　　(D) capable

(　) 13. She sued her husband for maintenance so that she could continue living the lifestyle to which she had become _____ .

　　　　(A) accumulated　(B) accosted　　(C) accustomed　　(D) accredited

(　) 14. The US is still a _____ military superpower, but its international influence is in steep decline.

　　　　(A) indispensable　(B) formidable　　(C) sustainable　　(D) accountable

(　) 15. Ignorance and _____ prevent them from benefiting from modern medicine.

　　　　(A) superstition　　(B) discrimination　(C) contamination　　(D) authorization

(　) 16. The _____ broke down because one side refused to play the game.

　　　　(A) endorsement　(B) investment　　(C) administration　(D) negotiation

(　) 17. In business, you've got to _____ how your competitors will act.

　　　　(A) anticipate　　(B) disintegrate　　(C) inaugurate　　(D) associate

( ) 18. Two pedestrians and a cyclist were injured when the car skidded.

    (A) Two pedestrians and a cyclist were all hurt and the car skidded out.

    (B) Two pedestrians were all injured by the car when a cyclist skidded.

    (C) It was the two pedestrians and a cyclist that had skidded out from the car.

    (D) It was the car that skidded out and hurt the two pedestrians and a cyclist.

( ) 19. Daniel: Kevin, do you want to stop now or should we try to finish the work?

    Kevin: _____

    Daniel: I think you're right.

    (A) Let's do it over now.   (B) Let's get it done now.

    (C) Yes, it's right on time.   (D) Yes, I'll take a look at it.

( ) 20. A: Why don't we eat here?

    B: This place looks expensive. You see, I'm not wearing a tie.

    A: _____ This is a casual place actually.

    B: OK, then. Why not?

    (A) No problem   (B) No way   (C) By no means   (D) You do?

模擬考題——第一回中譯解析

1.─ 5. 中譯：

　　酸雨是現在環境中的一個大問題之一，它有許多長期的影響，像是為害樹木及建築物，它也會導致皮膚及呼吸問題，也可能導致動物滅絕。

　　酸雨起因於汽車及工廠的空氣汙染，這些機器燃燒燃料作為能源，當燃燒時，燃料產生煙霧以及看不見的氣體而與雲混在一起。這些黑雲下了含有害化學物質的雨進入土壤裏。雖然雨沒有酸到會燒到皮膚，但它與有毒的水附著在樹葉、建築物及地上。

　　酸雨自從 1800 年代中期起就一直存在，它是被羅伯安・格斯・史密斯所發現的，史密斯發現酸與與空氣汙染之間的關係。然而，科學家直到 1950 年代才開始認真地研究酸雨，燃燒少一點的危險燃料可以避免產生酸雨，工廠也在實驗可以過濾有害化學物質的特殊過濾器，這些都是好方法，但政府必須快點行動，假如拖延時間，危害可能會無法停息。

1. A；中譯： 本篇文章的大意為何？(A) 酸雨的起因及對環境的危害 (B) 空氣汙染的危險形式 (C) 在1800年代中期的環境 (D) 羅伯安・格斯・史密斯發現酸雨

　　解析： 由一開始談到酸雨的為害，再來談到酸雨形成的原因及過程，及酸雨發現的經過，最後是如何防治酸雨，故主要是談到酸雨的起因及對環境的危害，答案為 (A)。

2. B；中譯： 依據本文，下列敘述何者為非？(A) 酸雨近來是一個嚴重的問題 (B) 酸雨可能導致氣候變遷 (C) 汽車及工廠是酸雨的主要原因 (D) 酸雨已經被發現超過150年了。

　　解析： (A) these days（近來），由Acid rain is one of the biggest environmental problems today.知酸雨近來是一個嚴重的問題，敘述為真。(B) 文中無提到酸雨及氣候變遷之關係，敘述為非(C) 由 Acid rain is caused by air pollution from cars and factories…知酸雨主要由汽車及工廠造成，敘述為真。(D) 由Acid rain has actually been around since the mid-1800s.…知酸雨在1800年中期就有了，故距今超過 150 年，敘述為真。故答案為 (B)。

3. C；中譯： 下列關於酸雨敘述何者為真？(A) 它可能使人類滅亡 (B) 從汽車及工廠中的有毒的水造成酸雨 (C) 大約從 60 年前才開始對酸雨作認真的研究 (D) 它可能讓人們得到肺癌。

　　解析： (A) 由It can also cause animals to become extinct.知酸雨會造成動物滅亡，沒說是人類，敘述為非。(B)汽車及工廠排煙造成酸雨，非有毒的水造成酸雨，敘述為非 (C) 由scientists did not start studying acid rain seriously until the 1950s, 知約 60 年前才開始認真研究酸雨，敘述為真。(D)文中提到會產生呼吸問題，沒有說會得肺癌，敘述為非。故答案為 (C)。

4. C；中譯： 誰需快速行動來預防酸雨？(A) 科學家 (B) 羅伯安・格斯・史密斯 (C) 政府 (D) 工廠

　　解析： 由…but governments have to act fast…，故政府必須快速行動，答案為(C)。

5. D；中譯： 下列哪一個字意思與第二段中的"corrode"最接近？

　　解析： corrode 意思為腐蝕（動詞），由 (A) comfort 舒適 (B) convict 宣判有罪 (C) convert轉換 (D)corrupt 使腐敗。故以 corrupt（使腐敗）最接近，答案為 (D)。

6.－10. 中譯：
　　在美國，讓學生能夠讀寫流利一直以來都是公立學校的中心職責，並且在學生的閱讀表現上，以強調「沒有一個小孩會落後」的觀念也正好增強了識字能力教育的中心地位。況且，學校過去以來也已經就他們學術上的訓練來編排課程，那是非常依賴文字來記憶並傳遞知識的。這種結果就是讀及寫的精通程度是檢視學生在學校學習有成的重要決定因素。事實上，精熟的讀寫技巧可能在各種訓練中有所不同：研究一個數學論文內涵畢竟與分析博爾赫斯文學作品是不同的。

6. A；(A) responsibility 責任 (B) profitability 利益 (C) adversity 苦難 (D) commodity 日用品
　解析：空格前為形容詞，需填入名詞。空格前後提到讓學生具備流利的讀與寫及公立學校的關係，選項中以 responsibility（責任）最適當，也就是公立學校的中心職責，故答案為 (A)。

7. D；(A) Otherwise 否則 (B) However 不論如何 (C) Whereas 反過來說 (D) Moreover 況且
　解析：空格置於句首，要用副詞修飾整句語氣，前一句談到學校的觀念為增強識字能力，後面談到學校過去以來也就已經這樣來編排課程，故需用加強語氣的副詞來表達，故以 Moreover（況且）最適合，答案為 (D)。

8. B；解析：空格需填入關係代名詞，引導依形容詞子句，修飾先行詞 disciplines（訓練），可用代表事物的 which 引導子句，故答案為(B)。

6. B；(A) efficiency 效能 (B) proficiency 熟練 (C) enthusiasm 熱情 (D) antipathy 厭惡
　解析：空格需填入名詞，本句表示學生的讀與寫的精通程度是學生在學校學習有成的重要決定因素，故答案為 (B)。

10. D；(A) adapt 使適應 (B) provoke 激怒 (C) change 交換 (D) vary 變化
　解析：空格需填入動詞。句中提到讀與寫的技能是因各種訓練而有所不同，選項中以 vary（變化）最適宜，故答案為 (D)。

11. C；中譯：他們已經搬了房子的傢俱因為他們要歸還房子。
　解析：本題考名詞用法，傢俱（furniture）為集合名詞，為不可數名詞，所以不可用複數，故本題應用 the furniture，答案為 (C)。

12. B；中譯：他是一個總是強詞奪理的人，難怪每個人都不喜歡跟他講話。
　解析：(A) cautious 謹慎的 (B) captious 強詞奪理的 (C) considerate 體貼的 (D) capable 能幹的
　本題考人格特質的形容詞，由後面提到沒有一個人會喜歡和他講話，選項中以 captious（強詞奪理的）最恰當，答案為 (B)。

13. C；中譯：她因贍養費而控告她的丈夫以讓她自己能夠過她已經習慣的生活。
　解析：(A) accumulated 累積 (B) accosted 勾搭 (C) accustomed 使習慣 (D) accredited 認可
　本題考動詞，maintenance 為生活費或贍養費，to which 後面說明他她可以繼續過的生活型態，依選項中以 accustomed（使習慣）最適當，且 be accustomed to 有習慣於之意，故答案為(C)。

14. B；中譯：美國仍然是個可怕的軍事強權，但他的國際影響力正在下滑。

解析：(A) indispensable 不可缺少的 (B) formidable可怕的 (C) sustainable可持續的 (D) accountable 有責任的

15. A；中譯：由於無知和迷信使得他們無法受益於現代醫學。

解析：(A) superstition 迷信 (B) discrimination 歧視 (C) contamination 汙染 (D) authorization 認可
本題考名詞，prevent from benefiting，在本句解釋為無法受益於…，依句意由於無知導致無法受益現代醫學，依選項推論還有superstition（迷信），故答案為 (A)。

16. D；中譯：因一方拒絕按章辦事，談判破裂了。

解析：(A) endorsement 背書 (B) investment 投資 (C) administration 管理 (D) negotiation談判
本題考名詞，broke down（破裂），play the game（遵守規則），因為雙方無法達成協議，所以談判會破局，答案以 (D) 最恰當。

17. A；中譯：在生意上，你必須事先估計你的競爭對手會如何行動。

解析：(A) anticipate 預測 (B) disintegrate 瓦解 (C) inaugurate 開創 (D) associate 聯合
本題考動詞，get to（必須），competitors（競爭者），要先知道競爭者會如何行動才能克敵制勝，故動詞用 anticipate（預測）最恰當，答案為(A)。

18. D；中譯：當那車子打滑後，兩個行人及一個自行車騎士都受傷了。
(A) 兩個行人及一個自行車騎士都受傷了而且車子打滑了。
(B) 當自行車騎士滑倒後，兩個行人因車子而受傷。
(C) 兩個行人及一個自行車騎士從汽車中滑出來。
(D) 車子打滑並傷了兩個行人及一個自行車騎士。

解析：skid 為汽車滑向一側，也就是汽車打滑，題目的意思是汽車打滑造成兩個行人及一個自行車騎士受傷，所以選項中以 (D) 最接近。

19. B；中譯：丹尼爾：凱文，你要現在停工或是我們要繼續把工作完成？
凱文：_____。
丹尼爾：我想你是對的。
(A) 我們現在重做一遍 (B) 我們現在把它完成吧 (C) 是的，現在剛好準時 (D) 是的，我會檢查一下。

解析：丹尼爾問現在停工或是我們要繼續完成，凱文可能的回答就是停工或繼續完成，依據選向來看，只有 (B) 是針對問題回答，且獲得丹尼爾認同，故答案為 (B)。

20. A；中譯：A：我們何不在這裡吃呢？
B：這地方看起來很貴。瞧，我沒有打領帶。
A：_____。事實上這是一個輕鬆不拘的地方。
B：那好。有何不可呢？
(A) 沒問題 (B) 決不 (C) 當然 (D) 是嗎？

解析：B覺得這地方會很貴，所以需要正式服裝，A告訴他這是一個輕鬆的地方，所以空格處應是請A不要擔心的話語，故以 (A) 最恰當，表示沒有他擔心的問題。故答案為 (A) 。

✒ NOTE

模擬考題 第二回

( ) 1. The plot was predictable, the actors were terrible, and the special effects looked really fake. The movie was _____ lousy.
(A) consecutively
(B) consistently
(C) consequently
(D) comprehensively

( ) 2. Judging from the position of the sun in the sky, the rock climber took an _____ guess that he had three hour of daylight left.
(A) abominable (B) unbelievable (C) educated (D) irrational

( ) 3. _____ the subways in this city dirty , but also confused.
(A) Not only (B) Not only do (C) Not only are (D) Not only is

( ) 4. The excellent communication skills are essential to be success in the _____ .
(A) convenience (B) commune (C) completion (D) commerce

( ) 5. No supportive words could ever _____ for the pain of being separated from her children for 10 years
(A) comprise (B) contradict (C) complete (D) compensate

( ) 6. Clerk:This is registration desk. May I help you?
John:Yes, I'm calling to reschedule an appointment I had with Dr. Ethan on Jun 6.
Clerk: _____ .I'll process for you right now.
(A) Hurry up!
(B) OK! Wait for a moment.
(C) I think it was in July
(D) Not at all!

( ) 7. Michael:Has'nt any one taken your order yet?
Ava:No, I'm still waiting.
Michael:The service in this restaurant _____ . I'm thinking whether we should left now!

(A) is terrific!　　　　　　　　(B) is as usual

(C) goes from bad to worse　　　(D) goes from strength to strength

(　) 8. Allen: I'm going out, John.

John: Where are you going?

Allen: A party in downtown. Could you take care of the cat when I'm out?

John: _____ ! I'm not your servant.

(A) No way!　　(B) Not at all!　　(C) No more!　　(D) No comment!

(　) 9. A: This is such a great program!

B: It is, isn't it? It helps my work a lot.

A: Is it all right if I copy this?

B: I think _____ . Don't you know it's illegal?

(A) that's out of my mind　　　(B) that's out of the date

(C) that's out of the question　　(D) that's out of the ordinary

(　) 10. He tried hard to shut all pessimistic thoughts out of his mind.

(A) He think pessimistically in his mind, and tried hard to get used for it.

(B) He did his best to think about everything he had pessimistically.

(C) He did his best to change the pessimistic thinking from his mind.

(D) He hardly changes his mind into a more pessimistic attitude.

(　) 11. Look out for pedestrians forced on the roadway when a pavement or footpath is closed or blocked by works.

(A) When a pavement or footpath is closed or blocked by works, look for people who walk on the roadway.

(B) Be careful to the pedestrians when they are forced on the roadway as a pavement or footpath is closed or blocked by works.

(C) When pedestrians are forced on the roadway by a pavement, look out for the blocked works on the roadway.

(D) Be careful to a pavement or footpath being closed when the pedestrians are forced on the roadway or blocked by works

請回答第12題至第16題：

Wine can be made with red grapes or white grapes, and, especiallyin the case of red wines. As new wine-shoppers browse the shelves of their local markets, they face a tough decision. Should they buy a wine with a cork or a screw top? Wineries are also facing tough choices in the best way to seal their products.

The root of the problem lies in "cork taint." Cork taint refers to a problem with wine that has been sealed with a bad cork. Traditionally, all corks are made from a special oak tree that grows around the Mediterranean. In the process of making the corks and sealing wine bottles, a certain type of mold may start to grow on some corks. Over time, this mold can produce a chemical that makes the wine inside the bottle taste musty. Some experts from the wine industry claim cork taint affects one out of every ten bottles of wine. Some wine makers see a possible solution to the problem of cork taint through adopting the tried and true method of sealing bottles with screw tops. However, many wineries are still playing it safe and sticking to corks for two reasons. First, there is the old belief among cork users that small amounts of oxygen are able to penetrate corks. This oxygen is necessary for the proper aging of fine wines, especially those aged 10 years or more. Screw tops do not allow for any oxygen to get into the bottles. Another problem arises from the image screw tops have with the public. In most people's minds, screw tops are only found on cheap, low-quality wines.

(　　) 12. What is the topic of this article?

(A) How can you choose a good wine?

(B) Where do the best wines come from?

(C) How should wineries seal wine?

(D) Why are some wines very expensive?

(　　) 13. What does "cork taint"affect?

(A) The age of wine   (B) The air in wine

(C) The color of wine   (D) The taste of wine

(　　) 14. Out of 100 wines sealed with corks, how many might be affected by cork taint?

    (A) One   (B) Five   (C) Ten   (D) Half

(　　) 15. Why do some wineries hesitate to use screw tops to seal wine bottles?

    (A) Screw tops are too expensive.   (B) Screw tops are difficult to open.

    (C) Screw tops can't seal in air.   (D) Screw tops give wine a bad image.

(　　) 16. According to the passage, which of the following is NOT true?

    (A) Small amounts of oxygen are able to penetrate corks.

    (B) "Cork taint" may affect wine that has been sealed with a bad cork.

    (C) Corks are traditionally made from a special oak tree that grows around the Mediterranean.

    (D) Most people think the corks are only found on low-quality wines.

請回答第17題至第20題：

    Baskin Robbins is the biggest ice cream store franchisein the world. Cousins Burt Baskin and Irv Robbins opened their first ice cream store in 1945. Burt Baskin died at a young age. His nephew, John Robbins, _____17_____ that his uncle died because he often ate ice cream as a main meal. Too much ice cream caused him to have a heart attack. After he found this out, John decided not to sell ice cream. He left home and stopped earning money from ice cream. _____18_____, John writes books about diet and health. He even became avegetarian to stay away from processed food. On a TV show, John said ice cream is not good for our health. It can cause heart disease, high cholesterol, high blood pressure, and diabetes. He _____19_____ that people should find out about the _____20_____ of the food they are eating.

(　　) 17. (A) found out   (B) found for   (C) found in   (D) found to

(　　) 18. (A) Whenever   (B) However   (C) Besides   (D) Nevertheless

(　　) 19. (A) assaulted   (B) advised   (C) advanced   (D) aggress

(　　) 20. (A) cosmetics   (B) conventions   (C) prescriptions   (D) ingredients

---

模擬考題──第二回中譯解析

1. D；中譯：情節是可預測的，演員是可怕的糟，而且特效看來很假，這部電影是完全地糟糕。

   解析：(A) consecutively 連續地 (B) consistently 堅定地 (C) consequently 必然地 (D) 全面地 comprehensively

   本題考副詞，用來修飾 lousy（adj.很差勁的），前面提到一連串失敗的地方，所以用 comprehensively（全面性地）來形容該狀況最恰當，答案為 (D)。

2. C；中譯：從太陽在天空中的位置研判，這位攀岩者依據所受的訓練判斷他離日落還剩三小時時間。

   解析：(A) abominable 討厭的 (B) unbelievable 不可信的 (C) educated 被訓練的 (D) irrational 無理的

   本題考形容詞。Take a guess（猜想一下），在此為大略估算之意，考量選項中的形容詞，以 educated最適宜，表示他是依據所受的訓練判斷，答案為 (C)。

3. C；中譯：這個城市的地鐵系統不但骯髒，而且令人搞不清楚。

   解析：本題考倒裝句型。Not only…but also（不但…而且），如 not only 至於句首，則要用倒裝句型，也就是動詞要置於主詞前面，且考量主詞為複數（systems），所以應該用 Not only are…，故本題答案為 (C)。

4. D；中譯：優良的溝通技巧在商場上成功是很重要的。

   解析：(A) convenience 便利 (B) commune 會談 (C) completion 完成 (D) commerce 商業

   本題考名詞，be essential to（對…很重要），好的溝通技巧對做生意很重要，所以選項中以 commerce（商業）最恰當，答案為 (D)。

5. D；中譯：沒有甚麼適當的字眼可以來補償她與小孩子分離十年所受的痛苦。

   解析：(A) comprise 包括 (B) contradict 反駁 (C) complete 完成 (D) compensate 補償

   本題考動詞，supportive（支持的）在此表示適合的，be separated from（與…分離），依句意知與小孩分離十年是很痛苦，所以動詞用 compensate（補償）來表示最恰當，答案為(D)。

6. B；中譯：櫃員：這裏是掛號臺，有甚麼可以為您服務的嗎？

   約翰：是的，我要重新安排我與伊森醫師在六月六日的預約。

   櫃員：＿＿＿＿＿＿，我馬上為您處理。

   (A) 趕快！(B) 好的，稍待一下 (C) 我想那是在七月 (D) 一點也不！

   解析：由談話中知這一場要更改與醫師預約的對話，櫃員最後雖然說我馬上為您處，前面應該還是會禮貌性的要請客人稍待一下，所以答案應為 (B)。

7. C；中譯：蜜雪兒：還沒有人來為您點菜嗎？

   艾夫：沒有，我還在等！

   蜜雪兒：這家餐廳的服務真是＿＿＿＿＿＿，我想我們是否要離開了。

   (A) 非常好! (B) 跟往常一樣 (C) 每況愈下 (D) 不斷壯大

解析：由對話中得知這家餐廳讓客人等很久都還沒有點菜，因此蜜雪兒才會說考慮是否要離開了，可見她已經不耐煩，所以對這間餐廳的服務意見應該是goes from bad to worse（每況愈下），答案應為 (C)。

8. A；中譯：艾倫：約翰，我要外出了。

約翰：你要去哪?

艾倫：鎮上的一個宴會，當我不在的時候你可以幫我照顧一下貓嗎?

約翰：_____，我又不是你的傭人。

(A) 免談！ (B) 一點也不！ (C) 不再！ (D) 無可奉告！

解析：由對話中得知約翰對艾倫要求他代為照顧貓的一事不以為然，所以才說他不是傭人，所以是拒絕艾倫的要求，故選項中以No way!（免談！）最適當，答案為 (A)。

9. C；中譯：A：這真是個很棒的程式！

B：是啊。它對我的工作很有幫助。

A：我可以拷貝嗎？

B：我想 _____。難道你不知道這不合法嗎？

(A) 我忘記了 (B) 那過期了 (C) 那是不可能的 (D) 那很新潮

解析：help a lot（對…很有幫助），illegal（不合法的）。對話中，A想拷貝這程式，但B說難道你不知道私下拷貝程式是違法的嗎，表示他是拒絕的，故選項中以that's out of the question（那是不可能）最適宜，答案為 (C)。

10. C；中譯：他努力設法讓悲觀的想法從腦海中消失。

(A) 他悲觀地想著，並設法去適應它 (B) 他盡其所能悲觀地思考他經歷的所有事情 (C)他盡其所能來改變腦海中悲觀的想法 (D) 他很難改變成更悲觀的態度。

解析：out of one's mind（忘記），題目意思是說他盡力不要讓悲觀的想法存在他腦海中，經比較答案的意思中，以 (C) 最接近題意。

11. B；中譯：當人行道封閉或因施工而有阻礙時，要小心被迫走上車道的行人。

(A) 當人行道封閉或因施工而有阻礙時，要尋找走在路上的人 (B) 當行人因為人行道封閉或施工而有阻礙時被迫走上車道，要小心他們 (C) 當行人被迫走沿著人行道的車道時，要注意車道上的施工 (D) 當行人被迫走上車道或被施工所阻礙時，要小心人行道被封閉。

解析：look out 為小心、注意之意，look for 為尋找，二者不能混淆，另 pavement 及 footpath 均可表示人行道。題目意思是表達行人可能會因為人行道封閉等狀況而走上汽車道，所以駕駛人要注意。經比較答案的意思中，以 (B) 最接近題意。

12－17. 中譯：

葡萄酒可以用紅葡萄或白葡萄製成，且特別是紅葡萄。當新的酒消費者在當地市場搜尋架上的產品時，他們面臨一個難題：他們應該買軟木塞或螺旋瓶蓋的酒？各酒莊對用採最佳方式來密封產品同樣也面臨難題。

問題的根源出在「軟木塞汙染」，軟木塞汙染意味著酒被不好的軟木塞封存產生的問題。

傳統上，所有的軟木塞都是由生長在地中海的一種特殊橡木所製成，在製作軟木塞及密封酒瓶過程中，一種特定的分子會開始生長於軟木塞中，一段時間後，這種分子產生一種化學物質並使酒瓶內的酒嚐起來有酸味。一些酒業專家聲稱每十瓶酒就有一瓶產生軟木塞汙染，一些酒商設法想出一個解決軟木塞汙染的可能方法，就是採用確實牢靠的螺旋瓶蓋來密封酒瓶。然而，許多酒商仍為保險起見而堅持用軟木塞有二點理由。第一，傳統上軟木塞使用者認為少量的氧氣可以穿透軟木塞，這些氧氣對酒適當的熟成是必要的，尤其是那些超過10年或更久的酒。而螺旋瓶蓋則無法讓氧氣進入到瓶子裡。另一個問題在於螺旋瓶蓋給大眾的印象，在大部分民眾心目中，螺旋瓶蓋只有在便宜，低品質的酒類上才看得到。

12. C；中譯：本篇文章的主題為何？(A)你如何選擇好的葡萄酒？(B) 好的葡萄酒從哪裡來？(C)酒莊應該如何密封葡萄酒？(D)為何有些葡萄酒這麼貴？

解析：由一開始談各酒莊對用採最佳方式來密封產品面臨難題，再來談到軟木塞汙染的原因及解討論如何解決這問題，最後提到認為軟木塞還是比較好的原因，故主要是談到酒類密封的問題，故答案為 (C)。

13. D；中譯：「軟木塞汙染」影響到甚麼？(A) 酒的年齡 (B) 酒裏面的空氣 (C) 酒的顏色 (D) 酒的味道。

解析：由Over time, this mold can produce a chemical that makes the wine inside the bottle taste musty…，知軟木塞會產生一種化學物質並使酒瓶內的酒嚐起來有酸味，故答案為 (D)。

14. C；中譯：每 100 瓶用軟木塞密封的酒中，有多少瓶會被軟木塞汙染有(A) 一瓶 (B) 五瓶 (C) 十瓶 (D) 一半。

解析：由 Some experts from the wine industry claim cork taint affects one out of every ten bottles of wine…知被汙染的比例大約十分之一，所以每 100 瓶約有 10 瓶會被汙染，故答案為 (C)。

15. D；中譯：為何有些酒莊對使用螺旋瓶蓋密封酒瓶感到猶豫？(A) 螺旋瓶蓋太貴了 (B) 螺旋瓶蓋不好打開 (C) 螺旋瓶蓋不能封住空氣 (D) 螺旋瓶蓋給酒一種不好的印象。

解析：由many wineries … sticking to corks for two reasons. First, …small amounts of oxygen are able to penetrate corks.… Screw tops do not allow for any oxygento get into the bottles…Another problem arises from the image …. In most people's minds, screw tops are only found on cheap, low-quality wines.可知酒莊不願使用螺旋瓶蓋的原因有二點，第一是螺旋瓶蓋無法讓氧氣進入酒瓶中，第二是人們對於螺旋瓶蓋的酒有便宜，低品質的不良印象。故本題答案為 (D)

16. D；中譯：依據本文，下列敘述何者是錯誤的？(A) 少量的氧氣可以穿透軟木塞 (B)「軟木塞汙染」可能會影響那些被不良軟木塞密封的酒 (C) 軟木塞傳統上是由一種長在地中海周圍的特殊橡樹作成的 (D) 大部分人認為軟木塞只有在低品質酒類才看得到。

解析： (A) 由small amounts of oxygen are able to penetrate corks…知少量的氧氣可以穿透軟木塞，敘述為真 (B) 由Cork taint refers to a problem with wine that has been sealed with a bad cork知「軟木塞汙染」就是被不良軟木塞密封的酒，敘述為真 (C) 由all corks are made from a special oak tree that grows around the Mediterranean.知軟木塞是由長在地中海周圍的特殊橡樹作成

的，敘述為真 (D) 由In most people's minds, screw tops are only found on cheap, low-quality wines.知螺旋瓶蓋只有在低品質的酒類上才看得到，本項敘述為非。故本題答案為 (D)。

17.－20. 中譯：

巴斯金・羅賓是全世界最大的冰淇淋店連鎖店，堂兄弟伯特・巴斯金與艾夫・羅賓在 1945 年開了他們第一家冰淇淋店。伯特・巴斯金很年輕就過逝，他的姪子約翰・羅賓斯發現他的叔叔的死是因為他時常將冰淇淋當正餐吃，太多的冰淇淋使得他心臟病發。在發現這種情況後，約翰決定不再賣冰淇淋了，他離家並停止賣冰淇淋來賺錢。另外，約翰還寫一些飲食與健康有關的書，他甚至變成一個素食者來遠離加工食品，在一個電視節目中，約翰說冰淇淋對我們的健康不好，它會造成心臟疾病，高膽固醇，高血壓及糖尿病，他勸告人們應當瞭解他們吃進食物的成分

17. A；(A) found out 查明，找出 (B) found for 作有利的判決

解析：空格需填入本句動詞，選項中均為動詞片語，依句意為約翰・羅賓斯確認他叔叔會早逝的原因…，故選項中以 find out（查明）最符合，故答案為 (A)。

18. C；(A) Whenever 無論何時 (B) However 然而 (C) Besides 另外 (D) Nevertheless無論

解析：空格需填入副詞修飾整句，並顯示與前句的語氣的關係，前句提到約翰不但停止賣冰淇淋來賺錢，後句表示他還寫一些飲食與健康有關的書，二句為更加強調的關係，故副詞用 Besides（另外）最適宜，答案為 (C)。

19. B；(A) assaulted 攻擊 (B) advised 勸告 (C) advanced 前進 (D) aggress 侵略

解析：空格需填入動詞，該句表示他要民眾了解吃進去的食物…故選項中的動詞以 advised（勸告）最恰當，故答案為 (B)。

20. D；(A) cosmetics 化妝品 (B) conventions 習慣 (C) prescriptions 處方 (D) ingredients 成分

解析：空格需填入名詞，表示民眾應該知道他們吃進去食物的性質，選項中以ingredients（成分）最恰當，也就是食物的成分（ingredients of the food），故答案為 (D)。

06
CHAPTER

附 錄

UNIT 01 鐵路專業詞彙

項次	英文名稱	中文翻譯
1	Baggage rack	行李架
2	Barrier	（平交道）柵欄
3	Berth, bunk	臥舖
4	Booking office, ticket office	票務辦公室
5	Buffet	自助用餐
6	Capacity	容量
7	Catering service	包車服務
8	Coach, carriage	車廂
9	Commuter electric multiple units	通勤電聯車組
10	Commuter train, suburban train	通勤列車
11	Conductor	車掌
12	Dining car	餐車
13	Dinner car	餐車
14	District	區段
15	Double-decker train	雙層列車
16	Down train	下行列車
17	Eastern railway	西部鐵路
18	Emergency button	緊急按鈕
19	Engineer	火車駕駛員
20	Excursion train	旅遊列車
21	Express train	快車
22	Fast train; express train	快車
23	Huatung line	花東線
24	Level crossing	平交道
25	Limited express	對號快車
26	Local train	普通車
27	Locomotive	火車機車頭
28	Lounge coach	客廳車廂
29	Luggage van, baggage car	行李車箱
30	Mail car	郵務車廂

項次	英文名稱	中文翻譯
31	Mother-and-child room	親子廁所
32	Night train	夜車
33	North link line	北迴線
34	One way tickets	單程票
35	Passenger	旅客
36	Platform	月台
37	Platform bridge	月台天橋
38	Platform ticket	月臺票
39	Railway gate	平交道口
40	Railway network	鐵路路網
41	Railway policeman	鐵路警察
42	Railway system	鐵路系統
43	Railway; railroad	鐵路
44	Round trip tickets	來回票
45	Season tickets	季票
46	Seat	座位
47	Sleeping car, sleeper	臥車
48	South link line	南迴線
49	Station hall	車站大廳
50	Station, railway station	車站；火車站
51	Stopping train, slow train	慢車
52	Taiwan railway administration	台灣鐵路管理局
53	Terminal	終點站
54	Through train	區間車
55	Ticket inspector	查票員
56	Ticket-collector, gateman	剪票員
57	Track	鐵軌，軌道
58	VIP room	貴賓室
59	Western mainline line	西部主幹線
60	Up train	上行列車

UNIT 02 鐵路標示、職位詞彙

項次	英文名稱	中文翻譯
1	Additional fare	補票
2	Adult Fare	全票
3	Advance Purchase (up to 7-Day)	預售七日內（含乘車日）車票
4	All Trains	各級列車
5	Arrival time	抵達時間
6	Arrivals waiting room	候客室
7	Baggage check	行李包裹託運
8	Baggage claim	行李領取處
9	Baggage clerk	行李員司
10	Baggage deposit	行李寄存處
11	Baggage service items	行李服務項目
12	Baggage services room	行李房
13	Bike check	機踏車託運
14	Boarding date	車票日期
15	Broadcasting room	播音室
16	Bus stop	公車轉乘站
17	Business Class	商務車廂
18	Business hours	營業時間
19	Children Fare	兒童半票
20	Chu-Kuang Express	莒光號
21	Coast line	海線
22	Coin change	兌換零錢
23	Conductor	列車長
24	Counter	窗口
25	Dangerous goods	危險品
26	Delay certificates	誤點證明
27	Delayed	列車延誤
28	Departure time	開車時間
29	Departures waiting room	候車室
30	Deputy station master	副站長

項次	英文名稱	中文翻譯
31	Destination	目的地
32	Diaper change	嬰兒換尿布檯
33	Disabled only	殘障專用
34	Disabled parking only	殘障專用停車位
35	Due stamps	到期日蓋章處
36	Duty office	值班站長室
37	East parking lot	東側停車場
38	Elevator	電梯
39	Emergency exit	緊急出口
40	Emergency phone	緊急電話
41	Entrance	入口
42	Escalator	手扶梯
43	Exit	出口
44	Express train	對號列車
45	Fares	票價
46	Fast Local Train	區間快
47	Fire distinguisher	滅火器
48	First aid	醫護室
49	Front exit	前站出口
50	Fu-Hsing Semi Express	復興號
51	General affairs office	總務室
52	Ground level	地面層
53	Hydrant	消防栓
54	Information	服務中心
55	Inspector	查票員
56	Local Train	區間車
57	Lockers	自動存物箱
58	Lost and found	遺失品查詢處
59	Military transport office	運輸軍官辦公室
60	Monthly passes	定期票

項次	英文名稱	中文翻譯
61	Mountains line	山線
62	No crossing	禁止進入（通行）
63	No pets	請勿攜帶寵物上車
64	North-bound line	上行線
65	Nursery room	哺乳室
66	Ordinary Train	普快車
67	Origin	起點站
68	Overpass	天橋
69	Paging	播音尋人
70	Parking lot exit	停車場出口
71	Parking tower	停車塔
72	Platform 2	第二月台
73	Platform level	月台層
74	Please Take a Number	預售叫號抽取號碼處
75	Police station	警察分駐所
76	Public telephone	公用電話
77	Railway restaurant	鐵路餐廳
78	Rear exit	後站出口
79	Receipt issuing	購票證明
80	Remarks	備註
81	Reserved parking	公務停車位
82	Reserved Tickets Pick-up	電話語音、網路訂票取票處
83	Reserved tickets and advanced purchase	預售窗口
84	Running on Mondays	週一行駛
85	Running on Saturdays	週六行駛
86	Running on Sundays	週日行駛
87	Service hours	服務時間
88	Service items	服務項目
89	Shop	販賣部
90	South-bound line	下行線

項次	英文名稱	中文翻譯
91	Station hall	車站大廳
92	Station Master	站長
93	Station staff	站務員
94	Suggestions	旅客意見箱
95	Taxi stand	計程車招呼站
96	Temporary ticketing windows	臨時售票窗口
97	The Elderly	老人
98	Ticket passenger only	無票旅客禁止進站
99	Ticket books	回數票
100	Ticket inspector	剪票員
101	Ticketing clerk	售票員
102	Ticket Counters	售票室（窗口）
103	Ticking hall	售票大廳
104	Time table	時刻表
105	Tour Trains	觀光列車
106	Train control room	行車控制室
107	Train crew	乘務員
108	Train information	查詢列車時刻
109	Train information display system	列車資訊顯示器
110	Train number	列車班次
111	Train type	車種
112	Tze-Chiang Limited Express	自強號
113	Underground parking	地下停車場
114	Underpass	地下道
115	Via	經由

好書報報－職場系列

Best Publishing

結合流行英語，時下必學的行銷手法與
品牌管理概念，讓你完全掌握行銷力！

全書分為**6**大章，共**46**組情境
★背景介紹＋實用對話
★練習題：中英對照，學習事半功倍
★相關詞彙：必備常用單字及片語＋文法加油站
★知識補給站：分析行銷策略＋重點訊息彙整
★**10**篇會議要點：對話急救包＋要點提示

題材充實新穎，增加語言學習和專業知識的深度！
行銷人要看，商管學院師生更不可錯過！

作者：胥淑嵐
定價：新台幣349元
規格：352頁 / 18K / 雙色印刷

旅館的客戶為數不少來自不同國家，
因而說出流利的旅館英語，是旅館人員
不可或缺的利器，更是必備的工具！

特別規劃**6**大主題 **30**個情境 **120**組超實用會話
中英左右對照呈現對話內容，閱讀更舒適！
精選好學易懂的key word＋音標＋詞性，學習效率加倍！
隨書附有光碟小幫手，幫助你熟悉口語、訓練聽力！

從預約訂房、入住，到辦理退房，
設計各種工作時會面臨到的場景，
提供各種專業會話訓練，英語溝通零距離！

作者：Mark Venekamp & Claire Chang
定價：新台幣469元
規格：504頁 / 18K / 雙色印刷 / MP3

Learn Smart! 030

鐵路特考
英文高分特快車

作　　者／方定國
封面設計／陳小King
內頁構成／菩薩蠻有限公司

發 行 人／周瑞德
企劃編輯／徐瑞璞
校　　對／劉俞青、陳欣慧
初　　版／2014 年 4 月
定　　價／新台幣 349 元

出　　版／倍斯特出版事業有限公司
電　　話／（02）2351-2007
傳　　真／（02）2351-0887
地　　址／100 台北市中正區福州街 1 號 10 樓之 2
Ｅｍａｉｌ／best.books.service@gmail.com

印　　製／世和印製企業有限公司
圖片來源／Dreamstime David Jones Elliott Brown

總 經 銷／235 商流文化事業有限公司
地　　址／新北市中和區中正路752號7樓
電　　話／（02）2228-8841
傳　　真／（02）2228-6939

港澳地區總經銷／泛華發行代理有限公司
地　　址／香港筲箕灣東旺道3號星島新聞集團大廈3樓
電　　話／（852）2798-2323
傳　　真／（852）2796-5471

國家圖書館出版品預行編目(CIP)資料

鐵路應試英語 /
　方定國著 — 初版. — 臺北市：
　倍斯特, 2014. 04
　　面；　公分. —
　ISBN 978-986-90331-4-5(平裝)

　1. 英語 2. 讀本

805.18　　　　　　　　　　103006033